ROOM 23

ROOM 23

A SECRET SERVICE AGENT'S STORY OF ESPIONAGE AND INTRIGUE

A NOVEL BY

SEAN QUARMBY

PALMETTO
PUBLISHING
Charleston, SC
www.PalmettoPublishing.com

Hardcover ISBN: 979-8-82295-974-3
Paperback ISBN: 979-8-82295-975-0
eBook ISBN: 979-8-82295-976-7

Dedicated to my wife and best friend, Lani. Our journey together is a cherished adventure that fills my heart with joy. To the Miller family, you continue to embrace this grateful soul with love and kindness. To my Niece Katie and Nephews Matthew and Michael, I love you all. May you find peace and comfort in this temperamental world. And to my beloved departed family, I feel your presence and imagine you smiling down from Heaven, amused by the mischievous things I still manage to get myself into.

Contents

Acknowledgements

This book is the culmination of a deeply fulfilling 25-year career as a Special Agent with the United States Secret Service. I hold immense admiration for the men and women I had the honor of serving alongside, and I extend my heartfelt thanks to all of them for their dedicated service to our country.

I would like to express my sincere gratitude
to the following individuals:
Lani Quarmby
Lisa Eckl
Heather Muckenfuss
Bill Murray
Sam Thumma

Your meticulous care, attention to detail, and selfless consideration in providing crucial feedback to the initial drafts of this novel were indispensable. Your honest and often critical input helped shape this book into the vision I had hoped for.

Index of Characters—Socialist Republic of North Korea

Pak Hyun Woo—New Supreme Leader of North Korea
Pak Sang Ho—Deceased Supreme Leader of North Korea and father of Pak Hyun Woo
Pak Hyun Mi—Sister of Pak Hyun Woo aka 'Akma Deja' (Demon Mistress)
Pak Soo Jin—Mother of the New Supreme Leader of North Korea Pak Hyun Woo
Soon Min Un—aka Tara Lee—Akma Deja's Operative
Wei Chan—Akma Deja's Security Officer (Triad Gang Member) aka 'Uncle' to Tara Lee

Remaining Characters in Alphabetical Order:

Stansfield "Stig" Anderson—British MI-5 Officer and Friend to Professor James O'Donovan
Sergei Bitrov—Russian Hacker Working for North Korea
Jeff Blake—NYPD Police Officer—Breezy Point
Rick Boland—Secret Service Special Agent New York Field Office
Mary Brooks—Secret Service Special Agent Newark Field Office
David Bryce—President of the United States
Helen Bryce—First Lady of the United States
Frank Cawley—Assistant Director of the Secret Service
Dave Cosby—AUSA/Federal Prosecutor
Jake Cutler—Secret Service Shift Leader on the Presidential Protection Division
Steve Evaden—Secret Service Special Agent Newark Field Office
Sue Faranato—Secret Service Forensics Specialist
Charlie Green—NSA Cryptanalyst and Intelligence Officer
Joanne Harkness—Owner of the House at Breezy Point
Jason Knight aka 'Kramton'—Breezy Point Assassin

Joe (Mack) Mackey—Secret Service Special Agent and Quinlan's Partner/Friend
Lana Miller—AUSA/Federal Prosecutor/Legal Advisor to DNSA Jan Townes
Carl Minelli—Secret Service Special Agent/Polygrapher
Mike Niego—DEA Agent/Group Leader
Phillip O'Donovan—Master Engraver at the Bureau of Engraving and Printing (BEP)
Anne (Annie) O'Donovan—Phillip O'Donovan's Wife
Patrick O'Donovan—Son of Phillip and Anne O'Donovan
Sean O'Donovan—Phillip O'Donovan's Deceased Father
James O'Donovan—Phillip's Uncle/Professor/Emerging Sinn Féin Leader
Adolpho Perez—Counterfeiter/Informant in NYC
Felix Perez—Father of Adolpho/Owner of 'Start to Finish Printing' in NYC
Sheila Priestly—NYPD Police Officer—Breezy Point
John Quinlan—Secret Service Special Agent/Supervisor of Room 23
John Reynolds—CIA Chief of Station—London, England
Jonathan Ridge—Secretary for the Department of Homeland Security
Bill Ross—FBI Liaison to the NSC
Beth Sales—Tara Lee's Boss at the Bureau of Engraving and Printing
Diego 'Carlos' Santana—Los Cazadores Leader—NYC
Tatiana Sokolov—Russian Spy Cultivated by CIA Station Chief John Reynolds
Rick Spencer—SAIC of PPD/Former Supervisor in the NYFO
Andy Stevens—White House Chief of Staff
Jake 'Nickalos' Stole—DEA Undercover Agent
Janise (Jan) Townes—Deputy National Security Advisor (DNSA) National Security Council
Molly Zurflueh—Contract Attorney to the Hollywood Industry

Acronyms and Terms:

BEP—Bureau of Engraving and Printing
CI—Confidential Informant
DNSA—Deputy National Security Advisor
FLOTUS—First Lady of the United States
GOV—Government Owned Vehicle
Juche—Korean Term for Self-Reliance
NSC—National Security Council
NSA—National Security Agency
NYFO—New York Field Office
POTUS—President of the United States
OEOB—Old Executive Office Building
PPD—Presidential Protection Division (Secret Service)
SAIC—Special Agent in Charge
SCI—Sensitive Compartmented Information
SCIF—Sensitive Compartmented Information Facility
VGTOF—FBI's Violent Gang and Terrorist Offender File

Preface

Having retired from the United States Secret Service in 2015, it has taken me nearly a decade to share this story. Many parts of this novel draw inspiration from my firsthand experiences, reflecting the authenticity of the events I encountered as a Special Agent with the United States Secret Service. I consider myself fortunate to have dedicated 25 years to serving as a Special Agent with the Secret Service, during which I had the privilege of protecting two sitting Presidents. I later advanced to the role of Supervisory Special Agent, overseeing Room 23 and the White House Access Control Branch.

The Secret Service bears the critical duty of protecting the President, Vice President, their families, all former Presidents and their spouses, as well as a diverse array of visiting foreign heads of state to the United States. Simultaneously, they are entrusted with securing the nation's financial system and cyber infrastructure—a formidable achievement orchestrated by its dedicated personnel. Their adeptness in fulfilling this dual mission with exceptional success underscores their unwavering commitment. It was a privilege to work alongside these outstanding individuals, each demonstrating unwavering excellence in their respective roles.

Upon retiring, I aimed for a private life, but conversations with family and friends about my experiences often led to the question, "When are you going to write your book?" Honestly, I had never seriously thought about it; I was not inclined to capitalize on the historical aspects of my journey with the Secret Service. Then, one evening over dinner in Kiawah Island, SC, my friends Heather, and Robert, along with my wife Lani, inadvertently encouraged the idea.

They planted a seed that would slowly grow over several years. This seed eventually blossomed into the novel you are about to read. I was advised to write about what I know, so I delved into a world—that is all too familiar to me.

Through this novel, I aspire to entertain readers while conveying my deep respect for the dedication of law enforcement officers and the clandestine operatives who navigate the complex world of intelligence. It is my earnest wish that this book pays tribute to the demanding missions they bravely tackle each day. My thoughts and admiration remain with them, always.

I hope you can enjoy: ***Room 23—A Secret Service Agent's Story of Espionage and Intrigue***

Sean Quarmby—Charlotte, North Carolina
July 1, 2024

CHAPTER 1

Abraham Lincoln

Nearly all men can stand adversity,
but if you want to test a man's character, give him power."
—Abraham Lincoln

His date etched on the desk calendar read April 14, 1865. The calendar was a poignant memento from his departed son, William, that Abraham Lincoln held dear. The morning unfolded with a series of meetings, one of which left a lasting impression. He sat in his office nestled in the southeastern upstairs corner of the White House. Lincoln, alongside his close confidant, Secretary of the Treasury Hugh McCulloch, deliberated on a matter that had been brewing for some time.

Months earlier, McCulloch had proposed the creation of a new agency to combat the widespread issue of counterfeit currency. The strains of the Civil War on the government's resources had exacerbated the country's woes. The startling revelation was that up to a third of circulating currency was counterfeit. It compelled Lincoln to seriously consider the idea. McCulloch's tenacity and sharp judgment on such matters had earned the President's admiration.

The proposal advocated for the establishment of an agency within the Treasury Department. It would be comprised of individuals with backgrounds in investigation, law enforcement, and military service. Lincoln, recognizing the urgency of the matter, agreed to the formation of this new agency. With utmost importance, he directed his aides to scrutinize the official proposal.

As the day progressed, Lincoln found himself in a cabinet meeting where McCulloch's proposal took center stage. McCulloch deliberated on the creation of an agency dedicated to addressing the rampant counterfeit currency problem plaguing the nation. At that historic meeting on April 14, 1865, Lincoln affixed his signature, bringing the United States Secret Service into existence.

Later in the evening, Mary Todd Lincoln reminded her husband of their plans to attend a performance of "Our American Cousin" at Ford's Theater. The theater was a short distance from the White House. Although Lincoln feigned interest, his thoughts lingered on the desire to spend time with his eleven-year-old son, Thomas. The young boy cherished his father's attention.

Unbeknownst to Lincoln, John Wilkes Booth was eagerly anticipating the play, setting the stage for a fateful turn of events.

CHAPTER 2

John Quinlan

"Patriotism is supporting your country all the time,
and your government when it deserves it."
—Mark Twain

John Quinlan's fascination with studying assassins started at a young age and stemmed from a deep curiosity about the human psyche. This was coupled with a belief in the possibility of predicting such extreme behaviors. His focus on creating a behavioral profile for potential assassins was fueled by the success of similar profiles in identifying serial killers, pedophiles, and rapists. However, he soon realized that predicting assassinations presented unique challenges. This was due to the diverse range of behavioral traits inherent in each individual.

The four Presidents—Lincoln, Garfield, McKinley, and Kennedy—who fell victim to assassinations, along with the attempted assassinations on F.D. Roosevelt, Truman, and Reagan, became the primary subjects of Quinlan's research. By carefully examining available data and evidence, he sought to identify patterns, commonalities, or red flags that could potentially lead to predicting future attempts.

The difficulty in predicting assassinations lay in the fact that individuals with such intentions often exhibited varying degrees of behavioral characteristics. Unlike other criminal profiles, the motivations behind assassinations were complex and multifaceted. Given the intricate nature of human behavior, Quinlan faced the challenge of discerning between potential threats and false positives.

Undeterred by the challenges, he dedicated numerous hours to his research. He was determined to uncover any correlations or indicators that might contribute to the development of a reliable behavioral profile for potential assassins. His journey involved delving into the intricacies of historical events, examining the psychological aspects of the perpetrators, and grappling with the limitations inherent in predicting such extreme and rare occurrences. He wanted to know what went wrong for the assassins and what went right for the Secret Service on those occasions.

Not many people even know about the attempt on President Franklin D. Roosevelt's life. On February 15, 1933, Roosevelt was giving a speech in Miami, FL from the back of an open car. An Italian immigrant, Giuseppe Zangara, fired five shots at close range. He missed Roosevelt but hit several bystanders. One of the bystanders was Chicago Mayor Anton Cermak who would eventually succumb to his injuries. It was later revealed that Zangara harbored profound anger and frustration toward the government, coupled with a deep sense of dissatisfaction with his own life.

The attempt on President Truman's life was on November 1, 1950, at the Blair House located across the street from the White House. President Truman had taken up temporary residence there while the White House was undergoing renovations. Two Puerto Rican nationals, Oscar Collazo and Griselio Torresola, attempted to storm the Blair House and assassinate President Truman. A shootout ensued between the assailants and White House police officers. This resulted in the death of Torresola and of Officer Leslie Coffelt. Officer Coffelt's steadfast determination was the reason the assassins were not able to gain access to the Blair House. Officer Coffelt, hailed as a hero, was able to wound Collazo and fatally shoot Torresola before he himself was fatally shot during the exchange of gunfire. Collazo would later say the motivation for the attack was to seek independence for Puerto Rico from the United States. Collazo faced a trial and was sentenced to death. However, President Truman commuted his sentence to life imprisonment. He was released in 1979 after serving twenty-nine years. During the shootout, President Truman was on the second floor of the Blair House. Some reports suggest he even peeked out the window to see what all the commotion was about.

Quinlan would recognize the motivation behind the attempt on President Ronald Reagan's life was quite a bit different. John Hinckley attempted to assassinate President Ronald Reagan on March 30, 1981. Hinckley's motives for the assassination attempt were complex. They stemmed from his obsession with actress Jodie Foster and his desire to impress her. Hinckley's mental health issues played a significant role in his actions. He believed that by assassinating President Reagan, he would gain attention and notoriety that would impress Jodie Foster. Hinckley's attack wounded President Reagan. Press Secretary James Brady was also shot by Hinckley. Many years later he would die from complications from his wound. Secret Service agent Timothy McCarthy and DC Metropolitan Police Officer Thomas Delahanty were also shot but recovered from their wounds. Hinckley was found not guilty by reason of insanity. He was confined to St. Elizabeths Psychiatric hospital in Washington, DC. On September 10, 2016, Hinkley was released with numerous restrictions as part of his ongoing treatment and supervision.

Quinlan's fascination with assassins took a deeper turn as he delved into his graduate thesis at Seton Hall University. The core of his research revolved around the intriguing concept that all assassins shared a common willingness to sacrifice their own lives for the life of their intended target. This idea lingered in his mind, haunting him frequently and with visceral intensity over the years.

As he navigated the intricate world of behavioral profiling for assassins, he couldn't help but reflect on the ironic origins of the United States Secret Service. The agency tasked with safeguarding the President was, in fact, established by President Abraham Lincoln who would later fall victim to an assassin's bullet on the very day he signed the Secret Service into existence. This historical twist added a layer of complexity to Quinlan's studies. It made him ponder the interplay between fate, security, and the constant threat to those in power.

It wasn't until later, after the assassination of President William McKinley in 1901, that the Secret Service would assume the responsibility of protecting the President of the United States. Until that time, they would eradicate most if not all counterfeit currency in the North and the South during the Civil War.

The evolution of the Secret Service's role in its infancy, transitioning from the eradication of counterfeit currency to the protection of the President, intrigued Quinlan. The agency's transformation mirrored the changing dynamics of security concerns in the country. This historical context further fueled his passion for understanding the motives and behaviors of potential assassins. Quinlan was hooked and his aim was set on being a Secret Service agent.

His academic journey, intertwined with the paradoxes of presidential security, solidified his determination. His aim was set on joining the ranks of the Secret Service. He was driven by a desire to contribute firsthand to the protection of the nation's leaders and to unravel the mysteries that surrounded the minds of those who sought to harm them. The path to becoming a Secret Service agent became both a professional aspiration and a personal quest for Quinlan. It would propel him into a world where history, psychology, and the ever-present threat of danger converged.

Earning the right to capture the attention of the esteemed agency was no small feat for John Quinlan; it demanded more than mere desire. At the tender age of seventeen, he found himself navigating the hallowed halls of West Chester University in Pennsylvania, his undergraduate pursuits shadowed by a burning ambition to join the ranks of the United States Secret Service.

His moment of reckoning unfolded at a job fair where he fortuitously stumbled upon the recruiting booth of the United States Secret Service. Agents Rodriguez and Stanford stood there, exuding professionalism and confidence in their dark suits, white shirts, and ties. The sleek, professional booth was adorned with the agency's emblem and informational banners. Their demeanor was approachable yet composed, reflecting their commitment to duty and public service. Equipped with brochures, posters, and a video presentation, the booth offered detailed information about career opportunities and the agency's mission. Their presence at the job fair showcased the agency's dedication to recruiting capable and dedicated individuals to join their ranks.

Quinlan engaged in a conversation with Agents Rodriguez and Stanford who were from the Philadelphia Field Office. They handed him a pamphlet and an application, a potential gateway to a future in the clandestine world. Yet, Agent Stanford's words lingered in the air, serving as a sobering reality check for the aspiring recruit.

In a frank exchange, Agent Stanford painted a vivid picture of the challenges awaiting a young man seeking entry into the prestigious agency during the tumultuous '80s. The prospects for a white Irish graduate fresh out of college were grim, according to Stanford. The advice offered was straightforward but profound, "Go be a cop, join the army, pursue graduate school; in essence, do something that sets you apart."

Undeterred by the daunting odds, Quinlan absorbed the wisdom imparted by Agent Rodriguez. He emphasized the fierce competition, the intense vetting process, and the grueling academies that lay ahead. The realization that only one in one thousand applicants would make it to the coveted status of recruit fueled Quinlan's determination.

Taking the agents' counsel to heart, he embarked on a dual path to distinguish himself. First, he became a police officer for the Jersey City Police Department, immersing himself in the challenges of law enforcement. Simultaneously, he attended Seton Hall University at night, diligently studying Education and Psychology to earn a master's degree.

The turning point arrived in April of 1989 when he received the pivotal call to undergo a polygraph examination by the U.S. Secret Service. This was the culmination of perseverance, strategic career choices, and unwavering dedication. Quinlan entered this critical phase of the selection process with a determined outlook. He carried with him the echoes of advice, the resilience of a police officer, and the intellectual prowess of a graduate student—all woven together in the tapestry of his journey towards an elusive dream.

CHAPTER 3

The Polygraph

"There are no secrets in the Secret Service."
—Unknown

As Quinlan stepped into the interview room, the door labeled Quiet Polygraph in Process, he was immediately struck by the atmosphere. The brightness of the room stood out, perhaps intentionally designed to keep everything visible and transparent. The space seemed clinical, akin to a doctor's office, yet with an air of heightened tension.

His gaze fixated on the polygraph device that awaited him. The setup was precise and sophisticated. A blood pressure cuff caught his attention, connected to a device placed on the table. This device, in turn, held a spool of graph paper with attached pencil arms, creating a visual representation of physiological responses. The whole system was interconnected, leading to a computer monitor displaying what appeared to be an electrocardiogram or EKG readout, reminiscent of a medical examination.

The details were meticulous. A breathing belt and electrodes completed the ensemble, all linked to the central device on the table. Quinlan couldn't help but notice the precision of the equipment, each element designed to capture and analyze different physiological indicators. The silent anticipation of the polygraph in process hung in the air, creating an environment where every detail seemed magnified.

This moment marked a crucial step in Quinlan's journey toward his goal of becoming a Secret Service agent. The bright room and the array of interconnected devices spoke to the gravity of the process and the significance of the role he aspired to undertake. As he prepared for the polygraph examination, the room became a symbolic threshold, where his dedication and sincerity would be put to the test in more ways than one.

"Mr. Quinlan," said a tall muscular fellow as he entered the room, "How are you feeling today? Are you nervous?"

"Uh a little, yes," was the best he could come up with.

"Try not to be, I am Special Agent Carl Minelli, and I am the polygrapher that is going to get you through this part of the applicant process."

Quinlan thought, *Get me through this,* as if bracing for some form of pain ahead.

"Before we get started on the actual polygraph exam using the polygraph device, I am going to brief you on the secrecy of this part of the application phase, do you understand?"

"Yes," he replied.

Moving in closer toward Quinlan, he said, "The specific questions asked during a Secret Service polygraph examination are not publicly disclosed in detail due to security reasons and the sensitivity of the information involved. The questions will revolve around topics related to your background, security clearance, potential involvement in illegal activities, loyalty to the United States, and any potential threats or risks you might pose to national security. Do you understand?"

Again, Quinlan replied, "Yes."

"I'll be asking you some example questions," Minelli began, his tone serious. "Such as: have you ever been involved in espionage against the United States? Have you knowingly associated with individuals or organizations involved in terrorism? Have you ever disclosed classified information without authorization? Have you committed a serious crime for which you were not caught? Have you intentionally lied on a security clearance form or during a background investigation? Have you researched ways to deceive this polygraph exam today, and is that your intention?"

Quinlan nodded, absorbing the weight of each question.

"That's where we'll begin. Any questions?"

Quinlan starting to perspire a little said, "Look, I am really nervous. Is that going to affect my results?"

Minelli replied in a serious tone but with a slight smile, "Not in the least. These questions are designed to assess your trustworthiness, reliability, and potential security risks. You have to understand that we may vary these questions based on your progress during the exam. Should you be a part of this agency as a Special Agent, your role will include access to extremely sensitive information. You will need to earn the highest clearance in the land, so to speak." Minelli let that sit there...

"So, my answer is yes, it is normal for you to be nervous, and I always take that into consideration when conducting these exams, alright?"

"Yes sir," was all Quinlan had left in him and the exam hadn't even started.

"John," Minelli's voice was firm, "I'm going to explain how this all works, okay?" Without pausing for a response, he pressed on, "The polygraph device records your physiological responses: changes in blood pressure, pulse rate, respiration, and skin conductivity, indicating fluctuations in perspiration. All these changes are revealed to me through the graph paper and the computer monitor."

Quinlan listened attentively, his nerves tingling at the gravity of the process unfolding before him, "Thank you for that information," he managed, his voice strained.

"Alright, let's begin," Minelli announced. "It is 1435 hours, Thursday, June 8, 1989. My name is Special Agent Carl Minelli, and today I am administering a polygraph to United States Secret Service Special Agent Applicant, John Quinlan. This exam is taking place in the New York Field Office of the U.S. Secret Service."

Several hours passed and after what felt like an eternity, Minelli rose from his chair. "Alright, Mr. Quinlan, we are done."

With no clocks in sight and his watch relinquished during the exam, Quinlan was left in the dark about the passing time. Urgently, he asked, "How did I do?"

"We're finished for today," Minelli replied calmly. "My charts will be sent to headquarters in Washington, DC. They'll be inspected for quality control to ensure my assessment of your truthfulness today is accurate."

"Did I pass?" he blurted out, the anticipation heavy in his words.

Minelli moved in to shake Quinlan's hand, and in that fleeting instant, Quinlan felt a surge of excitement, thinking, *Yes, I passed.* However, Minelli's words quickly tempered his enthusiasm,

"John, it is a process, and we will get back to you regarding the results of today's polygraph but for now, we are done."

The words hung in the air, indicating that the journey toward becoming a Secret Service agent involved several steps, including a thorough examination of the polygraph results.

For Quinlan, the wait for the outcome became a test of patience and resilience. The interview room, once filled with the brightness of anticipation, now carried a different encumbrance. The process was ongoing, and the final verdict on his suitability for the role would be delivered in due time. It was a reminder that the path to becoming a part of the Secret Service was not just about individual moments but an intricate series of evaluations that would ultimately determine his fate in this endeavor.

Quinlan later realized the arduous exam dragged on for five and a half excruciating hours, leaving him feeling demoralized and certain of his impending failure. *Why else would I endure such relentless questioning,* he bitterly pondered as he navigated the long drive back to his apartment in New Jersey. His mind churned with self-doubt, offering no solace from the relentless uncertainty.

I must have failed that one question, he thought, frustration boiling inside him, especially considering it concerned something he felt completely innocent about. *Why did the agent interrupt the exam so frequently, only to pose questions unrelated to...,* his thoughts abruptly halted as his phone shattered the silence with its ringing.

"John Quinlan," he answered, his voice strained with anticipation.

"Hey John, it's Agent Minelli..." The voice trailed off, and Quinlan's heart surged with hope. "Yes," he interjected eagerly, craving any news, regardless of its nature. *Either way,* he resolved silently, *I'll never endure that again. If I failed that damn test, that's the end of it. I'm done! No amount of anything is worth that level of humiliation.*

"Hey John, sorry, but I forgot to get you to sign an important document regarding today's exam," Minelli continued. "Can you come back and sign the form?"

Some form of relief flooded through Quinlan as he realized he hadn't received his verdict just yet. He exhaled deeply, grateful for the chance to return, albeit temporarily, from the brink of uncertainty.

He made a U-turn at the next exit and headed back to the New York Field Office. There, he met with Agent Minelli, who handed him the form to sign. As Quinlan scrawled his signature, Minelli couldn't shake the feeling of sympathy for him. Returning to sign the form was not part of any test, and Minelli recalled his own struggles with the polygraph, or the 'box,' as it was nicknamed.

"John," Minelli began, his voice tinged with empathy, "if my HQ finds nothing wrong with my charts, you can chalk today up as a win."

Quinlan's demeanor shifted instantly, gratitude washing over him as he thanked Minelli profusely.

But Minelli's tone turned solemn. "John, there are no secrets in the Secret Service. I know today seemed like a struggle for you. If all goes well with the remainder of the recruitment process, you'll endure some physical, mental, and maybe even some emotional pain during your initial training at the academy. Be careful what you thank me for."

Quinlan absorbed Minelli's words again, realizing that the road ahead might be even more challenging than he had anticipated.

CHAPTER 4

Under Investigation

Two weeks had slowly passed by when Quinlan's phone rang.

"Mr. Quinlan," the voice sounded stern. "Agent Steve Evaden here from the Secret Service. Congratulations on successfully passing your polygraph."

That simple statement served as Quinlan's only official acknowledgment of his polygraph results.

"I need to meet with you at your residence to go over your eighty-six and have you complete some additional forms. We'll also discuss your background investigation when we meet, sound good?" Evaden's tone was businesslike, yet not devoid of warmth.

"That sounds good," John replied, "When would you like to schedule this visit?"

"Tomorrow morning, 9:00am. Does that work?" Evaden suggested.

"Sure, I'll need to make some adjustments," He agreed, but before he could finish, Evaden cut in with a brisk, "Great, see you then," and the call ended.

Fortunately, Quinlan had the evening shift at the department, so the last-minute visit wouldn't be an issue. He felt a surge of relief at the confirmation of his polygraph results, even if it had come in an unexpectedly informal manner. He'd anticipated some sort of official notice, but instead, it was a brief phone call from Agent Evaden. The mention of an 'eighty-six' triggered his knowledge of government procedures—the Standard Form Eighty-Six, or SF 86, required by government employees seeking top-secret clearance. Completing it would furnish Evaden with the essential details for his background investigation.

Agent Evaden arrived at Quinlan's residence nestled in the quiet suburban enclave of Hawthorne, New Jersey. Quinlan rented the upstairs apartment of a quaint two-story home owned by Joseph and Nancy Chiello. The Chiellos, steeped in old-school Italian tradition, occupied the lower level. Quinlan often found himself amused by their thick accents, occasionally struggling to decipher their English. Nancy, a culinary virtuoso, treated him like one of her own sons, lavishing him with attention and hearty meals. Having graduated from Seton Hall two years prior, he had made this place his home. Joseph and Nancy, with their own grown children out on their own, took solace in having a police officer residing in their upstairs apartment, finding a sense of security in his presence.

"Hello, John, I am Agent Evaden," Quinlan greeted him with a firm handshake. "It's a pleasure to meet you," he said, welcoming him inside.

Over the next hour, the articulate and deliberate Agent Evaden explained the responsibilities of a Special Agent. He referred to this visit to Quinlan's residence as a 'home interview,' a customary practice where he typically met with both the applicant and their spouse or partner to outline the challenges and commitments of the role.

"John, you're single, or at least that's what you've indicated. But if there's someone significant in your life, they need to understand that the life of a Secret Service agent isn't a spectator sport. Eventually, the whole family gets to play," Evaden advised in a direct manner.

He would stress more than once during his visit that bringing work home was inevitable. It seeped into the mind and could affect one's personal life at times.

"Look John," Evaden began, his tone serious, "It's a twenty-four hour job. The Secret Service has the unfortunate distinction of having the highest divorce rate among all federal agencies."

The statement lingered with Quinlan, though it didn't fully sink in since he wasn't in a relationship at the time. Still, he grasped the importance of relaying this information, especially to recruits with families. They all needed to understand the reality of the commitment they were making.

Agent Evaden continued to outline the remainder of the background investigation process. "John, you'll likely hear from old friends, acquaintances, and individuals that are current in your personal and professional life that they've been contacted by the government."

"I see. Should I inform them that you or someone else might reach out to them?" Quinlan inquired.

"You can if you want," Evaden replied, "but I'll be sourcing names from those you've already provided on your SF 86. You know, the kid you had a scuffle with in grade school or the ex-girlfriend you had a falling out with recently. I'll be seeking out individuals you didn't list to gather their perspective on you."

Quinlan's surprise was evident as the situation began to feel like a peculiar game of chess. "Alright, I understand," he responded, unsure of what else to say in the face of this unexpected turn.

"I leave no stone unturned, John." Evaden's words hung heavy in the air as he stared directly into Quinlan's eyes for what felt like an eternity.

Quinlan had no reply.

Agent Evaden finally broke the silence as he rose to conclude the visit, "Sound good?"

He escorted Evaden to the door, inwardly remarking, *God, this guy is intense.*

Evaden assured Quinlan that he would hear from the Secret Service once the background check was completed.

Once again extending his hand at the door, Evaden added, "Be patient, no news is good news."

As Evaden departed, Quinlan's mind buzzed with thoughts of the people in his life, wondering whom he might have offended and what his sergeant at the Jersey City Police Department would say about his job performance.

In the following months, he began to receive inquiries from friends and acquaintances, just as Agent Evaden had predicted. Most expressed concern for his well-being. It seemed that when Evaden and the other investigators conducted their field inquiries, they were intentionally vague. They didn't indicate that Quinlan was seeking employment with the government. In fact, the specific agency, the 'U.S. Secret Service,' was not mentioned to any of the sources.

CHAPTER 5

The Call

"The two most important days in your life are the day you are born and the day you find out why."
—Mark Twain

Four months had passed by when Quinlan's phone buzzed with a call from the U.S. Office of Personnel Management. They provided him with the precise details of his upcoming medical examination—date, time, and location. It was another reminder of the impersonal machinery of the agency, seemingly indifferent to the concerns of its applicants. Nevertheless, the call suggested that his background investigation might have yielded favorable results.

Frustration gnawing at him, Quinlan retrieved Agent Evaden's business card and dialed the number listed under "Desk Tel."

"This is Agent Evaden," came the brisk response.

"Yes, sir, hello, John Quinlan here..." he began, but Evaden cut in smoothly, "Yes, John, how are you?"

"Good, but I wanted to check on the status of my background investigation because I was just given a date and time for a medical physical and..."

Once more, Evaden interrupted, "That is good, as it looks like you're in the home stretch."

"So, does that mean I passed the background check?"

"John, I can't discuss the results with you. It's not up to me to tell you how you did or if you got a passing grade. I submitted my report to Headquarters–Security Clearance Division about a week ago. I am assuming if they were not interested in continuing you in the recruiting process, you wouldn't have a physical. Am I right?"

Aggravated by the lack of transparency and any sense of encouragement, Quinlan simply replied, "Yes, sir, okay, thank you."

Quinlan completed the physical, but days passed without any word. Then, one evening after his shift at the police department, he checked his answering machine to find a message waiting. "Hello, this is Brian Gregory of the Secret Service New York Field Office. Please call me at your earliest convenience," the voice on the recording urged, leaving a telephone number.

It was already 6:30 pm when Quinlan dialed the phone number. He doubted anyone would answer at this hour.

"Hello, Agent Gregory."

"Yes, good afternoon. This is John Quinlan, and I have a voicemail message that you tried to reach me earlier."

"Yes, John, this is Brian Gregory with the New York Field Office, and I am pleased to offer you a conditional appointment to the New York Field Office of the Secret Service. I need a verbal for now, and we can discuss all the particulars when you come in, should you say yes to me now."

"Of course, YES!" an excited Quinlan replied.

Agent Gregory provided him with his EOD, or Entry on Duty date, marking the day he would officially begin his service with the U.S. Secret Service.

CHAPTER 6

Joseph 'Mack' Mackey

Quinlan found himself taking the oath of allegiance to the U.S. Secret Service amidst the imposing aura of the New York Field Office, nestled within the financial district of Manhattan. Beside him stood Joseph Mackey, another special agent whose significance would only reveal itself with time. Little did Quinlan realize; they were on the brink of forging a partnership that would transcend mere professional camaraderie. It would evolve into a steadfast friendship.

Their journey would commence with three rigorous months of training at the Federal Law Enforcement Training Center in Glynco, Georgia. This would be followed by an additional intensive three-month stint at the specialized Secret Service academy in Beltsville, MD. Anxiety coiled in Quinlan's gut as he anticipated the impending training, each step through the halls of the New York Field Office feeling heavier than the last. Amidst the hub of activity, a voice broke through the chaos, calling out his newly acquired moniker, "Hey Q!"

Turning, Quinlan was met with the sight of his newly acquainted colleague, Joe Mackey, occupying an unassuming cubicle within the Forgery Squad.

"Is this where you'll be stationed?" Quinlan inquired, his curiosity piqued.

"Yeah, the Forgery Squad. It's where they break in the greenhorns without causing too much damage. And you?" Mackey responded.

"I'm headed to the counterfeit squad," Quinlan revealed, his anticipation tinged with a hint of excitement.

"Were you in law enforcement before this?" Mackey asked, breaking the ice. "They told me I'd start off investigating stolen and fraudulent government checks since I don't have law enforcement experience."

"Yeah, I was a cop in Jersey City," Quinlan responded. "We all gotta start somewhere, right?"

Mackey suggested, "Since we're gonna be new recruits and probably bunk mates for the next six months, why don't we grab a slice of pizza for lunch and get to know each other?"

"Sounds good to me," Quinlan agreed.

Over lunch, Mackey painted a vivid picture of his roots, hailing from Newark, NJ. He spoke with the rapid-fire tempo of a true city dweller, often needing to repeat himself for clarity. He graduated with flying colors from Rutgers with a degree in Cyber Security and Network Intrusion. He believed his skills could land him a comfortable job in any of Newark's numerous banks or insurance companies. Opting for a lucrative cyber security position at Providence Insurance, he spent the last five years there. He confessed to Quinlan that the world of cyber security lacked the adrenaline rush he craved.

"One day, I'm sitting at my desk, and I get this call from a Special Agent Mary Brooks out of the Newark Field Office of the Secret Service," Mackey recounted to Quinlan. "She was looking into a guy who used to be in our sales department, you know, bigwig executive type. She swung by the office to chat with me. Turns out they were after him for conspiracy to traffic in child pornography or something like that."

Curiosity piqued, Quinlan asked, "What did she need from you?"

"That's what I wondered, too, until I remembered something from a couple of years back. See, my cyber unit conducted an internal audit of all the computers in the office. We started by focusing on employees visiting questionable websites. My unit got the go-ahead to install a network monitoring tool, which I happened to create myself, to keep tabs on internet usage within the organization."

"Wow, that's pretty technical stuff," Quinlan interjected, offering Mackey a moment to catch his breath.

"Wait, it gets better," Mackey continued. "We tracked the bandwidth usage and noticed patterns suggesting this guy was visiting some crazy sites during the day and at night when the offices were closed. You know, dark web shit. I suggested we put up web filtering software, again something I designed, to block access. But the higher-ups decided to let it slide, with a silent alert to a designated cyber unit investigator."

"Let me guess," Quinlan interjected, catching on, "you were the designated cyber unit investigator?"

"Of course," Mackey replied, his tone tinged with a hint of pride. "I planted a keylogger device on the target's computer and caught him red-handed trying to visit the sites we had blocked, completely unaware."

"Wow," Quinlan said, "Mackey, you've got to slow it down a bit. This is flying over my head. Either that or it's your fast Jersey speak."

"Yeah, I get that a lot. Just call me Mack, everyone does," Mackey said with a casual smile.

Quinlan nodded in agreement. "Got it, Mack."

Mackey leaned in, his demeanor growing more serious. "Alright, so here's the deal. We narrowed it down to this guy on the 30th floor. I got the green light to install monitoring software—another keylogger—on his office computer. It tracks everything—keystrokes, website visits, application usage. Did the whole thing after hours to keep it discreet."

Quinlan leaned forward, intrigued. "And then what happened to the guy?"

Mackey replied, "Next thing I know, they are walking him out the door. He was fired violating the clear policies and guidelines regarding acceptable internet usage in the workplace or that was the official line. He was trying to access child porn sites and other dark shit," Mackey said now, seeming reticent.

“So where does the Secret Service come into the picture?” Quinlan asked.

“Oh, yeah, so this Agent Brooks comes to visit me about the case because apparently after being released from Providence, he got deeper into buying and selling pornographic images of underage children. She requested my assistance and with the approval of Providence’s legal folks, I helped them image all of the hard drives from his computers they seized from his home. Man, he had about seven computers in total. We found thousands of images of child pornography. He was also part of a human trafficking operation out of Thailand.”

Quinlan was captivated by Mack’s narrative, hanging on every word as the story unfolded.

“Yeah, so I was essentially on loan from Providence Insurance as a private sector forensic examiner, delving into anything digital,” Mackey continued, a sense of pride evident in his voice. “My bosses were all for it; we were collaborating with law enforcement to improve the community’s safety. And for me, it felt like I was truly making a difference.”

Mackey took a moment to catch his breath, punctuating the tale with a bite of his last piece of pizza.

“Wow, that is some awesome stuff right there,” Quinlan exclaimed, admiration evident in his voice. “So, was she recruiting you the whole time?” he asked, curiosity brimming.

“Nah, I didn’t get that feeling,” Mackey replied thoughtfully. “But she did keep emphasizing the job’s highlights, and let me tell you, it wasn’t about the pay. Trust me on that. I’ve wanted to work for the Service ever since my time on that task force. Convincing my wife, though, that was another story.”

Quinlan nodded in understanding. “Yeah, how did she take it? The pay cut, the travel... all of it?”

“Not well,” Mackey admitted with a rueful smile. “The home interview was tough. By then, I’d passed the polygraph and the background check, and my wife knew how much I wanted it. But she kept reminding me, “Joe, you’re thirty-six now, right at the age cutoff for becoming a Special Agent." She'd say, "There's a reason there's a cutoff, Joe. It's dangerous."

"She's right," Quinlan exclaimed, struck by Mackey's words. He could empathize, recalling his own home interview. The thought of having family present during such a pivotal moment... it added an entirely new dimension. He remembered Agent Evaden's warning: "This isn't a spectator sport; eventually, the whole family gets to play."

Quinlan found himself growing fond of Joe Mackey. There was something refreshingly genuine and honest about him, qualities that he considered rare in the world they inhabited.

"It's your turn, Q," Mackey said with a hint of anticipation in his voice.

Quinlan began, testing out the new nickname for Mackey. "Mack, I don't have much of a family story. I'm not married and I'm not seeing anyone serious. My parents are retired and live in Northern New Jersey. I have a brother who is NYPD assigned to the 43rd Precinct in the Bronx. He is part of the Anti-Crime Unit. My sister lives a quiet life down in Georgia with her family."

"Fair enough," Mackey responded.

"But let's take a look at the last year of our lives," Quinlan said, shifting his gaze upward in reflection. "We had to pass an exam, and let's face it, that was no walk in the park. We survived an initial interview, only to endure an additional three-person panel interview. We—or I, barely survived the polygraph..."

"Barely is spot on, me, too," Mackey chimed in with a laugh.

Quinlan continued, "We had to spill our life stories on a thirty-page form, endure an eight-month background investigation that delved into every corner of our lives, and for what..." He paused, letting the weight of their journey sink in. "For a top-secret security clearance and the trust that comes with it."

"Yeah, but would you do it again?" Mackey interjected.

"Without a doubt," Quinlan replied, conviction ringing in his voice. "Without a doubt."

CHAPTER 7

Threat Case

"Insanity is often the logic of an accurate mind overtaxed."
—Oliver Wendell Holmes, Sr.

Quinlan completed Basic Agent Training in Glynco, Georgia, followed by the rigorous U.S. Secret Service Special Agent training in Beltsville, MD. He shed ten pounds through sweat and determination. On his first day as an agent, he found himself immersed in the vibrant atmosphere of the New York Field Office (NYFO), teeming with 210 Special Agents, and backed by a dedicated team of thirty support staff. Together, they represented a diverse array of expertise, covering everything from Counterfeit Currency and Cyber Security to Protection and Protective Intelligence.

Assigned to the Counterfeit Currency squad, Quinlan plunged headfirst into the gritty underbelly of the five boroughs that made up New York City. He was tasked with stemming the tide of fake counterfeit $50 and $100 bills flooding the streets of the city and beyond. His attention sharpened on a particular counterfeit operation stemming from the Dominican community nestled between Upper Manhattan and the Bronx.

However, despite the urgency of the case, his junior status in the office meant he was assigned to a temporary two-week rotation of night duty response. He was approaching his seventh month in the NYFO when he found himself partnered with seasoned Special

Agent Rick Boland for this temporary assignment. Although not the most sought-after assignment, the 10:00 pm to 6:00 am night duty response shift was crucial in a city as large as New York. Especially, given the continuous occurrence of crime around the clock.

At 3:05 am, Quinlan found himself immersed in reviewing counterfeit reports, dissecting the influx of fake $50 and $100 bills infiltrating the Dominican community. Suddenly, the overhead office speaker crackled, delivering a summons that pulled Quinlan from his analysis.

"Agents Boland and Quinlan, please respond to the duty desk for an urgent matter," echoed the dispatcher's call.

Recognizing the gravity of the situation, Quinlan swiftly made his way to the duty desk, where Agent Rick Boland awaited, already engrossed in conversation with Max Reeve, the office dispatcher. Reeve's notepad, littered with hastily scribbled notes, hinted at the urgency of the situation.

Boland's proximity to the duty room ensured his prompt arrival. He stood tall at 6'2" with the air of a seasoned agent. A former Marine and nearing the end of his twenty-five-year tenure, Boland wore his experience like a badge of honor, often joking about retirement with a twinkle in his eye.

"Don't expect me to take any risks. My wife has all the cruise brochures neatly organized, and unlike most of your husbands and wives, my wife still loves me," he'd quip to others in the office, a testament to his dry wit and enduring commitment to duty.

A team player through and through, Boland extended a firm handshake to Quinlan. Despite his seven months in the office, Quinlan had yet to meet every member of the office, including those in the Intelligence squad.

"Richard Boland, but you can call me Rick," he introduced himself, setting the stage for what seemed to be the beginning of a long and storied night.

Quinlan clasped Boland's hand firmly and introduced himself, "John Quinlan, part of the counterfeit squad. Pleasure to meet you, sir."

"Rick, not sir. Never sir," Boland replied with a grin, his demeanor casual yet authoritative.

Max wasted no time briefing the duo on the urgent matter at hand. "A short while ago, we received word from Secret Service Intelligence Division in DC regarding multiple threatening calls to the White House operator, targeting POTUS."

"Not to be a smartass, Agent Quinlan, but POTUS stands for President of the United States," Max interjected, his tone more informative than condescending.

Quinlan, nodded in acknowledgment. "Got it. Appreciate the info."

Max continued, "The calls began around 2:00 am and lasted until approximately 2:35 am. The caller, identifying himself as 'Jason,' made direct threats against POTUS in each call. Intelligence Division is currently transcribing the conversations and will send over the transcripts and call logs shortly."

Boland wasted no time in getting to the heart of the matter. "Where's this 'Jason' calling from?"

"The phone number has a 718-area code, and ISD traced it to an address in Breezy Point, Queens," Max explained, shooting a glance at Quinlan to preempt any misunderstanding. "ISD, or Information Support Division, pinpointed the number to 1329 Beach Avenue, Queens, NY 11697. And just to be clear, the calls to the White House originated from the same telephone number."

"Thanks, Max. Let's get moving," Boland said firmly to Quinlan, his mind already charting their next course of action.

Boland maneuvered his sleek black Ford Explorer, a government owned vehicle or "GOV" as it was called by most government agents, through the quiet streets of Queens, NY. The vehicle, carefully maintained by Boland, gleamed under the moonlit sky, a testament to his dedication to readiness. Quinlan rode shotgun, the two of them embarking on what promised to be a half-hour journey to Breezy Point.

Driving through the upper-class enclave, Boland couldn't ignore the stark contrast of the surroundings. "This part of Queens is breathtaking, but other parts of Queens are downright shit holes. John, have you ever been to Breezy Point?" he asked, breaking the silence.

Quinlan responded, "I haven't but I definitely want to come back and make a day of it."

Boland nodded, his gaze distant. "A lot of brave souls call this place home. NYPD, firefighters, they all live out here in this part of Queens. Probably one of the safest places in the five boroughs."

His thoughts were interrupted by a call from Max back at the duty desk, relaying concerning news of threatening emails sent to the White House, escalating the situation further. The sender, using the alias Jason Kramton, had made chilling declarations of violence.

Boland's mind raced as he pieced together the puzzle. "Jason Kramton...why does that name sound familiar," he muttered to himself, the memory inching closer to recognition.

Before he could articulate his thoughts, Max's voice crackled through the phone, confirming his suspicions. "Jason Kramton is an alias for Jason Knight. He's notorious for his numerous attempts to breach White House security and other Secret Service checkpoints."

Boland's grip tightened on the steering wheel as the intensity of the situation settled over him. Memories flooded back, vivid recollections of a past encounter at the Waldhorn Plaza Hotel.

"Jason Knight...the Waldhorn Plaza..." Boland murmured, his mind racing back to a chilling incident involving a small .22 pistol and a breach of presidential security.

With determination strengthening his gaze, Boland brought the Explorer to a stop by the edge of the roadside, attempting to gather his thoughts and focus. Realizing the urgency of the situation, he sensed a starting point for their investigation.

Boland remembered that evening now. Knight had effortlessly blended in with the hotel staff, slipping under the radar until an observant Secret Service post stander caught wind of his unfamiliar presence. Alerted by a vigilant hotel employee, the agent approached Knight, only to have him bolt. Swift action from a plainclothes NYPD detective, part of the security detail, brought Knight to the ground.

Boland shared this tale with Quinlan, breaking the silence with a pointed question. "John, forgive me for being blunt, but we're closing in on Jason's residence. I need to know—where do you come from? What's your background?"

Quinlan met Boland's gaze, understanding the implications. "You're asking about my background before the Secret Service?"

"Yeah, I need to know if you've got what it takes," Boland clarified.

Over the next few minutes, Quinlan recounted his stint as a Jersey City cop, detailing his experiences dealing with gangs and minor altercations. Boland seemed to relax slightly with this newfound knowledge.

"Here's the deal, John," Boland began, his tone grave. "We had Knight—aka Kramton—last year after he tried to breach security with a firearm at a POTUS event. We were gearing up to go to the grand jury for attempted assassination of POTUS, but a federal judge intervened. He ordered a psychiatric evaluation before we could even secure an indictment on the charges. And wouldn't you know it, he slipped out of the psychiatric ward at Presbyterian Hospital in White Plains. We've been chasing him ever since."

Quinlan's jaw tightened as he absorbed the significance of the situation. "Let's bring him in," he stated, his resolve unwavering.

Boland wasted no time, reaching out to Max at the duty desk to arrange backup from the NYPD. Max had already established communication with NYPD Sergeant Stan Nichols from the 100th Precinct. Sergeant Nichols assigned Officer Jeff Blake to the task, briefing him on the ongoing operation. Boland and Quinlan planned to meet with Officer Blake to strategize the next steps of their pursuit.

CHAPTER 8

Breezy Point

The brisk October air carried a chill as it weaved through the tranquil streets of Breezy Point like a delicate melody of nature. Quinlan, a stranger to this particular corner of Queens, found himself captivated by the quiet allure of the town. Despite the urgency of their mission, he couldn't help but appreciate the quaint charm that surrounded them. He silently contemplated the possibility of returning under more favorable circumstances.

Boland opted for Beach Avenue as they made their way to the precinct, a decision that allowed them to pass by Knight's residence. The clock ticked closer to 4:00 am, the streets devoid of life save for the parked cars lining Beach Ave. As they approached the 1300 block, Boland eased off the accelerator.

The neighborhood exuded an air of tranquility, a stark contrast to the turmoil brewing beneath the surface. Boland couldn't reconcile Knight's presence in this idyllic setting. "How does he fit in here?" he muttered, scanning the rows of houses bathed in darkness.

As they cruised past 1329 Beach Avenue, Boland's suspicions deepened. The dual entrances of the two-story home hinted at a landlord-tenant arrangement, confirming his earlier speculation. Only the glow of a solitary lamp illuminated the entrance to the lower level, while a faint light seeped from the upstairs, casting a mysterious aura over the residence.

"We'll be back," Boland declared, his voice tinged with determination as they continued on their journey, leaving the quiet streets of the neighborhood behind them—for now.

They navigated a few more blocks along Beach Avenue before veering onto the town's main street. It wasn't long before the well-lit precinct parking lot greeted them. A marked NYPD police vehicle flashed its headlights as they pulled in, prompting Boland to reciprocate before parking alongside the patrol car. With a flick of a switch, Boland illuminated the interior of their vehicle, a gesture aimed at easing the tension.

Stepping out, all four exchanged introductions under the glow of the precinct's parking lot lights.

"Rick Boland, and this is my partner, John Quinlan. We're with the Secret Service. You must be Officer Blake?" Boland initiated.

"Call me Jeff. Yes, good to meet you. And this is my partner, Officer Sheila Priestly," Officer Blake replied. "Max, your dispatcher, gave us the heads up on the address. I even dug into our precinct logs and found a noise complaint from Joanne Harkness, the resident downstairs, about five years back. Seems there was a bit of a ruckus."

Quinlan interjected; curiosity piqued. "Did you manage to dig up anything else? Tax records, maybe?"

Officer Blake smirked. "I do my homework, fellas. You're finally throwing us some action tonight."

Officer Priestly chimed in, her tone lighthearted. "My partner here is a regular Lieutenant Columbo. See, this is the only little resort town in the five boroughs, so we don't see much action out here. But Officer Blake's on top of it," she said, as she high fived her partner.

"Starsky, where's Hutch, right?" Officer Blake joked, then turned serious. "We did some digging. Joanne Harkness is indeed listed as the owner of the property and residing there."

Quinlan admired Officer Blake's thoroughness, reminiscing about his own days in uniform.

Boland acknowledged their findings, impressed.

"Great work, Jeff. More than we expected. Did you happen to find any info on the upstairs address, 1329 B?" Boland inquired.

"No luck there. No other address listed," Officer Blake replied.

"Now spill it. What's got our sergeant in hypertension mode?"

Boland launched into a detailed account, leaving no stone unturned as he recounted the intricate details of the case to the NYPD officers. Aware of the gravity of the situation, he spared no effort in conveying the seriousness of the threat. He emphasized the presence of weapons to the chilling intent to assassinate the President, likely exacerbated by the assailant's diagnosed psychosis. The two officers listened attentively, interjecting with questions and clarifications as needed.

As the clock edged towards 5:00 am, Boland couldn't ignore the impending dawn. Despite the comforting glow of the full moon in the October sky, darkness still enveloped the surroundings, providing crucial cover for their operation. With the briefing complete, Boland turned to the officers, inviting their input.

Officer Blake wasted no time inquiring about the tactical approach. Boland, ever diplomatic, presented the plan as a collaborative effort, soliciting their assistance rather than issuing orders. "Could one of you cover the rear of the residence in case our suspect tries to make a break for it?" he suggested.

Officer Priestly volunteered without hesitation. "I've got the rear covered," she confirmed.

"Excellent," Boland nodded, appreciative of her readiness. "Then Quinlan and I will approach the front door with Officer Blake. Hopefully, Ms. Harkness will answer, as your research suggests. Sound like a plan?"

The officers nodded in agreement, their resolve matching Boland's as they prepared to confront the unknown awaiting them behind the door of 1329 Beach Avenue.

Boland and Quinlan secured their issued ballistic vests, a precaution against potential small arms fire. Donning their blue windbreakers emblazoned with both "U.S. Secret Service" and "Police" markings, they projected an air of authority as they climbed back into the Ford Explorer. Officers Blake and Priestly, in their marked unit, joined them for the short journey back to the residence.

Within minutes, they arrived at the scene, positioning themselves strategically along the block. Boland, opting for a vantage point two houses down, while the marked NYPD unit parked even further away. Boland adhered to protocol, radioing their location to the field office dispatcher.

"New York, Boland," he announced.

"Boland, New York, go ahead," came Max's prompt response.

"Hold Quinlan and me out at 1329 Beach Avenue, Queens, NY for 30 minutes," Boland instructed.

"Roger that. Be safe, Boland," Max acknowledged before signing off.

Approaching the residence, Boland couldn't help but notice the drawn curtains on the second-floor windows, save for one. A faint glow emanated from the otherwise darkened room, hinting at the possibility of someone inside, perhaps Knight himself, observing their every move.

Meanwhile, Officer Priestly conducted a quick radio check with her partner and the precinct dispatcher before silently slipping behind the house. The trio approached the front door, passing by two residential mailboxes—one labeled 1329, the other 1329 B—confirming their earlier suspicions of a landlord and tenant arrangement. Boland rapped lightly on the door, opting for a gentle knock over the jarring ring of the doorbell.

As they waited for a response, Blake's radio crackled to life. "Blake, Priestly. A light turned on downstairs, repeat downstairs. Nothing upstairs. Copy?"

Acknowledging the update, Blake relayed, "Copy. We're knocking on the downstairs door now."

Officer Priestly turned from her post at the rear of the residence, her gaze sweeping over the tranquil scene before her. Beyond the row of boats docked on the bay that partners with the Atlantic ocean, she knew her presence was the only barrier between the peaceful waters and the potential threat posed by the individual they sought. Her vigilance heightened as she remained on high alert.

Inside the residence, a light flickered to life in the downstairs foyer, drawing their attention to the figure of a woman in her mid-70s. She was dressed in baggy sweatpants and an oversized sweater. She peered through the curtains, attempting to discern the identity of her unexpected visitors. Boland was silently thankful for having an NYPD uniformed officer present, especially at such an early hour.

As the woman cracked open the front door but kept the glass storm door closed, a muffled voice emanated from within. "Yes? What's the matter? Is everything okay?" she inquired.

"Police, ma'am," Officer Blake responded in a hushed tone, his breath misting against the glass. "We need to talk to you urgently."

It was as though the woman snapped out of a trance. Hastily unlocking the door, she exclaimed, "Yes, yes, come in! I'm sorry, I didn't realize you were the police, and I just woke up. It's early, you know?"

Boland stepped forward as they entered the foyer, mindful of the delicate situation. "Yes, ma'am, we're trying to keep it quiet. This matter may involve your tenant upstairs."

"Mr. Kramton," she interjected.

"Yes, that's right, Mr. Jason Kramton. Is he home?" Boland inquired.

"He should be up there. When I came to see who was knocking on my door just now, I heard him upstairs. He must have heard you knock," the woman replied.

With concern for his partner's safety, Officer Blake radioed Priestly, alerting her to the possibility of Knight being awake and attempting to flee out the back. Assuring Ms. Harkness of her safety, Boland explained that they needed to discuss a family matter with Kramton, urging her to remain indoors and refrain from contacting anyone.

As they conversed, Ms. Harkness revealed that Kramton had only been living there for four months, with minimal belongings and no apparent family in the area. Quinlan presented a smile and a gentle nudge on her shoulder which offered reassurance before asking her to return inside and secure the doors.

As the officers knocked on Kramton's door, however, they were met with silence. Ms. Harkness grew increasingly impatient, her concern mounting with each passing moment.

She stepped outside her house, joining the trio on the doorstep. "I have a key to the front door. If you want, you could yell up the stairs. Let him know you're the police. He's probably not answering the door because he doesn't know who you are," she suggested.

Quinlan exchanged a glance with Boland and Officer Blake before nodding. "She's probably half right. I say we take her up on that idea."

"That's a great idea, dear. Go ahead and get the key, and we'll talk with Mr. Kramton," Officer Blake affirmed.

Ms. Harkness retrieved her key and unlocked the door, ushering them into the foyer. Quinlan then instructed her to return to her apartment and lock the door and she readily complied. Officer Blake radioed his partner and relayed their plans for entry. She acknowledged and prepared herself by taking cover behind a solitary tool shed. He then led the way, his uniform lending an air of authority as they ascended the stairs to the second-floor residence. Arriving at another door, they discovered it lacked a lock.

"It's a privacy door-no lock," Officer Blake whispered to the others, his voice barely audible in the tense silence. "On three, we go in. Good?"

Boland and Quinlan exchanged determined nods; their resolve evident as they awaited Officer Blake's countdown signal.

CHAPTER 9

The Bomb

"Courage is resistance to fear, mastery of fear—not absence of fear."
—Mark Twain

Officer Blake silently counted down, "One, two, three!" They stormed into the apartment, voices commanding, "POLICE, POLICE, get on the ground, POLICE!"

Silence enveloped them, an eerie stillness. If Kramton or Knight by his actual name, had received any hint of their arrival, he would have swiftly vanished out the rear or sought refuge in a cunning hiding spot. Officer Blake keyed his radio, his voice tense. "Priestly, we've breached the upstairs apartment. Any signs of movement?"

"Negative. No activity on my end, unless our suspect has turned into a ghost."

Their flashlights cut through the darkness, casting long shadows. As Boland's eyes adjusted, he discerned the outlines of three rooms, one bathed in a faint, pulsating glow.

Officer Blake positioned himself by the front door, ready for any sudden movement. Meanwhile, Quinlan and Boland split up, moving cautiously along the perimeter walls, their senses alert. Quinlan approached the room with the glowing light, heart pounding with anticipation. As he neared the source, he realized it was emanating from a computer screen, casting an ethereal glow in the dimness of the room.

He located a switch on the wall and turned to his companions, his voice low but urgent. "I've found the light switch. When I flip it, let's all announce 'Police,' alright?"

With a click, the lights flooded the computer room, their beams revealing an empty space. The repeated shouts of 'Police' echoed, but there was no response. The illumination spilled into the rest of the apartment, guiding them to the remaining switches. As each light flickered to life, the apartment was bathed in brightness, revealing every corner.

In the kitchen area, they spotted two packed bags placed next to a round dining table, a silent testament to Knight's possible plans to travel.

Despite their thorough search, Knight remained elusive. They combed through every inch of the apartment, even venturing into the attic's crawl space, but found nothing. Their attention shifted to the two bags that resembled possible luggage.

Quinlan turned to Boland; his expression troubled. "We're treading on thin ice here, relying on what might be seen as a consent search, especially since we had the landlord open the door for us. If Knight isn't here, we'll need a search warrant. I'm itching to see what's in those bags, but..." Boland cut him off, determination in his voice. "There's no time for a search warrant. This is a matter of national security, and..."

In that crucial moment, Quinlan's voice shattered the tense silence like a bolt of lightning. "GUN! Gun in the couch!" Without hesitation, Officer Blake and the two agents dropped to the ground, their training kicking in automatically.

"Quinlan, what's going on?" Boland demanded urgently; his voice edged with concern.

Quinlan had spotted a glimmer of metal, the telltale shine of a .38 revolver peeking out from beneath a cushion on the couch. The word "gun" hung in the air, a chilling reminder of the still present danger.

Reacting swiftly, Officer Blake reached out and flicked off the room light, enveloping them in deeper darkness and silence.

"He's in the couch," Quinlan whispered to Boland, his voice barely audible in the darkness. Boland wasted no time, swiftly maneuvering to the far side of the couch. His imposing 6'2" figure loomed large in the dimness. With a powerful motion, Boland flipped the couch into the air with a strength that seemed almost superhuman. The couch crashed down, and Knight spilled out from his hidden refuge. Quinlan's training took over as he deftly kicked the revolver out of Knight's reach and placed him in handcuffs, with Officer Blake and Boland quickly moving in to assist.

As they lifted Knight to his feet, they couldn't help but notice the state of his pants. He had pissed himself, either due to the sudden and powerful toss of the couch or the prolonged confinement to his makeshift hiding spot.

Time seemed to return to its normal rhythm as they gathered their wits. Officer Blake reached for his radio, his voice steady despite the adrenaline still coursing through his veins. "Priestly, Blake here. We have the suspect. Could you please check on Ms. Harkness downstairs?"

"Roger that," Priestly's voice confirmed over the radio, her tone crisp and professional.

Jason Knight, known also as Kramton, appeared virtually unchanged from the day Boland had first restrained him at the Waldhorn Plaza Hotel. To confirm his identity, Boland demanded to see Knight's identification. Without a word, Knight nodded towards the bedroom, indicating where it could be found. Quinlan moved slowly, in that direction.

"Where do you think you're headed, Mr. Fed?" Knight's voice interrupted. "My passports in that backpack you tossed like a ragdoll when Goliath over there hurled me and the bag out of my hideaway. Quite the invention, wouldn't you agree?"

"What invention?" Quinlan inquired, intrigued.

"My hideaway couch," Knight said. "I dismantled the pull-out bed and fashioned a spot to hide and observe, hide and observe, hide and...." He kept repeating the phrase over and over.

Knight explained with a self-satisfied grin spreading across his face, "When I heard you downstairs bothering Ms. Harkness, I slipped into my hideaway and watched you stumble about. I could have taken you out with a single shot."

Quinlan redirected his attention to the backpack, now positioned prominently in the room's center. "Do you have any firearms in the house?" he probed.

"Oh, I have plenty. They're scattered all over," Knight replied casually.

With caution, Quinlan donned protective gloves and illuminated the backpack with his flashlight. Immediately, he spotted a Glock Semi-Automatic pistol in an outer pocket of the bag. Methodically, he disarmed it, ensuring it was safe before placing it on the kitchen table. Next, he reached in the bag and found a Sig-Sauer P229 Semi-Automatic 9-millimeter and repeated the process making the weapon safe. Finally, his fingers brushed against a heavier object.

Meanwhile, Knight stood in handcuffs, his grin widening into a slow, unsettling chuckle that echoed in the room. Simultaneously, Quinlan extracted the final item from the backpack—a pipe with a peculiar attachment equipped with a spring release. Gripping it firmly, Quinlan's senses sharpened. "I felt a click, I felt a click!" he exclaimed, his voice ringing out in the tense silence.

Knight was now laughing hysterically and when he could speak, he said, "Oh boyo you are fucked. That cop is dead, Goliath over there is dead, and so is poor Mrs. Harkness, all dead. Shit if I have played my cards right, this whole city block is fucked."

Boland spoke up, "Alright John, stand still. We don't know what that is but if it is a bomb, a pipe bomb, we have to treat it as such."

"Oh, it's a—" Knight's sentence was abruptly cut off as he collapsed to the ground.

Reacting swiftly, Officer Blake intervened, using his baton to silence Knight temporarily. "Enough out of you," he declared firmly. "Guys, I'm calling for backup. I'll inform my sergeant, and we'll get a bomb team here to handle this, John. We've got you, buddy. Just stay still."

Quinlan remained unmoving, a statue amidst the chaos. Officer Blake exited the room to relay the developments to his desk sergeant, his steps purposeful. The sergeant wasted no time, promptly alerting the NYPD bomb squad and Emergency Medical Services, ensuring a swift response.

Blake emphasized to his sergeant the involvement of a Secret Service agent handling the improvised explosive device, stressing the need for discretion. Understanding the severity of the situation, the sergeant agreed to a quiet approach, prioritizing the safety of all involved.

Officer Blake reentered the room, his voice firm yet reassuring. "John, the bomb squad and Emergency Medical Services are in route. We've got you, brother. We've got you."

Quinlan remained motionless, his outward demeanor betraying the turmoil within. Despite his stoic facade, he absorbed Blake's words.

Meanwhile, Boland seethed with a detached fury, his desire to inflict harm on Knight palpable.

"Rick. RICK!" Officer Blake's voice cut through the tension. "You with me?"

"Sorry, I'm here. I'm just pissed off," Boland admitted through gritted teeth.

"Okay, good," Blake responded calmly. "There's nothing you could have done differently. Backup has arrived, and they're taking this guy into custody. He'll be placed in the 100th precinct lockup. We won't question him, so we won't read him his rights. You can come with us—"

"Nah, nah, I'm staying here with Quinlan," Boland interjected firmly. "I'm not leaving him alone in this mess."

Quinlan grunted in response. "Rick, go. Just go. It is what it is."

Boland's excitement briefly surfaced before he composed himself. "I'm staying, John. And Officer Blake, I suggest you take Officer Priestly and Ms. Harkness and get the hell out of here."

There was no room for debate in such dire circumstances, and Officer Blake understood that. He acquiesced to Agent Boland's demand, knowing that the bomb squad would be coming from Maspeth, NY, a section of Queens closer to Manhattan. It would take them approximately thirty minutes, running lights and sirens until they reached Breezy Point.

"John, listen to me," Boland began earnestly. "I've only known you for the last several hours, but I am not leaving this room. I'm staying with you. Do not move."

Quinlan met Boland's gaze, his expression a mix of apprehension and determination. "During your time in training, do you remember that long bus ride to some strange location in North Carolina, right outside the small town of Conway?"

Quinlan's eyes flickered with recognition. "Yes," he responded.

"It was called TEFAM," Boland continued.

Quinlan nodded, recalling the acronym. "The Terrorist Explosives Familiarization Course. Yes, but what the hell has that got to do…?"

Boland interrupted, "Let's keep your mind off of what's going on here. We're going to practice what they taught us there. What did they say you should do if you're ever in a situation like ours?"

Quinlan recited the protocol. "Stay calm, breathe rhythmically, and do not move until someone more qualified can safely remove the device."

"Textbook, John, textbook," Boland praised with a reassuring smile. He was attempting to inject a sense of normalcy into the fraught situation.

Quinlan's tone turned urgent. "Rick, get the hell out. I'll do all those things, but I don't need you here if this thing goes off."

"John, remember how those CIA guys had us blowing things up with all kinds of improvised explosive devices during that training?" Boland reminded him. "They taught us to get out of our heads to control the matter at hand, especially in your situation. They taught us to meditate, remember?"

Quinlan sighed. "Yeah, we practiced it. But I'm not exactly a meditation guy."

"Then I want you to stand still and think of something in your past that brought you peace and calm," Boland instructed. "I want you to immerse yourself in that memory."

Quinlan knew exactly what Boland was referring to, but he wasn't wired to find solace in meditation. Instead, he retreated to a memory from his childhood—a time spent with his older brother, Paul, and their friend, Charlie or "Chuck" as he was known on the block. Quinlan went back to that time when life seemed simpler and troubles felt far away. He closed his eyes, transporting himself back to that moment, seeking refuge in the innocence of youth.

He remembered it well:

Lying down on the train tracks might have seemed reckless to some, but in that moment, I felt an unwavering sense of faith. Faith is the assurance of things hoped for and this night—I found faith! Paul and I laid down between the rails of the train tracks. Chuck looked on for cops then my brother tucked his head in. I did also, I was excited it was AMAZING! My faith in God forced the ruins of insanity to melt away from me on that day... I had peace. It would be a blessing to have this much peace always, I thought. The 200-hundred-ton locomotive and it's never ending cargo in tow flew over me as though I was not there—I wasn't... it was as though fear was gone. This amazing feeling would come back only when it was summoned through a complete lack of control like this one. I felt a warm presence beside me, but it wasn't Paul. The presence was inside me. Now it was with me again in this upstairs apartment. It guided me far away from my current desperation. Through the back window, I made my escape, venturing out over the boats and the vast expanse of the bay then the ocean. The warmth remained, a constant companion. I knew, deep within, that it would never abandon me, no matter what lay ahead.

Quinlan returned from his trance-like state to feel Boland's reassuring hand on his shoulder.

"John, you blacked out, man. Welcome back," Boland said, concern evident in his voice. "Where were you? You followed the bomb technician's instructions, but you weren't here."

Quinlan glanced over to see an NYPD bomb technician, clad in a protective Nomex-Kevlar suit, walking away with a steel case. The device was no longer in his hand and he couldn't recall the last twenty minutes.

That night, Quinlan found himself at Bellevue Hospital in Manhattan, undergoing both physical and psychological evaluations.

What of that lost time though, Quinlan thought. He remembered the click of the triggering device on the improvised explosive. Then nothing but a memory of the train tracks near his childhood home, the expanse of the ocean, and a companion of sorts. He would keep that all to himself. Meanwhile, Boland's case against Knight gained momentum, leading to the capture of a dangerous fugitive.

A search warrant was executed for Knight's residence, car, and computer. Inside the trunk of his vehicle, they uncovered four more improvised explosive devices made from 1" galvanized piping. Alongside were a bulletproof vest, a gas mask, flash-bang concussion grenades, his passport, and an AR-15 semi-automatic weapon modified for fully automatic fire.

Further investigation into Knight's navigation device revealed a chilling discovery—a programmed driving route from his home in Breezy Point to 1600 Pennsylvania Avenue, Washington, DC, the address of the White House. The luggage found near his front door suggested he had been preparing to embark on a deadly mission, joining the ranks of would-be presidential assassins.

As the details unfolded, it became apparent that Knight was on a path to infamy, a path that led to destruction and despair for countless lives. But thanks to the vigilance of Quinlan, Boland, and their NYPD colleagues, a catastrophe of unimaginable proportions had been averted.

The following week, Boland caught up with Quinlan at the field office, eager to share some crucial details about that night in Breezy Point. He explained to Quinlan how the NYPD bomb technician safely retrieved the bomb from his clutch. The technician had employed a device attached to the grip-trigger of the pipe bomb. This ingenious mechanism compensated for Quinlan's unresponsive grip allowing the technician to safely retrieve the bomb. By applying pressure to his wrist and hitting a specific pressure point, the technician managed to release the bomb from Quinlan's grasp. He transferred the device into a secure iron and lead case. The bomb was later detonated at the proving grounds in Rodman's Neck, averting a potential disaster that could have devastated a significant portion of Beach Avenue.

Quinlan's positive reputation was affirmed that day, solidifying his status as a calm, composed, and capable Secret Service agent. His inadvertent trial by fire demonstrated his ability to perform under extreme adverse circumstances, earning him the respect and admiration of his colleagues, particularly his supervisors.

Despite being shaken by the ordeal, Quinlan returned to the counterfeit squad with renewed determination. There, he fervently pursued leads on the counterfeit currency flooding the Dominican community in Upper Manhattan, near the Bronx borough. With his newfound recognition and resolve, he was ready to tackle whatever challenges lay ahead in his ongoing mission to protect and serve.

CHAPTER 10

The Continental Hotel

"Men are more easily governed through their vices than through their virtues."
—Napoleon Bonaparte

Quinlan, known as "Q" among his colleagues at the New York Field Office, had been steadily building his reputation by relentlessly pursuing counterfeiters throughout the bustling streets of New York City. It was during one of these pursuits that he stumbled upon his first breakthrough, a pivotal moment that would set the stage for unraveling a series of intricate counterfeit schemes.

Meanwhile, Professor John Irvine was wrapping up a lecture on postwar economic reconstruction in a Eurasian nation, with a particular focus on Ukraine. As a visiting professor at Manhattan College, he frequently delivered similar talks, offering a welcome change from his routine research endeavors at Syracuse University. Each visit to Manhattan also afforded him the luxury of staying at the Continental Hotel, nestled in the heart of midtown Manhattan.

Janet Irvine, John's wife of two decades, often voiced her desire to accompany him on his trips to Manhattan. However, John's steadfast response remained consistent. "Who will manage the salon back home in Syracuse while I'm gallivanting around the Big Apple?" Janet had inherited a thriving salon business from her late parents and found fulfillment in running it, especially with their teenage son to tend to.

After wrapping up his lecture, Professor Irvine made his way to the campus pub, The Wiggly Tooth, a clever nod to both the college's renowned hockey team and the inevitable facial injuries that often accompanied the sport. Settling into a booth, he ordered a sandwich and a frosty cold beer before settling his tab with a crisp $100 bill. Leaving a generous tip, he pocketed his change and retrieved a business card from the depths of his overstuffed wallet.

Dialing the number on the card, a voice on the other end greeted him, "At Your Leisure Massage, this is Cassie speaking, how may I assist you today?"

"Hello Cassie, it's John Irvine, and my member number is 2424," he replied smoothly.

"Ah, Mr. Irvine, pleasure to hear from you. What can we arrange for you today?" Cassie inquired.

"I'd like to schedule a massage for 8:00 pm tonight in my suite at the Continental Hotel, room 453. Do you need the address?" John asked.

"No need, Mr. Irvine, we have that address and your credit card is on file with us ending in 3216. Is that still valid?" Cassie confirmed.

"Yes, that's correct. And who will be the massage therapist this evening?" John queried.

"Sandra will be your therapist, and as usual, any additional services can be arranged directly with her for cash payment. The massage service itself will be billed at $220.00 to your credit card. Is that satisfactory?" Cassie inquired.

"Thank you, Cassie, that's perfect," John acknowledged before ending the call.

Arriving at the Continental Hotel, John phoned his wife to update her on his day. He shared details of his successful lecture and at least some of his plans for the evening. Keeping the conversation brief, he subtly hinted that he had more work to attend to before turning in for an early night. He ended the call and turned his thoughts away from the busy day. Now, he desired privacy, eagerly anticipating the arrival of his massage therapist. After showering and donning the plush Continental Hotel robe, he settled in to await his guest's arrival. Anticipation mingled with the quiet hum of the city beyond his hotel room window.

A gentle knock rapped on the door, and John approached cautiously, peering through the peephole. His gaze fell upon a striking young woman with luscious dark hair, likely in her mid-twenties. He opened the door with anticipation, revealing a radiant Sandra, her demeanor brimming with warmth.

"Hello, you must be John Irvine?" Sandra's smile was infectious as she extended her hand in greeting. "I'm Sandra, your therapist for the next ninety minutes."

Returning the smile, John shook her hand softly, impressed by her professional demeanor. "Pleasure to meet you, Sandra. Please, come in."

As Sandra stepped over the threshold, she gracefully balanced a portable massage table with ease. Setting up the table, she glanced at John, her expression earnest. "Before we begin, I just want to confirm the payment policy that was discussed over the phone."

Nodding in understanding, John affirmed, "Yes, everything is in order. Thank you for reminding me."

With that, she continued prepping to deliver a massage, ready for whatever came next. For John, the atmosphere was charged with anticipation for the therapeutic session ahead. As Sandra prepared her equipment with practiced efficiency, John settled into the plush armchair, ready to indulge in a much-needed moment of relaxation amidst the hustle and bustle of city life.

"So, will there be an additional service?" Sandra asked, as though she was offering something other than a sexual gratuity.

"Yes." He reached for his wallet and gave her $150.00 in cash. She immediately placed the money in her backpack. She set up her massage table, lowered the lights in the hotel room and started to massage his naked body. Clearly, she was comfortable with the arrangement and quite skilled as a massage therapist. She was gliding her hands over his skin; the warmth of the massage oil helped the tension of the day melt away with each soft stroke. She could hear his sighs of relief and feel the easing of muscle tension, and the growing sense of relaxation. She was attending to his physical and emotional well-being.

She is good, he thought.

She moved on to the pressure points on his upper back and shoulders, kneading oil deeply into the tense muscles. He savored the deep tissue massage, feeling the relief as her, now strong hands worked out the tension in his shoulders. She slowly glided her hands down to his buttocks where she spent a lot of time lightly massaging in and around his groin. After a half hour of play, she quietly said, "I'm going to need you to roll over on your back."

He rolled over clearly aroused and she gently whispered, "We still have time for that in a little bit, honey."

She continued to massage his legs and worked her way up to his torso. She gently massaged him and started to kiss his ear at the same time. She removed her tight spandex yoga top and seemed to carry herself with confidence, her ample curves accentuating her large breasts, full and inviting. He gently caressed them feeling more aroused now.

She whispered again, "We can finish like this if you would like," as she gently massaged his groin, "or I can do more."

"More," he managed to utter. It wasn't long before he found release, fulfilling their contractual obligations.

As Sandra tidied up after the massage, she draped a soft blanket over John's torso, casting a comforting warmth over him. With a gentle flick, she adjusted the dimmed lights, casting a soft glow throughout the room, before excusing herself to the bathroom suite.

Feeling rejuvenated, John rose from the massage table, his muscles loose and his mind at ease. Sandra had reappeared and John, moved by a surge of gratitude, found himself leaning in for a kiss as he now seemed drawn towards Sandra. His heart fluttered with an impulse. Before he could act upon it, however, Sandra subtly recoiled, her demeanor shifting from professional warmth to polite reserve as she offered him a handshake instead.

Flushed with embarrassment, John quickly withdrew, stammering, "I'm sorry, I didn't mean to—"

But Sandra interrupted him with a gentle smile, her voice soft yet reassuring. "It's okay, I understand. It happens sometimes. I do hope we have the chance to meet again soon."

With those parting words, Sandra gracefully departed, leaving John to his thoughts. Pouring himself a generous measure of whiskey from the minibar, he reflected on the evening's turn of events. This was only the second time he had availed himself of the services of At Your Leisure. The first experience had left him equally impressed, having been recommended by a trusted colleague at the college.

As he settled back into the plush armchair, the soothing warmth of the whiskey enveloping him, John's eyelids grew heavy with fatigue. Little did he know, his night was far from over, as the city outside his window hummed with life, beckoning him into the embrace of its nocturnal mysteries.

* * *

Professor Irvine was jolted awake by the insistent knocking on his door, his senses still clouded by sleep. "Sir," a voice boomed from the other side, "Hotel security, please open up."

Rubbing the sleep from his eyes, Irvine stumbled towards the door, hastily grabbing his robe from where it lay discarded on the floor. Peering through the peephole, he observed a man in a navy-blue sports jacket with a Continental Hotel name tag. He was accompanied by Sandra, her expression grave. With a sinking feeling in his gut, he reluctantly unlatched the door.

"Good evening, sir. My name is Vince Grinds, and I'm with hotel security," the man introduced himself, his tone businesslike. Irvine couldn't shake the feeling that Vince sounded more like a cop than a security officer.

Before Irvine could gather his wits to respond, Sandra interjected sharply, her demeanor now tinged with accusation. "You paid with a $100 bill and a $50 bill, but this $50 is counterfeit!" she declared, holding up the suspect bill with a mark from a counterfeit detection pen.

Irvine's heart sank as he examined the bill, his mind racing to comprehend the accusation. How could this have happened? His thoughts churned with a whirlwind of confusion and panic as he struggled to piece together the events of the evening.

Vince interjected, his voice carrying a hint of weariness that suggested he had encountered similar situations countless times before. "Look, it's just a misunderstanding. If you have $50.00 to settle this, we can all move on. Sound good?" Both Vince and Irvine turned their attention to Sandra, awaiting her response.

"Yeah, fine," Sandra agreed tersely, her irritation evident.

As Irvine reached for his wallet, his hands trembled with nervous tension. His fingers fumbled through his wallet until he realized he only had a $5 bill to offer. Panic seized him as he contemplated the implications of this unexpected turn of events. Offering his credit card or writing a check would undoubtedly raise suspicions, particularly with his wife managing their finances. The prospect of explaining the additional charge loomed over him like a dark cloud however the circumstances were grave.

"Look, I can give you my credit card or write you a check," Irvine stammered, his voice betraying his growing anxiety. He felt as though he were teetering on the edge of something unfamiliar, desperately searching for solid ground amid the chaos of the moment.

Sandra now angry exclaimed, "Are you shitting me? I went down on this asshole; I want my money!"

Vince intervened, his tone firm as he urged Sandra to calm down. But before the possibility of resolving the situation could be discussed, Sandra abruptly stormed off, leaving Vince and Irvine in her wake.

"Now, Mr. Irvine, I'm going to need you to put on some clothes and come with me to my office," Vince stated, his voice carrying an air of authority. "This has escalated into an official security incident. I don't know what transpired in this room, and I can't guarantee this is the last we'll hear of that young lady, but you need to accompany me."

Feeling a wave of shock and disbelief wash over him, Irvine complied silently, hastily dressing himself under Vince's watchful gaze. As Vince instructed him to bring his driver's license or some form of identification, Irvine felt as though the ground beneath him was slipping away, his mind reeling with uncertainty.

Vince had witnessed similar events countless times during his tenure as a security officer at the Continental Hotel. He knew this would make for an intriguing tale when he regaled his old cop buddies at his neighborhood bar in Astoria, NY.

Meanwhile, Irvine found himself seated in the hotel security office, his mind consumed by a whirlwind of questions and anxieties. "What's going to happen now?" he asked, his voice tinged with apprehension.

Vince wasted no time. Unbeknownst to Irvine, he quietly directed another security officer to contact the NYPD. Soon, a patrol unit from the Mid-Town North precinct would arrive on the scene. Vince knew better than to divulge this information to Irvine, understanding that the impending arrival of the police would soon become apparent.

Vince responded, his voice calm but authoritative, "I need you to sit tight while I try to reach the woman you didn't pay. In the meantime, think about how you came into possession of that counterfeit $50."

Shortly after, NYPD Officer Jim Bailey arrived at the Continental Hotel and was guided to the security office by one of Vince's colleagues. Upon seeing the police officer, John Irvine's heart sank, his mind racing with fear and uncertainty. "Shit! Are you here for me? This is a misunderstanding," he blurted out nervously.

"Relax," Officer Bailey said with a reassuring smile. "I'm sure it is. Why don't you tell me what happened?"

Irvine proceeded to recount the events of his day in detail. Officer Bailey's interest piqued when Irvine mentioned his visit to the campus pub.

"Okay, at the Wiggly Tooth, how did you pay for your food and drink?" Officer Bailey inquired.

Irvine explained "I paid with a $100 bill. Yes, that's right, and I received a $50 bill and some change, including a $10 bill that I left as a tip for the bartender."

"Alright, this is good," Officer Bailey remarked thoughtfully. "Can you identify the person you paid at the pub?"

"Yeah, but it was around 4:30 in the afternoon, so I'm not sure if they'll still be there now," Irvine replied with uncertainty.

"Let me handle that. I'll need to take your picture now, and then I'll have to place you under arrest for soliciting a prostitute. Once that's settled, we'll get to the bottom of the counterfeit," Officer Bailey stated matter-of-factly.

Irvine's world seemed to crumble around him as he sank back into his chair in disbelief. Officer Bailey proceeded to place him under arrest, reciting his Miranda rights before escorting him to the police vehicle.

Once outside the vehicle, Officer Bailey made a call to his precinct sergeant. "Hey Sarge, it's Bailey. Do we still have that card from the Secret Service guy? The one who was handing out counterfeit notifications? Yeah, I can't remember the name. Yes, that's the one, Quinlan. Can you give me his contact number?"

CHAPTER 11

College Pub

Quinlan stirred from a deep slumber, the shrill ring of his phone slicing through the silence of the night. Yet, he welcomed the call from Officer Bailey. The case of the counterfeit $50 and $100 bills plaguing the upper west side of Manhattan had kept him restless for nights on end. Finally, a breakthrough seemed imminent.

Within the hour, Quinlan found himself at the Manhattan North Police Precinct lockup, interviewing the unfortunate John Irvine, now a detainee. Officer Bailey stood by his side; the strain of anticipation from Irvine was heavy in the air. Once done, they made their way to the Wiggly Tooth, determined to uncover more leads.

As they stepped into the dimly lit bar, they were met by Anne Marie, a young and sassy bartender in her twenties. "I didn't do it, but hey, we're closing up. How can I help you, gentlemen?" she quipped, her demeanor brimming with confidence.

Quinlan wasted no time showing Anne Marie a photo of Irvine. "Was he here today?" he inquired.

"He sure was," Anne Marie replied enthusiastically. "Left me a generous tip. Paid his tab with a big bill, too. Not something you see often in a college pub. Pretty sure it was a $100 bill. Is he alright?"

"He's fine," Quinlan reassured her before asking to inspect the contents of the cash register. Anne Marie obliged, emptying the drawer and revealing a stack of bills, predominantly comprised of eight $50s and two $100s.

"Are these all from today?" Quinlan probed; his gaze fixed on the suspicious bills.

"No, the big bills would come in throughout the week and it being Thursday, yeah, probably since Monday," Anne Marie explained.

"Bingo, these are counterfeit," Quinlan remarked, a glimmer of satisfaction in his eyes as he inspected the bills from the cash drawer. He expressed his gratitude to Anne Marie and proceeded to fill out a receipt for the counterfeit notes she had retrieved from the register—five $50s and one $100.

An astonished Anne Marie held up the receipt. "Hey, what am I supposed to do with this?" she asked incredulously. "What do I tell my manager? A Secret Service guy and a cop walk into a bar… it's a joke, right? Seriously, what do I tell my boss?"

"I don't want to get you in trouble with your boss, here's my card," Quinlan offered, extending it to her. "I'm seizing the counterfeit currency because it's considered contraband and therefore illegal to possess. You can explain that to your boss, or I'd be happy to do so if you'd prefer."

"That's fine, I'll handle it," Anne Marie replied. "Look, if you guys are looking for the guy spending counterfeit money all over the west side, the rumor in the restaurant circle is that it's a student at the college. I go to Manhattan College myself, and that's the word there, too."

Quinlan thanked her and urged her to stay vigilant. With this breakthrough in the case, he intended to brief his superiors and organize surveillance at the Wiggly Tooth.

* * *

During the second day of surveillance, Quinlan spotted Anne Marie, the bartender, entering the pub around 4:00 pm. By 7:00 pm, his phone rang, and a woman's voice whispered on the other end, "Is this Special Agent Quinlan?"

"Yeah, who's this?" Quinlan replied.

"It's Anne Marie from the Tooth. You spoke to me last week at the pub."

"Are you okay?" Quinlan asked, concern evident in his tone.

"Yeah, fine. Listen, a group of college kids are in the pub at a table. One of them just paid using a $50 bill. I'm pretty sure it's fake. Can you get here, like NOW?"

"On my way," Quinlan responded promptly since he was right outside conducting the surveillance. He radioed the other two agents assigned to the surveillance, briefing them on the situation. All three agents entered the pub casually, spotting Anne Marie at the far end of the bar. Quinlan approached her, and she discreetly led him into the office in the back. There, she revealed the counterfeit $50 bill and Quinlan was able to confirm it was part of the batch circulating on the west side. She pointed out the suspect sitting at a table.

Quinlan, along with agents Jimmy West and Eric Dougherty, approached the table. When he began to identify himself, one of the suspects attempted to flee. Quinlan swiftly tackled the suspect and slapped on the handcuffs. A search yielded five more counterfeit $50 bills on the runner, identified as Stanley Monroe. He and the other two suspects were arrested and transported to the New York Field Office for questioning. As Quinlan began to recite the Miranda rights, he noticed Stanley had pissed himself.

Quickly improvising, He grabbed a plastic garbage bag from the trunk of his government vehicle, known as the G-ride, and wrapped it around Monroe to prevent any further mess. Quinlan mused; *Shit is this going to happen every time I arrest someone?*

During the drive to the office, Monroe spoke up, "I want to talk. I want to tell you what I know. My parents live in Westport, Connecticut, and they will have a fit when they find out what I've done," he confessed, the somberness of his admission evident in his tone.

Quinlan had already Mirandized Monroe when he was placed under arrest, so Monroe had either forgotten or didn't realize he had the right to remain silent. "What have you done?" said Quinlan.

Monroe hesitated before divulging the name Flaco, painting a picture of him as a Dominican enforcer dealing in counterfeit bills at discounted rates.

"You're in deep on this," Quinlan remarked, his gaze steady. "Can you set up a meeting with Flaco and get him to talk?"

"Yeah, but it's not like I can just give him a call. I usually run into him on campus and ask if he's got any monopoly, which is what we call fake money," Monroe explained, his nerves palpable.

"Where does he get the monopoly from?" Quinlan probed further, sensing a potential lead.

"I honestly have no clue," Monroe admitted, his shoulders slumping in defeat.

With a nod of determination, Monroe agreed to wear a wire, attempting to orchestrate a chance meeting with Flaco while under surveillance.

* * *

One Wednesday afternoon, near the bustling campus quad, Monroe spotted Flaco sporting his signature red Boston Red Sox cap and baggy jeans. He relayed the description to Quinlan via his hidden microphone. Quinlan and his team swiftly adjusted their positions, ready to tail Flaco should he make a move off-campus. Meanwhile, a Secret Service surveillance technician began discreetly capturing photos of Flaco as Monroe slowly closed the distance.

Just as Quinlan held his breath, Monroe's voice pierced the tension. "Hey, hey Flaco," he called out, a mix of nervousness and determination in his tone. It was a pivotal moment, one that could either move the case along or shatter their carefully laid plans.

For Fuck's sake, is all Quinlan could think, *don't force this thing, kid.*

Just then Flaco stood still and agents started to hear the conversation, "Hey Flaco, you got some monopoly?"

For the first time, a second voice pierced through the static. "Nah, it's getting hot around here, so no. I don't even know what you're talking about."

Shit, Quinlan cursed inwardly, sensing the missed opportunity. But just then, Flaco walked off the campus, heading North on Broadway. The agents swiftly adjusted their positions, closely trailing Flaco as he navigated the bustling streets. He led them on a meandering path, taking several turns until he finally arrived at a storefront, 'Start to Finish Printing.'

Unaware of the prying eyes tracking his steps, Flaco stepped into the print shop. A swift LexisNexis business search unveiled two figures associated with Start to Finish Printing, Felix Perez, aged 65, and Cortina Perez, aged 62.

Bingo, Quinlan exulted inwardly, piecing together the puzzle.

Delving deeper, he discovered that Felix and Cortina Perez had a son named Adolpho Perez, aged 22, known on the streets as 'Flaco.'

Quinlan and his team dedicated countless hours to surveilling the print shop, thoroughly documenting the traffic in and out, capturing video footage, and snapping photographs. They observed suspects entering the shop, later spreading counterfeit bills at bars and restaurants across the upper west side of Manhattan. Surveillance teams conducted interviews with restaurant staff, retrieving the counterfeit bills that had just been passed. Statements were collected, and numerous interviews were conducted, unraveling the intricate web of deception.

Adolpho Perez was becoming careless. He brazenly sold counterfeit bills right from his father's shop, emboldened by his unchecked activities. Realizing the need to escalate the case, Quinlan decided it was time to involve the U.S. Attorney's Office. He reached out to Lana Miller, his trusted federal prosecutor in the Southern District of New York, laying the groundwork for the legal battle ahead.

CHAPTER 12

Forensics

"It is a capital mistake to theorize before one has data. Insensibly one begins to twist facts to suit theories, instead of theories to suit facts."
—Sir Arthur Conan Doyle

In the undercover world of law enforcement, Agent Quinlan would soon forge an unlikely alliance with this counterfeiter. But for now, it was a delicate dance of pursuit and evasion, akin to a game of cat and mouse. Adolpho Perez was known simply as Flaco among his circle for his slight and gaunt physique. Their initial encounter, as Perez would later attest, was far from ideal. Yet, from this rocky beginning, Quinlan gleaned invaluable insights into the case.

As Quinlan unraveled the intricate threads of the investigation to Assistant U.S. Attorney Lana Miller, a formidable presence in the Southern District of New York, he couldn't help but appreciate her penchant for attacking his cases in the same spirit as he. For Quinlan, meticulousness was second nature, and Miller's appreciation for his work served as a validation of his tireless attention to detail and thoroughness.

Miller was a resolute prosecutor, an imposing figure to many adversaries in the courtroom. She exuded confidence, always impeccably dressed in tailored suits that complemented her slender frame. When litigating a case, her mission was always zero-fail. Courtroom regulars often watched the tall woman with piercing emerald, green eyes scan the jury and the defendant's table with practiced precision. Her auburn hair framed her face in soft waves. Quinlan, was beginning to see her differently—not as a stern prosecutor or a professional colleague but as a captivating woman with an allure that increasingly commanded his attention.

The majority of Quinlan's cases never saw the inside of a courtroom. Faced with overwhelming evidence, most defendants chose to plead out rather than face trial. And for the few who dared to challenge the system, their fate was sealed with convictions leading to lengthy prison sentences.

Quinlan's method of presenting the case to AUSA Miller was through a narrative format, a technique he believed offered the most comprehensive understanding.

"Agent Quinlan, I have an hour before I'm due at an arraignment. Let's focus on what the grand jury needs to hear to indict this case," Miller instructed.

And so, Quinlan began his recounting. "Adolpho Perez, son of Felix Perez, a respected figure in the Bronx printing community, appeared to be a typical Manhattan College student. However, away from his studies, he operated a shadow business within his parent's establishment, Start to Finish Printing. When the day's work was done, Adolpho would secretly employ his father's sophisticated printing equipment to churn out counterfeit bills—$50s and $100s—and sell them at half their face value. His clientele? College students, eager to partake in the nightlife across boroughs and even state lines, armed with fake currency and a penchant for pocketing the change."

In the hushed ambiance of the meeting room, AUSA Miller occasionally raised her hand, signaling Quinlan to slow down as she diligently transcribed his words. Undeterred, Quinlan pressed on, his voice steady and deliberate.

"Counterfeit for genuine was the name of the game for the low-level 'passers' in this counterfeit scheme," he explained, his words punctuated by the scratch of Miller's pen on paper. "Under the dim lights of bars, restaurants, and strip clubs, the counterfeit was passable. The notes flooded the Bronx area, especially in the Dominican establishments, earning them the moniker Dominican Note by the Secret Service. But what most novice counterfeiters like Adolpho failed to realize is that all that counterfeit currency had to end up somewhere."

"The banks," Miller interjected, her tone knowing.

"Exactly. Which is where the buck stops," Quinlan quipped, knowing Miller would appreciate the wordplay.

"Pun intended, I guess," Miller chuckled, confirming Quinlan's intuition.

Quinlan's pace slowed as he continued, "Most tellers handle genuine currency all day long, making them adept at detecting the subtle discrepancies of counterfeit bills. To the seasoned eye, the unraised texture of the ink on counterfeit notes has a distinct feel, a telltale sign of something amiss. Counterfeit notes detected at the bank are then routed to the New York Field Office of the U.S. Secret Service, directly to my desk."

"Chain of custody?" Miller queried; her voice raised slightly.

"Yes, I understand the chain of custody," Quinlan responded calmly. "The New York Field Office support staff would log each note into the Secret Service Counterfeit Database and submit select samples to the Forensic Services Division for ink and paper analysis."

"The ink and the paper?" Miller probed further; her interest piqued.

"Lana, I know you are not familiar with this side of our operation, but the Secret Service has the largest library of ink samples in the world. Sometimes there can be a connection between the ink used on the counterfeit bill in question and the ink used on previously submitted counterfeit bills in unrelated or related cases."

Quinlan was well aware that the Secret Service's renowned ink library was more than just a resource for combating financial crimes—it was a symbol of the agency's broader mission. Protecting the

President, Vice President, and other dignitaries was paramount, often considered the cornerstone of the Secret Service's dual mandate.

The ink library's significance extended beyond the realm of counterfeit currency. In cases where individuals threatened the lives of those under the Secret Service's protection by sending letters, ink analysis served as a crucial starting point. By comparing the ink from threatening letters to the vast array of samples cataloged in the Service's ink library, investigators could begin to unravel the identity and location of potential suspects.

As Quinlan pressed on with his presentation to AUSA Miller, he emphasized another crucial aspect: The Forensic Services Division's (FSD) analysis of the paper used in the counterfeit bills. "FSD's scrutiny of the paper is equally vital," he explained. "Every commercial-grade standalone printer leaves behind a microscopic dot pattern on the actual paper that is unique to the machine being used to make the copies. This pattern forms a distinct footprint, if you will, revealing details such as when and where the printer was purchased, to whom it was delivered, and even the shipping address."

Miller looking surprised interrupted, "Seriously, every copy machine has its own DNA"?

Quinlan replied, "Sort of—you see when these high-end machines were created, they became so proficient at recreating even the subtlest nuances of the original document that industry technicians and the executive boards became paranoid."

Miller said, "So they realized they created a machine that could counterfeit not just money but priceless documents, even the Declaration of Independence?"

"I guess but we can stick with counterfeit for now," Quinlan replied. "The technicians that built these machines saw the possibilities of these advancements in replication. They saw these copiers as so precise and accurate with the color ratio, there would need to be a tracking system for each machine of this caliber. There would need to be a record of such transactions exactly for the purpose we need as investigators of counterfeit currency. Usually, however, gaining this information from the manufacturers of commercial printers required a subpoena and depending on the mood of the U.S. Attorney's Office, maybe even a search warrant."

AUSA Miller interrupted, her tone slightly incredulous, "What do you mean by my mood? When was the last time I gave you grief about getting you a search warrant or, hell, a subpoena? Seriously, I could do that over a cup of coffee!"

Quinlan paused, briefly entertained by the idea of sharing a cup of coffee with Lana. A smile tugged at the corners of his lips as he replied, "Sorry, I didn't mean to strike a nerve. What I meant to say is that I have a good partnership with the copy machine manufacturers."

This was one of Quinlan's talents. He possessed a knack for forging connections, whether it was with individuals in the private sector or, in this case, partnering with technicians in the commercial copier industry. He understood the importance of these relationships and nurtured them with care.

Quinlan's approach was strategic yet personal. He would extend invitations to company CEOs for events attended by the President or Vice President of the United States, ensuring they were positioned on the rope line for a photograph opportunity. These snapshots, later autographed and personalized through his contacts at the White House, solidified the bond between Quinlan and the copier industry personnel.

Quinlan relished the dual mission of protecting these political figures. With these influential contacts at his fingertips, he found that the need for subpoenas or search warrants often became obsolete. Yet, he made a point to keep this information close, allowing AUSA Miller to handle the legal proceedings with the proper paperwork, unaware of the behind-the-scenes efforts.

Quinlan pressed on, laying out the findings to AUSA Miller. "Upon analyzing the counterfeit notes sent to FSD, it was determined that they were not produced using a traditional printing press method, as seen with seasoned counterfeiters. The ink lacked the raised feel characteristic of such presses. Additionally, the paper used was a low-grade blend of 80% cotton and 20% linen, devoid of the red and blue fibers found in genuine currency. Authentic bills are printed on a 75% cotton and 25% linen blend, with distinctive red and blue fibers that can be physically extracted with some degree of effort. This specialized paper is exclusively manufactured by the Crane Paper Company in Dalton, MA, and delivered under stringent security measures directly to the Bureau of Engraving and Printing (BEP)."

Quinlan continued, citing the FSD report, "The counterfeit notes in this case were likely printed on a Canon commercial-grade color printer, Model 3540, identified by a dot matrix pattern linked to the copier's serial number 2345768."

AUSA Miller's interruption was swift and sharp. "WAIT, WAIT, WAIT! How did you obtain this information without a subpoena," she demanded, her voice rising in urgency. " This could blow the case before we even present it to my boss. YOU WILL NOT proceed until I get the subpoena to cover your lone wolf ass."

Quinlan started to chuckle, and he tried to hide it but to no avail, "Look" he said sheepishly, "I work in the gray and things move fast."

Miller interrupted and said sternly, "Yea well I am a rule follower and that certainly applies to the rule of law, or have you forgotten that I am a federal prosecutor!"

Quinlan now a little less cocky quietly offered, "I will hold back, and I won't do another thing until I can cover my people at Canon with a subpoena."

"Good" Miller said as though she taught him a lesson on the Bill of Rights. Then there was a long pause...and a slight tension in the room.

"Well, what did you find out about where the printer is?" Miller asked in a slightly lower tone.

Quinlan's smile took on a coy edge as he responded, "The data from Canon indicates a purchase made roughly two years ago, coinciding with the emergence of the Dominican Note. The commercial-grade copier, valued at $6,500.00, was delivered to 3132 3rd Avenue, Bronx, New York—the very address of Start to Finish Printing.

AUSA Miller's voice was quiet but firm as she spoke, she reiterated, "No reports, no discussions, not even a fleeting thought on this matter until I secure the subpoena to cover your ass, as well as those at Canon."

As Quinlan was leaving AUSA Miller's office, she offered unsolicited advice to him, in no uncertain terms, "I want bodies in bracelets! None of this shit where we indict the property, seize it, and have nobody arrested. The media loves to bash us on things like that. We are not in the business of asset forfeiture without arrests—got it?"

"I got it," he said in a voice lower than hers.

Quinlan knew this to be a reference to numerous cases investigated federally where it appeared the big bad federal heat was only in the business of seizing assets from ill-gotten gains and liquidating it for purposes of government use. Believe it or not, some government agencies were involved in that kind of thing, but Quinlan did not play that game. He did, however, realize early on in his career that most criminals facing federal prison will do the time rather than snitching out someone higher on the food chain. However, if you take away their shiny toys, they are more likely to talk. Many a time an organized crime low life reminded Quinlan that they could do federal time standing on their head. Threaten to take away their house in the Hamptons, their bloated bank accounts, their boat, and their Mercedes E class, you may be surprised how motivated even the most loyal of criminals can become.

CHAPTER 13

Grand Jury

"Let justice be done though the heavens fall."
—William Watson

Quinlan was privy to a wealth of information regarding the illicit transactions swirling around Start to Finish Printing. It appeared that Flaco, whether out of laziness or sheer ignorance, had opted to keep the counterfeit sales perilously close to their point of origin. Rather than discreetly distributing them elsewhere, he brazenly directed his clientele to his father's print shop. AUSA Miller's reminders about the necessity for arrests were unnecessary. Quinlan already had federal arrests in mind when he initiated the process with the New York Field Office Technical Security Division (TSD).

The directive was clear: install a pole camera discreetly positioned just down the street, taking advantage of the myriad streetlight poles in the vicinity of Start to Finish Printing. In the silent hours of the morning, at 3:30 am, Secret Service TSD technicians, disguised as AT&T Telephone workers, executed the operation seamlessly. The installation remained undetected, and the covert cameras diligently captured every movement in the vicinity of the print shop.

Quinlan orchestrated surveillance efforts with his handpicked team, ensuring round-the-clock coverage in twelve-hour shifts. Their vigilance paid off, revealing a pattern of suspicious activity predominantly unfolding after the shop's official hours. Quinlan maintained this watchful eye, allowing the camera to document the comings and goings for nearly a month.

As the evidence mounted and the pressure intensified from both the U.S. Attorney's Office and his superiors within the Secret Service, Quinlan knew it was time to act. With an estimated involvement of fifteen to twenty individuals in the counterfeiting network, the impending arrests loomed large. The urgency to dismantle the operation resonated deeply, driving him to expedite the shutdown as demanded by the powers that be.

Agent Quinlan brought the investigation to a decisive close by executing a thoroughly planned search warrant on the print shop. He effectively seized the premises and all associated assets through criminal asset forfeiture. Within the confines of the shop, Quinlan stumbled upon a staggering $500,000 cache of counterfeit bills, predominantly in $100 and $50 denominations. In the ensuing days, Quinlan and his team orchestrated the arrest of a total of twenty individuals linked to the nefarious counterfeiting enterprise. Of all the targets, the one Quinlan coveted most was the printer himself, Adolpho Perez. He had him firmly in his grasp.

Quinlan subjected Perez to exhaustive interrogation sessions after ensuring his arrest occurred late on a Friday afternoon. This calculated move delayed his appearance before the Federal Magistrate Judge until the following Monday, granting Quinlan and his team the entire weekend to coax Perez into cooperation. They dangled the prospect of leniency in exchange for valuable information on other active counterfeit operations plaguing the area.

The necessity of administering Miranda rights to any individual in police custody and subjected to custodial questioning about their involvement in a crime was a procedural cornerstone. However, the timing and manner of delivering these warnings remained shrouded in ambiguity. Quinlan, through hard-earned experience, gleaned that promptly issuing the Miranda rights, practically upon the moment of arrest and cuffing, proved most efficacious. By the time interrogation ensued, often hours later, the weight of the Miranda rights had typically dissipated, conveniently slipping the suspect's mind amidst the chaos of their circumstances.

Perez fancied himself a cunning operator who had outwitted the system with his counterfeit scheme. He thoughtfully sourced the finest quality paper available, courtesy of Crane Paper Company, a staple among print shops like his father's. Yet, despite his efforts, the discerning eye of vigilant bank tellers saw through his facade. The absence of the distinct red and blue fibers, characteristic of genuine currency, immediately raised suspicions. And what of the lack of raised ink on the counterfeit notes? It was a glaring oversight. The enhanced security features like incandescent color shifting ink, embedded security threads, and watermarks would not be introduced to more modern currency for several more years.

However, Perez proved a formidable adversary. He promptly invoked his right to legal representation and steadfastly refused to cooperate with Quinlan's inquiries. Unphased, Quinlan ensured Perez's lodging at the Metropolitan Correctional Center (MCC) in Manhattan. There, he would spend the weekend awaiting his appearance before the Federal Magistrate Judge on Monday. It was a calculated move, designed to instill a sense of urgency and provide a preview of the consequences awaiting Perez should he remain obstinate in Quinlan's case. At 9:00 am on Monday morning, Perez stood before the Magistrate Judge for his arraignment, visibly shaken from his brief stint at MCC. Much to his dismay, the Judge remanded him to the custody of the U.S. Marshals Service. He would be detained at the MCC while awaiting his initial appearance scheduled in two weeks' time.

Since the arrests stemmed from a complaint drafted by AUSA Miller and signed by Agent Quinlan as the affiant, the case required presentation before a Grand Jury for indictments. AUSA Miller managed to secure a slot with the sitting Federal Grand Jury just two days after Perez was remanded to the MCC. Her aim was to obtain the indictment and utilize it as leverage to encourage Perez's cooperation.

* * *

Agent Quinlan would stand before the Grand Jury, offering expert testimony in the federal case against the young Adolpho Perez. He articulated, with precision, the intricate process involved in printing genuine currency.

"Genuine currency," he explained, "is deliberately crafted using an Intaglio printing method. This technique involves engraving an image onto a metal plate, typically fashioned from copper or steel. The engraved sections retain the ink, while the unengraved portions are wiped clean. When pressed onto paper, the ink is transferred from the recessed areas, resulting in a raised image with a distinctive texture discernible to the touch."

As the Grand Jury delved deeper into the labyrinth of the case, one member had a question. "Could the defendant truly have wielded such sophisticated counterfeiting techniques?"

Quinlan, armed with a wealth of training and research, responded with unwavering authority. His reply, "Within the Bureau of Engraving and Printing, perhaps only ten individuals possess the expertise of qualified Intaglio printers. It's a journey spanning roughly a decade of apprenticeship before one earns the coveted title of qualified master engraver."

Another member of the jury posed a pivotal question. "How much of the counterfeit currency can be traced back to Perez?"

Quinlan recognized the seriousness of the question and stated, "Thus far, we've confiscated $500,000 in counterfeit currency during the execution of the search warrant at Start to Finish Printing. Additionally, we've retrieved over $150,000 already in circulation. By this, I mean these bills were successfully passed in New York and New Jersey but were later flagged as counterfeit by different banks. Nevertheless, it's crucial to acknowledge that additional counterfeit currency may still be in circulation within the community and could emerge at financial institutions. The tally might gradually increase over time."

Now it fell upon AUSA Miller to steer the discourse. "Agent Quinlan, could you expound upon the specialized paper utilized in genuine currency compared to the subpar material employed by Perez in his counterfeiting endeavors?"

Without hesitation, Quinlan delved into the intricacies of the paper analysis conducted by the Forensic Services Division. "Our investigation revealed that the counterfeit currency was printed on inferior-grade paper—a blend of 80% cotton and 20% linen—devoid of the distinctive red and blue fibers synonymous with genuine currency. In stark contrast, authentic currency is crafted from a superior blend of 75% cotton and 25% linen, meticulously embedded with the signature red and blue fibers. This exclusive paper is manufactured under strict security protocols by the Crane Paper Company in Dalton, MA, and subsequently entrusted directly to the Bureau of Engraving and Printing (BEP)."

Both AUSA Miller and Agent Quinlan concurred that the confidential procedure involving distinct dot matrix patterns connecting certain high-end color copiers should not be presented to the Grand Jury. Revealing the integrity and confidentiality of this investigative technique was deemed inappropriate at this juncture. AUSA Miller suggested that perhaps it could be disclosed during the trial, but it ought not to be divulged during the Grand Jury proceedings.

AUSA Miller's voice cut through the silence of the courtroom. "Thank you, Agent Quinlan. Does anyone in this Grand Jury have any further inquiries for Agent Quinlan or myself?"

The room remained silent, and without hesitation, the Grand Jury returned with an indictment against Perez and nineteen accomplices, charging them with violating Title 18, United

States Code, Section 471—the federal statute criminalizing the manufacture of counterfeit currency.

The following day, Miller reached out to Perez's retained legal counsel and scheduled a meeting in her office. Reading aloud the indictment to Perez and his counsel, AUSA Miller's tone remained firm. "Your client stands accused of violating Title 18, USC, Section 471—manufacturing counterfeit currency. This section specifically pertains to the offense of 'uttering counterfeit obligations or securities,' prohibiting the creation, possession, or dissemination of counterfeit U.S. currency or securities."

Directing her gaze squarely at Perez, AUSA Miller continued, her words carrying an earnest sternness. "Whoever, with intent to defraud, falsely makes, forges, counterfeits, or alters any obligation or other security of the United States, shall be fined under this title or imprisoned not more than 20 years, or both."

But AUSA Miller wasn't finished. With a steely resolve, she addressed Perez and his legal representation. "Shall we entertain discussions about additional federal conspiracy charges, or do you believe you can offer assistance to Agent Quinlan in another counterfeit operation he's currently investigating?"

Upon hearing the grave charges levied against young Adolpho Perez, he and his legal counsel agreed to a proffer agreement to be conducted within the Southern District of New York.

This proffer agreement, as explained to Perez, stood as a formal legal accord between AUSA Lana Miller as the prosecutor and he, Adolpho Perez as the defendant. It granted him the opportunity to divulge pertinent information, typically pertaining to criminal activities, in exchange for specified assurances or concessions from the prosecution. In reciprocation for cooperation, the prosecution might extend immunity from prosecution for certain offenses, a reduction in charges, or a recommendation for a mitigated sentence. This proffer agreement held the promise of being an invaluable asset to the unfolding case.

Quinlan was immersed in another case within the Dominican community, one significantly more intricate. He was intimately acquainted with the challenges of infiltrating the tightly knit community, but he saw a potential avenue through Adolpho Perez as a confidential informant. He found himself immersed in the intrigue of a peculiar counterfeit operation. The emergence of counterfeit $100 bills, produced with an offset printing press on genuine paper—a rarity in the counterfeit world—had sent ripples through the community. With an estimated $50,000 already circulating, as per the weekly count from the Secret Service's Criminal Investigations Division (CID), the situation demanded swift and decisive action.

Quinlan held hope for the prospect of Perez's cooperation dangling before him courtesy of AUSA Miller's carefully orchestrated proffer agreement. Both Quinlan and Miller clung to a flicker of optimism. The looming shadow of a potential twenty-year sentence, unaided by conspiracy charges, loomed large for Perez and his counsel. A constant reminder of the importance of the situation.

Adolpho Perez didn't take long to consider the options laid out by AUSA Miller. He could either go to trial and risk facing a twenty-year sentence in federal prison or cooperate with the United States Government, hoping for leniency with a potential downward departure. He opted for the latter.

Quinlan embarked on a field-generated investigation, that would later be dubbed 'Operation Wipe Out.' He now was able to enlist the assistance of a freshly recruited confidential informant, or CI known as Flaco. He teamed up with his trusted comrade and fellow agent Joseph 'Mack' Mackey, now also a rising star within the NYFO Counterfeit Squad. Quinlan set the intricate machinery of the operation into motion. Little did he anticipate that Operation Wipe Out would thrust the Secret Service into uncharted territory, presenting challenges unlike any they had faced before.

CHAPTER 14

Flaco

"The informant knows where the bodies are buried,
because he helped bury them."
—Robert D. Novak

In the complex world of counterfeiting, 1993 marked a turning point. The Bureau of Engraving and Printing (BEP) unveiled a groundbreaking weapon against illicit replication. They introduced a 'thread' interwoven within the fabric of the $5 bill. Though discernible when held aloft to light, its message—etched with the letters "USA" and the singular word "FIVE"—eluded all but the most astute observers. Yet, under the piercing scrutiny of ultraviolet light, it pulsated with a brilliant hue. This triggered a wave of installations of UV lights at cash registers throughout the bustling expanse of New York City. What appeared to be a mere addition held profound implications within commerce. The security thread was an anti-counterfeiting measure that proved pivotal in reducing the amount of counterfeit in circulation.

Adolpho 'Flaco' Perez, his identity shrouded beneath the guise of a CI number, vanished from official records, a ghost in the eyes of the government. Concurrently, within the corridors of the counterfeit squad, a once fledgling investigator named Joe Mackey emerged as a beacon of promise. He had an impressive string of over twenty federal arrests, eighteen culminating in successful convictions. Mackey's intelligence and prowess rendered him essential in the fight against counterfeiters. It was inevitability, clear as daylight, that he belonged in the counterfeit squad, where the stakes were high and the puzzles grew ever more intricate.

Mack's presence in the squad was a gain for Quinlan, as he would inject a fresh wave of enthusiasm into their investigations. United in purpose, they delved into their latest case with an unwavering resolve. Each was fueled by a shared determination to unravel its complexities. Quinlan dutifully kept AUSA Lana Miller apprised of their progress, ensuring she remained privy to every development, no matter how small.

Within the intricate web of counterfeit investigations, the Secret Service Forensic Services Division (FSD) held a pivotal role. It served as the linchpin in Quinlan's pursuit of justice. Quinlan had been seizing an inordinate amount of a particular kind of counterfeit currency from the various shops, bars, and restaurants within the Dominican community. He submitted the numerous counterfeit samples to FSD for forensic analysis and awaited their precise analysis with bated breath. FSD's scrutiny pierced through the veneer of deception, dissecting the intricacies of patterns, materials, and printing techniques, each revelation shedding light on the operation's sophistication. The use of the offset print method hinted at a level of craftsmanship mirroring the Bureau of Engraving and Printing's authentic currency production. The offset print method offered the counterfeit bills a lifelike three-dimensional allure. This was a testament to their authenticity that confounded all but the most discerning eyes. While Quinlan acknowledged the technological prowess of commercial printers, he remained cognizant of their inherent limitations. This was the case especially when juxtaposed with the unparalleled realism of the offset printing press. In the discerning gaze of a seasoned investigator, this advanced style of manufacturing counterfeit currency stood as an undeniable benchmark for gauging a bill's legitimacy.

* * *

Gathering at Lincoln Square on Manhattan's Lower East Side, Quinlan and Mackey sought peace and quiet amidst the tranquility of the open expanse. They decided to blend in by squaring off to a game of checkers at one of the many checker tables. Quinlan was happy just to be away from the field office. The purpose for this retreat was to introduce his newfound informant, Flaco, to Mackey. There they would strategize their next move in the unfolding saga of their investigation.

They arrived at their meeting spot a good half-hour ahead of schedule. Mack found himself engrossed in the detailed forensics report furnished by FSD regarding the specific counterfeit they were up against. Almost immediately, a particular term leapt out at him from the pages, 'bleached.'

"Hey, Q," Mackey called out, a quizzical look on his face with one eyebrow raised. Quinlan turned his attention to his partner.

"Have you gone through this report from forensics?" Mackey inquired, holding up the document.

"Oh, yeah, completely," Quinlan nodded in confirmation.

"Well, it seems we're dealing with a genuine $5 bill that's been bleached," Mackey pointed out, his brow furrowing in concentration. "They've stripped away the original ink from the paper to create a clean slate."

"Yes, bleached, like a blank canvas," Quinlan affirmed. "Then they're using an offset printing press to layer on images of a $50 and a $100 onto the bleached genuine paper."

Mackey's eyes widened in realization. "So, they've essentially repurposed the genuine $5 bill paper. This gives them the genuine cotton and linen consistency, the red and blue fibers, and the clear strip.

Quinlan looking amused replied, "Mack it's the real McCoy. Only difference is, their strip on the $100s reads 'USA FIVE' in microprint. And no one's bothering to check that detail at the cash register."

"That's some serious ingenuity," Mackey marveled, shaking his head in disbelief. "Even the bank tellers could be easily fooled, especially since they rely heavily on the feel of the paper when processing cash at their stations."

"Yeah, most of these counterfeits have sailed right through to the Federal Reserve Bank before getting flagged," Quinlan chimed in. "It means the majority of banks aren't catching these fakes when they first come through."

It was now Mackey's turn to finish the thought. "These notes have a longer lifespan on the streets since the banks are unwittingly recycling the counterfeit notes back into circulation. Incredible, Q, did you catch this?" Mackey thrust the forensic report towards Quinlan, directing his attention to a specific passage: "Of the ten samples of counterfeit specimens examined by this lab, three revealed trace amounts of anhydrous ammonia, lithium, and pseudoephedrine."

"Are those the chemicals used to bleach the genuine notes?" Mackey inquired; his brows knit with concern.

"That was my initial thought, too," Quinlan responded, his tone thoughtful. "But the presence of pseudoephedrine threw me off. I reached out to my contact at the DEA, and he confirmed that these are chemical precursors used in the production of methamphetamine. It seems whoever's behind this counterfeit operation might also be involved in manufacturing methamphetamine."

As the heightened level of this revelation settled between them, Flaco made his entrance into Lincoln Square. Spotting Quinlan engrossed in a game of checkers with an unfamiliar figure, Flaco's apprehension eased upon meeting Quinlan's gaze.

Before even being properly introduced, Perez picked up one of the sample counterfeit notes that was on the checkers table and argued, "This is fucked! How am I supposed to get a sample of this shit? I don't know these..."

Quinlan interrupted, "Flaco, relax. Can I introduce you to my partner, Joe Mackey? Mack, this is Flaco. Flaco, this is Joe Mackey."

Perez settled into his seat with a heavy sigh. "Hey," he murmured, his tone laden with uncertainty. After a moment of silence, he continued, "My lawyer said I gotta cooperate with you, but I don't even know where to begin. It's not like I have connections for this kind of stuff."

"Alright, let's figure this out together," Quinlan responded, his demeanor calm and approachable.

Quinlan had a principle. Never talk down to informants. He treated them with respect unless they proved unworthy of it. He understood early on that the most potent incentive for truthfulness wasn't money, revenge, or some glamorous espionage fantasy. No, the most compelling motivation, in his opinion, was the prospect of avoiding prison time.

Quinlan researched the geographic spread of the counterfeit notes. He noted their prevalence in the northern reaches of Manhattan, the Bronx, and White Plains. Collaborating closely with FSD, he directed their focus towards identifying the specimens contaminated with methamphetamine precursors. As their findings unfolded, an alarming pattern emerged. A growing number of counterfeit bills bore traces of methamphetamine. This revelation led Quinlan and Mackey to speculate that they were dealing with a narcotics distribution network doubling as a sophisticated counterfeit ring. Specialists from the headquarters counterfeit section floated the theory that the counterfeit currency might be used to exploit or frame rival gangs.

It was one possibility, Quinlan mused, *or perhaps they were simply leveraging both enterprises for maximum profit.*

Quinlan leaned forward, his tone firm but measured. "Alright, Flaco, here's the plan, keep attending your classes at the college, stay plugged into the neighborhood, but steer clear of your dad's printshop—we've seized it."

"What exactly am I supposed to focus on?" Perez retorted; his voice tinged with sarcasm.

Mackey's voice dropped to a low growl. "Focus on helping us help you stay the fuck out of federal prison."

Perez sighed, his demeanor shifting. He now focused on Quinlan, "Alright, listen up. Los Cazadores are making some serious moves in the Bronx, and all over the five boroughs, for that matter. They're nasty hombres. You guys familiar with them?"

"The Dominican gang, right?" Quinlan confirmed.

"Yeah, they've been pushing a lot of meth lately, maybe some heroin, too, but I can't confirm if they're tied to the counterfeit money," Perez admitted.

Quinlan and Mackey exchanged glances, silently agreeing to keep the information about the drug residue found on the counterfeit notes under wraps. Quinlan knew all too well that a wise informant could quickly become a dead one.

"Alright, get out there. Make some calls, but..." Quinlan paused, his gaze locking onto Perez. "Keep your eyes and ears open. Stay grounded, and don't go playing Elliot Ness."

"Elliot who?" Perez looked puzzled.

"Just see if you can dig up anything on where the drugs and the counterfeit are coming from," Mackey interjected. "

Quinlan chimed in, "And don't make a move without letting us know first. I mean it. None of this matters if we can't cover the operation or keep you safe. Got it?"

"Yeah, got it," Perez replied, his tone resigned. "I'll check in with you soon, Quinlan."

CHAPTER 15

DEA

Quinlan had some work to do back at the office. He was waiting for a report from FSD on what chemicals were being used to remove the legitimate ink from the $5 bills. He thought, What solvent could remove ink but not damage the paper? He also wanted to put a call into his contact at the DEA to check on any information about the Los Cazadores.

The phone was ringing then a voice announced, "DEA Agent Niego."

"Mike, it's Quinlan. How's your day?" Quinlan greeted.

"Hey, good. What's up? Anything new on that counterfeit case you mentioned the other day? We suspect it's tied to meth, right?" Agent Niego inquired.

"Yeah, it's getting more serious. We're seeing a surge in the same counterfeit bills, contaminated with those meth precursors you mentioned. Quite a significant number of notes. We've got a CI who's thinking it's a Dominican group that's distributing methamphetamine and heroin. Thinks they might be Los Cazadores," Quinlan informed him.

There was a brief silence on the line, "Mike, you still there?" he prompted.

"Yeah, let's discuss this in person. Can you make it down here tomorrow morning, say 9:00 am?" Agent Niego suggested.

"How about in an hour?" Quinlan proposed.

With the urgency of the situation at hand, Quinlan quickly briefed Mack and they set off southbound on the West Side Highway. The journey to the DEA's office in the heart of the Meatpacking District would take them about forty-five minutes at this time of day. The strategic location of the office, deliberately situated away from the bustling Manhattan traffic, boasted easy access to underground parking for discreet comings and goings of personnel. Equipped with cutting-edge biometric security measures, the building blended seamlessly into its surroundings. It looked like any other meatpacking plant. In a historical nod, the building had even hosted President George H.W. Bush as its keynote speaker and master of ceremonies upon its opening in 1989. With Bush's administration ramping up the war on drugs and coining the term Narco-Terrorism, the DEA garnered increased funding and attention.

Pulling into the surface lot adjacent to the unmarked building, Quinlan guided his Government Owned Vehicle (GOV) to a stop. He knew the unmarked fenced-in lot was reserved for guests visiting the building.

He began speaking into the intercom, "Secret Service, Agents John Quinlan and Joe Mackey here to see..."

Before he could finish, the voice on the speaker interrupted. "Please show your agency identification to the camera above the speaker." Quinlan and Mackey presented their Secret Service credentials, "Thank you. Now, who are you here to see?"

They provided Niego's name, and after a brief pause, they were buzzed in, granting them access to the parking lot and the building's foyer. Upon entering the foyer, Quinlan couldn't help but notice the surveillance cameras positioned in each corner, their lenses trained on the entranceway. The large portraits of the President and the Attorney General hanging on the wall were impossible to miss, casting an authoritative presence over the space.

They didn't have to wait long before a young woman emerged. She showed some distress when holding the door open as she greeted them. Quinlan surmised that the door, and likely the walls, were heavily armored and reinforced—a telltale sign of the encounters typically faced in such a space.

"Hi, I'm Donna. And you are here to see?" she inquired.

"Hello, Donna. I'm John Quinlan, and this is Joe Mackey. We're with the Secret Service, here to see Agent Mike Niego," Quinlan replied.

Donna nodded, and in a professional demeanor said, "I just need to see your Secret Service identification, gentlemen."

Quinlan and Mackey showed their credentials once again, and Donna led them into another waiting room.

"Gentlemen, Agent Niego is currently occupied, but he's expecting you. I will let him know you're here," she informed them before disappearing back through the door.

Quinlan and Mackey settled into the more comfortable confines of the waiting room, where a flat-screen TV mounted high in the corner showed the local news. Quinlan's gaze drifted to the imposing DEA insignia adorning the wall. Beside the insignia, hung a framed photo of a fallen agent. Beneath the image were the solemn words, 'In Memory of Enrique 'Kiki' Camarena.' Quinlan knew the tragic tale of Camarena all too well—a poignant reminder of the sacrifices made in the war on drugs. Camarena's untimely demise in 1985 at the hands of the Guadalajara Cartel had sent shockwaves through law enforcement circles. This, of course, sparked outrage that reshaped the political framework between Mexico and the United States. Yet, Quinlan could not shake the sobering realization that as long as there was a demand for drugs, the cycle of violence and corruption would persist.

Their wait was interrupted by the appearance of Agent Niego, who emerged through the lobby door connecting the outer and inner sanctums.

"Sorry for the delay, John. I didn't mean to keep you waiting. When you mentioned Los Cazadores, I knew we needed to talk," Niego explained as they exchanged greetings.

“I understand, Mike. Thanks for making time for us. This is my partner, Joe Mackey.”

“Call me Mack,” Mackey chimed in, extending his hand for a firm shake.

As they walked to Niego’s office, he couldn’t resist a playful jab at Quinlan’s past. “John, looks like you’ve made it to the big leagues. I remember when you were just a new cop in Jersey City, fighting against all that corruption across the river. Bet he didn’t fill you in on that, Mack,” Niego teased, winking at Quinlan.

Mackey’s response was a hesitant chuckle. “Uh, no, we haven’t had a chance to discuss that.”

Upon reaching his office, they settled in as Niego took a seat behind his desk, a folder bearing the DEA insignia prominently displayed before him.

“So, John, do you think your CI has any ties to Los Cazadores?” Niego inquired, his tone now serious.

“Not directly, but he suspects they might be behind the counterfeit operation we’re investigating,” Quinlan replied, launching into the heart of the matter.

“Is he working off a beef or being paid?” Niego inquired, fixing his gaze on Quinlan.

“He’s working off a beef. We nabbed him on federal 18 USC 471 charges, so he’s working to avoid a prison stint,” he explained.

Niego’s expression shifted to one of confusion, his face blank. “John, if it’s not drugs, I’m completely lost.”

“Sorry, manufacturing and passing counterfeit bills. He used his father’s legitimate printing business as a front. We caught wind of it, slapped him with the charges, and seized the business,” Quinlan clarified.

“His father’s business? Printing you say?” Niego probed further.

“A legitimate print shop that makes copies for customers. My CI had access to top-notch commercial copy machines. But the quality of those fakes pales in comparison to what we’re seeing now. The

CI suspects Los Cazadores are behind the high end counterfeit bills surfacing within the Dominican community," Quinlan elaborated.

"My guys haven't mentioned anything about high-end copy machines at their club," Niego countered.

"How about an offset printing press?" Quinlan suggested. "That's what the manufacturers of these counterfeit notes are using. It's a sophisticated piece of equipment that produces high-quality notes with raised ink, just like genuine currency, but it requires skill."

Niego replied, "Damn John, I'm out of my depth here. Let me get my guy, Jake Stole, the undercover on the Cazadores meth case. Maybe he can shed some light on this." Niego reached for the phone to summon assistance. "Jake, this is Mike. Can you come to my office?"

Agent Niego opened the folder that was sitting in front of him. He turned it around so Quinlan and Mackey could see the 8 X 10 image of a naked corpse. They both recoiled at the bloody emasculated body.

Niego, now laughing, "Sorry, too early in the day for you?"

"And the point is?" Quinlan asked with a puzzled look.

"Glad you asked. Niego said, "This is Cheecho. He was our informant. He was in good with Los Cazadores or so we thought. Fortunately, prior to Cheecho's untimely death, he was able to get our agent, Jake Stole, into the club. Jake is still undercover so he is a bit uhhh, ripe as you will soon see."

Mackey now holding the photo asked, "Are those his balls in his mouth? I'm guessing that since it appears his genitals are missing and somewhat mutilated."

"Oh yeah," Niego affirmed. "When Los Cazadores wants to send a message, they make sure it hits home."

He continued, "Looks like Cheecho got a little too cozy with Diego Santana's lady. Diego's street name is Carlos. We think that's because his last name is Santana. You get it, like Carlos Santana," Niego teased. "Anyway, Carlos is the boss, or El Jefe, of the Bronx chapter of Los Cazadores."

Mackey, still focused on the photo, questioned, "Why didn't they mess up his face? Apart from what's in his mouth and his missing... uhh parts, he looks relatively untouched."

Before anyone could respond, Agent Jake Stole strode into Niego's office, with a very much alive and unharmed Cheecho by his side.

Looking up and seeing Cheecho alive, Quinlan shouted, "WHAT the fuck?" as he sank back into his chair.

"See, gentlemen," Niego said, "All his kibbles and bits are in the right place."

Agent Jake Stole was standing next to his informant, and both appeared mildly amused.

"Jake Stole," he said extending his hand to greet the still shocked agents and this is Cheecho the CI with nine lives. Don't worry, Niego's a sick fuck; he pulls this charade with everyone."

After giving Quinlan and Mackey a moment to collect themselves, Niego's tone turned serious.

"There was growing distrust against Cheecho within the Cazadores inner circle," he began, his tone now serious. "But despite that, he managed to get Agent Stole well-positioned with Carlos and his crew. Stole's cover is Nickalos, a fully 'patched' Outlaws biker club member."

Agent Stole now interjected, "I am Greek, so originally my name was Stolesnos, but my grandparents shortened it to Stole when they emigrated. They were the only Greeks in Queens who were not keen on running a diner," he explained with a warm smile, his imposing 6'2" stature adding to his affable sense of humor.

Niego continued, "Stole has been doing exceptional undercover work for the past year. He's the muscle for Los Cazadores." Niego glanced at Quinlan. "Before you reached out, John, we were on the verge of pulling the plug on this case. We have more than enough to take Carlos and the whole methamphetamine distribution operation down."

He paused, his gaze flickering between Quinlan and Mackey. "We staged Cheecho's 'death' to protect him and basically save his life. As far as Los Cazadores are concerned, Cheecho is dead and out of the picture. Stole, or Nickalos as they know him, will be our star witness. With Cheecho effectively out of the picture, it gives us a head start in relocating him through the Marshals' witness security program."

Niego turned to Stole. "Jake, why don't you fill them in on the details?"

Looking at Stole, Quinlan interjected, "How did Carlos handle the photo as being proof of Cheecho's death?"

"Hook, line, and sinker. He looked at that picture for a long time. He flipped it over thinking he would see the back of his head or something. He ain't the sharpest tool in the shed, trust me. Then he just laughed, enjoying the revenge. He wanted me to recount the entire ordeal for him over and over again. So, I did, with great flair."

Cheecho rolled his eyes at Stole's evident amusement, clearly unimpressed by the retelling of his alleged demise. Cheecho interrupted, "I was in the middle of lunch, Jake. Mind if I get back to it?" With that, the DEA informant, very much alive, exited Niego's office.

Over the next hour, Stole delved into the intricacies of Los Cazadores for Quinlan and Mackey. He revealed that the U.S. Attorney's Office believed they had enough evidence to indict Diego 'Carlos' Santana and his entire crew. They were running a sophisticated methamphetamine lab known as the Factory in the Bronx, near the corner of 180th and 3rd Avenue. The building boasted its own ventilation system, minimizing the telltale stench associated with meth production.

Quinlan exclaimed, "So they're running some Breaking Bad Hollywood-level operation?" He referenced the popular series featuring a high school science teacher turned methamphetamine drug lord.

Niego grinned. "Exactly. That's what we thought, too. Stole, tell them about our little Hollywood act with Cheecho."

Stole began to explain, "So, it was time to safely get Cheecho out. I spread the rumor he was fucking LaSandra, Carlos' girlfriend. I then put that bug in Carlos' ear, and I suggested I take him out."

Niego interrupted, "At first, Carlos had a problem with that. Cheecho was a good earner. He okayed the plan only after Jake agreed to do the hit. Jake also had to get Cheecho's replacement to cover the meth sales."

Smiling, Stole said, "It was perfect. We staged the rendition in the woods up in Harriman, NY. We stripped our boy naked and got all Hollywood on him. We used pig entrails and other specifically selected items from the butcher down the street. It pays to be in the meat packing district. Our technical security team took a lot of photos of the corpse." Quinlan and Mackey were eagerly absorbing every word that Agent Jake Stole uttered. He continued, "They were able to doctor the photos to make it even more gruesome. The whole balls in the mouth thing was Niego's idea."

"This kind of thing was done before, by the FBI I think," said Niego.

Agent Stole spoke up, "Those pinheads would never come up with something genius like this. It was done by an ATF undercover agent. He and his CI got deep into the Hell's Angels motorcycle club."

"Stole is right," Mackey said. "It was an ATF agent by the name of Jay Dobyns. He did the same thing as you guys. Except in his case, he staged a bullet to the back of the CI's head. A lot more understated. His genitals remained where God put them."

Quinlan inquired, "Jake, during your time undercover, did Los Cazadores, especially Carlos, ever give you or pay you in cash?"

Agent Niego swiveled around in his chair, reaching for an evidence bag sealed with the chain of custody tape still intact. With deliberate care, he sliced open the sealed container, causing bundles of currency to cascade onto his desk. Among the spilled contents were \$50s, \$100s, and even \$1s—a testament to the integrity and accuracy of Agent Jake Stole's record-keeping. Every bill had been logged into evidence.

"I wanted to wait until you guys got down here, but this is every bit of money that Agent Stole logged into evidence as part of this case," said Niego.

Quinlan reached over and picked up a bundle of $50s and Mackey looked at the $100s. Right away they could see a few bleached counterfeit notes bundled in with genuine currency. They now had enough evidence to link the counterfeit to the meth lab.

"Stole, did you ever see a printing press in the factory any time you were there?" asked Mackey.

"Shit guys I wasn't looking for that kind of thing. I'm not sure I would know what a printing press was if I tripped over it. I know there is an office upstairs. I am not allowed up there, hell no one is except Carlos and whatever lady toy he wants to get private with. The meth lab is downstairs and that's where I hang," replied Agent Stole.

Mackey looked at Stole and said, "We think they are using $5 genuine notes. They bleach them in a solution that we are still trying to figure out. This solution removes the ink without damaging the paper. They get the bleached paper with the strip and other security features so they can print $50-dollar and $100-dollar images. You ever see bundles of $5s coming in?"

Niego glanced at Stole and instructed, "Jake, go get Cheecho again. I want him to give his input on this."

A short while later, Cheecho returned with Agent Stole. Eager to share his insights, Cheecho felt like he was playing the role of Dick Tracy. He eagerly mentioned having seen bank envelopes filled with new $5 bills but hadn't thought much of it until now.

"Cheecho, tell them about the acetone," Niego prompted.

"Yeah, we always had gallons of that stuff lying around. I remember the name on the cans—acetone. You know, the stuff for cleaning up paint," Cheecho explained.

Quinlan inquired further, "Have you ever been up to the office or seen what goes on there?"

"Nope, never been up there. But I know something is happening when we're not around. Why else would it be off-limits? Also, sometimes the cans of this acetone would be lined up at the bottom of the stairs, like they were ready to be taken up," Cheecho replied.

"Thanks, Cheecho," Niego said, dismissing him again. Agent Stole escorted Cheecho out.

Turning to Quinlan, Niego asked, "Think we could use your CI to get inside? He might be familiar with the counterfeit operation or at least know what to look for."

Quinlan replied, "Absolutely. Plus, we've got a reason to bring a new face in. Isn't Carlos in the market for a new salesman, especially after Stole's little 'altercation' with Cheecho?"

As Jake returned to the office, Niego inquired, "Jake, do you think you can get their CI into the operation without setting off any alarms with Carlos?"

"I'll have to meet him first. What's his name?" Jake inquired.

"Adolpho Perez, but he goes by Flaco," Mackey answered.

"Flaco, huh? Is he skinny? Let me meet him first, and I will let you know," Jake said. Then, looking at Niego, he asked, "Is that okay with you, boss?"

Niego responded with a thumbs up.

Turning to Stole, Quinlan inquired, "They've got a ventilation system to mask the smell of the meth production. Do you think it's possible for the residue to contaminate the counterfeit? Like, could it flow through the ducts?"

Stole nodded emphatically. "Oh, hell yeah. That stuff seeps everywhere. There's no escaping it. Sometimes I walk out of there so buzzed, I gotta take a walk around the block before I can even think about driving."

"Alright," Niego interjected. "This was productive. I'll reach out to AUSA Dave Crosby, who's handling our case. Who's the AUSA on your end, John?"

"AUSA Lana Miller. I will inform her, too. Hopefully, they will both collaborate on this," Quinlan replied, nodding in agreement.

CHAPTER 16

Chemistry 101

Quinlan and Mackey were navigating the city streets back to the field office when Quinlan's phone rang.

"Agent Quinlan, Sue Faranato here from FSD," crackled a voice through the receiver. "I'm sending over the forensics report, but I wanted to touch base. The counterfeit bills you submitted for analysis. They've been bleached using a basic acetone and baking soda concoction. Pretty amateurish work. Whoever's using this solution to bleach the notes is far from a pro."

Quinlan glanced at Mackey, who leaned in with interest. "Hey, Sue, Joe's here, too. Lay it on us. What's a more sophisticated method of bleaching?"

Sue's voice took on a professorial tone. "Well, you'd want a solution containing ether-based glycol, antioxidant DOT 3-4-5, boric acid, and ether. No scrubbing required, just a nice, long soak."

Quinlan chuckled. "You're hitting us with some serious chemistry here, Sue. I only took Chemistry 101 in college. I'm thinking of introducing our confidential informant to these printers. Figured if he can bring in a more efficient method of ink removal, it might be a good opening."

"Oh, my apologies, John," Sue responded. "That would be brake fluid. Common automotive brake fluid. The nomenclature comes with the territory when you spend all day in the lab."

"Alright, Sue, how long should these bills soak for?" Quinlan inquired.

"If you submerge a genuine $5 bill in brake fluid overnight, the ink that the Bureau of Engraving and Printing uses will seep into the solution. Afterwards, the notes need to be transferred straight into a vinegar solution to halt the process, or the bills will start to deteriorate. The vinegar will also neutralize any lingering chemical odors. I'll draft a detailed report and send it your way," Sue replied.

With a determined expression, Quinlan ended the call, his mind racing with plans.

Mackey always marveled at the speed of Quinlan's thought process. *Introducing Flaco to Los Cazadores as a bleacher via the undercover operation was a stroke of brilliance,* he thought. *If Flaco could introduce a more simplified bleaching method for the $5s, it might just be their ticket in.*

Quinlan swiftly dialed DEA Agent Niego.

"Did you solve your case without me and so quickly?" Niego teased.

Quinlan explained his plan, and Niego was immediately onboard. He summoned the undercover agent to his office to hear Quinlan's proposal. Agent Stole also embraced the idea, recognizing its potential as an icebreaker.

"John, it sounds promising, but I need to meet Flaco in person. When can you bring him down here?" Stole inquired.

"Would tomorrow at 9:00 am work for you," he suggested.

The following day, Quinlan and Mackey picked up Flaco and drove him to the DEA Field Office. After introductions were made, they left Flaco in Stole's capable hands to become acquainted. Over the ensuing days, Stole and Flaco frequented popular locales in Northern Manhattan and eventually the Bronx, ensuring they were seen together. Stole advised Flaco to maintain a rough appearance. He told him to stop grooming and avoid preppy attire in favor of a more rugged look. The directive was to distance himself from his usual associates, including his girlfriend, and to temporarily suspend his college enrollment. All of this proved to be challenging for Flaco.

Nonetheless, Stole emphasized the importance of these actions for the success of their operation.

* * *

Quinlan received the FSD report, complete with an addendum from Forensics Specialist Faranato. The addendum laid out a specific step-by-step guide for removing ink from genuine Federal Reserve notes. To their surprise, it even recommended a specific brand of brake fluid, Arcon Brake Fluid, as being the most effective.

Taking a calculated risk, Quinlan and Mackey set up shop at Quinlan's house, away from the prying eyes of the office. They understood their actions bordered on breaking federal law by defacing United States currency. Nevertheless, they proceeded with caution, cutting the brake fluid with water to the prescribed consistency before submerging the notes into the solution. With bated breath, they waited approximately eight hours for the bleaching process to take effect, then transferred the bleached notes to a vinegar-water solution to neutralize the chemical reaction.

To their astonishment, the process worked like a charm. Mackey marveled at the transformation as the once tainted bills emerged clean and bright. The red and blue security fibers now stood out prominently against the pristine paper. The embedded security strip gleamed with the unmistakable imprint, USA FIVE. Stripped of ink, the remaining security features became even more pronounced and obvious.

Quinlan wasted no time in arranging several repeat sessions of the bleaching process with Flaco. Agent Stole observed the process, thoroughly impressed by the efficacy of the method. Quinlan and Stole diligently coached Flaco, quizzing him on the chemical composition of the brake fluid. They knew they had to craft a cover story for Flaco's involvement as a printer. They would have to be mindful not to reveal his true connection to his parents' business, Start to Finish Printing. Everyone in the neighborhood knew the shop was officially closed down by the feds.

* * *

Stole stood before Niego, Quinlan, and Mackey, unveiling the cover story with practiced ease.

"So, Flaco used to handle the books for my motorcycle club until he got nabbed for forgery," Agent Stole began, his tone casual yet convincingly natural. "At least, that's the word around the club. We never got the full story. All we know is he spent some time up north at a juvenile detention center. Served a year, and I picked him up at a bus stop in White Plains as a favor to a friend. During the ride, he spilled the beans about why he got sent up: making counterfeit money. Turns out, he's been sitting on a method to make fake money using real cash. Beyond that, your guess is as good as mine."

The low murmur of approval rippled through the DEA conference room as Stole's cover story unfolded. It was a tale woven with just enough truth to sound plausible yet shrouded in enough mystery to avoid further scrutiny. All present agreed that this narrative would serve as the perfect cover to introduce Flaco to Los Cazadores.

But as the applause subsided, a new sense of urgency permeated the room as Stole pivoted to more pressing matters. "I've got some new intel to share," he continued, his voice taking on a grave undertone. "Diego 'Carlos' Santana's been slipping. He started hitting the heroin hard after his woman left him. The junk's become his crutch. He used to be all about the meth, but now he's nodding off more than he's tweaking. Word is, he's becoming a liability to the senior management of Los Cazadores."

Niego interjected, his tone resolute. "Another reason to move quickly on this. Let's get Flaco into the factory sooner rather than later."

As the meeting ended, the weight of their mission hung heavy in the air. Quinlan couldn't shake the feeling that the tide was turning, that their operation was hurtling towards a pivotal moment.

* * *

Quinlan had been diligently keeping AUSA Miller in the loop, updating her on their joint operation with the DEA. She welcomed the opportunity to prosecute a narcotics case, a refreshing change from her usual white-collar work. Quinlan admired her professionalism and made a mental note to ask her out for a cup of coffee once the case wrapped up, though he quickly dismissed the idea as a fantasy. "She was way above my pay grade," he would say.

"John, if Flaco starts bleaching or printing bills, or even spots the printing press, we'll follow it up with a search warrant," AUSA Miller informed him over the phone, her voice serious and determined. "If we get visual confirmation from your CI, we'll have enough to raid the place. Right now, the DEA's undercover operation has gathered sufficient evidence. Also, we've heard Diego Santana is getting sloppy. Dave Cosby and I are concerned. We agree you may need to arrest him before Los Cazadores has their chance to take him out."

"We're on the same page. Let's see what Flaco uncovers once he's inside," Quinlan affirmed, his mind already racing with anticipation for the operation ahead. "And after the raid, who knows? It might lead us to more counterfeit operations in the five boroughs."

"Keep me posted," Miller instructed before signing off, leaving Quinlan to contemplate the significance of their impending actions.

As he hung up the phone, Quinlan felt a surge of adrenaline coursing through his veins. The pieces of the puzzle were finally falling into place, and the prospect of bringing down a major counterfeit operation was within their grasp. But amidst the thrill of the chase, a sense of caution lingered. The stakes were higher than ever, and any misstep could jeopardize the entire operation.

He glanced over at Mackey, who shared his sense of determination. Together, they were ready to gear up for the task ahead, but Quinlan could not shake the nagging thought that their journey was far from over.

CHAPTER 17

Los Cazadores

The DEA was ready to move on this since their best evidence against Los Cazadores' narcotics operation was the DEA undercover who had been quite successful. Tacking on federal counterfeit charges would be even better for all parties. The U.S. Attorney's Office as well as the brass from the Secret Service and the DEA would applaud the spirit of cooperation. Quinlan knew this case would mean suppressing the counterfeit plant. That would be a feather in their cap. Right now, that printing press was responsible for over $200,000 in counterfeit money currently in circulation.

Friday night Stole knew Carlos would be high on something and he thought that would be the best time to introduce Flaco. At that late hour, Stole also thought maybe there would be activity upstairs. Cheecho always told him that area comes alive after midnight.

The outside roving cover team for the introduction were Mack and DEA Agent Stan Jameson. The DEA had already installed pole cameras covering the front and rear doors of the factory. The cameras had been up the whole time Stole or his alter ego, Nickalos, was undercover. The cameras were connected to monitors situated within a DEA control room, strategically positioned just a block away from the target factory. To facilitate round-the-clock electronic surveillance of the factory, the DEA transformed a second-floor factory office into a dedicated operations center. Its monitors and cutting-edge equipment ensured uninterrupted video surveillance and recording capabilities. Countless individuals had been identified through recordings captured at the factory's front and rear access points.

As midnight approached, the control room hummed with anticipation. Agents Niego, Quinlan, and NYPD Narcotics Detective Dan Blanchard maintained their vigilant watch. Each member of the team stood ready, their senses heightened, poised to execute the intricately laid plan they had prepared.

Shortly thereafter, Stole and Flaco pulled up in Stole's sleek BMW M3. Stole would often joke that the vehicle was a perfect match for his imposing 6'2" frame. He parked the M3 half on the curb and half on the street near the factory entrance. Stole knew the Cazadores lookouts were accustomed to his car and paid it no mind. Entering the factory, Stole wasted little time in announcing his intention to introduce Flaco to Carlos and his cohorts.

"Hey, where's Carlos? Stole shouted slipping into his undercover persona, Nickalos, "I need him to meet my boy, Flaco!"

One of the low hanging fruit assholes with a gun, as Stole would describe him, stepped up. "Who the fuck is this, Nickalos, and who the fuck are you to just bring someone..."

Nickalos grabbed the low hanging fruit by the shirt and cocked back his fist, "You ever fucking talk to Nickalos like that again, Nickalos will fuck you up. He will chain your arms to a light pole and your legs to a rear bumper and yell 'Andale' motherfucker."

Meanwhile, Flaco, equipped with special knock-off Michael Jordans wired with a Phantom Tag 5 transmitter, discreetly relayed audio back to the cover team.

Niego chuckled, turning to Quinlan. "I forgot to mention, Nickalos has this thing where he refers to himself in the third person. It's all part of the undercover persona Stole's crafted for him—a Greek biker vibe with an air of superiority."

"Hey, if it works," Quinlan replied with a smirk, fully immersed in the tense yet strangely exhilarating atmosphere of the operation.

Nickalos, now scanning the room shouted, "Carlos, Carlos, where you at, man? I got someone for you to meet."

A short time later, Carlos emerged from the second-floor office, a cigarette dangling from his lips. His figure was obscured by coveralls splattered with what seemed to be a mixture of paint and ink. "What the fuck you doing here? You don't come here at night and who the fuck is that?"

"This is Flaco, man, we were partying, and I wanted to introduce you, man..."

"No, no, get the fuck out, man. Come back tomorrow in the afternoon but without anyone. Come on, man, you know the rules."

Stole immediately sensed that he had overstepped his bounds, and Carlos's demeanor didn't indicate he was high, at least no more than usual. Covered in what appeared to be paint, a chilling realization dawned on Stole, could Carlos be the printer? It was a startling thought. Stole had been around this guy for a year. He only ever knew him to go upstairs when he wanted to get laid. The notion of him being involved in counterfeiting had not crossed his mind until now. "Alright man, my bad. Tomorrow."

"Yeah, tomorrow," said Carlos.

Niego got on the radio and ordered all units to report back to the control room via the rear entrance for a debrief.

Agent Stole briefed the group and thought Carlos reacted in a way he could anticipate given the hour. He opined, "We forced the meet by bringing Flaco in. Sometimes it works, sometimes it doesn't. Tonight, it didn't. I am thinking he is more involved with that printing press and counterfeiting, though. Seeing him come out of that upstairs office. I've never seen him in coveralls or whatever that was."

Niego chimed in, "Alright, let's give it another shot. Stole, perhaps it's best if you go solo tomorrow."

The following day, Stole arrived at promptly 11:00 am, noticing immediately that Carlos was pissed off.

"Man, what the fuck was that last night?" Carlos shouted.

"What? Sorry, man, just wanted to bring this kid in. Ya know Cheecho's replacement. This kid wants to move shit like Cheecho and I know he can because he was with us at the club before he got pinched."

Carlos seemed dazed, "What, wait what are you talking about?"

"Man, you alright? You seem out of it," Nickalos said with concern.

"Yeah, up all night with some other shit. Who'd you bring by?"

"The kid I was telling you about," Nickalos was clearly gaslighting Carlos now. He tried this before with Carlos and it worked so he figured what the hell.

Looking directly into Carlos' bloodshot eyes, Nickalos said, "I told you he's out of juvie and he kept our books at the Outlaws? He can move shit, too. A kid worth looking at, no?"

Carlos now excited, "Oh, Cheecho's replacement," he said and started to laugh. He snorted a line of meth from a plate on the table. "Yeah get him back in here and we can talk. What do you mean, he kept your books?"

It was the perfect opportunity, Nickalos thought.

"Yea he kept our ledgers at the club, and we even made him an honorary pledge. He was too young to be patched or anything..."

Carlos interrupted, "Hey, don't talk that biker shit. I don't get it, patched, pledged whatever. I just know you crazy fucks are good paying meth junkies."

Look who's talking, Nickalos thought.

"Yeah, so anyways, he is also into making funny money or that's what he said he got pinched on."

Stole knew this was a dangerous shot in the dark. As far as Carlos was concerned, Nickalos knew nothing of the counterfeit operation he was running out of the upstairs office.

Carlos, now locking eyes with Stole, uttered, "What does he know about counterfeiting?" Stepping closer into Stole's personal space, Carlos maintained his intense stare. Stole sensed he might have crossed a line. Then Carlos slumped and said, "Can you bring him down here now, man? I'm fucking exhausted."

Nickalos stepped outside and called Flaco and told him to stay put and be ready for a call from Quinlan. His next call was to his Group Leader, Agent Niego. He told Niego he needed Flaco delivered and wired if possible. Niego had been prepared for this and he called Quinlan, and the second undercover operation was hastily put into action.

Nickalos reentered the building and approached Carlos, assuring him that help was on its way. He observed Carlos's weary demeanor. He looked like shit. Carlos confided in his top soldier that he was into something else. He had been making fake money and selling it to markets in the Dominican Republic, Mexico, Peru, and other parts of South America. He did this at the direction of Los Cazadores bosses. When they found out he knew how to make counterfeit, they took advantage of the situation. They were now pressuring him to produce an additional twenty percent profit above what the meth sales were bringing in.

After hearing this, Nickalos wanted to get him to stop talking until Flaco arrived. Flaco would be wired up and recording. He wanted to record Carlos saying all of this.

"Carlos, hold on man. My guy told me about some advanced shit with removing the ink so you can reuse the paper. Does that sound right? Anyways, he's on his way. I know meth, man; I don't know this shit."

Aside from the arrival of the liquid disposal truck to haul away the byproduct of meth production, the factory floor was eerily silent. Today marked cleanup day, and a truck bearing a resemblance to a port-a-potty disposal service rolled in. Its purpose was obvious. With a methodical efficiency, it siphoned the liquid waste into its bladder-like container. Nickalos often pondered where it all ended up, but he was never privy to that information.

Looking at Carlos, Nickalos asked, “Hey, if you’re making fake money, did you ever pay me with that shit?” He was trying to get Carlos to admit he paid his own guys with the counterfeit to make him feel even worse than he was feeling.

“What? No,” said Carlos. “Unless I was so high, I might have paid you guys with some of that shit. Man, I didn’t mean to if I did.”

“Look, I don’t give a shit, Carlos, I spent whatever you gave me. I just don’t want you tripping up and ruining the whole meth business.”

Carlos, now looking defeated, said, “Alright, man. Sorry, but all these pinche cabrons working me, man. You the only hombre to last a year. I trust you. LaSandra left me, I’m down on my count for sales, I can’t fill the phony money orders.” He snorted another line of meth from the plate on the table.

Nickalos grabbed a beer out of the fridge and sat down with Carlos.

Carlos now feeling a little more himself, continued, “What time was it that you come by last night?”

“About midnight, man, sorry about that.”

“Yeah, no shit, man, just freaked me out. I was douchey with you, man. I hope I wasn’t a dick in front of your boy, what’s his name?”

“Flaco,” Nickalos said.

“Flaco, is he skinny? Oh shit, yeah, he’s skinny. I remember that.”

Just then Flaco walked in with one of the Cazadores stooges saying, “he was clean.” Nickalos didn’t know if that meant he wasn’t wired, or they missed it. The Phantom Tag five embedded in his fake government issued Jordans was high-end, and he was wearing them.

Carlos walked over to Flaco and said, “Boy, you are skinny. Now I know you is Flaco.”

Moving in closer to Flaco, Carlos continued, “What you know about funny money?”

Flaco gave him a full resume of his capabilities to include the rehearsed part about bleaching $5 bills. He explained the best way was with brake fluid. There was no need for scrubbing the ink off.

Nickalos didn't know if Carlos was high, tired, desperate, or all three. He walked away towards the stairs leading to the upstairs office space.

He shouted to no one in particular, "Everyone get the fuck out! Get the fuck out of the building. Not you two. You two come with me."

Nickalos and Flaco followed Carlos up the stairs and into a room that had sound foam on the walls. It was well lit and the obvious beast in the room was a fully operational printing press.

Flaco's eyes lit up, "This is an S&G Emerald Back second generation press. This is sweet."

Then Flaco walked to the vats of the acetone mixture, "Whew, I can smell this shit. It's acetone, man! I can help you with that."

Flaco explained the solution he would use to make the operation clean and easier.

Nickalos thought to himself, *this kid is a natural.*

Nickalos exclaimed, "He can move our shit, too. He's got the juvi connections..."

Carlos cut him off, "Fuck that! Kid you want to make some money? Ha, you assholes, get it, make some money?"

This was a rare occasion when Nickalos actually saw Carlos laugh or even crack a joke. Flaco was wired for sound, and everything was recorded.

Quinlan and Niego were two blocks away sitting in Niego's Audi A4. The A4 was compliments of a previous drug seizure. They were listening to the whole exchange. It was being recorded in the nearby DEA operations room. Quinlan wanted to get Flaco more involved in the counterfeiting process. He wanted to record Carlos instructing Flaco on how to make the counterfeit.

"Mike, imagine the evidence. It would be gold for the Secret Service," Quinlan said. "We would have the counterfeiter actually teaching the informant how to work the press while the informant teaches the counterfeiter how to bleach the notes."

"I hear you but how long are you thinking? The U.S. Attorney's Office wants to shut this down since we have more than enough on the drugs alone."

Quinlan replied, "One-week tops. Shit, at this point, Carlos is tired, depressed and on so much dope he would probably let me print the paper if your boy Nickalos introduced me."

Niego, now looking at Quinlan, said, "Yeah, THAT ain't happening."

AUSAs Miller and Cosby agreed to give it one more week to see if Flaco could be more involved in the counterfeiting process. Cosby was thinking of the splash this would make in the New York Post.

Hell, he thought, *even the New York Times would run with this. A joint Secret Service—Drug Enforcement Administration investigation prosecuted by the United States Attorney's Office for the Southern District of New York.*

Miller was more practical about it, not really concerned with the splash it would make with the media. She was more concerned with protecting the prosecutive integrity of the case. Everything had to be tied up with no procedural snags. She once lost a case on a search warrant technicality and it haunted her.

Quinlan's phone rang.

"John, Lana Miller. Hey, we are good to go for one week, then we are drawing up search warrants for the factory. Start working with Niego and his team to have your raid plan down. When we agree it's time, we hit it. Sound good?"

"Sounds good. Be in touch," he said.

AUSA Miller talked like a cop because she was surrounded by them. She knew their way of thinking. Her way, however, was guided by procedural law and having all the evidence standing up in court.

After ending the call with Quinlan, she staired out her office window in lower Manhattan, *Justice is blind,* she thought. *These days justice is also leaning towards liberal, social restorative justice policies and away from good, solid facts supported by the evidence.* She would see so many good federal cases get downward departures from federal judges seeking higher office in a town run by liberal millionaire political activists. *Justice was blind but for the wrong reasons.*

Carlos had taken a liking to Flaco. He looked at him as an apprentice of sorts. Flaco impressed Carlos with the new bleaching solution that required no scrubbing. This put Flaco in good standing with Los Cazadores, at least the tribe that Carlos controlled. Was Carlos in control though? While undercover as Nickalos, Agent Stole started to see Carlos using more heroin. He was now shooting up the junk.

His judgment was off. He would say to Nickalos, "I got Flaco, man, Flaco is the Mona Lisa of the printing press man, look at him." A reference to his obvious lack of art appreciation or just the drugs warping his mind? With Flaco around, Carlos loosened his rules on printing only after hours. He was now running that printing press day and night.

It was all about the bottom dollar. Carlos had to pay up to the Cazadores bosses. They didn't give a shit if the profits came from meth or counterfeit. Hell, they didn't even ask, Nickalos thought.

Flaco was now bleaching notes and printing the counterfeit on the highly sophisticated S&G printing press. It was time to shut it all down, thought undercover Special Agent Jake Stole.

The life and times of Nickalos might be coming to an end, he thought to himself.

CHAPTER 18

The Raid

All agreed the raid on the factory would take place on Friday afternoon. Diego 'Carlos' Santana and his trusted Los Cazadores would be making meth. Flaco would be making counterfeit bills upstairs. Carlos would most likely be strung out and not in control. The decision was made to keep Agent Stole as Nickalos in the factory for the raid. He would be arrested like everyone else. This would confuse Los Cazadores. They wouldn't see Nickalos again until he morphed into DEA Special Agent Jake Stole. His appearance as such would be in a federal court room.

AUSAs Miller and Cosby would monitor the raid from the DEA operations room across the street. Also assigned to that post would be DEA Supervisory Agent Brad Collier, Supervisory Secret Service Agent Jason Steele, and NYPD Detective John Flemming.

Quinlan's squad was bolstered by two Secret Service agents, among them Rick Boland. Boland, edging closer to retirement, half-jokingly cautioned Quinlan, "Let's skip the makeshift bombs this time, Q. I'm three weeks from retirement, after all."

Mackey and Niego each had two agents assigned to their teams. The NYPD provided their elite Emergency Services Unit (ESU) to breach the front door of the factory. The plan was comprehensive.

The last situation report via cellphone from Nickalos to the DEA operations room was, "Eight inside, six armed with semi auto pistols, Flaco and Carlos, second floor, no one at the rear entry, no long guns observed. I will be at the front door. Chemicals are flowing and meth is being made so NO STUN GRENADES!"

Nickalos knew that the non-lethal explosive grenades were typically a safe and effective way to disorient and temporarily incapacitate anyone within their immediate vicinity. However, he also knew the device could trigger an explosion when exposed to the chemicals present.

It was 12:45 pm when Niego signaled a go. NYPD ESU entered through the doorway first and no breach was necessary as the doors were unlocked. They drew down their Colt M4 Carbine Rifles and shouted "POLICE" as they advanced inward to the center of the factory floor. Quinlan and Mackey's team followed while Niego and his team had the rear entrance. Agent Boland could be heard, "POLICE drop your weapon," followed by a single gunshot. Boland was down and rolling on the ground in pain. Mackey returned fire on the shooter, and he was down. Quinlan and his team moved towards the stairs which was part of the plan. The remaining teams placed flexi-cuff zip ties on the two that were at the meth tables. Three others tried to run out the rear door but were quickly apprehended and cuffed by Niego's team. Supervisory Agent Brad Collier already had Emergency Medical Services on the way and sirens could be heard in the distance.

Quinlan and his team were slowly moving up the stairs. They reached the second floor landing and turning the corner, they realized there was no door separating the office from the landing. Cautiously, Quinlan entered the upstairs office. The lights were off and it was pitch black. Quinlan stood in place and shined his flashlight. He could not immediately discern any movement or presence of anyone in the room. As he moved closer to the printing press, he redirected his flashlight and saw movement right in front of him from under the table. It was Carlos and before Quinlan could respond, he felt a piercing pain in his right thigh, "I'm stabbed," he shouted. Whatever it was it was sharp, and it only stopped when it hit the bone. Just then the lights went on in the room and Carlos was running toward the landing. He made the sharp turn just outside the room but lost his balance and tumbled down the stairs. He came to a stop on the factory floor landing. He was now staring down the barrels of several raid team members' weapons. Quinlan was now able to see a hypodermic needle sticking out of his leg. It was so deep; the syringe had bent into his leg. He was bleeding heavily, and he thought the worst. It might have hit the femoral artery. It was a deep cut and it felt like his leg was in flames.

He was writhing in pain when a call went out on the radio, "We have three down, two friendly and one suspect. Gun shots and stabbing."

"Roger that. EMS is two minutes out."

Quinlan shouted, "WHO WAS SHOT? WHO WAS SHOT?" over and over.

Niego, arriving next to Quinlan, who seemed calmer and responsive said, "John, your boy, Boland, was shot but his vest took the hit. Mackey put down the shooter. Boland had the wind knocked out of him. Looks like he's alright. EMS is on their way. How are you?"

Quinlan tried to grab the syringe to pull it out when Niego stopped him, "Don't, John, we don't know what's going into your leg from that syringe. We sure as shit don't know what's coming out if you pull it out. Leave it be brother. Leave it be. Let EMS work on you."

EMS split their response and called for additional EMS units. Boland had a cracked rib and Quinlan's needle puncture, although deep and to the bone, did not hit any arteries. He was told by EMS that the aggressive blood flow was most likely from his heightened blood pressure and adrenaline. The person Mackey shot was not so lucky. He was dead on arrival. Mackey put two rounds center mass in the Cazadores lieutenant. A testament to his firearms training for sure.

Boland now sat next to Quinlan on the factory room floor. They were awaiting transport to Montefiore Medical Center.

Boland said, "Q, what the fuck man? Pipe bombs, gun shots, stabbed with a needle. I am done. Working with you is a death wish. My wife is going to be pissed at me."

Quinlan replied, "You can make it up to her if you just retire."

* * *

Two days later, AUSA Dave Cosby got his press conference. Standing right alongside him on the steps of the Southern District of New York was a stunning redhead named Lana Miller. Quinlan was watching NY1, the local news network, when he saw this all unfold. He was resting in his apartment, sitting in his guy chair with his leg up.

He was now looking at Lana as a woman. A beautiful one at that, and no longer a federal prosecutor. She is pretty, he thought to himself.

The public relations arm of the Southern District of New York would not disappoint.

AUSA Dave Cosby stood at the microphone, "This joint investigative effort put forth by the Drug Enforcement Administration and the United States Secret Service could not have happened without the direction and coordination of the United States Attorney's Office. Operation Wipe Out was planned over a year ago when the Southern District of New York..."

Just then Quinlan's phone rang, and it was Mike Niego, "John, you watching this?"

"I am," he replied. "I am glad for them, but I can't really hear anything because I am too focused on AUSA Lana Miller."

Niego replied, "Ha, I gotta say she is pretty. Pretty good at what she does for a living, too. Did everything go alright with your medical follow up?"

"Yea no Hep C, HIV or any of the other shit that could come with a needle stick. Not going to lie, the follow up shots I needed were no walk in the park. Boland had it far worse though. Cracked rib. He's putting in his papers."

"Yeah, good for him," Niego said. "He's one of the good ones."

Still watching the press conference Quinlan thought to himself, *she is fun to look at*. "Alright Mike, talk to you when I get back into the office."

Niego ended the call, "See ya, pal."

CHAPTER 19

Quinlan's Goodbye

Boland retired, and Quinlan had taken his place in the New York Field Office Protective Intelligence Squad. He moved to intelligence because it was believed his art of interviewing and interrogation was beyond reproach. He would later be expected to apply those skills to his assignment in Room 23.

Mackey was on administrative desk duty following the shooting of Los Cazadores member, the late Juan 'Loco' Lopez. The Secret Service Internal Affairs and the Department of the Treasury—Office of the Inspector General cleared him after a three-week investigation. Mackey's shooting was deemed justified. Mack would continue in the Counterfeit Squad taking up the slack that Quinlan left behind. Adolpho 'Flaco' Perez had paid his debt to the federal government. His attorney requested that AUSA Miller put in a dismissal for the case. Miller countered with a downward departure to six months' probation that included community service, fines, and court costs.

Quinlan always made it a point to steer clear of the head office. The time came when the Special Agent in Charge of the New York Field Office summoned him. He gave him the news.

"John, congratulations, headquarters called. Shine your shoes because you are going to the show!"

The term "show" referred to the Secret Service—Presidential Protection Division. John had certainly earned the prestigious opportunity. With seven years of dedicated service in one of the nation's busiest offices, he had proven himself worthy. To bid him farewell, the New York Field Office organized a gathering at Jeremy's Ale House, a beloved spot tucked under the Manhattan side of the Brooklyn Bridge. It was a cherished tradition for NYFO agents to gather and toast their departing colleagues as they embarked on new assignments. Quinlan smiled as he spotted his DEA pals, Niego and Stole, the latter still donning his Nickalos persona.

Standing beside his partner, Joe Mackey, was Lana Miller, impeccably attired. Amidst the clamor of the crowd, she shouted to Quinlan, "I couldn't resist!" Her gaze swept across the pub, settling on the multitude of ties dangling from the ceiling pipes of the lively establishment.

Quinlan explained to her, "It was customary for the staff to literally cut your tie off if you were stupid enough to come in here with it still on. Did Mack tell you about my going away?"

She began, "He did, and I wanted to say...," however, her sentence was cut short as a crowd converged around Quinlan. Just then, Rick Boland raised his glass in a toast, "To the most fearless man I've ever known. Just remember to keep your distance from the President!" Quinlan couldn't help but think it wasn't Boland's finest toast, but it did carry a grain of truth.

"Sorry Lana, you were saying...?"

"John, just be careful." Lana moved in closer and held Quinlan's hand, "You're a thoughtful guy, John. You're also quite good at what you do." Her green eyes now widened, "I hear DC can be a difficult place. I read once it was described as a soul sucking bubble." She laughed and so did Quinlan. At that moment, to Quinlan, Lana was the only person present in the otherwise noisy room.

She continued, "I think your addition to DC might make the place a little bit better. Stay in touch and who knows maybe I will come your way."

Quinlan gave Lana an embrace perhaps too long for a professional relationship. As his arms dropped, he couldn't help but hold her hand.

He walked her to the door of the pub. He watched as she hopped into her BMW 740i which was illegally parked. It had an 'Official Business—U.S. Attorney's Office' placard on the dashboard.

At that moment, the Agent in Charge produced a pewter NYFO Tavern Plate, embellished with the iconic Secret Service five-pointed star and inscribed with the words 'New York Field Office—Department of the Treasury.' It was engraved with Quinlan's tenure at the NYFO, a symbol of honor for those recognized. Tradition dictated that the plate would vanish at some stage during the evening, only to reappear later, bearing a bullet hole for each year served. As Quinlan left Jeremy's Ale House later that night, he was delighted to find his tavern plate marked with seven bullet holes—a testament to his dedicated service and the fond admiration of his peers at the NYFO.

CHAPTER 20

Pyongyang, North Korea

"The best way to destroy an enemy is to make him a friend."
—Abraham Lincoln

A Friday's shadow stretched long over the jagged mountains and barren landscape on the Korean Peninsula. The eyes of North Korea turned in masse towards Pyongyang. Those were drawn to the figure of Pak Hyun Woo, their newly proclaimed 'Supreme Leader.' The air was thick with confused mourning and celebration. The citizens marking the dawn of a new era even as they absorbed the loss of Pak Sang Ho. The father, the elder, breathed his last breath. At the age of 81, his heart yielded to the strain of time and rule.

Amidst this pivotal moment, Pak Hyun Woo stood as a stark contrast to the legacy left behind by his father. At just twenty-seven, the young leader was an emblem of change. He had aspirations that diverged from his family. With the new mantle of leadership, he harbored a vision. North Korea should reform its state of impoverishment and dilapidation, steering the nation towards a reimagined future.

Young Pak was intimidated by his father and equally intimidated by his older sister, Pak Hyun Mi. It was she who was appointed by their father, as the republic's Deputy Department Director of State Affairs. She would have been the desired choice if it were not for being born a woman. She thought there was no room for her brother, the heir apparent. She always thought of her brother as detached and apathetic towards the "Juche" or socialist ruling ideology which meant self-reliance until the end.

Until his demise, Pak Sang Ho espoused political, economic, and military autonomy as the cornerstone ideals of North Korea. The Korean Armistice, signed on July 27, 1953, marked the conclusion of U.S. involvement in the Korean War. A conflict where North Korea had paid a heavy toll in pursuit of self-reliance and sovereignty. North Korea remained steadfast in its identity as a socialist state, advocating for the equitable distribution of wealth among its populace. Furthermore, its supreme leader asserted control over industries, agriculture, and the military. It followed a strict, military first policy that permeated every aspect of society, from politics to economics to culture.

The Pak surname is linked to the *bon-gwan*, a term denoting the ancestral home, which traces back to the ancient kingdom of Buyeo, now part of present-day North Korea. Historical records and legends suggest that the Pak name originated from the royal house of the Gaya confederacy, where it was adopted by the ruling elite. Now, the mantle of this illustrious name, imbued with nobility and centuries of history, was bestowed upon Pak Hyun Woo, the newly anointed Supreme Leader, as his birthright.

Pak Hyun Mi, the sister, was adamant about maintaining the legacy of the enduring Pak dynasty, regardless of its newest, more progressive successor. Her determination lay in ensuring a seamless transition, safeguarding the Juche ruling class identity. She would do this through the existing state propaganda, political education, and the media. She had already gained control of the media through serving in her father's cabinet. She will continue to uphold the legitimacy and authority of the ruling regime.

My quiet resolve, she thought, *will exact her personal agenda of removing the United States from the map through a thousand cuts.*

Even she recognized that confronting a formidable force like the United States would be an asymmetrical and imprudent undertaking.

However, unbeknownst to her naïve brother, her plan was about to be put in motion.

* * *

The recently anointed Supreme Leader, Pak Hyun Woo, had studied at Tipperary College in Dublin, Ireland. His chosen field was Political Science, a subject that ignited his intellectual curiosity. It was during his time as a student that he crossed paths with Professor James O'Donovan. The young future leader was captivated by O'Donovan's lectures, specifically the professor's perspectives on libertarianism. Pak Hyun Woo found resonance with his teachings and gradually became enthralled by his mentor's ideas. The ideology of libertarianism intrigued him. Open markets, increased individual liberties, and less government. An extremely hard sell to his father and dictator of North Korea, much less his tyrant sister. In truth, it was a closely guarded secret that he was even enrolled at Tipperary College. The Pak dynasty went to great lengths to keep this information under wraps. Pak Soo Jin, the quiet yet resolute mother of Pak Hyun Woo, played a pivotal role in this clandestine arrangement. While fiercely loyal to her husband and the regime, she was unwavering in her insistence that her son be allowed to live and study far from the oppressive environment of North Korea. Under pressure from his father's insistence, he reluctantly left Tipperary College before completing his bachelor's degree. The reasons primarily owed to the mounting economic and political turmoil brewing in North Korea. Some speculated that the elder Pak Sang Ho harbored fears of his son being swayed by Western political ideologies. However, during his time studying at Tipperary, Pak Hyun Woo found himself increasingly intrigued, even admiring the concept of democracy. Yet, he remained cognizant of its limitations. He reasoned that in its current form, democracy primarily served the interests of the affluent capitalist class. This would render its concepts as incompatible with the existing political landscape of North Korea.

Pak Hyun Woo closely followed American politics, developing a fondness for the newly inaugurated American President, David Bryce. Upon assuming his role as the Supreme Leader of the Republic of North Korea, it would be his desire to extend an olive branch to America. He intended to use his time in office to demonstrate good faith to the Western world, particularly the United States. His overarching objective was to suggest a summit to be convened in the village of Panmunjom. The village was strategically situated in the heart of the current demilitarized zone (DMZ) that divides North and South Korea. This location held profound significance as the site where the Armistice was signed.

By selecting Panmunjom for the summit, Pak Hyun Woo aimed to offer President Bryce a unique opportunity. The village's proximity to the DMZ would afford the President an occasion to address his stationed troops. This would provide a plausible pretext for a meeting with the new North Korean Supreme Leader. The young Supreme Leader saw it as a mutually beneficial arrangement, one that would facilitate a dialogue between North Korea and the United States. However, he understood that building trust with President Bryce was a necessary first step and it would take time before moving forward with such a meeting.

President David Bryce was a pragmatist at heart. His victory in the recent election was attributed to his independent stance. Unlike adhering strictly to conservative or liberal ideologies, Bryce championed libertarian principles. This resonated with voters across the political spectrum. His third-party candidacy emphasized the vision of a streamlined government. It structured a capitalist framework that prioritized the empowerment of individual citizens. Bryce's message struck a chord with the American populace. It propelled him to a landslide victory over the Democratic incumbent. The outcome of this election did not escape the notice of the new North Korean leader. Recognizing the significance of the moment, he believed that now, more than ever, was the opportune time to establish a connection with the United States.

His sister, Pak Hyun Mi, vehemently disagreed with such sentiments, leaving her bitter and resentful. In her eyes, she saw her brother as nothing more than a puppet manipulated by the ideals of an open American democracy. To her, he was devoid of true leadership qualities and merely serving as an ignorant tool. She was aware that her treasonous remarks could inflict severe consequences, including banishment or execution. However, Pak Hyun Mi harbored no fear except for her brother's perceived weakness. She believed it would spell the downfall of socialism in North Korea.

She discovered the derogatory moniker bestowed upon her within her father's administration, *Akma Deja*, or the Demon Mistress. Rather than shy away from it, she defiantly embraced the title. She wore it like a badge of honor. In an act of boldness, she insisted on being addressed by this very epithet. She would think it a symbol of her strength and defiance.

One might say with this new moniker, Pak Hyun Mi was reborn as Akma Deja. She was tall about 5'8", her presence commanding attention with an air of quiet confidence. Her long, jet-black hair cascaded down her back, kept in place by a simple, elegant clip. Her almond-shaped eyes, a striking shade of dark brown, were both sharp and observant, always seeming to assess her surroundings with a keen intelligence. A subtle scar on her right eyebrow, a remnant of a childhood misadventure was the only visible flaw to her otherwise smooth complexion. She always wore a conservative, well-tailored charcoal gray designer suit. A favored color by the republic. The fitted blazer and matching pants highlighted her graceful athletic figure. She moved with the grace of someone who has trained in martial arts for years, a skill she often attributed to her disciplined upbringing. When she spoke, her voice was soft yet firm, each word measured and deliberate, reflecting her thoughtful nature.

With a determined smile, she reached for her office phone and uttered two words into the receiver, "activate her." Observing the unfolding events with a sense of satisfaction, Pak Hyun Mi, now Akma Deja's, smile widened.

CHAPTER 21

The Southern Border

The Southern border connecting Mexico to the United States was wide open. It had become a political hot potato leading to a failed reelection bid for the incumbent President. The administration lost sight of the fact that Americans like hand-outs and government aid, but they like safety and security much more. Crime was up in the country and Presidential candidate Bryce attributed everything and anything to the failed Southern border. He won the election handily on high crime and the failed and unsafe Southern border. The newly elected President Bryce ran on closing the border, but he knew it could not happen overnight. The border would still have to process migrants until a permanent plan was put in place by the new administration. This was not lost on the evil North Korean sister, Akma Deja.

A scared and exhausted twenty-six-year-old North Korean woman and her uncle appeared at the Southern Border in Eagles Pass, TX. They had traversed the Rio Grande River. Their appearance startled the U.S. Immigration and Customs Enforcement (ICE) Officers. They both had bruises and open wounds on their necks and faces. Both were attended to by Immigration and Customs medics. They were eventually brought to the nearby trauma unit. They were treated for dehydration and wounds attributed to being in the desert for weeks, if not months. They were released from the trauma unit and brought back to the ICE registration building. The woman started to complete the form given to her by the ICE agents and she struggled to understand what the ICE agent was saying to her. There were no officers available at Eagles Pass that day that spoke Korean. She wrote the name Soo Min Un in broken letters on the form and just waited in despair. She could not continue filling out the form as she started to shake. Her uncle was able to provide more information on the form, cautiously offering his alias, the name of the person that would be sponsoring them, and the address where they could be contacted while in the United States. The uncle seemed more organized and prepared to expedite the process.

On the U.S. Immigration form, their identity was stamped as "No identification documents provided." Their citizenship was listed as "South Korean," and their status as "refugee." After enduring four hours of waiting in a detention room, an ICE agent finally escorted them to an adjacent office. There they were interviewed by a U.S. Immigration officer who did not speak Korean. Despite the language barrier, their refugee status was approved and officially documented. Both were provided packets containing instructions on their immigration hearing. The hearing was to be held four months from the date at the Superior Court of Houston, TX.

In the lot adjacent to the DHS processing facility, there were buses in a queue that were designated as transportation to various cities throughout the United States. The transportation of the migrants crossing the border was the brainchild of the conservative Texas Governor Ronald Rathbone. The state was witnessing 5,000 migrants entering the country through the Southern Border each day. Fearing no government aid to the burgeoning border crisis, Rathbone organized buses that would transport the processed migrants to various 'sanctuary cities.' Today, all buses would be going to New York City.

Sanchez operated as a Mexican Coyote, thriving in the lucrative trade of smuggling migrants for the Mexican cartels. His current mission was to guide Soon Min Un and her uncle across the perilous Southern Border. Sanchez cautiously orchestrated and timed every detail of this operation, ensuring that New York City would be the migrants' ultimate destination this week.

After a two-and-a-half-day journey, the bus and its sixty undocumented passengers pulled into the Port Authority Bus Station in Manhattan, NY. There was no fanfare nor anyone waiting for them. Soo Min Un went to the ladies room and removed a locker key she had secreted in her anal cavity. She had memorized the number of the Penn Station locker, given to her by the Mexican Coyote.

She and her uncle exited the Port Authority building. They took a taxi to Penn Station. This was the main hub of the interstate railroad system that serviced contiguous cities and states. Arriving at the locker bay, Soo Min found the locker that contained $2,000.00 in cash, a cellphone, identification documents, a note with instructions, and an address. They both boarded the Northeast Regional Amtrak 101 to Union Station in Washington, DC. This seemingly circuitous route to New York City then to Washington, DC was a necessary precaution to muddy their trail.

Four and a half hours after departing from New York City, they finally arrived at Union Station. There, they were met by another man who drove a van labeled Chang's Catering Service. The van transported them to Anacostia, a notorious high-crime area in Washington, DC. Renowned for its anonymity and lawlessness, it was an ideal location for a Triad safe house, discreetly situated at 1516 W. Street SE.

* * *

The Triads, a Chinese organized crime syndicate with far-reaching international ties, including connections in North Korea, were infamous for their involvement in a range of illegal enterprises such as drug trafficking, human trafficking, extortion, and gambling. Akma Deja, recognizing their malevolent reputation, knew she could depend on the Triads, particularly Wei Chen, for support. He had been handpicked by her as the most adept member of the Triad network. For this portion of the plan, Wei Chen was the designated "uncle."

His mission was to ensure the secure transit of Akma Deja's vital asset, Soo Min Un, to Washington, DC.

* * *

After a prolonged nap, Soo Min Un retrieved the envelope containing a Virginia driver's license adorned with her picture and the name Tara Lee. Using the cellphone provided to her, she proceeded to dial the number as instructed upon her arrival at the safe house.

"Hello, America's Talent, how can I help you?"

With only a slight Korean accent, Tara spoke up, "Yes, I'm Tara, and I heard I could take acting classes to improve my accent, or, I should say, get rid of my accent?"

"Ha—yes, that's right. Not all our students are aiming to be the next Scarlett Johansson. Some just want to shed that pesky accent."

Tara chuckled, "Yes, caught me red-handed! I do want to pretend I am from the Midwest and get rid of this Korean accent. I'm hoping this will help with that."

"It sure will, hon. Let's see, your name sounds familiar... yup, I see it here. You have a class with us next week on Monday at 9:00 am. Do you need the address?"

"No, I have it. See you."

Hanging up the phone, Soo Min Un was acutely aware that her English proficiency far surpassed the conversation she just had. She understood the imperative of shedding any remnants of her Korean accent. To maintain her cover, she would fabricate a backstory of being born and raised by her grandparents in Bellevue, Washington. Her acting classes would be instrumental in refining her speech, rendering it malleable and devoid of any discernible accent.

Soo Min Un had been groomed her entire life as a sleeper operative for the Pak dynasty. Now, under the guise of Tara Lee, she would finally have the opportunity to demonstrate her unwavering loyalty to Akma Deja.

CHAPTER 22

Indoctrination

"The greatest trick the devil ever pulled was
convincing the world he didn't exist."
—Charles Baudelaire

Perched on the edge of her bed in the Triad safe house, Tara Lee set aside the heavy dossier detailing her past. Memories flooded back, transporting her to the moment when her life took a sharp turn at the tender age of nine, marked by a chance encounter with Akma Deja, the Supreme Leader's daughter.

Deja had singled her out, sensing potential where others saw only a child. With a mix of assurance and expectation, she had offered Tara an alternative path, a path paved with promises of power and privilege.

"I'll shape you," Deja had declared, her tone devoid of sentimentality. "Teach you the tricks of the trade, the art of control."

The alternative, Deja had made clear, was a bleak existence on the farm, a life bound by the regime's suffocating grip. Tara would be condemned to a future devoid of choice, forced to toil under the watchful eye of the Supreme Leader.

"Follow me," Deja had urged, her words a lifeline in a sea of uncertainty, "and escape awaits."

But freedom came at a cost, a test of loyalty and obedience. Tara recalled the trial Deja had orchestrated, a risky maneuver that would ultimately spell ruin for her family. They, like many others, had dared to defy the regime's laws, hoarding rations of their farmed crops to ward off hunger in a world of scarcity.

Yet, amid the shadows of oppression, these types of defiant acts occurred quietly. Each one a testament to the resilience of the human spirit and survival. Young Soo Min found herself caught in the crossfire, torn between duty and desire, the allure of power versus the tug of conscience.

Amid oppression, even minor acts of defiance like hoarding food were met with severe consequences. Soo Min understood the significance of her choices, realizing they would not only determine her own destiny but also influence the fate of those who dared to envision a better world.

Young Soo Min was summoned before Akma Deja and questioned about the stolen crops. To her it would be a test of loyalty and allegiance. It would eventually turn the young farm girl, Soo Min, into Tara Lee.

"Soo Min, after everything I have offered you," Deja said with a gentle tone, "I need you to tell me if your parents have done anything wrong of late."

Soo Min, her demeanor softened and eyes brimming with tears, asked, "What happens to them if they've wronged you?"

Deja responded with a chilling clarity, explaining they would face consequences proportional to their actions.

Soo Min's next question quivered with uncertainty, "And what of me? Will I face punishment?"

Deja's reply was stark and direct, "Only deceit would draw punishment upon you."

Deja knew that the young Soon Min would be loyal. So much so, in the next room, she already had her parents in custody. They were kneeling with their legs shackled and their hands bound behind their back. They were positioned facing each other, staring longingly into each other's eyes, they knew no other life apart from one another. Their mouths were gagged so neither could speak nor share comforting words. They were in shock having been pulled from their field by Deja's security squad. They were blindfolded during the thirty-minute car ride and thrown into a cold jail cell. They endured this state for the past four hours. Deja guided young Soon Min into the dimly lit room, her hand firmly clasped in hers. The air hung heavy with the stench of decay, a reminder of the oppressive atmosphere that permeated the space.

The lights came on and she saw her parents through a glass window bound and gagged in the next room. The blindfolds had been removed. The nine-year-old looked up at Deja in confusion and terror.

"Please don't hurt them, please don't hurt them," the terrified young girl would repeat.

Akma Deja, now with a commanding voice said, "Tell me their offense."

The young girl went silent. She looked down and stiffened as though she was no longer in her own body. She paused letting the tears run off her face. She could not control herself and her body heaved, then she said in a whimper, "They put crops in the root cellar of our hut. They refused to share them with the state."

Deja, looking pleased, said, "That is very good, my darling." She moved close to Soon Min and shoved her face closer to the glass holding her head steady. Forcing her to watch, an assassin appeared. He raised the Hwando sword and in a single stroke decapitated her mother's head. The blood sprayed like a whip across her father's face as he looked on in disbelief. He fell over in emotional pain and shock, crying and shaking uncontrollably as a result of what he just saw. He was lifted upright, and the execution was repeated.

And so began the indoctrination of young Soo Min Un. She was instructed to hold the ruling Pak family in the highest regard, while perceiving the outside world, especially the United States and South Korea, as hostile adversaries. Training sessions in the martial art of Krav

Maga honed her ability to neutralize physical threats, while English language lessons expanded her linguistic repertoire. Countless hours were dedicated to studying the intricacies of the American political system, its economy, and cultural nuances.

Now numb to the whirlwind of emotions from those memories, Tara Lee drifted into slumber, despite the pressures from her new reality settling upon her shoulders.

CHAPTER 23

Tara Lee

There would be a week of relaxation and a good nutritious diet before the acting class started. This would allow her wounds from the crossing to heal. She would shower and drift back to when she first met Sanchez, her Mexican Coyote. The beating she and her Triad bodyguard endured was for the cause. She even thought, *This fucking Mexican is enjoying this.* It would leave them looking like they had just spent a month in the Mexican desert seeking refuge at the southern border. In fact, they were led in an airconditioned van to the small Mexican city of Piedras Negra. One mile from the southern border in Eagle Pass, TX. There, the cartel had a safehouse. It was there, they received their beating. Yet, she understood the necessity of thoroughness. No detail could be overlooked, not even the faintest hint of her Korean accent. In her new role, every trace of her former identity had to vanish.

* * *

After the fall of the Soviet Union in 1991, KGB computer hacker, Sergei Bitrov's services were no longer required. He became a hired gun. His option was quickly picked up by the North Korean government, specifically the now deceased leader Pak Sang Ho. Akma Deja wasted no time in using Bitrov's talents to hack the Virginia DMV, the National Crime Information Center (NCIC), the Department of Homeland Security Immigration/Customs Enforcement, and the Social Security Administration. All to turn the spy Soon Min Un into Tara Lee. She would have no criminal background or any background at all for that matter. Oddly enough, Bitrov found it easy to hack these systems as they were all somewhat interconnected. After the attacks of 9/11, all U.S. law enforcement agencies became somewhat interoperable.

It was a kumbaya thing, Bitrov thought. He also relished the fact that there was very little compartmented encryption or dual authentication. There was an algorithm-intrusion detection system that was part of the NCIC however a simple code overrode the 'protective' measure.

* * *

Under the guidance of her Triad handler, Wei Chan, Tara Lee's initiation into her new life began with lessons on driving in the United States. Navigating the bustling streets of Washington, DC, and its outskirts became her classroom, with Wei Chan as her instructor.

Tara Lee was no stranger to the world of espionage, having been groomed by the enigmatic Akma Deja from a young age. Akma Deja had molded her into a sleeper agent, biding her time until the opportune moment to activate her.

According to Akma Deja's well-planned scheme, Tara Lee's role would be that of a submissive lover to a particular man possessing a unique skill set. But Tara's training extended far beyond mere interrogation techniques. She had honed her abilities in the subtleties of mastering the art of crafting resumes, navigating job interviews, and engaging in the casual banter that endeared people to one another in the American social landscape.

Tara was toweling off from her long, soothing shower when her phone rang. She quickly grabbed it and answered, "Hello, this is Tara."

"Tara?" said the voice on the other end. "This is Joy from DCjobs.com. If you have a moment, I believe we have a job posting that matches the questionnaire you completed online."

"Yes, please go ahead. I am all ears," Tara replied.

Joy continued, "You mentioned you were specifically interested in seeking employment with the Bureau of Engraving and Printing, correct?"

"Yes, that would be my preference," Tara responded.

She learned the job was for a GS-4 Clerk Typist position at the U.S. Bureau of Engraving and Printing. She grew excited and knew she could not fail this interview. The headhunting representative at DCjobs.com provided her with the appointment time, the name of the person conducting the interview, and the exact location.

Tara Lee interviewed with Human Resources, and it went well. They loved hearing that she was fluent in Korean. She was told the job was a General Scale 4 or GS-4 which paid $32,000 a year with health insurance, a Thrift Savings Plan, and life insurance, if she elected for that option. She was given a packet of additional paperwork to complete. Since the job was classified sensitive, it would require that she complete the forms and return them for further processing. It was explained that a routine criminal history check was mandatory for the position.

A week had passed when Tara received the call for her second interview. Armed with her thoroughly prepared packet, she arrived on time, ready to impress. The meeting with Beth Sales unfolded seamlessly. Beth wholeheartedly endorsed Tara's performance, anticipating becoming her direct supervisor should she secure the position.

The seriousness of the position became apparent when Tara was informed that it was a bonded job classification. This would necessitate the standard procedure of fingerprinting as part of the vetting process.

The Bureau of Engraving and Printing security office administered the fingerprinting. The technology was that of the latest biometric identification system known as AFIS or Automated Fingerprint Identification System. The palms of Tara Lee's hands were placed on the black glass. A faint red laser ran across her hand capturing the friction ridges of the tips of each finger as well as her palm. This information was captured and uploaded. The data would be compared against the database of known prints to identify potential matches. If there was a known match in the system, the security office would receive a printed account of the information. The estimated turnaround time for the fingerprinting process stretched to an hour. Tara received the option to either wait in the cafeteria or be contacted later in the day. Politely declining the offer of lunch, she mentioned an errand she needed to tend to. With a nod of understanding, security escorted her to the public foyer, wishing her luck with the impending process.

Now, all that was left was to await the call. Tara anticipated that the background check would yield no record. This would be as a result she owed to Akma Deja's Russian.

Tara would spend time driving with her handler, Wei Chan, as a passenger. They drove on I-495, or the Capital Beltway as it was called by many. They drove on I-95, I-295, and even through the dreaded 'mixing bowl'. This was the nickname commonly used for the interchange where all three of those interstate highways merged. Curious to Tara, Chan made her drive up and down the George Washington Parkway that ran along the Potomac River. He would have her pull in and out of the rest stops at high rates of speed. He would stress caution, however, to avoid a moving violation. He also wanted to avoid the attention from the joggers on the path that ran adjacent to the parkway.

While at a rest stop, Tara's phone suddenly rang.

"Hello Tara, this is Beth Sales from the Bureau of Engraving and Printing. How have you been?"

Tara feigned excitement, glancing in Chan's direction. "I'm doing great, Beth. It is wonderful to hear from you," she replied smoothly.

"Well, I have some fantastic news for you. I am sending you an email with a conditional job offer right now, but I always like to call, too," Beth explained.

Tara chuckled. "I see. And what is the condition?" she asked, playing along.

"Oh, just whether you accept the job or not," Beth replied with a laugh.

"Well, count me in! Thank you so much!" Tara exclaimed.

"Fantastic!" Beth said. "The email has all the details. The start date is Monday, two weeks from today. Does that work for you?"

"It works perfectly. Thank you again, Beth. See you then," Tara confirmed.

As Tara ended the call, Chan, now gazing out towards the Potomac River from the Virginia side, remarked, "This is good. Very good. We need to kick off the second phase of the operation."

* * *

It was a crisp Monday morning when Tara Lee and Chan set up surveillance in the beautiful Old Town area of Alexandria, Virginia. They sat in an old Ford van which was on loan from the local Triad leader. Chan had carte blanche and any request he made of the local gang was a singular priority. They stationed themselves at the intersection of Cameron Street and North Lee Street, right next to the venerable Carlyle House. From this vantage point, they had a clear view of Phillip O'Donovan's residence. However, their attention was not on him today. Instead, for the next several days, they would be focusing on his wife, Anne. Like clockwork, at 7:00 am, Phillip O'Donovan would come out of his two-story walkup at 392 North Lee Street. He would slip into the driver's seat of the blue Ford Bronco, steering towards the direction of Interstate 395. Soon after, Anne O'Donovan would emerge, clad in her running gear, and commence a light jog. She would head towards the George Washington Parkway running path. A favored running path cherished by Virginia and Washington, DC enthusiasts, it hugged the curves of the Potomac River. Without deviation, Anne O'Donovan adhered to this routine five days a week. Their son, Patrick, would remain inside the residence and his schedule was erratic at best. Lee and Chan witnessed this schedule for a full week and the following Monday, their plan was a go.

Monday morning arrived, but today, it was Chan behind the wheel of the van, while Tara Lee piloted a sleek black Chevy Suburban. This vehicle had been sourced from the Triad gang in New York City. Its New York license plates had been deliberately weathered down through an arduous sandblasting process. The vehicle had slightly tinted windows. The vehicle identification numbers (VIN) were discreetly removed from both the engine block and the dashboard beneath the windshield. The Suburban was designed to be untraceable if hastily abandoned. Chan had suggested the Black Suburban for its abundance in the DC area. This brand of vehicle would seamlessly blend in with the numerous security details speeding around the district.

Chan was set up in the van covering the O'Donovan residence. Lee was parked in the Belle Haven Comfort Station lot waiting for Anne to start her run on the trail. Both Chan and Lee would be communicating using prepaid mobile phones often referred to as 'burners' so they could not be traced. Anne O'Donovan started her daily run heading down the same route towards the Potomac Running path and as she neared the comfort station, Lee called Chan and kept an open line. Anne moved closer to the first trail head parking lot. Lee slowly drove her Suburban along the same route shadowing her pace. As Anne reached the designated second trailhead, Tara Lee accelerated the Suburban into the parking lot, hurtling the SUV directly toward her. To bystanders, it appeared as though the vehicle had veered out of control. In a split second, Tara noticed a jogger with a baby in an elite jogging stroller. Instinctively reacting, she jerked the steering wheel to avoid hitting the stroller, ultimately colliding with a tree. The force of the impact caused the vehicle to careen into a group of six people, leaving them motionless on the ground. Lee sped from the lot and heard Chan screaming, "Get out of there, get out of there."

As Lee sped away traveling north on the parkway, then onto 395 towards Anacostia, her training kicked in, prompting her to slow the vehicle down. A whirlwind of thoughts swept through her mind, yet one persisted at the forefront. *Why hadn't the airbags deployed upon impact with the tree? That would have surely marked the end of the operation,* she pondered.

She made it back to the safe house in Anacostia where Chan had already arrived. Chan demanded an explanation for her erratic behavior. Nothing she offered would satisfy. She let him vent.

In a deliberate, lower-than-usual tone, he addressed her as if reprimanding a child in public, "Be thankful the airbags were removed for such a situation as this. Your emotions must not lead you astray from the mission, not even for a moment. Do you understand?"

Tara remained motionless, absorbing the words and the lesson imparted by Chan. Together, they awaited the local news coverage of the incident.

Later that morning, Phillip O'Donovan was called into his supervisor's office at the Bureau of Engraving and Printing and was informed his wife was hit by a vehicle, the accident was fatal, and the police have deemed it a hit and run. He was told his wife died instantly.

Lee and Chan listened to a similar narrative as they watched Fox 5 DC. Despite their frayed nerves, they knew that part of the mission had been accomplished. The wreckage of the Suburban had already been processed by a vehicle salvage yard and was now in route for recycling in West Chester, PA.

Tara Lee devoted the week to calming her nerves and thoroughly preparing for her inaugural day at the Bureau of Engraving and Printing. *Anne O'Donovan was no longer a factor, and Phillip O'Donovan's emotional scars would mend,* she considered. Her anticipation of meeting Phillip O'Donovan grew, fueling a stronger sense of purpose in executing Akma Deja's plan. However, beneath her enthusiastic anticipation, she recognized the significance of the upcoming phase in Akma Deja's complex scheme. It was a long-haul commitment, set to span two years, demanding patience and careful execution.

CHAPTER 24

Phillip O'Donovan

It was late March. Another cold, gray morning in the nation's capital. Phillip O'Donovan, Phil to his friends, left his home in Old Town Alexandria. He considered sitting in traffic on Interstate 395 as a necessary evil. It was also his reflection time as he used to kid about the necessary part of DC known as traffic. Today would be the two-year anniversary since his wife was struck by a hit-and-run driver who veered off the George Washington Memorial Parkway. According to police reports, the vehicle collided with a tree at a high rate of speed before hitting Annie, who was halfway through her daily run along the Parkway running path. At the tragic scene, Anne Patricia O'Donovan was pronounced dead, succumbing to internal blunt force trauma. Witnesses watched helplessly as the black Chevy Suburban bolted away, leaving chaos in its wake. Despite two years of relentless investigation by the Virginia State Police, the hit-and-run driver remained elusive, a ghost.

Witnesses' testimonies offered little solace; their voices overshadowed by the lack of unanswered questions. "It was over in an instant," they would recall to investigators, their words a painful echo of the event's swiftness. "The driver showed no remorse, no intention of stopping," they would recount, grappling with the callousness of the act. "They simply vanished."

Yet amidst the fog of uncertainty, crucial details remained elusive. No description of the driver emerged, nor could anyone confirm the presence of passengers, obscured behind tinted windows. However, what puzzled investigators most was the absence of any visible license plate, both front and rear, confounding their efforts.

The Virginia State Police investigator was baffled by the absence of skid marks on the parkway. It appeared as if the driver had surrendered control, the vehicle hurtling forward without restraint. The absence of airbags was glaring; they surely would have prevented the vehicle from continuing its course. Instead, the collision with the tree redirected the three-ton mass onto a busy running path, where Annie's life was tragically cut short in an instant. But the vehicle's rampage did not cease there. It struck three more runners with brutal force, leaving behind a trail of devastation. O'Donovan knew the case was growing cold as he heard less and less from the VA State Police. The memories, although not fading, were somewhat tolerable now. He would move on for his son, he would tell himself.

His mind drifted to his son, Patrick, who was on the cusp of completing his junior year at American University. A summer spent together beckoned, a precious interlude before Patrick embarked on the final leg of his undergraduate journey in International Studies. Beyond that lay the hopeful pursuit of Georgetown Law, a path that brimmed with promise and ambition. Annie's absence loomed heavy, but in the quiet recesses of his mind, O'Donovan found solace in the thought that she would be immensely proud of their son. *He's definitely inherited his mother's intellect,* he would think to himself, a bittersweet acknowledgment of the legacy they shared.

Traffic was moving a bit now as he approached the Rochambeau Bridge that connected the 395 inbound traffic to 15th Street. This segment of the journey always brought him joy. The sight of the Jefferson Memorial, gracefully overlooking the Tidal Basin, never failed to uplift his spirits. With Spring soon arriving, the cherry blossoms started to adorn the landscape in a vibrant display of nature's beauty. Memories of Annie flooded his mind once more, her fondness for the cherry blossoms during their late March bloom resonating deeply within him. O'Donovan would think to himself, *One last look at God's creative gift*, before pulling into the 15th Street entrance to the underground parking deck. The parking deck served the United States Bureau of Engraving and Printing (BEP).

Phillip O'Donovan held the esteemed title of one of the ten Master Engravers at the BEP. His journey to this prestigious position was marked by dedication and perseverance. Hailing from Dublin, Ireland, Phillip pursued his passion for graphic and industrial design, earning his bachelor's degree from Tipperary College. During his time at Tipperary College, Phillip found solace in the company of his uncle, James O'Donovan, affectionately known as Uncle Jimmy. A prominent figure at the college, Uncle Jimmy was a tenured professor in Political Science and International Studies. He shared a deep familial bond with Phillip, being the younger brother of Phillip's late father, Sean O'Donovan. The O'Donovan family history bore witness to the tumultuous era of the 1970s in Northern Ireland. Both brothers, Sean and Jimmy O'Donovan, were active members of the Irish Republican Army, (IRA). Tragedy struck when Sean lost his life during a protest in Derry, a pivotal moment that left a profound impact on Phillip and his family. In the aftermath of the violence, the town of Derry underwent a renaming, becoming known as Londonderry, a move that some perceived as an attempt to distance themselves from the turbulent past.

The uprising ignited riots across Belfast and the surrounding towns of Northern Ireland. It was a dark chapter in history famously labeled Bloody Sunday by the local media. Uncle Jimmy, however, remained reticent about the harrowing events of that fateful day. While he distanced himself from the IRA, he found assurance and purpose in the more moderate political sphere, aligning himself with Sinn Féin.

Sinn Féin, often viewed as an extension of the IRA by many, was a political party Uncle Jimmy believed in, despite the shadows of its past. He never shied away from acknowledging the party's roots. In fact, he often encouraged his nephew, Phillip, to consider relocating to Northern Ireland. He could immerse himself in local politics, and perhaps even contemplate a future within Sinn Féin's ranks.

Phillip harbored different aspirations. Following his graduation from Tipperary College, he returned to the United States to pursue further studies, enrolling at Georgetown University in Washington, DC. There, he embarked on a path toward a Master of Fine Arts degree, focusing his studies on engraving, etching, and the intricacies of intaglio processes. He really enjoyed lithography and screen printing; however, intaglio etching would be his passion. It was that interest that got the attention of the BEP. He ranked among the nation's top five graduates. A distinction acknowledged by the BEP as they designated him and his peers as winners of an apprenticeship in the esteemed Master Engraving Program. This program was dedicated to training engravers in the precise art of etching and crafting the plates essential for producing United States currency.

* * *

It was at Georgetown where he would meet Anne Archer. She was also a fine arts major at the university. She focused more on developing a relationship with Phillip than focusing on the study of art appreciation in the post-modern world. What began as a casual connection quickly blossomed into a deep and abiding love. As Phillip neared the completion of his degree at Georgetown, they exchanged vows, embarking on the journey of marriage. Anne, affectionately referred to as Annie by Phillip, soon found herself embracing the joy of pregnancy. With motherhood on the horizon, she gracefully transitioned away from her graduate studies, finding fulfillment and contentment in supporting her husband's unwavering pursuit of becoming a Master Engraver for the BEP.

He would try to explain to her that intaglio was a printmaking technique where the image was created by incising or engraving lines and textures into metal. He would say that intaglio was the Italian word for 'engraved'. Annie loved how he looked at engraving as a form of art and he was overly passionate about it. She would try to follow his explanation of the process but got lost every time. She would laugh and say, "You know, when I want to brighten up a room, I don't need to understand how electricity works. I just flick the switch, and presto, there's light." They always laughed while poking fun at each other.

O'Donovan would study under a Master Engraver working with steel alloy plates. He would polish them to a smooth surface then coat the plate with a thin layer of acid-resistant material called the ground. Using various instruments such as etching needles and engraving tools, he would draw and incise the image of a $100 federal reserve note directly into the ground, exposing the metal surface beneath. This would lead to the etching phase which required all the patience O'Donovan could muster. The alloy plates were immersed in an acid bath, which bites into the exposed metal. This would create recessed areas where the lines and textures had been etched. The longer the plate remained in the acid bath, the deeper and wider the lines would become. Once the desired lines and textures had been etched onto the plate, it was wiped clean and inked. Specialized green ink exclusive and proprietary to the BEP was then forced into the recessed areas of the plate. The surface of the plate resembling the $1, $5, $10, $20, $50, or $100 was then wiped clean, leaving ink only in the etched lines and textures. The inked plate was then placed on a printing press along with dampened proprietary paper. The paper was considered exclusive because it was delivered under armed escort directly from the Crane Paper Company in Dalton, MA. The paper had security features already embedded when the paper was crafted. Under pressure, the paper was forced into contact with the inked plate. This transferred the ink from the recessed areas onto the paper, creating the perfect genuine $100 federal reserve note or whatever denomination was ordered by the Federal Reserve.

His excitement would bubble over as he explained to Annie, "Intaglio printmaking transcends mere craftsmanship; it's an art form in its own right. When you master the precision of the craft, the lines and textures come alive, transforming the images into dynamic, three-dimensional pieces of art." That, at least, was Phillip O'Donovan's perspective.

It was the perfect method for manufacturing the United States currency and a process almost impossible to replicate by counterfeiters. O'Donovan cherished his work at the BEP. To him, the process of creating currency was nothing short of an art form, where every detail held significance and every stroke contributed to the masterpiece.

Upon completing the engraving apprenticeship program at the BEP, O'Donovan ascended to the rank of Journeyman engraver. However, before he could transition to the currency section, he needed to hone his skills further. This involved engraving highly detailed and intricate designs, including portraits, symbols, and patterns, for various government agencies. It is a lesser-known fact that agencies like the FBI, Secret Service, CIA, IRS, and Department of Homeland Security, among others, use intaglio printing for their employees' identification cards and other official documents. This printing method is employed as a security measure to prevent counterfeiting.

After five years of dedicated effort, O'Donovan achieved the prestigious title of Master engraver, earning him a coveted place in the currency section. His accomplishment filled both Annie and their five-year-old toddler, Patrick, with immense pride. For many years to follow, they reveled in their life together in the charming Old Town area of Alexandria, VA. Their world was as close to perfect as could be until two years ago when a black Chevy Suburban changed his and Patrick's life forever.

His friends, with well-meaning intentions, encouraged him to move on as best he could. "You're still young," they would remind him, offering words of consolation amidst the pain. It was through this support network that he was introduced to a striking woman who also worked at the BEP. Despite being several years his junior, she exuded a sense of maturity and worldly wisdom that captivated him. They even lived close to each other in Old Town Alexandria. This made carpooling a natural choice, which in turn facilitated the growth of their friendship. As days turned into weeks and weeks into months, their bond deepened into something far more meaningful.

But what truly mattered to Phillip was Patrick's acceptance of her. The young boy found in her a confidante, eagerly absorbing her stories of travel to Seoul and her upbringing in Washington State. As their bond grew stronger, Phillip was falling in love with Tara Lee.

CHAPTER 25

The Presidential Protection Division

"Failure is not an option."
—Gene Krantz—Apollo 13

Quinlan touched down in Washington DC in February, ready to assume his new position on the Presidential Protection Division. Within the Secret Service, it was known simply as PPD. His role would place him among the select few entrusted with the monumental task of protecting the President of the United States. President David Bryce was completing his second year in office. He secured victory two years prior on a platform as a self-identified libertarian, running under the independent party ticket. His resounding victory had seen him triumph over the Democratic incumbent with a significant margin. The wide-open Southern border, inflation, and the high crime rate would secure Bryce the Office of the President. Quinlan would serve his first year as a shift agent on Bryce's detail. His focus was providing arms reach protection on all the President's movements. This was a 24-hour, 7-day a week assignment, so Quinlan would have to frequently rotate shifts. He also came to appreciate the rigors and exacting attention to detail required in formulating a comprehensive security plan well in advance of any presidential visit. He quickly realized that this task became even more challenging when the trips involved foreign countries. Some of these nations were friendly, while others were outright adversarial, adding layers of complexity to the security preparations.

During the PPD new agent orientation, he remembered senior agent Jake Cutler saying, "PPD is like living in dog years. Every year on PPD is like seven years in any other assignment the Secret Service has to offer."

Senior Agent Cutler would be a mentor and guide to Quinlan. Cutler took a liking to him right away. Maybe this was because like Quinlan, Cutler, too, was experienced in complex investigations. Quinlan's reputation was that of a hard charging investigator from the New York Field Office. Cutler's philosophy was simple. If you could investigate complex criminal cases and successfully navigate the world of intelligence assessment, the likelihood existed that you would be an excellent protection agent.

Quinlan realized early on that the few coveted spots on PPD were filled with aggressive type A personalities. It seemed they had to prove something to someone. Out of 3,600 agents working for the U.S. Secret Service, only a fraction of that amount would serve on PPD. Quinlan earned recognition from his supervisor as an out-of-the-box thinker. He was never one to settle for mere checklists. His advance security plans were always timely and comprehensive, reflecting his dedication to thoroughness. His paperwork was impeccable, a testament to his attention to detail.

Despite the demands of constant travel and the temptations of unhealthy eating habits on the road, he remained committed to his fitness regimen. He soon realized that maintaining his physical well-being was an essential aspect of his new role.

Jake Cutler observed Quinlan during his mandatory physical training while on PPD. He pulled his fitness reports from his days at the academy. It was then that he realized, Quinlan might be able to keep up with President Bryce during his daily runs. To be sure, he had him report to the Secret Service training facility in Beltsville, MD.

While there, Quinlan suited up in his running gear that included a customized running belt. The running belt held his Sig Sauer P229 .357, issued radio with surveillance harness, extendible baton, hand cuffs, and light armor vest. All in, about twenty pounds of equipment. During the tryout, Quinlan faced the demanding task of running a 6:50 mile for three consecutive miles while also responding to simulated attacks along the way. Though he passed, it was a close call. In a moment of unexpected intensity, an overly enthusiastic role-player charged at the role-playing President during the final stretch of mile three. With swift reflexes, Quinlan managed to respond and aggressively address the situation before returning to the run for the final sprint. Despite the unexpected challenge, his performance earned him a spot among Turnkey's runners.

Turnkey was the code name given to President David Bryce by the Military Office. The Military Office carefully assigns those names to the protectees of the Secret Service. Quinlan reminisced about one particular run he shared with President Bryce at Camp David, the Presidential retreat. Bryce had a penchant for running in extreme weather conditions, whether it was enduring scorching 105-degree heat at his Texas Ranch or braving the icy cold snowstorms that swept through Camp David during the winter months. Despite the challenging conditions, Quinlan was among the select few Secret Service agents who could keep pace with Bryce as they confidently maintained a sub-7-minute mile. Quinlan would always trade harmless verbal jabs with President Bryce. Bryce never missed an opportunity to take snipes at the familiar members of his protective detail. On one particular day, President Bryce couldn't help but remark on Quinlan falling behind. "You're getting old," he quipped with his distinct Texas drawl. Quinlan shot back, reminding President Bryce that he was carrying a hefty twenty-pound load of equipment. One time, during a snowstorm at Camp David, President Bryce was rounding his third lap. As they approached Big Bertha, the steep hill that the President loved to conquer, the snow intensified, coming down horizontally and stinging the faces of the runners. Typically, the runs consisted of three laps around the Camp David Marine base, totaling 3 ½ miles. However, as they reached the foot of Big Bertha for the fourth ascent, President Bryce shouted to Quinlan, "We're going to add an extra lap for good measure!" Quinlan, seizing the chance to banter, shouted back, "If we do another lap, I won't need to squeeze in my more serious workout this afternoon!"

With that remark, President Bryce came to an abrupt stop and looked at Quinlan with serious eyes. Both were out of breath. Quinlan thought he might have overstepped trying to match wits. Bryce laughing, slapped his back and said, "Q, you are truly a bad ass!"

Quinlan enjoyed working on the shift, but it was time for him to move to a satellite section of PPD where he would be for another two years. PPD essentially had three tiers. When you first arrived as a new agent on PPD you were assigned to one of four shifts. The shift comprised a highly trained cohort of twenty-four men and women tasked with providing within arm's reach protection. The term bodyguard carried a misleading connotation, evoking a sense of disdain among agents assigned to the shift. This was because their duties extended far beyond merely working within arm's reach of the President. In addition to close protection, they were also responsible for conducting security surveys in advance of presidential visits. This often involved being dispatched up to two weeks ahead of time to formulate comprehensive security plans for the sites to be visited by the President.

After approximately one year on the shift, PPD agents would undergo a selection process to move on to a specific satellite section within PPD for an additional year or two. These second-phase sections included the First Lady Detail, the Counter Assault Team, and the Transportation Section, known as TS. Once their time in these specialized sections was completed, agents would return to their original shift as seasoned and experienced PPD agents.

Agent Quinlan's tenure on the shift ended, and he was selected to attend the Protective Operations Driving Course (PODC). Successful completion of this rigorous two-week program would result in his assignment to the Transportation Section (TS). The PODC was notoriously challenging, with one-third of candidates failing to pass.

During the course, candidates were tasked with maneuvering a ten-ton armored vehicle in various simulated conditions at high rates of speed. The final practical exam included vehicle evade and escape maneuvers conducted at night on a skid pad made of Teflon-infused Macadam. Following the evaluation period, which lasted two days, eight out of the twelve candidates passed, including Quinlan. With his successful completion of the course, he was now qualified to work in TS.

TS was where Quinlan spent his second phase and true to its reputation, it offered the most challenging assignment on PPD. He understood that most attacks on the principal occurred during motorcade movements, where the principal was most vulnerable. In this role, he encountered numerous challenges, particularly when assigned to drive the President in various countries.

The Presidential limousine, often referred to as the Beast, earned its nickname for a reason. Quinlan vividly recalled the day the name was unofficially bestowed upon the extra-large vehicle. He was stationed at the TS operations desk in Headquarters at the time. His supervisor, Bob Rally, had just returned from the secured parking garage where the new armored Cadillac had been delivered. With a wide grin, Bob exclaimed, "That limo is a Beast!" Little did anyone know that the media and anyone else with an eye for Presidential news would adopt and perpetuate that moniker. From that moment on, it would never again simply be referred to as the Presidential Limo without the term the Beast being attached.

* * *

During a trip to Rome and Castel Gandolfo, Italy, Quinlan was tasked with conducting the motorcade security advance. Immediately, he observed that the archways in the ancient cities were too narrow. Memorizing the exact measurements of the Beast, he realized that the planned route would not accommodate it. Furthermore, the entrance route to the Pope's Summer retreat in Castel Gandolfo also proved too narrow for the Beast. Last-minute adjustments to the motorcade arrival became necessary. This challenge would surface in numerous other countries as well. Quinlan emphasized the importance of Secret Service personnel responsible for driving the secured package to carefully rehearse the arrivals and departures at all sites visited by the President.

He worked closely with the elite Secret Service counter-sniper teams and all other units to ensure secure arrival and departure locations, identifying, and addressing any potential vulnerabilities. These mandatory exercises were conducted well ahead of each visit, enabling swift adjustments to be made as needed. For Quinlan, this level of preparation was non-negotiable, a principle he staunchly upheld.

Quinlan meticulously inspected the motorcade routes alongside his local police counterparts. He would identify vulnerabilities ensuring that all street covers were securely welded shut on the day of the visit to prevent the placement of hidden explosive devices. He ordered the removal of all trash receptacles, mailboxes, and any other items that could potentially contain improvised explosives.

The training that had once given him a semblance of control while handling an explosive device several years ago in Breezy Point remained deeply ingrained in his memory. He understood the importance of thorough preparation and vigilance. Securing the motorcade routes was essential, but practicality was also paramount. With as many as thirty vehicles in a Presidential motorcade, each vehicle housed occupants deemed essential to the President's function.

The Secret Service always travels with its own armored vehicles, known as the secured package. These vehicles accompany the President wherever he goes. Under no circumstances does the President travel in vehicles provided by the host country. These vehicles do not meet Secret Service security standards and are likely equipped with bugging devices. It is crucial that the secured package always arrives before the President. This is the case whether the President is in Washington, DC or New Delhi, India. Close coordination with the White House Military office allows the Air Force to fly the secured package ahead of the President. The Air Force utilizes C5, C141, C17, and sometimes C130 aircraft as the main means of transporting vehicles, Secret Service personnel, military personnel, and other vital assets essential to the mission. The logistical planning for these trips is nothing short of astounding. The responsibility lies with the Secret Service Presidential Operations Section, where agents possess the highest organizational skills. They must be analytical thinkers, adept problem solvers, and possess a keen eye for detail. Failure is not an option for them—they are tasked with ensuring the safety and success of every operation. Indeed, they represent the best the Secret Service has to offer.

Quinlan's tenure with the Transportation Section was drawing to a close. Soon, he would return to the shift where his journey on PPD first began. Though the faces and names may have changed, Quinlan was accustomed to such transitions. Now regarded as an experienced PPD agent, he anticipated being entrusted with greater responsibility upon his return.

* * *

At 5:30 am on Monday morning, Quinlan reported to W6, a small office located under the stairway in the West Wing of the White House complex. Real estate at the White House was highly sought after, with long waiting lists for coveted spaces. However, the Secret Service was an exception; they had secured this office long ago. Presidential administrations may change, but the Secret Service always managed to retain their real estate. Their office in W6 was a testament to this.

Every shift would start with a briefing in W6. Agents coming on duty would get briefed by a representative from the shift going off duty. Usually, a designated proxy from that shift would relay the current location of the President and the First Family. Other important information about incidents worthy of note would also be conveyed. Today, it was the midnight shift agent providing a briefing to the day shift coming on duty.

After the briefing concluded, Quinlan's shift leader, Supervisory Special Agent Jake Cutler, addressed the team.

"Everyone, listen up," he began. "This is Special Agent John Quinlan, back from the Transportation Section. We all know TS can be stressful, so let's be patient with him. He might be a bit worn out, possibly dealing with some mild PTSD." The crowded room now lightened up with laughter, "He goes by Q and I am glad he's back to work with us protecting Turnkey. Welcome to the Cutler Shift, Q."

Cutler and Quinlan had previously worked together when Quinlan first arrived at PPD, so it was no surprise that he found his way back to his shift. After the morning briefing concluded, Cutler pulled Quinlan aside. "Q, good to have you back, seriously," he said. "Do you happen to know a Joseph Mackey?"

"Of course, I do, he was my running mate in the NYFO, Mack's a great guy, why?"

"It looks like he's got his orders to PPD! Should I take a run at him for our shift?"

Quinlan felt a surge of excitement upon learning that his friend and partner would be joining PPD. Anticipating the opportunity, he responded, "Absolutely, boss. He'll be a good fit for our team."

Quinlan was thrilled to see his trusted partner coming down to DC. Moreover, he would be a part of the same shift of twenty-four close knit agents. He hoped for Mack's sake his wife and kids would be happy as well. A transfer could be a blessing and a curse. It was a blessing because your option was picked up by the next rung on the ladder. It means you were checking all the boxes towards promotion. It was a curse because no family starts their day hoping this is the day we uproot and leave all that we are familiar with.

Agent Cutler interrupted Quinlan's train of thought and said, "Q, I am responsible for scheduling twenty-four little Indians and making sure I know what they're up to 24/7. What are you up to tomorrow because my Excel spread sheet is showing you have not attended the mandatory Air Force 1 (AF1) briefing out at Andrews?"

Without waiting for a response, Cutler continued, "I have you going on an all-expense paid voyage on AF1 to Tokyo, Japan then onto Seoul, South Korea with Turnkey and Tullamore."

"I guess I'm reporting to Andrews Air Force Base for my AF1 briefing, but why? I've been on AF1 before," Quinlan remarked.

"New agency Director at the Secret Service, and she is a by the book, no nonsense leader. We follow her rules. She was never happy with how much we didn't know about AF1 and its capabilities. Everyone must go through this briefing. Besides, it's pretty cool. I think you'll enjoy it," Cutler replied.

"Whatever you say, Jake. Here to serve at your pleasure," Quinlan responded.

"That's my boy," Cutler said with a nod. "You'll be on this trip as part of the day shift when we get to Tokyo. We reside overnight (RON) in Tokyo, then onto Seoul, South Korea for two nights. Turnkey will want to run, so keep up that magnificent pace of yours. Lord knows he still is."

Quinlan replied confidently, "I still have my running chops and all of my running gear. I'll be good to go."

"Great," Cutler said, giving Quinlan a thumbs up. He continued, "This will be a pretty cool trip. He's going to visit with the Emperor and Empress of Japan, at their Palace, so pack clean underwear, Q."

Cutler carefully reviewed the preliminary schedule for the upcoming foreign trip provided by the Presidential staff. One note caught his eye. He stood up and addressed his shift. "Hey, everyone, listen up," he said, scanning the room. "We need to keep the Korea part of the POTUS schedule under wraps until the administration announces it publicly. That portion of the trip might be handled as an OTR. That's off the record for Q since he may have forgotten what that meant. Rare, for any portion of an overseas trip to be OTR I know, but we will adapt."

A few of Cutler's agents were confused. It was highly unusual for any portion of an overseas trip to be handled as an unofficial OTR. This meant that the administration, particularly the POTUS, wanted to keep that part of the schedule away from the media. Such occurrences typically happened in response to unforeseen or sudden events, such as funerals or when the President wanted to personally address troops in a warzone.

After his shift ended, Quinlan went to the gym located in the New Executive Office Building which was part of the White House Complex. He found running on the treadmill a great stress reliever. He also knew he needed to keep up with the POTUS should he decide to go for a run.

The flat screens in the gym had their volume turned down, but CNN and Fox News were on display. Both networks showed closed captions, accompanied by a chyron banner at the bottom of the feed reading, "Special Alert: President to Attend North Korean Meeting at Peacehouse." Quinlan glanced at the closed captions:

"This is a special alert. Breaking news from Pyongyang suggests a potential meeting between the U.S. and the North Korean Supreme Leader Pak Hyun Woo. Woo, son of the late North Korean Dictator Pak Sang Ho, has held the position of Supreme Leader for the past two years. During his brief tenure, he has forged positive relationships with many world leaders once considered adversarial. Now, he is extending what is perceived as an olive branch to the United States. The proposal comes in the form of a meeting between the North Korean Supreme Leader and

President David Bryce and will take place in the North Korean village of Panmunjom. This village is also part of the demilitarized zone or DMZ that shares the South and North Korean border. It was the location where in 1953 an armistice ending the three year war between the United States and North Korea, was signed. More news on this historical event will be the subject of our next report."

Quinlan kept pace with the treadmill's 6:30 minute-per-mile speed, musing to himself, *Wow, sometimes the best intelligence sources can be the cable news networks*. He sensed this information would likely be relevant to his upcoming trip to the Far East. Over the next twenty minutes, he observed various reports pinpointing the historic 'Peace House' as the likely venue for such a meeting. As the treadmill gradually slowed to a cool-down speed, Quinlan's final thought lingered, *This could be a very interesting historic event, and I may just be a fly on that proverbial wall.*

CHAPTER 26

Andrews Air Force Base

Quinlan adhered to the 9:00 am directive, finding himself amidst the exclusive confines of the VIP lounge at Andrews Air Force Base. Alongside ten other PPD agents, he was ushered through the labyrinthine corridors to the Presidential Airlift Group hangars. This elite unit, under the umbrella of the White House Military Office, bore the weighty responsibility of managing and overseeing the aircraft designated for Presidential travel.

The crown jewel of their fleet was Air Force One or AF1, a Boeing 747 transformed into the venerable military aircraft with the call sign VC-25A. Deliberately outfitted to serve as the presidential vessel, it was more than just an aircraft; it was a flying bastion of executive authority. Its inner workings were shrouded in layers of classified technology and security measures. The mere presence of the President aboard instantly changed its military call sign from VC-25A to the revered AF1. Within its fuselage lay an operating room theater, stocked with blood tailored to match the President's own, as a precaution against the unforeseen exigencies of high office.

Following an exhaustive tour of the hangars, Quinlan and the rest of his cohort convened for a comprehensive briefing on the intricacies of Air Force One. Amidst the sea of uniformed Air Force personnel, one figure stood out distinctly; Colonel Rick Patterson, a luminary in his own right, having once commanded the cockpit of AF1. With a tenure spanning two preceding administrations, Colonel

Patterson now assumed the mantle of educator, imparting his wealth of knowledge to the incoming cadre of PPD agents.

Colonel Rick Patterson introduced himself and wasted no time diving into the heart of the matter.

"When the President takes to the skies aboard Air Force One, the entourage of accompanying aircraft can fluctuate based on mission specifics, security protocols, and the nature of the President's journey. However, as a standard practice, there are typically two additional planes flying alongside. These serve as the support aircraft and the backup to AF1. The support aircraft is tasked with ferrying Presidential staff, media personnel, and any other individuals who couldn't secure a spot on AF1."

A ripple of amusement swept through the room, accompanied by muttered remarks about "scrubs" and references to junior varsity. Colonel Patterson chuckled, gently reminding them that even the lesser aircraft played a pivotal role, and agents often found themselves on those flights, their missions no less critical.

"Now, let's talk about the Back-Up Air Force One," Colonel Patterson continued, his gaze sweeping over the small gathering of agents. "This second aircraft mirrors AF1 in both equipment and configuration. It serves as a shadow or spare, ready to step in should mechanical issues, emergencies, or other contingencies necessitate the President's transfer. The specifics of accompanying aircraft can be adjusted based on threat assessments, airspace restrictions, logistical factors, and the President's itinerary."

Pausing for questions, Colonel Patterson emphasized the informality of the briefing, despite its classified nature. "Feel free to interrupt with any questions," he encouraged before segueing to the next speaker.

"And now, I'd like to introduce Major Roy Stephens," Colonel Patterson said, gesturing towards the unassuming figure who resembled anything but a typical pilot. Major Stephens appeared more akin to someone fresh from a gaming convention than an engineer responsible for the defense systems of Air Force One.

"Good afternoon, ladies and gentlemen," Major Stephens greeted the assembly. "I may not look the part, but I assure you, I've had a hand in crafting the defense systems of this aircraft and a few others." With a nod to simplicity and an assurance of patience, Major Stephens delved into the intricacies of Air Force One's security measures. He reminded his audience that no question was too trivial in their pursuit of understanding.

"Alright, let's dive into the nitty-gritty," Major Roy Stephens began, his tone matter of fact. He discussed Air Force One's countermeasures, carefully designed to fortify its security against potential threats, especially during flight. "First off, we've got electronic countermeasures geared towards detecting and neutralizing incoming signals, be it radar or communication waves, emanating from potential threats like missiles or hostile aircraft."

He paused, the sincerity of his words settling over the audience before continuing. "Then there are the infrared countermeasures, tailored to detect and foil heat-seeking missiles by emitting infrared energy to disrupt their guidance systems. Flare Dispensers come into play, releasing decoy flares to divert heat-seeking missiles off course. Chaff dispensers follow suit, spewing out strips of aluminum or metallic material to create false targets and confound radar-guided missiles or enemy aircraft."

Major Stephens underscored the secure communication systems onboard, facilitating encrypted exchanges among the President, officials, military commanders, and government agencies on the ground.

"We've also got armor and structural enhancements to fend off ballistic threats and physical assaults," he added, his voice resonating with assurance. "And let's not forget the sensitive compartmented information facility (SCIF), providing a secure area for uninhibited discussions during flight."

As the information settled in, a hand tentatively rose, inquiring if there were any handouts available before retracting in embarrassment. Major Stephens quashed any discomfort with a reassuring smile. "No handouts, but absolutely no dumb questions either."

With a brief segue, Major Stephens relinquished the stage to the next speaker. "Now, before I bid adieu, allow me to introduce our final presenter. Captain James Tilson, hailing from the Special Operations Wing of the Air Force. Take it away, Captain."

Captain Tilson wasted no time in making his presence known. "Folks, I'm here to shed light on the unseen aspect of this entire operation," he began, his tone carrying an air of authority. "I oversee the air wing responsible for housing and operating the Airborne Warning and Control System, better known as AWACS. These aircraft are the backbone of airborne surveillance, commanding, and controlling military operations."

He explained the AWACS provides continuous surveillance of the airspace. Equipped with potent radar systems and sensors, it detects and tracks aircraft movements. It identifies potential threats and announces early warning of any unauthorized or suspicious activity.

Captain Tilson underscored AWACS' function as an aerial traffic controller, a lifeline in congested or fraught airspace. "Should the unfortunate occur, and air traffic control is incapacitated, AWACS steps in to ensure safe separation between guiding AF1 and other aircraft along proper routes." Now, injecting a hint of levity he inquired, "You all still with me—this is easy listening stuff compared to what we will eventually cover? Anyone lost? Just kidding, no tests today."

The small audience, rapt with attention, absorbed the information with awe. Captain Tilson pressed on, delving into AWACS' contributions to security and defense. Several minutes passed by and despite the critical nature of his briefing, Captain Tilson sensed the need to draw it to a close. He recognized the danger of delving too deeply into the technical and extremely classified minutiae of the

AWACS capabilities. After all, his task for the day was to provide a comprehensive overview of the resources available in the event of an Angel Fallen scenario, and nothing more.

"In summary, folks, AWACS aircraft are pivotal in bolstering situational awareness and command capabilities for AF1," Captain Tilson declared, his gaze sweeping across the small assembly. "Any questions?"

Agent Quinlan's hand shot up. "Where is the AWACS positioned during an AF1 movement?" he inquired.

"During AF1 flights, the AWACS operates well beyond visual range, cruising at approximately..." Quinlan interrupted, "sorry sir I meant where is the AWACS positioned on the ground during such presidential movements?"

Undeterred, Captain Tilson redirected the conversation with a genial chuckle. "That's need-to-know, son," Tilson said. "Any other questions I can address?" he offered. "Alright then, I'll hand you over to Lieutenant Greer, who will guide you through a tour of AF1 and acquaint you with your future accommodations."

CHAPTER 27

Emperors Palace

Quinlan would say after flying on Air Force One, or Angel as was its call sign, you could never get used to flying commercial again. There was an obvious absence of the nauseating safety briefing all commercial airlines had to adhere to. Nope, when POTUS got onboard and was securely fastened in his seat, the awesome 747-200B series would start its roll to the runway. The runway was always within close proximity to the tarmac. This made the time to takeoff even more brief. Often more than a few of the plane's passengers would not be seated before the plane engaged its rapid ascent. It always made Quinlan laugh. He and his eight Secret Service shift mates would sit in their section, watching as VIP passengers stumbled around the cabin. The press, seated in the next cabin behind the agents, would join in the laughter. However, nothing like that happened on this flight, as most of its passengers were more senior and experienced AF1 travelers. The flight to Japan, departing from Andrews Air Force Base, would take fourteen hours.

At 10:00 am, Angel touched down at Yokota Air Force Base in Japan. Shortly after, the President left the base in a motorcade bound for the Tokyo Imperial Palace. This was the principal residence of Emperor Akito and Empress Maskato. This journey, and many others would constitute essential diplomatic initiatives under the Bryce Administration aimed at fortifying U.S. relations around the world.

Arriving promptly at 10:35 am, the motorcade pulled up as planned, and the Emperor and Empress warmly welcomed the President and the First Lady.

As a shift agent, Quinlan's duty mandated that he always remain within arm's reach of the President. In the event of an attack, it fell upon him and his team of agents to shield and evacuate the President and First Lady to safety. However, discretion was paramount, particularly during formal ceremonial occasions such as this. Quinlan managed to maintain proximity to President Bryce, while his fellow agents found themselves inadvertently excluded and unable to enter the holding room area. They found themselves physically blocked by the overenthusiastic palace guard, a departure from the agreed-upon arrangement. Consequently, Quinlan found himself alone with the President and Mrs. Bryce in the holding room, a situation he quickly relayed to the detail leader through his discreet radio. With clear instructions, his task was straightforward; stay close to Turnkey and Tullamore, the designated code names for the President and First Lady, respectively.

He grasped the situation almost instantly. It dawned on him that, despite extensive planning with the host country's security detail in the lead-up to such events, on game day, the individuals involved in the preparations were often replaced by higher-ups who were unaware of the arrangements. This phenomenon seemed particularly prevalent in foreign countries. *So, chaos ensues, and the best laid plans turn to shit,* Quinlan mused to himself. Nonetheless, he found solace in the fact that the President and First Lady were never endangered.

After some time, an irate advance person from the Presidential staff stormed into the holding room. Quinlan overheard President Bryce demanding to his staff, "What the hell happened?" Following a tense ten minutes, Quinlan, the President, and the First Lady were ushered into a spacious ballroom where the Emperor and Empress awaited to formally greet the esteemed couple.

Relieved by a somewhat irked and flustered Detail Leader, Quinlan took the opportunity to step outside for a breath of fresh air. Standing on the veranda, he viewed the boundless rolling hills, Japanese Maples, and verdant gardens that embellished the Tokyo Imperial Palace grounds.

In that instant, a voice pierced the air, remarking, "They'll let anyone into this place." Quinlan turned to find none other than Assistant United States Attorney Lana Miller. Shock surged through him; seeing Lana was unexpected enough, but in Japan? At the Imperial Palace? It left him utterly bewildered.

After finally ceasing her laughter, she asked, "Hi John. Are you hungry? I have an extra boxed lunch I got from the Embassy...Hello, John?" Lana waved her hand in front of his face, as if trying to rouse him from unconsciousness.

When he regained some composure, he said, "I am at a loss. What are you doing here? Why are you here?"

She chuckled once more before explaining, "I was with the arriving entourage, and somehow, I got swept into the event room. When I realized I wasn't supposed to be there, I stepped out onto the veranda and bumped into you."

Quinlan, now gesturing with his hand in circles, clarified, "No, I mean why are you here in Japan?"

Lana nodded slowly, the way one does when faced with a confused person. "I know what you meant," she said. "Oh, where to begin. I was offered a very good position working for the National Security Advisor, or more specifically, Jan Townes. Do you know her?"

"I know the name, but I don't work on that side of things. I'm still on the President's detail. Wait, wasn't she with you in the U.S. Attorney's Office up in New York?" Quinlan asked, his memory stirring.

"That's right she was actually my boss as the first assistant to the U.S. Attorney, but she took on a position with the Bryce Administration.

She is presently the Deputy National Security Advisor in a new enforcement roll created by your very own DHS."

Quinlan, still a little distracted by the whole thing and now smiling like a schoolboy in a crush again asked, "What are you doing here?"

"Wow, okay," Lana replied, somewhat amused by their back-and-forth. "Let me start again. I'm Jan Townes' Legal Advisor. Jan should be around here somewhere. We're both here in Japan because we hitched a ride from Andrews on AF1. We were then manifested in the motorcade, and that's how we got here. However, our main focus is the next stop in North Korea."

"Lana," John paused, a mixture of emotions evident in his expression. "It's good—so good to see you, and I have questions, but we both have jobs to do. My cell isn't turned on at the moment, but I'll get your number, and I'll call you, okay?"

"More than okay, John."

Back at his hotel room, he attempted Lana's number twice, but both times it went to voicemail. *Probably the international cell coverage*, he thought. On the second attempt, he left a message, "Hey, it's John. Just wanted to follow up. Uh, wow, so good to see you today. I'm sure we'll be busy, what with the DMZ visit in North Korea. Okay, so I'll see you in who knows where? Be safe." John placed his cellphone on the nightstand, plugged in the charging cord, and instantly fell into a deep sleep. He would need to be up in less than six hours.

CHAPTER 28

DMZ—Panmunjom

"In the midst of chaos, there is also opportunity."
—Sun Tzu

Air Force One departed from Yokota Air Base in Japan, heading towards Osan Air Base in Pyeongtaek City, South Korea. The journey from Osan Air Base to the village of Panmunjom, where the summit was scheduled to take place, spans forty-eight miles. The White House Military Office, alongside the Secret Service, concurred on the transportation plan for the President. Consequently, the President would be flown via Marine One to the demilitarized zone (DMZ) in Panmunjom, North Korea, aboard Marine One, a move that consistently raised logistical challenges. The Secret Service would be manifested on Marine One along with the President and First Lady. The remaining shift agents would be manifested on the backup to Marine One. The remaining delegation would utilize three additional Marine helicopters. President and First Lady Bryce arranged to address the troops and personnel stationed at Osan Air Base. This arrangement permitted delegation members and media not assigned to helicopters to board large buses. Korean police would escort these buses on the forty eight-mile journey to the DMZ, ensuring they arrived ahead of the official delegation. The timing was precise, prearranged, and always impeccable. Quinlan observed the proceedings, reminiscing about similar tasks he had undertaken in the past as an advance agent.

Following a thirty-minute address to the troops, the President, the First Lady, and the official delegation, accompanied by the Secret Service, boarded the five helicopters, and departed from Osan Air Base. They touched down at Camp Casey on the South Korean side of the DMZ just fifteen minutes later. Tensions were palpable on this day for numerous reasons. Serving as a dividing line between North Korea and South Korea, the DMZ is one of the most heavily fortified borders globally. Considerable military forces are deployed along both sides of the DMZ, under close surveillance and frequent patrol by both nations. As a result, military tensions remain high in the region.

Quinlan was aware that the agents tasked with advancing the security at the Peace House for the upcoming summit were carefully chosen. Despite their talent for advance security planning, the sudden nature of the event provided only a week to devise a security plan that would typically demand weeks, if not months, of preparation. The qualifications of the advance agents, contrasted with the limited time to prepare, offered little comfort.

Meanwhile, the First Lady pursued her separate agenda and remained at Camp Casey. The President, accompanied by a small official delegation, entered the Peace House. Each guest had a designated seat reserved by name markers on the table. Seated at the center of the table was the President, flanked by his Chief of Staff, Military Aide, and National Security Advisor. Agents Cutler and Quinlan were stationed on either side of the room. Positioned nearby, a small media pool from both North and South Korea had already taken their places, their cameras' shutters constantly fluttering. Quinlan understood the historical significance of the room. Constructed in 1953, the Peace House was designed to document the end of the Korean War. It was where the armistice was signed, effectively ending the conflict. The North Korean delegation had yet to take their seats on their side of the table, which Quinlan interpreted as an obvious snub. After fifteen minutes, several North Korean security personnel positioned themselves in all corners of the room, prompting the media to readjust their positions.

A figure resembling a senior North Korean official entered the room and took position by the vacant center seat designated for the new Supreme Leader of the Socialist Republic of North Korea. He announced, "The Supreme Leader, His Excellency Pak Hyun Woo." With a smile, the youthful Supreme Leader entered the room, extending his hand to Bryce. They shook hands before he took his seat across from Bryce. Following him was the announcement of his sister, Pak Hyun Mi. Quinlan could not help but notice her striking beauty almost immediately. She seemed to be in her late thirties, older than her brother. She effortlessly captivated the camera, and the media thoroughly relished her presence. It was widely acknowledged that Pak Hyun Mi was a very private person. She was seldom seen at public appearances. Two additional men in Republic of North Korea military uniforms appeared next without any introductions, completing the delegation. With all parties now seated at the table, the media fervently captured this historic event. Smiles and seemingly friendly exchanges filled the room. However, after approximately ten minutes, the man who had introduced the North Korean delegation made a loud announcement in Korean. The media were promptly ushered out of the room, leaving some of the American press startled by the urgency and assertive manner of the security escorting them out.

The room fell silent. Quinlan believed this marked the beginning of the official bilateral talks. Everything preceding this moment had seemed more like a show for the cable news networks and whatever propaganda the sister would permit to be disseminated to the citizens of North Korea.

"Mr. President," Pak Hyun Woo spoke in flawless English, "I am pleased that you have taken me and this meeting seriously. I come with no predetermined expectations of how this will unfold. Unlike my father, I consider myself a pragmatist. It is imperative for our countries to reconcile and cooperate. You may be aware that I studied at Tipperary College in Ireland. My education there was kept discreet at my father's choosing. It was during my time there that I learned the inherent instability of oppressive governance in sustaining long-term development."

Over the next hour, Woo meticulously outlined his comprehensive plan, delving into its various layers. Central to his vision was his desire for North Korea to "have a seat at the table," a phrase he reiterated multiple times throughout the meeting. His ultimate ambition was for North Korea to become a member of the United Nations Security Council (UNSC). Woo embraced the prospect of participating in the global balance of power alongside the major regions of the world. He emphasized to his American counterparts that North Korea could serve as a valuable partner within the UNSC's agenda to effectively address international peace issues.

President Bryce and his staff had not anticipated this nearly impossible proposition. It seemed inconceivable, especially considering the dictatorial rule of Woo's tyrant father.

President Bryce, a keen player of cards, particularly Texas Hold 'Em, remarked, "Leader Woo, if you're genuinely committed to your proposition, a positive step would be to release the two American exchange students your country accuses of political dissent. You have imprisoned them for the past year and a half. Additionally, you need to release Jackson Taylor, the CNN foreign correspondent your country alleges is a spy."

The Supreme Leader glanced around the room with a slight smile and said, "Mr. President, I encourage you to consult with your aides after this meeting. You will discover that a planned release is already underway for the three individuals you mentioned. Furthermore, my council is currently reviewing applications for the release of six other individuals who hold German and Italian passports."

President Bryce felt skeptical. He had not anticipated the young Supreme Leader's diplomacy, or more precisely, his willingness to seek redemption.

Bryce proceeded with his impromptu demands, "I insist on you granting free access to United Nations Weapons Inspectors on-site in all North Korean military installations. They should have complete, uninterrupted access to all weapons stockpiles within your country, as well as to the locations our current intelligence has pinpointed as hostile to American interests. Additionally, we seek to inspect your prisons and address the longstanding concerns regarding human rights violations spanning decades."

Woo lowered his gaze momentarily before locking eyes with President Bryce. In a solemn tone, he responded, "I understand. Yes, this would be acceptable to the People's Republic of North Korea."

The Supreme Leader's sister, Pak Hyun Mi, sat in the room, her disbelief palpable as she listened to the unfolding negotiations. She had anticipated her brother's ridiculous strategy at the Peace House summit, but not this. In that moment, she realized she was out of the loop. She would have no official role in her brother's cabinet, and her carefully laid plans would be rendered futile. The thought of inspectors scrutinizing every aspect of the Pak dynasty's regime filled her with dread. Operating in Camp 15 or anywhere in North Korea would become impossible under such intense scrutiny. She feared that her brother's rule would spell the demise of the Socialist Republic, and she could not shake the feeling that their father would curse them from beyond. With so much racing through her mind, she resolved to contact Stansfield Anderson in Belfast. She realized that changes to the plan were now imperative. *We must relocate,* she thought. *Anderson wanted us to move the American currency printing operation to Belfast anyway.* With her brother's unexpected olive branch, this would finalize the decision. Her mind raced as she contemplated the adjustments that needed to be made.

The media was readmitted to the Peace House, capturing numerous photos of the President shaking hands and nearly embracing Leader Pak Hyun Woo. Meanwhile, the sister remained isolated from the group. Despite the condescending nature of the media spectacle, she wore it with a mild smile. Quinlan observed her closely, noting that her smile seemed to mask a busy mind.

Quinlan could not believe what he had just heard, but he would keep it to himself. He believed that the news media could do a better job of reporting what had transpired. He realized that this was where having a top-secret clearance could be put to the test. In his mind, what happened at the Peace House would stay at the Peace House.

It did not take long for the sister to shed her facade and revert back to Akma Deja. As the cameras were turned off and the media departed from the Peace House, so, too, did Deja's feigned gratitude for her brother. She was escorted to her awaiting armored vehicle, a Mercedes S580. Once inside the quiet privacy of the car, she reached for her secure satellite phone. There would be changes, but the plan would still move forward.

The journey back to Andrews on AF1 was marked by a celebration at 37,000 feet. President Bryce and his advisors quietly reveled in the events of the day, knowing that there would be a lot of planning ahead. With North Korea literally opening its books to the West, particularly the United States, Bryce would be hailed as a hero and assured of a two-term presidency.

CHAPTER 29

Stansfield 'Stig' Anderson

"You cannot solve a problem with the same mind that created it."
—Albert Einstein

Stansfield 'Stig' Anderson occupied his desk within the confines of his Tipperary College office. His door bore the official designation, Staff Assistant—International Affairs. Engrossed in online research concerning the unfolding events in Kyiv, Ukraine, he was interrupted by an MSNBC news alert flashing onto his screen: Peace House Summit Ends in Surprise...

Just then, his encrypted satellite phone buzzed, signaling an incoming call. "Anderson here," he answered.

The voice on the other end dripped with anger, unmistakably belonging to Pak Hyun Mi, now known as Akma Deja within her circle. "Are you keeping tabs on the developments at the Peace House?"

"I am," retorted the man, his British accent sharp and perhaps unwelcome in the current situation.

Akma Deja's response dripped with venom. "There will be adjustments, but Tara Lee will adhere to the plan's timeline. She's swiftly progressing with Mr. Phillip O'Donovan, and that momentum must not be disturbed."

She refrained from discussing any aspect of the new plan, recognizing it was conceived in anger. Anger was her Achilles' heel; it clouded her ability to think rationally and with order. She understood the folly of planning in such a state, so with that, she abruptly ended the call.

* * *

Akma Deja was once a young Pak Hyun Mi who faced a significant disadvantage in life; she was insane. She was fully cognizant of her condition, her mind often a tumultuous sea of distorted values and destructive tendencies. At the age of seventeen, her father appointed a psychiatrist to aid her, acknowledging her struggles. Growing up in a socialist republic devoid of companionship was challenging enough. Being the daughter of a ruthless dictator only compounded her hardships.

She tried to drown her younger brother in the bathtub on two occasions. Several acquired pets would turn up dismembered or suffering from severe burns. Her own security team would act as an assassin squad at her command. The situation was spiraling out of control, escalating beyond even the standards set by her dictator father.

After undergoing therapy for several months, the psychiatrist diagnosed her with extreme psychopathic tendencies. He would often suggest to the dictator that psychopathy wasn't inherently negative. "Many world leaders," he'd say, "exhibit psychopathic and even sociopathic traits." He explained that Pak Hyun Mi lacks empathy. Violence would calm her and, in some cases, offer excitement. She had the ability, if she wished, to feign joy, happiness, and even compliance, but such emotions would merely be a charade. This veneer of emotion was only worn to manipulate situations to her advantage. When her father inquired about the origin of her condition, the doctor, hesitant yet compelled to answer the Supreme Leader, suggested that psychopathy often has roots in inheritance.

Two days later the doctor was executed by way of the Hwando sword.

* * *

Back in Anderson's office at Tipperary College, the secured call ended, and Anderson looked at the satellite phone receiver in frustration,

"A real charmer that one. She could knock a buzzard off a shit wagon with that personality, ay Jimmy?"

Professor James O'Donovan settled into one of the two chairs in Anderson's office. He had been privy to Anderson's end of the short phone conversation, but now waited to hear the rest of the discussion.

"Look, mate, I know what the evil demon has on me but what's she got on you?" Before he could allow James to speak, he continued, "Hey, by the way, do you know she is now making everyone call her 'Akma Deja' as some sort of warped compliment, I guess?"

His response always measured as if James O'Donovan was assembling a delicate puzzle, "She is a complicated woman, old friend. She is also a fragile woman with needs. Her ends will always justify her means. The degree of pain tied to those means however," he exhaled, "are not palatable to blokes like you and me."

"Spoken like a true professor," Anderson remarked, his gaze drifting down to his friend's increasingly gray beard and weary eyes. "It does make one wonder, mate. How does being a tenured and full-time professor allow you the time to also serve as one of the few Vice Presidents of Sinn Féin? That's a demanding role for anyone, isn't it?"

"I am a figure head here at Tipperary for fucksake. I haven't earned an honest day's wage in a long time. My grad students handle everything," James confessed. "The college seems more interested in having an arm in Sinn Féin than they are in having an international relations professor. And as for my fragile Pak Hyun Mi, she's impressed by my role within the new government. I dare say it's more useful to her than being a professor of..." His voice trailed off, tinged with a sense of resignation, as if he had sacrificed loyalty and allegiance to Northern Ireland. Through his connections with Sinn Féin, he would provide whatever information she required.

"Fragile, mate," Stig shouted with wrath, "She is anything but fragile. Again, I ask you What the fuck does she have on you?! Are you going to give me that love shit? She kept me as her strung out stooge for a long-time mate, way too long. I only have disdain for that..."

O'Donovan interjected; his tone laced with hostility. "Yes! I feel trapped by her. It's love. Remember?" He paused, reflecting on the past. "Her brother, Pak Hyun Woo was attending the college, and I grew fond of the lad. One day, she accompanied him to settle back in after the break. We were introduced, and despite being many years her senior, things took off. She made several visits over the years. I was trapped."

"Trapped? Mate, a capricious psycho bitch can't love you back. It's quite unrequited I assure you," said a defiant Stig. He continued, "Was it the love or the idea of being in love? You know blokes like you will jump at the first thing that comes along."

"How would I know her brother would someday be the Supreme Leader of the Socialist Republic of North Korea," O'Donovan sighed.

"How the fuck could you not know? Did you think Papa would be immortal?" Now looking directly into his old friend's eyes, he said, "Jimmy, I guess the trappings of love is still better than what she has on me."

* * *

Stansfield 'Stig' Anderson earned an advanced degree in economics and political science from Cambridge University. He began his career as a graduate assistant, providing support to various faculty members at Tipperary College. When Professor James O'Donovan advertised a permanent graduate assistant position, Anderson proved to be the ideal candidate. They collaborated closely for the following two years.

During a dinner party hosted by the college's dean of the economics department, Anderson found himself engaged in a lengthy conversation with an older acquaintance of the dean. They delved into the intricate politics and economics of Northern Ireland, discussing topics such as the IRA, Sinn Féin, nationalism, and loyalties to the Republic and the Crown. Anderson noticed he was enjoying his own single malt scotch way too much while the other gentleman slowly sipped something clear. *At least one of us is trying to keep a sharp wit*, Anderson mused thinking the man was sipping water. Two weeks later, that same man paid him a visit at the college with an interesting proposition. "How would you like to serve Her Majesty?" he would say.

* * *

MI-5, the United Kingdom's official domestic counterintelligence and security agency, recruited Anderson to safeguard the nation against threats to national security. His role primarily involved addressing foreign terrorism, espionage, and cyber-attacks. At times, he collaborated with intelligence agencies representing foreign interests to combat shared threats.

His initial training lasted close to a year. He would say the training nearly killed him. His classmates were top notch in their field. It was then when he was given the nickname Stig. More than a few times during training exercises, instructors would scold him for not paying attention. One instructor, hailing from Scandinavia, likened him to a wanderer. Stig—the Norwegian word for wanderer—became his moniker. Dispatched to the Northern Ireland directorate, he crafted his covert identity as Staff Assistant—International Studies amidst the familiar environs of Tipperary College. Maintaining a second office at the College's Belfast campus, he operated under the radar. Little-known to many, Northern Ireland had once served as a breeding ground for spies from the Russian KGB. During the early days of the Irish Republican Army (IRA), espionage activities of this nature were common. Anderson often remarked, "The teams may have changed their jerseys, but the game is still being played the same." Indeed, the Russians, now represented by the Federal Security Service (Federal'naya Sluzhba Bezopasnosti or FSB), and the IRA, which had evolved into the more politically acceptable Sinn Féin, continued their maneuvers, albeit under different guises.

Stig maintained a somewhat hesitant rapport with John Reynolds, the CIA's Station Chief in London. Aware of Reynolds' prowess in gathering information as per his needs, Stig knew to tread carefully around him. Reynolds' frequent visits to Northern Ireland, to see family in Donegal and Londonderry, were noted by Stig. Educated in the rules of espionage, Stig was well-versed in the theory of M.I.C.E. as the primary motivators for turning an individual into a mole. It was a craft perfected by the CIA, Israeli Mossad, the Russian FSB, and MI-5. Coercion often targeted weaknesses: M for money, I for ideology, C for compromise/blackmail, and E for ego/excitement. Stig would fall prey to almost all of them.

After five years as an MI-5 operative, he monitored the Belfast police radio frequency from his office at the college. A call came in for an urgent response to a 'suspicious package' left in the lobby of the World Bank Headquarters. Stig responded, but only as an observer, keen to be close in case it was tied to a state-backed terrorist organization. While discreetly taking pictures of license plates on parked vehicles, a bomb exploded.

The explosion catapulted him fifty feet into the air, slamming him against a parked car and injuring the cervical and thoracic parts of his spine. Despite months of physical rehabilitation, he struggled to cope with the pain. Reliant on opioids, particularly oxycodone and fentanyl patches, for relief, he found himself addicted when access to the painkillers was abruptly cut off. Keeping this dependency a secret from his beloved MI-5, he grappled with the challenges it posed.

It emerged that the improvised explosive device wasn't planted by a state-backed terrorist group. Instead, responsibility fell on an anarchist group from Portland, Oregon. It marked their next move in an escalating war against capitalism and international banking. Tragically, five others lost their lives in the attack.

Stig's descent into opioid addiction began insidiously but soon spiraled out of control. Unable to obtain prescription drugs through official channels, he turned to heroin sourced from an evidence vault. Initially, he experimented with snorting it, finding relief for his phantom pain. However, the addiction tightened its grip, compelling him to resort to injecting it directly into his veins.

Despite maintaining a facade of functionality, he knew deep down that being a functioning addict was an oxymoron. His adversaries recognized his fragile state and exploited it, leveraging his access to valuable intelligence. His impaired judgment became evident, and in the throes of heroin withdrawal during a visit to Dublin, he was compromised.

* * *

His old friend, Professor James O'Donovan, extended an invitation to a dinner party in Dublin. Stig felt a weekend away might be just what he needed, so he boarded the 2 ½ hour train ride to arrive just in time for the gathering. James hadn't seen his friend since the hospitalization following the blast nearly seven months ago. Stig's appearance was unsettlingly emaciated, nothing like his former self.

"Stig, old boy, you look worse for wear," the professor remarked. Stig could only nod, fully aware of the reasons behind his deteriorated appearance.

"You remember Pak Hyun Mi" James said, reintroducing her to Stig. He looked stunned. He had suspected their dalliance to be fleeting, yet there she was. Stunningly beautiful yet hideously destructive at the same time. He harbored no fondness for her. Somehow, she seemed to know exactly what plagued the spy. Yes, she even knew all about that, a fact not revealed to her by her elder gentleman professor friend. No, O'Donovan had not yet known his friend was an addict, a full-blown junkie. However, she knew. She learned about it from a Russian contact at the FSB. In the black-market underworld, vendors for illicit drugs and information were plentiful, particularly in the UK. Pak Hyun Mi operated her counterfeiting operation while selling secrets to the Russians. Payment typically arrived in Bitcoin, but sometimes in valuable information as well. Details that could be used to blackmail a

British spy were considered priceless. She devised a scheme to ensnare such a spy.

The next morning, James had arranged to meet with Stig for breakfast at his hotel. The Fitzwilliam Hotel, situated directly across from the college, was Stig's favorite place to relax and recharge—neither of which were available in his current state.

"Brass tacks, old friend, you look like shit. Is it more than just the pain?" James remarked, eyeing Stig with concern.

Stig's eyes, usually bright and lively, now held a somber intensity. "Stress from the job, mate. The pain is always there, but I have another surgery scheduled."

With a careful look of concern, O'Donovan looked directly at Stig and said, "You would tell me if there was anything I can do to help, wouldn't you? Are you suffering from post-trauma? I have an excellent doctor..."

Stig couldn't take the inquisition any longer and he held up his hand gesturing for his friend to stop. Just then, the beautiful black widow spider, Pak Hyun Mi appeared in the lobby dining room. She peered around the room until her eyes landed on their table.

She walked over, kissed James on the cheek and said, "I have an errand to run my love." Then looking at Stig, she extended her hand which held a bag from the lobby gift shop. She said with a wry smile, "Stansfield, you do not look well. I got you some lozenges and medicine for your illness." She left the bag with him and smiled as she left.

Stig returned to his room, unsettled by her stare from the previous night and the strange gesture this morning. Fumbling to open his bag, he pulled out its contents and threw the lozenges on the floor. Grabbing the bottle of aspirin, he discovered it had already been tampered with. Pouring out the contents, he found among the blue gel caps five 80-milligram pills he knew all too well. Hastily, he downed three of the opioid tabs. The potent drug began to take effect, and he picked up the packet of lozenges to find a small note containing a phone number. Dialing the number, he heard a phone ringing in the hotel hallway just outside his room. Peering through the door's peephole, he couldn't locate the source of the ringing. Turning his attention to the adjoining door to the next room, he noticed the faint ring growing louder. With caution, he approached the door, and as he moved closer, the ringing intensified. Placing his ear against the adjoining door, he heard a voice, "It's me, Stansfield. Please open the door," she requested.

He complied with her request. Standing in the adjoining doorway was Pak Hyun Mi, dressed in delicate black satin and lace lingerie. Stig couldn't help but notice how the contours of her body accentuated her curves. Initially taken aback, he backed away out of surprise, bordering on shock. As he took in her ensemble, which included a lace bralette, matching panties, garters, and stockings, confusion swept over him. The opioid began to mask the phantom pain, creating the illusion of safety. She stepped into his room, extending her hand below his waistline, caressing the exterior of his pants. The alluring fragrance of jasmine emanated from her body, enveloping him. As she unbuckled his pants, she nibbled and kissed his ears removing any effort to resist. She continued to explore his erogenous area and she moved to take him in. This ignited a cascade of sensations that enveloped him into the next phase of her plan. She guided him to her own hotel room bed that had already been turned down awaiting this inevitable outcome. She was aware of her attractive features that men desired. *Such beauty is not wasted*, she thought to herself. As long as she could use it to achieve her goals. What a psychopath desired could be dangerous, and in this moment, for Stig, was perilous.

The video recorded every embrace of the moment. Her body intertwined with his in a rhythm that mirrored the hearts of so many who had been compromised before. As passion continued and the opioids flooded the limbic system of his brain. Stig surrendered to the moment and released.

He woke from his temporary escape to find the room empty. The scent of jasmine lingered, but she was gone. Realization washed over him; he had crossed a line, not just with his friend James O'Donovan, but with the British Government as well. An MI-5 operative couldn't easily justify having a relationship with an adversarial North Korean cabinet member. He lay there thinking of his friend, pondering, *I can understand. I can now see what she could do to make you fall in love with her. Maybe not love, but definitely something close to it.* Out of the corner of his eye, he noticed an envelope with the name Stansfield Anderson written across it. Inside was a USB flash drive.

Without delay, he headed to his room and fetched his computer. After inserting the flash drive, he proceeded to examine its contents. The entire act played out before him in digital format. In that moment, he realized he was compromised. Pak Hyun Mi had obtained her latest asset in the form of a British Intelligence officer, one with access to valuable information about the state of Ukraine. Questions about their military readiness and strategic vulnerabilities now had answers. Her leverage would be profitable if she could keep his brain fed with the drug he desired. With this kind of information, she could keep the Russians on a short leash, always ready to serve her interests.

In no time, Pak Hyun Mi began passing on Stig's intelligence to the Russians. The secrets identified the dynamic vulnerabilities of Ukraine's political and military infrastructure. It provided Russian President Petrov with the necessary timeline for their attack on Ukraine.

On that fateful day, Stansfield 'Stig' Anderson's friendship with his dear friend, Professor James O'Donovan, was also compromised. Pak Hyun Mi would now have the leverage to manipulate Stig however she pleased, potentially pitting him against the United Kingdom and her older gentleman lover.

CHAPTER 30

The APEX Note

On this day, Phillip O'Donovan commuted to work alone, his regular carpool companion, Tara Lee, was absent. She claimed she was staying at her grandparents' residence in Bellevue, Washington, but, in truth, she was residing at the Triad safe house in Anacostia. Akma Deja was briefing her extensively on the next phase of the operation, necessitating a thorough discussion of background and objectives over a secured, encrypted satellite phone. The operation had to be modified due to recent events at the Peace House. Tara's involvement, however, would go forward as planned. Akma Deja thought she was being careful to avoid specific names during the call. She felt even with a secured encrypted phone line, she couldn't be too careful. One symptom of her psychopathy was paranoia and it served her well for many years.

She deemed it the opportune moment to fully brief Tara Lee on the entirety of the operation. She recounted her initial conversation with Phillip's uncle James, the professor, several years prior at Tipperary College. How she learned about Phillip's role as a master engraver at the Bureau of Engraving and Printing. Over the course of subsequent hours, the professor inadvertently divulged everything necessary for her plan to progress. Just like any other asset under her control, she intended to manipulate the professor to her advantage. Her objective? To lure the American master engraver to North Korea to fix a very specific problem. Though she initially spoke in vague terms about the necessity of the American's involvement, she made it clear he would be fulfilling the unfinished business her father started.

She explained to Tara Lee that North Korea had been making American currency since 1990. Her father's plan, before his demise, aimed to undermine the American economy by saturating the global market with counterfeit U.S. currency. The intended consequence? To render the American dollar practically worthless. While the world's attention remained fixated on nuclear weaponry and cyber warfare, North Korea would execute a stealthy assault through economic sabotage. North Korea's deliberate manipulation of inflation could gradually erode the strength of the United States dollar and inevitably its economy. Tara Lee was rendered speechless by the revelation. She had been taken aback by the intensity of Akma Deja's words. It was instances like these that underscored Tara's unwavering deference and respect for Akma Deja. She listened intently.

Deja proceeded with the briefing, recognizing the imperative for Tara Lee to be thoroughly informed. Aware of the potential consequences, her father regarded it as a calculated risk, even amidst the looming possibility of it being perceived as an act of war amid escalating tensions between North Korea and America. The counterfeit was nearly flawless. American intelligence dubbed the $100 bill as the APEX note. Employing their own master engraver, Akma Deja's father embarked on the task of fabricating the note, yet a crucial element eluded him. The engraver devoted every waking hour to dissecting the intricacies of the note, striving to replicate the plate-making process mirroring that of the Americans. Concurrently, her father's team of chemists scrutinized the paper, affirming that the cotton-to-linen ratio was impeccably matched to the composition of authentic American currency. The deliberately crafted plates were seamlessly integrated into the very model of printing press utilized by the Bureau of Engraving and Printing. Everything appeared impeccable. The master engraver flawlessly replicated the $100 bill, even down to the minutiae of the red and blue security fibers seamlessly woven into the paper. Yet, despite this meticulous craftsmanship, how did the Americans manage to discern these counterfeit notes from the genuine? Akma Deja realized the necessity to fulfill what her father had initiated. She required Master Engraver Phillip O'Donovan's expertise to identify and rectify these imperceptible flaws. Her brother's aggressive pursuit of peace inadvertently expedited her plans. With UN inspectors scheduled to conduct their inspections in less than six months, the timing was critical. During the call, there was a moment when Akma Deja momentarily lost her grip on discretion over the supposedly secure line, while Tara remained steadfastly attentive.

"Tara," Deja began, "I've just received information from my contact that Phillip's son, Patrick, will be studying abroad. Are you aware of this?"

"Yes, I've heard about it," Tara confirmed. Akma Deja now placed significant reliance on the phone's encryption to obscure the content of her forthcoming message.

"Tara," Deja's voice seemed to carry a deliberate sense of authority with each syllable, "Phillip's Uncle James is leveraging his position at Tipperary College to steer young Patrick O'Donovan towards enrolling in a foreign exchange program at the National University of Korea in Seoul, South Korea. Unwittingly, he's delivering Patrick into our hands." Deja continued, each syllable thoughtfully orchestrated like pieces of a puzzle, "Your task is to bring him to Seoul. Once you both arrive, the college will arrange transportation to the campus. James has already arranged these details, and Patrick is aware. Once Patrick checks into the college, ensure he contacts his great Uncle James to confirm his arrival. Do you understand the plan thus far?"

Tara listened attentively, confirming that she did.

Akma Deja persisted, "It's imperative that James remains unaware of my involvement in the next phase, which involves Patrick's abduction and transfer to my compound in Pyongyang. Initially,

Patrick will spend the first few days participating in college orientation while following the foreign exchange student itinerary. This will give the impression that he is safe and occupied. At a designated time, you and three members of my security team will incapacitate Patrick and transport him to Pyongyang. The journey will take three hours by road, during which Patrick will be sedated. Do you understand the importance of your role and your involvement in this operation?"

Tara drew in a deep breath, then exhaled slowly before saying, "I understand. I'm eager and thankful for the opportunity to serve you. I owe you a great deal, and now I'm honored to repay you by playing a role in your ingenious plan."

Akma Deja was gratified to hear Tara's response, reaffirming her confidence in Tara Lee.

Tara added, "I'll have a conversation with Phillip in two days, when I return. I can propose accompanying Patrick to Seoul, mentioning a recently discovered ailing relative."

Deja responded, "Perfect. Keep me updated on how that conversation unfolds," and then the call concluded. Despite her usual well-founded paranoia, Akma Deja's fragile ego and contemptuous nature prevented her from masking her otherwise calculated and secretive demeanor.

* * *

National Security Agency (NSA) Cryptanalyst Intelligence Officer Charlie Green monitored and documented the twenty-eight-minute conversation. The source code originated from a site in Pyongyang, North Korea. The targeted satellite phone, positioned at coordinates 38.8638926–76.9832416 (1516 W. Street SE), alerted Officer Green to an incoming call, triggering the digital recording of the discussion. Officer Green had been tasked with monitoring these coordinates a year prior following the issuance of a Foreign Intelligence Surveillance Act (FISA) warrant. The request was initiated by the FBI/CIA International Joint Terrorism Task Force, with a focus on monitoring

Triad organized crime activity at that specific location. Initially, there had been only a handful of intercepted satellite phone transmissions from the surveilled location. As of late, however, Green noticed a spike in recent telephonic activity.

The satellite telephone encryption was crude, originating from Russia, and posed little challenge to decrypt. Green observed that the majority, if not all, of the conversations were conducted in Korean. NSA Officer Charlie Green operated from a windowless SCIF situated in the underground levels of Fort Meade, MD. Having served in the U.S. Navy, Green had developed expertise in communication analysis, cryptography, and counterintelligence. Following his military service, he seamlessly transitioned into a civilian role at the NSA. With his active top-secret clearance, it was a no brainer. He would effectively continue his role from the U.S. Navy, now as a civilian assigned to the NSA's Counterintelligence Unit, enjoying twice the salary.

The digital recordings of conversations would be transcribed and provided to the task force in both Korean and English formats. Typically, the turnaround time for these transcriptions to reach the FBI's joint terrorism task force was three days. Following this delivery, Green's involvement in that communication would come to an end. He found the process frustrating, as he would not receive feedback on whether the intelligence he analyzed was acted upon.

Furthermore, Green felt frustrated with the current environment at the NSA. He noticed an influx of personnel coming directly from Ivy League colleges. He believed that the current cohort of intelligence officers lacked the same level of patriotism that was once considered essential for working at such a prestigious agency. Green held the belief that most, if not all, intelligence positions should be filled by former military or law enforcement personnel, rather than individuals lacking in patriotism and a strong work ethic.

Officer Green's decision to enlist and subsequently attend the Navy's Officer Candidate School was greatly influenced by the events of September 11th, 2001. However, his frustration grew over time due to the lack of coordination among our nation's intelligence and law enforcement agencies. Despite the passing of the USA Patriot Act, which aimed to reduce fragmentation between these "premier" agencies, Green observed little improvement in their collaboration and cooperation. "Did anyone even read the act," he thought to himself. "If they did, they would know that the name USA Patriot Act was itself an acronym. It stood for Uniting and Strengthening America by Providing Appropriate Tools Required to Intercept and Obstruct Terror."

Officer Green held a firm belief that the events of 9/11 could have been prevented with better communication among the nation's intelligence agencies. He was adamant that the CIA and FBI had failed to share crucial information that might have thwarted the attacks on that tragic day. In response to this communication breakdown, the administration established the Department of Homeland Security (DHS), aiming to house numerous agencies under one umbrella for improved cohesion, efficient communication, and reduced fragmentation.

Green often remarked on the irony of the situation, noting, "The only two agencies that were still not part of this cooperative effort were the FBI and the CIA."

Green would dutifully pass along the digital recording, the transcription, and his summary regarding the intercepted conversation between the two parties. He didn't mind if it was slow walked however since no one, certainly not the FBI or CIA cared about his efforts.

CHAPTER 31

Tara Lee's Plan

"Plans are of little importance, but planning is essential."
—Winston Churchill

Phillip reached Washington National Airport ahead of time, eager for Tara's plane from Seattle to touch down. Two hours before, Chan had ensured Tara was at Washington National Airport, setting the stage for her to appear as if she had just landed according to the flight schedule. They had carefully planned everything, leaving nothing to chance. Phillip waited in the cellphone lot. Tara, traveling light with just a carry-on, would call him once she was at the pickup/drop-off area.

Thoughts of Annie flooded Phillip's mind, bringing with them a familiar wave of guilt. *It had been two years,* he thought, *but whoever said time heals all wounds was full of shit.* He was grappling with conflicted emotions. Was he betraying his beloved wife by considering moving forward? Would she want him to find happiness again? Patrick, sensing his dad's loneliness, offered reassurance that it was okay to let go. With Patrick soon departing for his final semester abroad, Phillip fretted over the prospect of solitude. It was a relentless cycle in his fragile psyche. *She'll always have a special place in my heart,* he acknowledged to himself, *but I must find a way to move forward.* His train of thought was interrupted by the ringing of his cellphone, prompting him to make his way towards the pickup area. "Hey, welcome home," he answered, "I'm on my way." Tara now had a specific agenda away from the day in and day out mindless rendition of grooming a romance. She now knew her purpose in the grand scheme, and it made sense now. She was enlightened and could focus on the plan to get Patrick to Seoul.

"Hi, my Philly," an excited Tara said as she got in the car. She kissed him on the lips and lingered there for a while. She said, "What did I miss, catch me up?" She now spoke like a true American. She picked the name Philly because it was her name for him. No one else called him that. Not Patrick, not Uncle Jimmy, and certainly not his late wife, Annie. She believed it gave her purpose in his life and it made him feel needed once again. He felt loved; he liked that. She started to find unique ways to inject herself without being too pushy. These lessons were part of her social engineering strategy. She was trained in such subterfuge while being indoctrinated. She knew not to replace Annie but to introduce Tara.

She wasted no time, "So listen," she said. "My grandparents are fine, and the visit went really well but I have to head to Seoul to see my cousin who has been diagnosed with multiple sclerosis. She is older and needs me to come visit to help her from time to time."

Phil, feeling genuinely sorry looked at her as best he could while driving, "Tara, I'm so sorry to hear that. That's awful. Whatever you need. What can I do?"

Now it was Tara's turn, and she had to tread carefully. "Has Patrick given more thought to his study abroad?" she inquired; her tone measured. She knew Patrick hadn't mentioned it, but this was a bluff she had to make. Tara understood the importance of this moment, particularly after the briefing she had just received from Akma Deja.

Phillip, feeling a sense of satisfaction, remarked, "Well, as luck would have it, he's decided on a college in South Korea for a four-month exchange. My Uncle Jimmy and he have discussed it extensively. Perhaps we can turn this unfortunate situation into something positive. Can you arrange your trip to coincide with his? You could go together."

Excitement bubbling within her, Tara exclaimed, "Yes, that's exactly what I was thinking. I know you mentioned you couldn't accompany him, and you were worried about him going alone. Problem solved."

Phillip nodded, saying, "I'll need to confirm the travel plans with Patrick, but I believe he intends to start over the summer in three weeks."

During the ride back to Alexandria, Tara invited her Philly over for dinner at her place. Her house was located around the corner from his own home in the quaint village of Old Town Alexandria. A cobblestone alleyway linked their two houses so impromptu visits became the norm. On this occasion, however, she wanted the evening to be special. She was very patient with the slow pace of the intimate part of their relationship. She detected that Phillip preferred to proceed cautiously. He was mindful of Patrick's feelings and didn't want to rush into anything. Phillip was sensitive to Patrick witnessing him in a new relationship. He wondered aloud to Tara if Patrick might interpret it as leaving his mother behind. He believed that kids, especially ones Patrick's age, were perceptive and could pick up on these nuances. All of this had previously prompted Tara to proceed slowly, but now she felt compelled to be more assertive, driven by a greater purpose.

Phillip and Tara had finished dinner. Tonight, he seemed less concerned about Patrick as he was going to spend the night at his friend's house in Fairfax. She tried to steer the conversation away from his son. She wanted all of Philly's attention. He was very much attracted to Tara but only infrequently acted on it. He was attracted to her youthful and graceful facial features. Smelling the fragrance on her he likened it to clove and cardamom. She moved closer to him, and he relished her smooth skin, almond shaped eyes, and high cheek bones. She was kissing his neck. He moved his hand along her long, straight, and dark silky hair. He seemed to have dismissed this beauty in the past perhaps because he was insecure about his desires. He hadn't been prepared. Tonight, he resolved to surrender to his desires. She led him to her bedroom, where they embraced each other passionately. They woke and he felt joy once again. Later that morning, Phillip decided to call Uncle Jimmy to update him on the latest news about Patrick's travel plans to South Korea.

* * *

Across the Atlantic in Dublin, Professor James O'Donovan was enjoying his late afternoon tea, though he felt somewhat sluggish and unwell. Four months earlier, he had been diagnosed with thyroid cancer. Although the doctors believed they had caught it in time, he was undergoing aggressive chemotherapy. He had just received a call from his nephew, who shared the wonderful news that Patrick had been accepted into the exchange program at the National University of Korea. Patrick joined the call, and together they expressed their gratitude to Uncle Jimmy for orchestrating everything. However, Phillip couldn't help but notice that Jimmy didn't sound well. "You don't sound too good, Uncle Jimmy. Are you okay?" he asked with concern.

"Oh, it's just a cold. Everything's fine," Jimmy reassured them.

Professor O'Donovan was not going to inconvenience anyone with his health issue. Not even his beautiful Pak Hyun Mi. He would never refer to her as Akma Deja. He hated that she liked being called Evil Demon. He felt equally uneasy about the notion that she had, through her brother, secured an invitation for him to attend the upcoming White House Iftar Dinner. He couldn't grasp why she would desire his attendance at an event commemorating the end of the Muslim fast, Ramadan. She elaborated, "President Bryce will soon extend an invitation to my brother to visit the White House. It will be a historic occasion and you will accompany him as a representative of Sinn Féin. My brother holds you in high regard. The only thing he loves about me," she remarked, "is my proposal for an alliance between the Socialist Republic of North Korea and Sinn Féin of Northern Ireland.

Until that celebratory occasion arrives, I believe your attendance at the Iftar dinner will demonstrate solidarity between Sinn Féin and the Bryce Administration." Professor O'Donovan couldn't help but wonder, "what was she up to."

Stansfield 'Stig' Anderson had informed Akma Deja that her professor had been diagnosed with thyroid cancer a few months earlier. He hadn't learned of this directly from his friend, but rather through one of his numerous covert arrangements with Deja. She instructed Stig to conduct weekly 'sweeps' of the professor's offices in Dublin and Belfast. During one of these sweeps, Stig stumbled upon the professor's medical diagnosis, revealing that he had been undergoing aggressive radiation treatment at St. Luke's Hospital in Dublin. As always with Deja, this information would undoubtedly serve a purpose.

CHAPTER 32

Room 23

Quinlan had been serving on the Presidential Protection Division (PPD) for nearly four years now. Throughout his tenure, he had successfully completed numerous protective assignments, both domestic and foreign. Along the way, he had witnessed many significant historical events and navigated his fair share of nerve-wracking close calls.

After completing his day shift at the White House, where the President happened to be that day, Quinlan was on his way back home to Fairfax, VA. He was coming to the realization that his tenure with PPD was coming to an end. It was becoming increasingly evident that he would soon have to ready himself for a potential return to a field office. As he drove, his cellphone rang, prompting him to pull over to the far-right westbound lane of Route 66. On the other end was Rick Spencer, the Special Agent in Charge of the Presidential Protection Division. Rick was well-liked and commanded the respect of those he supervised. He recalled Quinlan from their days together in the New York Field Office, where Rick had supervised the young agent in the protective intelligence squad.

"John," SAIC Spencer spoke in his calm but brisk New York City accent. "Are you off duty? Are you home? Got a minute to talk?"

"Yes, Sir," Quinlan replied promptly. "I heard your voice and pulled over! Is everything—"

Spencer interrupted him, "No, no, no, all good. Good news. Look, I'm promoting you to my supervisory team on PPD. YES, you'll be a GS-14 Supervisory Special Agent on the Presidential Protection Division! A rare occurrence, John."

Quinlan was overwhelmed with disbelief. He had been vying for a promotion for years, thoroughly compiling his qualification statements, often referred to as his brag sheet. He had always assumed that a promotion would necessitate a transfer back to the field or, worse yet, a headquarters assignment.

"No one gets promoted in place," Quinlan muttered to himself.

"What's that, Q?" Spencer's quick but assertive tone prompted Quinlan to speak up.

"I said, wow boss, I did not see that coming."

Spencer wasn't one to leave long gaps in conversation, especially not on phone calls. He concluded the call by saying, "Look, enjoy the weekend and be in my office at the OEOB Rm. 220 at 8:00 am on Monday."

The OEOB, Washington speak for the Old Executive Office Building, would soon become more familiar to Quinlan than he anticipated.

"Sir, before you hop off this call, where will I be working?" He inquired.

"Room 23," replied the agent in charge.

Quinlan was eager to share the news of his promotion with someone, but he realized he knew very little about Room 23 other than its location in the OEOB. He understood that it housed the access control branch of the Presidential Protection Division. Essentially, they were the gatekeepers of the eighteen acres, which was a colloquial term for the entirety of the White House grounds. This encompassed the West Wing, the Mansion, the East Wing, and the Old Executive Office Building, as well as the surrounding grounds from Pennsylvania Avenue to Constitution Avenue. Room 23 would be responsible for vetting who could access this area. This office also conducted background investigations on all workers, from the custodial staff to the Chief of Staff. Room 23 assessed the suitability of those seeking access to the White House.

The number of people vetted at the White House each day can vary significantly depending on various factors such as scheduled events, meetings, tours, and official visits. On a typical day, the White House staff, visitors, contractors, and guests undergo various levels of security vetting before gaining access to the grounds. This vetting process includes background checks, security screenings, and clearance procedures all coordinated by Room 23. Quinlan would supervise four special agents and twenty administrative personnel. Those were the responsibilities of Room 23 personnel according to the paperwork available to him. He would soon come to realize, however, that there was much more to the role than what appeared on the surface and a lot of it was in the gray area.

* * *

At 7:30 am, Quinlan strode through the southeast gate of the White House. There, he encountered Secret Service Officer Ron Doty, a respected colleague at the White House. Doty greeted him with a beaming smile, declaring, "Congratulations, Boss! Looks like it's Mr. Quinlan for all of us now, huh?" Doty's southern charm and amiable nature endeared him to both the White House staff and the Secret Service.

"Never the case, Ron—never the case," Quinlan responded, acknowledging Doty's remark with gratitude. He couldn't help but marvel at how quickly word spread within the tight-knit community of the Secret Service. Memories of Agent Minelli's words about the lack of secrets in the Secret Service flooded Quinlan's mind, a stark reminder of the organization's transparency.

Quinlan proceeded to the office of SAIC Rick Spencer to discuss his new role overseeing Room 23. Spencer welcomed Quinlan with a warm smile and a firm handshake.

"Have a seat, John," Spencer offered, gesturing towards a plush leather chair in his office.

"Did you enjoy some celebration this weekend?" he inquired, letting the question linger for a moment. When Quinlan couldn't respond quickly enough, Spencer continued, "John, let's get to it. There are some matters concerning your new role in Room 23 that we must address."

"Sure and no boss I have no one really to celebrate with."

"Jesus, Quinlan, that's sad. You divorced? Oh, wait you never married, you haven't met that special person yet right? Don't you have anyone in your life?" SAIC Spencer's inquiries lingered, filling the air with curiosity.

Quinlan opted to allow SAIC Spencer to continue his line of questioning. He couldn't help but notice Spencer's characteristic New York demeanor, reminiscent of their interactions back in the New York Field Office—always direct and no-nonsense.

"Well, I haven't had much personal time, sir. At least not with all the travel. There is one girl I would..." He trailed off, abruptly halting his sentence mid-thought. He realized, why am I divulging my personal life to the SAIC? Quinlan quickly shut down the conversation in his mind.

"Well, I guess if the Service wanted you to have a family, they would have issued you one," Spencer remarked casually. Quinlan understood that Spencer's comment wasn't meant to be offensive; he simply hadn't anticipated the personal line of questioning. After all, he and Quinlan shared a history that spanned several years. Quinlan had worked for him at the New York Field Office, where he had grown accustomed to Spencer's unfiltered speech. He was never one to mince words or filter his thoughts; he spoke his mind without any regulatory restraint.

SAIC Spencer cut to the chase. "Listen, John, we need to raise your clearance level to Sensitive Compartmented Information or SCI," he began. "Room 23 is like the black sheep of Secret Service assignments. You'll be dealing with all White House access-related issues, yes. But you'll also be tasked with..." Spencer paused, his tone now more measured and deliberate as he chose his words carefully.

"Well, you'll be navigating in the gray area, so to speak. Matters not explicitly assigned to other Secret Service sections will fall under your purview in Room 23. Does that make sense to you, John?"

"Yes, but sir, if I may," Quinlan interjected, seeking clarification. "Who was the supervisor over Room 23 before me? Perhaps meeting with that person could provide me with a better understanding." He simply aimed to gain deeper insight into his new responsibilities.

Spencer tilted his head upwards, as if searching the sky for a suitable response, before replying, "That's going to be difficult since the responsibilities we're discussing... The non-access related ones used to be managed by the National Security Agency. We advocated for and obtained permission to assume these responsibilities, effectively bypassing the NSA. You see, the traditional access-related duties were handled by the Joint Operations Center Supervisor along with the Uniformed Division of the Secret Service. With your promotion, we've integrated those overt responsibilities into Room 23's jurisdiction. However, this move wasn't just about overt duties; we've also absorbed the NSA's more covert responsibilities. And now, John, those responsibilities will be yours. Is this making any sense to you?"

"So, if I may, sir," Quinlan interjected, his tone akin to someone strategizing their next chess move, "While access control-related functions are undoubtedly integral to my new role here at the White House, they also serve as a veil for the undisclosed, darker operations previously managed by the NSA. I suspect our acquisition of these responsibilities wasn't exactly welcomed by the NSA, hence their reluctance to provide thorough briefings."

"Or any briefings at all, John," SAIC Spencer began, nodding in acknowledgment, "Yes, that's one perspective. The National Security Advisor also supported the transfer of these responsibilities to us. He essentially wrested them from the NSA and entrusted them to the Secret Service. It wasn't coincidental that I recommended you for this assignment. I detest the cloak-and-dagger aspects of this job, but we'll uncover more as we go. Over the years, you've demonstrated a knack for thinking beyond conventional boundaries. You don't rely on checklists; you seek solutions. You're at home in the gray area—hell, I believe you thrive there."

"Yes sir, I think I understand and thank you for the opportunity," was all Quinlan could muster at the moment.

SAIC Spencer had scheduled a security briefing for Quinlan later that day at Secret Service Headquarters. It was standard procedure for Secret Service personnel to have their top-secret clearances updated every five years. This involved updating the Standard Form 86, or SF-86, followed by a field investigation to ensure ongoing clearance suitability.

During the briefing, Supervisory Agent John Quinlan would be briefed on the same motivations that led to the compromise and betrayal of MI-5 operative Stansfield 'Stig' Anderson. The briefing would underscore the sobering reality that individuals could be compromised without even realizing it.

As a preventative measure, the Secret Service implemented the five-year security update to mitigate the risk of compromise and betrayal among its personnel.

Spencer briefed Quinlan on the responsibilities of Room 23, including matters related to White House access. However, he also introduced another unique aspect of the role: Quinlan would be involved in missions with higher stakes. As a result, his clearance would be elevated to SCI level, granting him access to sensitive compartmented information.

Quinlan would have a seat at the table in the West Wing Situation Room and become an associate member of the National Security Council. This would expose him to the nation's most sensitive secrets, making him the eyes and ears of the Secret Service. His role in Room 23 would involve cleaning up anything that fell through the cracks.

SAIC Spencer escorted Quinlan to the Assistant Director of Investigation's office in Headquarters, where they were formally introduced.

"John, I believe we've crossed paths before," Frank Cawley greeted, extending his hand. Quinlan reciprocated with a firm handshake. "I want to bring you into the loop on something that could be crucial to our nation's security, though we're still in the process of assessing its significance."

Cawley continued, emphasizing the rationale behind Quinlan's promotion. "You've been promoted because you're the right person at the right time to assume the responsibilities of Room 23 and safeguard the White House. The President holds you in high regard; he sees you as the only individual on his protective detail who can keep up with him during his death runs," Cawley chuckled, glancing at SAIC Spencer. "And truth be told, he's probably right."

Cawley's tone turned serious as he addressed Quinlan directly. "John, it might sound peculiar given your current focus on protection, but you possess an exceptional talent for solving counterfeit cases."

Quinlan found himself thoroughly confused. He understood the Secret Service's dual mission of safeguarding world leaders and preserving the nation's financial infrastructure. However, he never anticipated these two realms intersecting within a single office.

"John," Cawley pressed on, his tone serious, "We've received intelligence indicating a surge in the circulation of the APEX note, particularly in Europe and domestically. This near-perfect counterfeit $100 bill demands our utmost attention. Oh and for the time being, refrain from discussing this with anyone except me and SAIC Spencer."

Quinlan shifted his gaze to AD Cawley, his mind swirling with questions. "Sir, I understand, and I do have some questions. Why wouldn't our field offices or international branches handle this note?"

"They will be involved, but there needs to be a direct link to us here at the White House, and that link is you," Cawley replied.

Quinlan furrowed his brow. "Is the White House read in on this?" he asked.

"Not at the moment," SAIC Spencer interjected, "But the Bureau of Engraving and Printing, our currency producers, have a vested interest that goes beyond what I'd consider typical. John, you'll need to obtain that SCI clearance before we can delve any deeper into this matter."

Quinlan sat in silence. AD Cawley could tell he had blindsided Quinlan, especially considering the recent news from SAIC Spencer about his new management role in the esteemed Presidential Protection Division.

Standing up from behind his desk, AD Cawley extended his hand to Quinlan once more. "John, your dedication, and hard work, both in the field and here on the President's detail, have brought you to this point. It's not a conventional career path, to say the least. One might even call it a journey born out of the gray area."

SAIC Spencer suggested they walk back to the White House, breaking the tension. "Let's head back, John. For now, your main concern is access control and matters involving the security of the eighteen acres. The White House is a delicate beast that balances on a tight rope—a challenge I'm well acquainted with."

Quinlan smiled warmly. "That's right, boss. You held the access control portion of the Room 23 position for a couple of years before taking on your current role as the Agent in Charge!"

"Well, not quite," SAIC Spencer clarified. "My responsibilities didn't quite overlap with what you'll be handling, but managing access control at the White House was certainly a handful in itself."

Seizing the moment, Spencer escorted Quinlan to his new office. The plain placard on the door simply read "Room 23," without a nameplate or any other distinguishing marks. Yet beyond that door lay a bustling network of personnel stationed in small offices and cubicles, manned switchboards, and active computer terminals. This would be the team Quinlan would oversee to ensure the safety of the White House.

SAIC Spencer reassured him, "I'll always be available to offer assistance whenever you need it."

Quinlan expressed, "Sir, I have so many questions right now."

"John, we have to get you that bump in clearance before we can go any further. I have my own clearance to maintain, and I don't want to be careless about these things."

"Got it, and thank you again, sir."

With that, Spencer left Quinlan's new office. Quinlan's thoughts raced with the recent conversation. He understood attaining a higher clearance, specifically SCI, would entail undergoing another polygraph. He swore he would never subject himself to that again.

It would be several months before he would receive the SCI clearance necessary to be briefed in on the APEX note. In the meantime, he was fast at work as one small part of an elaborate and dynamic security plan designed to protect the eighteen acres and all those that frequented it.

* * *

Quinlan immersed himself in numerous meetings aimed at fortifying the security of the White House, establishing a solid rapport with his liaison at the National Security Council (NSC), Ms. Janice (Jan) Townes. She served as the Deputy National Security Advisor to Secretary Jonathan Ridge of the Department of Homeland Security. Townes had ascended to her current position as DNSA after making a significant impact in the battle against human trafficking, primarily along the eastern corridor of the U.S. Townes received her appointment from Secretary Ridge while she was serving as the Deputy United States Attorney for the Southern District of New York, marking a pivotal step in her career. Ridge was in search of an individual capable of establishing an enforcement arm within the NSC, one that would effectively translate policy into action. He required a leader with a prosecutorial background who possessed the unique ability to communicate effectively with both law enforcement and intelligence operatives. Jan was the ideal candidate for this role.

Quinlan exited the OEOB heading towards the West Wing when he spotted Lana Miller on West Executive Avenue. This bustling thoroughfare, often teeming with pedestrians and occasional vehicle traffic, serves as the boundary between the OEOB and the West Wing. Lana was engrossed in conversation with another council member, clutching a leather-bound portfolio. Deciding to catch her attention, John positioned himself within her line of sight. Almost instantly, Lana noticed him and greeted him with a warm smile. She moved towards him, pulling him into a heartfelt hug. She said, "How are you, my friend? We meet in the coolest places, don't ya think?"

Smiling ear to ear, John replied, "We certainly do," By now he had lost his normally reserved Secret Service agent composure. "What are the odds that our worlds would somehow align again?" he asked.

"It's meaningful, I think, don't you?" she asked.

"I do, Lana, I really do. Hey, I see you have a temporary T pass which will give you only limited White House access for now. We need to get you your permanent pass," he said.

"I just came from access control, and they said a review of my file needs to be completed before getting the proper credentials."

"I can help you with that. That's what I do now!"

During their lunch at the OEOB dining hall, John and Lana had a chance to catch up on the cases she had worked on in New York since his departure. Lana recounted her experiences working alongside Jan Townes as a legal advisor and her recent transition to a new role at the White House, specifically within the NSC. Amused and intrigued, John shared that he, too, would be joining the council. Lana also mentioned her new townhome in Alexandria, VA. She expressed excitement for beginning anew in the very bubble she warned John about at his going away party a few years ago. They agreed to meet for lunch again and, schedules permitting, possibly for dinner, eager to continue reconnecting.

Upon returning to his newly assigned office in Room 23, Quinlan was greeted by a hefty stack of files on his desk. These were the comprehensive FBI background checks for individuals seeking permanent White House and presidential access, pending clearance reviews for top-level administrative officials. A chuckle escaped him as he noticed Lana's file within the pile. He floated that file to the top and opened it for review. He paused. He realized his job was to go through each file meticulously, judging suitability for close access to the President. Each file contained the same completed SF-86 form he had to complete for a top-secret security clearance. The file would contain the official's whole life in the form of an FBI agent's background investigation. Their entire life, both personal and professional, was condensed into a single folder. Yet, within that folder lay concealed every aspect, both the good and the bad, of their being. Quinlan shut the file and carried it over to his group leader, William Gonzalez.

"Willie, could you take a look at this one for me?" Quinlan requested.

Willie grinned, "I noticed you and Ms. Miller together on West Executive Avenue earlier today, and then again in the dining hall." With a knowing smile, he added, "Perhaps it's best I handle this review. I'll pass it back to you for the final sign-off."

"Thanks, Willie," Quinlan expressed his gratitude. He was eager to learn all about Lana Miller, but he preferred to hear it directly from her, rather than through the impersonal lines of an FBI dossier. He marveled at how quickly he'd encountered a moral gray area in his new role, thinking, it's only been a week, and I'm already navigating the complexities that seem to find me.

CHAPTER 33

Taken

"Nothing external to you has any power over you."
—Ralph Waldo Emerson

Tara had slept the night at her own home in Old Town. She knew she would never see this place again. Today would be the day she accompanied Patrick to Seoul, North Korea. The week leading up to this trip was hectic. Patrick was excited about his trip and Phillip was nervous and sad he was leaving. This would be the first time Patrick would be away from his dad for any length of time. Feeling selfish Phillip realized this would also be a transformative journey for himself as he must relive the sense of absence and the emptiness that comes with it. He paused those emotions to remember how much Tara has become a part of his and Patrick's life. *This is a good thing,* he thought, *Patrick will be immersed in a new culture and taken under the wing of his hosts. He will be in the excellent and loving hands of Tara all the way to Seoul.* Phillip was falling in love with Tara and her endearing journey with Patrick made him love her even more.

Akma Deja made sure there would be no missteps during this part of the operation. Once Tara's uncle during the border crossing, Wei Chan now served as her Triad handler. In his current role, he embodied courtesy and professionalism as the chauffeur for Gold Signature Limo Service. During their conversation the previous night, Tara had casually informed Phillip that she had arranged transportation to the airport, intending to surprise Patrick with a stylish journey. As the Cadillac

Escalade rolled up to Phillip's house, Tara, bubbling with anticipation, eagerly stepped inside, her excitement palpable.

Phillip helped Patrick with his luggage, trying to match the enthusiasm his son felt for the upcoming journey. He was fulfilling both his and his late wife's dream for Patrick to experience living abroad. They wanted him to see the world and embrace its opportunities.

In the modest foyer of their home, Phillip and Patrick met Tara and were greeted by the sight of the awaiting Escalade.

Phillip turned to Tara and said, "What have you done?"

Unbeknownst to him, these words would reverberate in his mind with mounting anguish in the days to come. He would gradually uncover the truth about Tara's role in the kidnapping scheme, repeatedly revisiting the phrase like a haunting refrain.

In two days, Tara's house in Old Town Alexandria would be thoroughly cleared of any remaining belongings. The Triad team would meticulously scrub and disinfect every corner, ensuring that all traces of her presence were eradicated.

Tara and Patrick stepped out of the Escalade, the moderate morning breeze hitting them as they approached the bustling drop-off area at Dulles Airport. The sound of suitcases rolling across the pavement echoed through the busy terminal.

"Thanks' for the ride," Tara said as she made eye contact with Chan. "The tip is included on the credit card."

The Escalade pulled away, leaving them standing in front of the imposing airport entrance. They turned towards the curbside Sky Cap and waited in the first of many lines that day. The Sky Cap tagged their bags, securing them for their journey. Tara was now trying to shake the anticipation building within her. She made a space for herself in Phillip's world so she could take Patrick to Akma Deja. *Killing a wife and mother was the hard part, this is the easy part,* she would say to herself. *Stay focused. This is for the cause.* Was there some apprehension building up? Maybe the same apprehension that caused her to swerve and miss an innocent jogger with a baby in a running stroller that day? The same day she took the life of Patrick's mother. She dismissed any sense of self-doubt. "It was for the cause," a phrase she would repeat to herself against her self-doubt. Changing her thoughts, she checked her watch while their bags disappeared on the conveyer.

"We've got some time before our flight. Want to grab a coffee?" Patrick nodded and they went inside the terminal.

Meanwhile, Phillip was deep into his Monday routine. The Escalade's departure coincided with the start of his workday. He had already left for the Bureau of Engraving and Printing where his responsibilities now included oversight of quality control for currency reproduction.

The Monday morning meeting loomed, a crucial session that always seemed to set the tone for the week. He took his responsibilities seriously, especially when inspecting the craftsmanship of the plates used in currency production. Akma Deja would soon be counting on Phillip to focus on her own currency manufacturing product line. He would eventually be compelled to help with her cause.

The long flight to Seoul proved uneventful for Patrick. He passed the hours engrossed in movies he had downloaded onto his iPad, finding solace in the cinematic distraction. Meanwhile, Tara remained steadfast, her attention consumed by the intricacies of the next phase of their plan. In the hushed hum of the cabin, her mind buzzed with anticipation. Her thoughts switched to the little girl who was once nine years old. *Stop she said stop,* a small trick to keep her from going to the vivid place where her parents took their last breath. She moved her thoughts to Phillip. He was a kind and patient lover. For it to be her first time with him as a virgin would be out of the character created for Tara. Akma Deja even thought of that. She removed her virginity before her crossing to America. It was painful and nothing more than a necessary task completed with the assistance of Deja's male companion. As she pondered Phillip's patience, she drifted off to sleep.

After a brief layover at the San Francisco International Airport the plane touched down at Incheon International Airport in Seoul, South Korea.

Patrick felt a mix of excitement and nervousness as he stepped out of the airport terminal, the crisp air of a new country hitting him. Tara stood by his side, a familiar face in this foreign land. The van that would take him to the Seoul National University campus awaited him curbside. He noticed a man holding a sign, 'Shuttle—National University of Korea.'

Tara's reminder about calling his uncle resonated with Patrick. He appreciated the concern, knowing it was a thoughtful gesture from someone who had become a comforting presence in his life.

"Thanks, Tara. I'll make that call once we get settled," Patrick replied, a genuine smile breaking across his face. He felt a sense of gratitude for Tara's companionship during the journey, and her reminder about his uncle was a testament to the caring bond they had formed.

As they leaned in for a warm embrace, Patrick said, "I'll catch you for lunch on Tuesday, right after I get things sorted out at the dorms."

Tara nodded, her eyes reflecting mixed feelings knowing the upcoming lunch would be the beginning of a dark and harrowing journey for Patrick. She blocked the thought, "Absolutely, Patrick. Just focus on getting yourself registered and settled in. Have fun and take in the experience."

With those words of encouragement, they parted ways temporarily. Patrick headed towards the waiting shuttle, while Tara made her way to her own transportation. The adventure at Seol National University was about to begin, and Patrick couldn't help but feel a surge of anticipation for the new chapter unfolding in his life. Tara's visit on Tuesday would change all of that.

After she saw Patrick leave in the awaiting shuttle bus, Tara was met by two members of Akma Deja's security team. Their demeanor serious and efficient. They greeted Tara with a nod, and without exchanging a word, they guided her toward a discreet vehicle that would transport her to the apartment rented under an alias.

Once inside the vehicle, the security team briefed her on the abduction plan that would take place in two days' time. The atmosphere was tense, and every word spoken was measured. The plan was laid out with precision, detailing the sequence of events, potential obstacles, and contingencies. Tara, though experienced in her line of work, couldn't shake the gravity of the situation.

The apartment, a temporary refuge, provided a covert space for her to wait as the plan unfolded. The security team ensured the surroundings were secure, leaving her to go over the details in her mind. The strain of the mission pressed upon her, she convinced herself the hard part is over. A refrain she would repeat several more times.

As she reviewed the plan, Tara couldn't help but wonder about Patrick and his experiences on campus. The stark difference between their situations was a reminder of the delicate balance she maintained between her personal life and her covert assignment. The apartment, with its nondescript exterior, shielded Tara from prying eyes as she prepared for the imminent operation that would alter the course of events for both her and Patrick.

As Patrick settled into his new life on campus, the anticipation of the exchange program mingled with the lingering uncertainty about his father being alone. He spoke with Uncle Jimmy on two occasions. The phone calls with him had been informative yet somewhat odd because it seemed dad had not shared much about Tara with him.

During one of the phone conversations, Uncle Jimmy expressed support for his father's decision to move on but admitted, "Your dad didn't go into much detail about Tara. I reckon he's still grappling with the idea of dating again. It's good he has someone like her, especially to accompany you to Seoul. What can you tell me about her?"

Patrick hesitated for a moment, processing his own limited knowledge about Tara. "Well, she's been a great friend during this whole journey to Seoul. Dad met her at work and they spend a lot of time together. She's been really helpful and supportive. She's got this lively energy, and we've had some good laughs together. Dad seems to trust her a lot."

Uncle Jimmy chuckled, "Sounds like she's made an impression on you already. Your dad deserves to be happy, and if Tara brings joy to his life, that's a good thing. Just make sure she's looking out for you, too. And hey, when you have the chance, try to get to know her a bit better. It might put your dad at ease, you know?"

Taking Uncle Jimmy's advice to heart, Patrick resolved to learn more about Tara. Despite any lingering concern for his father and the upcoming exchange program, he couldn't help but feel grateful for Tara's presence in their lives and this unfamiliar city.

Patrick listened to Tara's voicemail with a smile, her enthusiasm for the day was contagious. He quickly texted her back, confirming the meeting spot and expressing his anticipation. The light blue Honda minivan arrived at the campus, and Patrick, standing by the fountain as instructed, eagerly watched for Tara's familiar face.

As the van pulled up, Tara waved from the front seat passenger window, a grin lighting up her face. Patrick felt a sense of ease at her welcoming gesture. He approached the van, its doors sliding open to reveal the interior where Tara's cousins sat.

"Hey, Patrick! Meet my cousins," Tara said with a cheerful introduction. The atmosphere in the van was lively as introductions were exchanged. The cousins, eager to include Patrick in their plans, greeted him warmly.

Patrick took a seat. The prospect of lunch, sightseeing, and spending time with Tara's family added a touch of normalcy to his new life in Seoul. As the van set off, conversation and laughter filled the air, creating a sense of camaraderie that temporarily overshadowed the covert missions and hidden agendas that lurked in the background of Tara's life. Little did Patrick know that the events of this day would become a pivotal point in the unfolding drama that connected their worlds in unexpected ways. As the conversation in the van waned, one of the men reached over with a damp cloth. Patrick caught a whiff of a chemical scent just before feeling a sharp prick in his thigh. The drive to Akma Deja's compound would take at least four hours.

* * *

As the young student regained consciousness, a dull throbbing in his head mirrored the disorienting haze that clouded his senses. Unbeknownst to him, he had been drugged and unconscious for five hours. Blinking against the harsh artificial light, he found himself confined within what appeared to be a dormitory-style cell. Cold metal walls pressed in around him, and the air held a clinical, antiseptic scent.

His hands reached but only found an unfamiliar surface beneath him. It was a thin, unyielding mattress. The room's only features were a small desk bolted to the wall and a solitary chair, both stark and impersonal. The lack of windows intensified the feeling of isolation.

Attempting to make sense of the situation, his memories flickered like distant shadows. A shadowy band of faceless men, the prick of a needle—fragments of a bewildering puzzle. Fear crept through him as he realized the seriousness of his predicament. Why had they subdued him? What the hell had he stumbled upon?

The door to the cell remained locked, a seamless length of metal with no visible handle or mechanism. Panic began to claw at the edges of his consciousness, but he forced himself to focus. Observing his surroundings more closely, he noticed a small intercom embedded in the wall.

Summoning courage, he pressed the button, the cold surface yielding slightly to his touch. A crackling voice emanated from the intercom, "You're awake, I see. Welcome to Akma Deja's containment facility. Your questions will be answered in due time."

The cryptic message offered little solace, and the young student's mind churned with apprehension. Hours passed in uneasy silence, punctuated only by the sterile hum of unseen machinery. Eventually, a mechanical whir signaled the unlocking of the door.

As it swung open, a group of stern-faced individuals accompanied by a woman clad in black attire stood outside.

The woman spoke, "I am Akma Deja, and you are Patrick O'Donovan." She then turned around and gestured for him to follow. The young student hesitated for a moment, a flicker of defiance in his eyes, but the unwavering gazes of the security personnel left him with no choice.

He rose abruptly, perhaps too hastily, only to slump back onto the bed. His head still throbbed from whatever drug continued to course through his system. He tried again slowly. Stepping into the sterile corridor, he wondered about the secrets concealed within the confines of this facility. The journey ahead promised answers, but with every step, the shadows of uncertainty clung to him like a haunting specter.

Patrick felt a cold shiver down his spine as he was led into the larger cell, the stench of decay assaulting his senses. The dim light barely revealed the damp and squalid conditions that surrounded him. The two-way glass added an element of mystery, leaving him unaware of the ominous presence on the other side.

Inside the cell, the air was heavy with tension, and the oppressive atmosphere seemed to cling to him like a suffocating cloak. Patrick could scarcely fathom the horrors that awaited him within what he would soon discover was a notorious political prison camp. The distant cries and muffled whispers that echoed through the narrow corridors served as a chilling reminder of the desolation that engulfed his surroundings.

Little did Patrick know, on the other side of the two-way glass, Tara Lee observed him in silence. As Patrick tried to make sense of the situation, he couldn't shake the feeling of being watched.

Tara Lee's eyes widened in horror as Akma Deja cruelly forced her to witness the brutal treatment of Patrick. The sounds of the vicious beating echoed through the cold, damp cell, sending chills down Tara Lee's spine. The vivid brutality unfolding before her eyes made her stomach churn, and she struggled to maintain composure.

The realization struck Tara Lee like a bolt of lightning. This was the same horrifying spectacle that some forgotten nine-year-old girl had endured, watching her parents being executed. The cruel symmetry of the situation weighed heavily on Tara Lee's conscience, forcing her to confront the unimaginable cruelty that occurred within the confines of the Yodok Political Prison Camp.

Akma Deja, seemingly devoid of any remorse, stood impassively beside Tara Lee, watching the sadistic scene unfold. The two security team members took turns punching and kicking the defenseless teenager. They continued their merciless assault on Patrick, leaving him battered and broken. Tara Lee's eyes filled with tears as she witnessed the brutality, unable to intervene. The video cameras in the room recorded the entire spectacle.

As the harrowing scene played out, the atmosphere in the cell became suffocating, each strike resonating as a cruel reminder of the merciless regime that governed the lives of those trapped within the confines of the prison camp. The silence that followed was heavy with the severity of shared trauma, and Tara Lee couldn't shake the haunting images etched into her memory.

* * *

As the sun dipped below the horizon in Old Town Alexandria, Phillip was easing into yet another evening without Patrick and Tara. The silence was more than he preferred, yet there was comfort in knowing Patrick was abroad, living out his and his late wife Annie's dream for him—to gain a full education while enriching his life experiences. Just as Phillip settled deeper into his thoughts, a knock at the front door interrupted the quiet. Feeling uneasy, Phillip approached the door and peered through the side glass of the threshold, spotting two Asian men, one of whom was carrying a computer satchel. He hesitantly opened the door, and one of the men immediately relayed that they had news about his son, Patrick. Compelled by concern, Phillip stepped outside to listen. The men revealed they had his son and insisted on coming inside. Overwhelmed and torn, Phillip's initial instinct was to return inside and slam the door shut, secure it, and call 911. But the mention of his son's name halted him. Reluctantly, he allowed the two men into his home. The two Triad members were integral to Akma Deja's plan, each compensated generously for their roles in the next phase of her operation.

Once inside Phillip's home, one of the men retrieved a laptop from the satchel and placed it on a nearby table. Tension filled the room as Phillip braced himself, his anxiety mounting as he awaited what was to come.

The video displayed a chilling scene of his son being beaten and tortured by two men. The gruesome images unfolded on the screen, while the two Triads watched impassively, their faces displayed a lack of emotion. The brutal beating went on for nearly fifteen minutes, though to Phillip it felt much longer. He was frozen in place, overwhelmed by the harrowing realization of the extent of Patrick's suffering.

"Is this some kind of sick joke?" he managed to stammer out.

"No joke," replied one of the Triads coldly. "If you want to see your son alive, you'll take the contents of this envelope and prepare for a trip to Seoul, South Korea."

The other Triad then added, "Pack an overnight bag and come with us. We're on the 11:00 pm flight out of Dulles."

Phillip pulled the contents out of the envelope. It was a one-way plane ticket to Seoul, South Korea.

"When we reach Seoul," the Triad thug said, "you'll be reunited with your son, and all will become clear," he instructed.

Phillip, driven by panic, dropped the envelope and dashed toward the bedroom to grab his cellphone, aiming to barricade himself and call for help. However, before he could secure himself in the bedroom one of the Triad enforcers tackled him to the ground. The enforcer's voice was cold and firm as he warned, "Your actions are understandable, but this trip is unavoidable. Try something like that again, and I will kill you, and your son will rot in a Korean prison camp."

Phillip broke down in tears, perplexed and alarmed. He grasped the severity of the situation, and fully realized the urgency at hand. The ominous presence of the two large men along with the airline ticket hinted at the perilous journey ahead. He began to comprehend that the circumstances surrounding Patrick's captivity were far more intricate than he had initially imagined.

With a heavy heart and a mind racing with fear and determination, Phillip O'Donovan prepared himself for the journey. The heavy-handed escort, undoubtedly a menacing presence, awaited to usher him into a world of uncertainty. The distance of 6,500 miles felt like an insurmountable chasm, but he needed to be with his son, and this propelled him forward.

Phillip couldn't shake the haunting images of Patrick's suffering from his mind. The magnitude of the situation bore down on him heavily. Departing from Dulles International Airport that night, it seemed as if Phillip had vanished into thin air. The Triads' careful orchestration and ominous presence made any attempt by Phillip to reach out to friends, family, or authorities a perilous endeavor. Questions swirled in his mind: Who was behind this? Where was Tara? He recalled the phone conversations from the days following her and Patrick's arrival in Seoul, when he spoke with Tara every morning and evening. His last contact with Patrick was on Tuesday morning, discussing lunch plans with Tara and her cousins. It was all too overwhelming to process for now.

CHAPTER 34

Perfecting the APEX Note

Akma Deja received a comprehensive briefing on the incidents that occurred at Phillip O'Donovan's residence in Alexandria, VA. O'Donovan, upon witnessing the harrowing torture his son endured, was fully prepared to journey to Seoul. Indeed, he was already in route with her security team providing the necessary escort. "O'Donovan must refrain from contacting anyone from this point forward," were her orders to her security team.

She had already outlined the plan for him to complete what her father had started. She would leverage the release of his son against refining the APEX $100.00 note. This, she thought, would ensure the longevity of her late father's scheme to undermine the American economy. They would flood the world with the unmistakable worthless currency. He dubbed it death by a thousand cuts. He would explain to his daughter that she needed to complete the plan. She would siphon the lifeblood from the capitalist stronghold of America. In this orchestrated economic erosion, their wealth would lose its purpose, rendering them unrecognizable as the colossal financial giants they professed to be. The U.S. economy would be destroyed.

* * *

Lying on the frigid cement floor, Patrick writhed in pain from the beating he endured. Transported onto a gurney, he returned to the room of his initial captivity. Akma Deja's doctor examined him, detecting signs of impending shock. With Patrick's life hanging in the balance, she issued a dire threat against any potential loss. Urgent measures were taken as he underwent treatment, tethered to life support for the next critical twenty-four hours.

* * *

Phillip O'Donovan grappled with his muddled thoughts, his mind still reeling from the shock of the video he saw of his son being beaten. Held captive and flanked by imposing escorts, he struggled to focus amidst the fight-or-flight response consuming him. The flight from Dulles Airport to Seoul, with a brief stop in San Francisco, offered no reprieve as answers eluded him, leaving his mind fixated on Patrick.

As the plane touched down in San Francisco, jolting him back to consciousness, Phillip contemplated slipping away and reaching out for help. The instinct to call Uncle Jimmy surged through him; he needed someone to know about this ordeal. However, his bargaining thoughts were halted by the stark reality—he had no money, no phone, stripped of everything useful. The nameless captors made it clear that any deviation from the plan would result in Patrick's brutal fate.

The plane resumed its journey to Seoul, and Phillip's mind raced with unprecedented anxiety. He pondered whether the Bureau of Engraving and Printing would involve the police. His expertise in a critical field for America added a layer of concern—would this jeopardize Patrick's safety? Thoughts of Annie, his beloved wife, flooded his mind. The inability to protect her and now Patrick weighed heavily on his conscience.

With his mind spiraling, Phillip considered reaching out to Tara Lee. He even questioned her role in the unfolding crisis. *Could that have been her voice on the video?* he thought. *The voice on the video, however, belonged to an older woman. Shit I don't know what to believe anymore.* Desperate and uncertain, he wondered, *What would Annie do in this situation?*

After what seemed like an interminable flight, the plane finally touched down again. This time in Seoul, South Korea. Phillip

O'Donovan was guided through the bustling terminal and directed to a waiting van. Once seated inside, he wrestled against a damp cloth pressed to his face. He detected a chemical odor and felt an unexpected prick in his thigh. Gradually, his consciousness faded away.

* * *

When Phillip regained awareness, he found himself in a windowless room. A voice over a speaker welcomed him to Camp 15 in North Korea. Soon after, the door opened, revealing an Asian woman in her late thirties accompanied by two security officers. In her hand, she held a remote control, directing it towards a monitor displaying Patrick in what appeared to be a hospital room. Patrick was connected to an EKG monitor, receiving oxygen, and on IV fluids. He was badly bruised and had several bandaged lacerations.

"I know this is confusing for you. You feel groggy and out of sorts. I assure you that is your son, Patrick, and he is being well taken care of. We needed you to come. It is unfortunate what we had to do to Patrick. You came and now that is over with," the woman said.

Phillip attempted to speak, but she interrupted, "I need you to listen for now, only listen. You can call me Akma Deja. If you do exactly as I say, everything will go back to normal in your life. Do you understand?" Phillip nodded, his heart heavy with concern for Patrick and a sinking realization that his life had taken a dark turn.

"How are you feeling?" she inquired of Phillip.

"I'm scared and deeply concerned for my son. Where is Tara? Why am I here? What do you want? I'm willing to do anything, just please give me a chance to bring him home safely. I want my life back...," Phillip implored.

Interrupting him once more, she asked, "Can you stand and walk with me?"

He stood up slowly. As they moved, one security man led the way while the other flanked them. They entered a spacious factory equipped with printing presses. A workbench showcased familiar items—engraved plates revealing $100 U.S. currency images. An older Asian man operated a press, actively printing sheets of $100 federal reserve notes, indicating an intricate counterfeiting operation. Shelves stacked with paper rolls and ink bins in the corner emitted the same ink scent Phillip recognized from the Bureau of Engraving and Printing. Slow to process it all, he attributed his foggy state to the sedative wearing off.

"I need you to be alert. You've been sedated for several hours," Akma Deja explained, underscoring the urgency of the situation.

She summoned the man standing near the printing press. She conversed with him in Korean.

"This is the Socialist Republic of North Korea master engraver, Huan Jung So. He has been the engraver for the entire time of my father's reign as Supreme Leader. He has been making your currency since the early 1990s. You are aware of this, no?"

Phillip, slowly understanding what might be happening, said, "Of course. We call it the APEX note, if that's truly what this is. The APEX is very good, but it's not perfect. The note enjoys good circulation, but it is always eventually identified as counterfeit and pulled out when it reaches the federal reserve."

"You understand then why you are here. You will make this note perfect," she said with a sense of entitled confidence.

Phillip, looking startled, replied, "You've got to be fucking kidding me! Is that what this is about? This is about me perfecting your counterfeiting operation," he said incredulously. We had some idea that a rogue country was behind this because the note was that good, but I'll be damned if I am going to be the one that...," and just like that, Phillip remembered where he was and what was at stake.

She finished his thought, "Yes, you will examine the plates, point out the imperfections, and fix them. You will train our printer to manufacture the perfect $100.00 note."

"I'm willing to comply if you allow me to see my son," he pleaded.

Time pressed on, especially with her naive brother on the verge of granting access to U.N. Inspectors in less than three months, exposing her counterfeiting operation. Her plan to relocate the operation to Belfast, Ireland, had already been set in motion. The logistics were orchestrated by her soulless British traitor, Stansfield Anderson. For the moment, however, she would accommodate a certain father's request.

Phillip received a twenty-minute reprieve with Patrick. Although he felt better, a sense of disorientation lingered. Questions swirled in his mind, yet he struggled to articulate them coherently. Phillip did all the talking but was prohibited from divulging the plan or its purpose. His role was confined to offering comfort and ensuring that all would be well. Patrick was able to grasp his dad's hand. It made all the difference for Phillip. That slight touch made him want to get them out of there at all costs.

* * *

The following morning, Phillip meticulously examined the expertly crafted currency plates. They bore the unmistakable mark of a master engraver, precision evident in every detail. Requesting a magnification loop and a microscope, he already knew precisely where to focus his scrutiny on the note. The BEP and the Secret Service had long been laboring to trace the origin of the APEX counterfeit note. They already were aware of its imperfections. In a fleeting instant, his undivided focus fixated on the present. His gaze shifted to the plate responsible for generating countless near perfect \$100 counterfeit bills. A challenge that had tormented the BEP and the Secret Service for years. The pursuit of truth demanded countless hours of investigation and careful analysis. Now, ironically, Phillip found himself at the heart of the operation, compelled to perfect it under the metaphorical threat of a gun to his head.

As he scrutinized the note printed earlier in the day, Phillip, aided by the loop, identified the few imperfections he had known about. They were located in the upper right-hand quadrant. These imperfections manifested as bloating; an excessive depth carved on the plate that caused the lines to appear heavier when printed. Another imperfection, more elusive, demanded the precision of a microscope. Carefully examining the lower left quadrant, he spotted the microscopic line that deviated from the patterns of all other lines.

Raising his gaze from the table, Phillip addressed an array of spectators, with Akma Deja among them. "The plates you are using cannot be fixed; your engraver will need to recreate new ones with the corrections I will point out to him."

She seemed satisfied and requested a briefing with the engraver present. O'Donovan disclosed the imperfections, both on the actual note and on the plate. The engraver worked tirelessly through the night, with Phillip by his side. In one additional day, the time it would take the plates to cure, they would be ready for use. Phillip sought another visit with his son. However, he had to settle for a monitor in his room, providing a live feed to Patrick as he continued his recovery.

The moment arrived when the plates were completed and affixed to the printing press. Phillip marveled at the quality of the cotton/linen blend paper they produced in-house. Even noting the correct amount of red and blue fibers embedded in the uncut spool. His focus was solely on finishing this task to be reunited with Patrick. By day's end, they had amassed close to a half a million dollars in uncut sheets that convincingly resembled genuine United States currency. Phillip knew these would soon be cut and introduced into the economy, but he couldn't grasp the full ramifications of this reckless act against the freedom of his son. It felt almost like an act of war, and he was emotionally drained. Despite the uncertainty in his life, regaining control and bringing his son back became his solace.

Akma Deja delivered the grim news. Neither he nor his son would be leaving North Korea anytime soon. It was during this revelation that

Akma Deja disclosed her relationship with his uncle. She recounted the entire story of how Professor James O'Donovan embraced her brother as a student. How this led to a romantic relationship between her and the professor. She explained how Uncle Jimmy would accompany her brother, the Supreme Leader, to a private White House ceremony, signifying the commencement of the next phase of her plan.

She had dispatched the initial set of perfected APEX notes to Stansfield 'Stig' Anderson in Belfast. He had explicit instructions to place the $500,000 in counterfeit $100 bills into the Northern Bank of Ireland account under the name of James O'Donovan. As she reflected on the situation, she couldn't help but pity the oblivious professor. Unbeknownst to him, substantial amounts of counterfeit currency had flowed through his bank account. Stig's cunning schemes had significantly enriched James, especially through the profitable sales of Ukrainian secrets to Russian intelligence. These funds were also laundered through the professor's bank account. However, James O'Donovan remained blissfully ignorant of the fraud committed against his bank account or the clandestine operations unfolding within his financial sphere.

CHAPTER 35

Iftar Dinner

During Monday morning's National Security Council Enforcement meeting, chaired by Deputy National Security Advisor (DNSA) Jan Townes, the topic of access control at the White House was raised. Typically, Supervisory Special Agent (SSA) John Quinlan would spearhead discussions on such matters, but Townes felt the need to intervene on this occasion. As the discussion unfolded, Townes cited information sharing as a unique challenge that required immediate attention.

"The sharing of information between our intelligence agencies and Room 23 is of paramount concern," she would say. Without hesitation, she shared her insights and suggestions, showcasing her deep understanding of the complex access control dynamics at the White House. This unexpected contribution demonstrated Townes' keen awareness and expertise in the field, leaving Quinlan impressed.

Their collaboration grew increasingly seamless as they navigated the complex web of security measures and access protocols essential for the White House's safety. Their shared responsibilities brought them closer, forming a formidable professional alliance. Together, they addressed access-related issues with a blend of creativity, expertise, and a touch of camaraderie that defined their efforts in Room 23.

As the mutual partnership between SSA Quinlan and DNSA Townes progressed, Quinlan began to notice a recurring issue with the FBI's handling of information. Specifically, there was a lack of timely communication when individuals on the FBI's Violent Gang and Terrorist Offender File (VGTOF) sought entry to the White House. This raised significant concerns for Quinlan, as it compromised the security protocols in place.

Frustrated with the apparent oversight, he faced a dilemma. He didn't want to appear as if he were complaining, but the safety of the White House and its occupants was paramount. The secretive nature of the FBI's lists added an additional layer of complexity to the situation. Quinlan knew he needed to address the issue diplomatically, finding a way to improve communication without straining the working relationship with the FBI.

In discussions with Townes, he sought to develop a strategy to bridge the communication gap. Together, they explored avenues to streamline information flow between the FBI and Quinlan's office. His proactive approach demonstrated his commitment to overcoming challenges and maintaining the highest standards of security. He aimed to find a resolution that would strengthen their joint efforts in safeguarding the White House and this was all about to be put to the test.

The upcoming annual Iftar dinner held considerable political and cultural significance for the President and his administration. This was primarily due to the persistently strained relations between the U.S. and the largely Muslim Middle East. This yearly occasion consistently served as a constructive outreach to the Muslim world. Quinlan, at the helm of Room 23, knew that ensuring the security of such a high-profile gathering, especially in the post-9/11 era, was paramount.

The specific vetting process for the invitees was a routine part of his responsibilities. The White House Social Office, charged with identifying esteemed members of the Muslim community, collaborated closely with Room 23 to perform thorough background checks. The information provided by the invitees underwent rigorous scrutiny. The deadline was set two months prior to the event to allow ample time for a thorough vetting.

The Iftar dinner garnered substantial funds and was considered a standout event within Washington DC circles. Attendance costs fluctuated based on several factors, and the proceeds from the event were directed towards supporting diverse charitable initiatives.

The invitees would provide their biographical information, typically their date of birth, place of birth, social security number or passport number to the social office. They, in turn, would then forward it on to Room 23 for vetting. Quinlan established a rule with the staff that the deadline for submitting the particulars for the Iftar dinner would be one month out to ensure proper and thorough criminal and intelligence background checks.

On this occasion, the list was reviewed, and aside from typical DUIs and minor misdemeanor charges, there were no alerts barring access to the White House and the Iftar dinner. Quinlan found this unusual because in the past, individuals on FBI, CIA, or even NSA watch lists would trigger actions to exclude them from the event. On those few occasions, the staff would retract invitations to such individuals due to safety concerns for the President and all attendees. A senior staff member would discreetly inform the disinvited person or their assistant without providing further explanation. Quinlan appreciated the rigorous security screening process for anyone entering the White House grounds. This measure significantly reduced the risk of physical threats. However, there still existed the potential for embarrassment to the President and his team by allowing access to uninvited or potentially problematic individuals. Such incidents could be exploited by the media for prolonged periods.

Quinlan poured over the list of forty-five attendees to the Iftar dinner and saw a name that stood out—James O'Donovan. A departure from the typical Muslim names, it caught his attention for reasons beyond the surface. Determined to ensure the safety and integrity of the Iftar dinner, he swiftly issued orders to his intelligence research specialist in Room 23, emphasizing the urgency of a deep dive into O'Donovan's background.

Intelligence Specialist Clair Daniels uncovered potential FBI scrutiny regarding money laundering allegations. Furthermore, he had ties to the North Korean government and had recently been elected as a senior member of Sinn Féin. However, nothing more was available at the time. More importantly the FBI had not conveyed any of this information directly to Room 23. She relayed this information to Quinlan.

He absorbed the information with a mix of concern and intrigue. The revelation that James O'Donovan had been flagged by the FBI only added complexity to an already perplexing situation. The dual concerns of potential involvement in money laundering and ties to the North Korean government were unsettling, especially given O'Donovan's high-ranking position in Sinn Féin. This intel stemmed from Analyst Daniels' investigation with the Financial Crimes Enforcement Network (FinCEN). The report concluded by stating that FinCEN and Scotland Yard had informed the FBI's International Joint Terrorism Task Force of this information as standard protocol.

Quinlan acknowledged the gravity of the situation, realizing that this story had the potential to overshadow O'Donovan's role in Sinn Féin, which is considered to be the Irish Republican Army's new political landscape. The intersection of financial impropriety and dubious connections to North Korea created a narrative that went far beyond the typical guest list for the Iftar dinner.

Quinlan knew that navigating the delicate balance between security concerns, diplomatic considerations, and the potential political fallout required a nuanced approach. The unfolding narrative surrounding James O'Donovan had elevated the stakes. Room 23 would need to act judiciously to ensure the safety of the Iftar dinner while managing the broader implications of O'Donovan's background and affiliations.

Quinlan again inquired with the intelligence research specialist in Room 23, "Claire, check the notifications from the FBI again.

O'Donovan should have been flagged as being on the FBI's 'VGTOF' list as a person of interest. That should have prompted a call from them alerting us!"

"Two calls boss, we ran him twice in the system, we should have received two calls," proclaimed Intelligence Analyst Daniels.

Quinlan's frustration mounted as he realized that the FBI had not provided any information regarding O'Donovan's status in their databases. This was contrary to the established memorandum of understanding. Per the agreement, Room 23 was supposed to be promptly notified if someone on a terrorist watchlist was being screened by the Secret Service.

Upon further investigation, Quinlan discovered that O'Donovan was indeed present in the FBI's system, marked as a silent hit. This revelation raised a new set of questions and concerns. A silent hit meant that the FBI was aware O'Donovan was undergoing screening by the Secret Service for an event at the White House but had chosen not to notify the Secret Service.

Quinlan pondered the reasons behind the FBI's decision to keep this information under wraps. Was it a matter of ongoing investigations, national security considerations, or perhaps a complex web of diplomatic intricacies? Room 23 found themselves in a precarious situation, with the need to balance national security concerns against the potential risks posed by O'Donovan's presence at the Iftar dinner.

As Quinlan delved deeper into the mystery, he knew that untangling the web of motivations behind the FBI's silence was crucial. Room 23 would have to navigate the complexities of intelligence sharing and interagency cooperation to uncover the truth.

It was 7:30 pm and the event was to start at 8:00 pm. The Secret Service had already opened the line and started screening the attendees for the event. Quinlan quickly dispatched two of his agents that were already in their tuxedos to put eyes on O'Donovan and keep a loose surveillance on him.

Agent Quinlan reluctantly found himself in the office of White House Chief of Staff Andy Stevens. As he briefed Stevens on the situation surrounding James O'Donovan, he could feel the heat from the roaring fireplace behind him. He believed it was necessary to inform the Chief at this moment despite it being a judgment call. Stevens keenly sensed the urgency in Quinlan's demeanor.

Reacting promptly, Stevens stood up from behind his desk, fully aware of the possible importance of the situation. Addressing Quinlan, he remarked, "If O'Donovan is truly linked to North Korea and possibly engaged in money laundering, among other potential offenses, the consequences could extend widely and pose embarrassment for the administration."

The two men huddled in a room charged with tension, acknowledging the need for a strategic approach. They reached a consensus that, despite the concerns, O'Donovan would be allowed entry to the Iftar dinner. However, Stevens, with his political acumen, decided to take matters into his own hands. He proposed giving O'Donovan a personal tour of the White House, diverting attention from the main event where other guests interacted with the President.

Chief Stevens recognized the potential embarrassment and political fallout if O'Donovan's presence became a public spectacle. By offering a personal tour, he aimed to control the narrative, ensuring that the media focus remained on the positive aspects of the event and sparing the President and the administration from unnecessary scrutiny.

Quinlan agreed to the plan, knowing that O'Donovan would have undergone rigorous security screening before entering the White House grounds. As the fireplace continued to cast its warm glow, the two men finalized the details of a carefully orchestrated plan to navigate the delicate balance between national security concerns and political optics. The events of the Iftar dinner would unfold with a calculated dance. Each step aimed at preserving the integrity of the administration in the face of potential challenges. *How can this night get any crazier,* Quinlan thought to himself.

As the flow of guests formed a queue for entry into the White House, Quinlan received an urgent transmission through his radio from the Joint Operations Center (JOC). The message conveyed, "abnormal radiological levels had been detected upon the entry of a specific guest at the security checkpoint," instantly elevating the night's complexity. Reacting swiftly, he proceeded to the checkpoint where a Technical Security Officer had already singled out a guest for additional screening. Upon his arrival, Quinlan found that officers had isolated James O'Donovan, subjecting him to enhanced magnetometer screening. Not wishing to disclose his presence to O'Donovan just yet, Quinlan recognized that such a radiation spike might be indicative of medical treatment, possibly for an illness like cancer.

The relatively low levels of radioactivity made it improbable to consider it as an attempted radiological attack, akin to a dirty bomb. Adding to the puzzle, the FBI had failed to notify Room 23 that O'Donovan was on a watch list. Considering these factors, Quinlan made the pivotal choice to grant access. His decision to withhold information about potential FBI or CIA scrutiny from O'Donovan displayed Quinlan's strategic discretion, as he aimed to avoid tipping off any covert surveillance activities. The decision weighed heavily on his mind, as he delicately balanced security concerns with the necessity of keeping O'Donovan unaware of the scrutiny.

The Secret Service shift report logs reflected that the last guest had left the dinner and the White House at 11:05 pm. President Bryce and the First Lady, Helen Bryce were not big on parties and had returned to their private residence two floors up at about 10:00 pm. At 11:00 pm, Quinlan received a call from the Deputy National Security Advisor Jan Townes,

"John, what the fuck! My office tomorrow at 7:00 am," exclaimed DNSA Townes. It was at that moment Quinlan realized that Chief of Staff Stevens had conversed about the matter with DNSA Townes earlier in the evening.

Quinlan's phone buzzed again, this time with a message from Rickey Miller, the Secret Service supervisor from the Technical Security Division, stationed at the JOC. The message conveyed that the report on the radiological incident would be discussed in the National Security Council Enforcement meeting scheduled for Monday morning, and a copy was already accessible at the JOC. Realizing the significance of the situation, Quinlan made the decision to turn around and return to the White House promptly to examine the report. It became clear to him that the night would be long and challenging, consumed with unraveling the incident's details and preparing for the high stakes meeting ahead.

CHAPTER 36

Iftar Dinner Fallout

Back at the White House, Quinlan braced himself for the impending fallout from the previous night's Iftar dinner. Unable to shake off the significance of the looming consequences, he had spent the entire night at his office, opting for a few hours of sleep amidst the chaos. As he cautiously peered out onto the relatively deserted West Executive Avenue, he noted the early risers—the President's closest aides—already at work on this Saturday morning. Jan Townes' distinctive Mercedes 300 occupied its usual space, signaling her presence.

Familiar with the Olde Executive Office Building, Quinlan navigated the corridors with ease, taking advantage of shortcuts ingrained in his memory. His thoughts were consumed by the encounter he had just experienced with one of the uniformed Secret Service officers.

"Hey Q," Officer Ron Doty greeted him with a friendly smile and a hearty slap on the back. "Heading to see Ms. Townes? She's in a... well, let's just say a hurried mood!"

Quinlan inquired, "More hurried than usual?"

"Oh, yeah, and we all heard about what went down last night. It's not every day the Chief of Staff offers a guided tour of the White House to a high-rolling political donor. Rumor has it he didn't get within fifty feet of the old man."

Doty added, "The desk Sergeant outside the Chief of Staff's office overheard him talking on the phone to Ms. Townes around 11:00 pm last night and they discussed the details of the entire evening."

"Thanks, Ron. At least I have a better understanding of how this got her attention. I owe you, buddy," Quinlan acknowledged sheepishly, already putting some distance between himself and the officer, determined to face the challenges awaiting him in Jan Townes' office.

He approached her office door located on the third floor of the OEOB and the name plate to the right of the door indicated, "Janice Townes—Deputy National Security Advisor." Quinlan followed the familiar routine, securing his two cellphones in a lockbox just outside Townes' office. Leaning his chin on a cup device, he submitted to a retina scan, the audible click confirming the unlocking of the secure door. Her entire office was a Sensitive Compartmented Information Facility, known as a SCIF in the intelligence world. The stringent measures, including reinforced walls and ceilings, soundproofing materials, access controls, biometric scanners, and secure communication systems were all aimed to ward off unauthorized access. Eavesdropping and electronic surveillance would be a hard play in such a facility.

Entering the SCIF with practiced ease, Quinlan found Townes standing in front of her desk as she extended her hand. He responded with a steady handshake.

"Ms. Townes," he began, but his words were swiftly cut off.

"Seriously, John?!" Townes blurted out, setting the tone for a challenging morning. "John, call me Jan. How many times do I have to remind you that we work together, and it's Jan! Now, tell me whose judgment lapsed last night, causing the FBI to avoid playing ball."

Caught off guard by the informal address, Quinlan mentally reassured himself, *Calm down, you've got this. You did nothing wrong, but you have a lot to tell the deputy right now.*

He appreciated Jan Townes' inclusive use of us, extending beyond just the Secret Service. She was a true patriot on a mission to protect the country and the President.

"Where to start Ms., uh, Jan," Quinlan replied. He didn't want to lead an informed response by throwing the FBI under the bus. Townes realizing her initial question didn't offer much in the way of preventing that, initiated another line of questioning.

She continued. "I've heard the FBI's side of the story. After I spoke with Andy last night. Now I need yours."

Quinlan interjected, "Andy?"

"Sorry, Chief of Staff Andy Stevens. After speaking to him, I called Agent Bill Ross, who, as you know, is their representative to the NSC Enforcement group, to get his version of events."

He replied, "Well, I do know him, but not really. I'm too new to the council to have established a working relationship with him."

"Yeah, well, that seems obvious, doesn't it?" Townes remarked curtly. "Look, I told him to be in my office by 8 am, so before he gets here, tell me your version of events last night."

Quinlan embarked on a methodical explanation, choosing his words with care. "The FBI maintains a Violent Gang and Terrorist Offender File, also known as VGTOF, as part of its National Crime Information Center database, which we have access to. However,..."

Townes interjected, finishing his thought, "However, the FBI won't disclose the VGTOF list openly to the agency that is running the name. Instead, it sends a silent hit to their own agency, notifying them that a specific law enforcement agency is checking a name on that list. Am I right?"

"Yes," Quinlan affirmed, "and they can decide whether to notify that agency or not if such a hit exists. We didn't receive any communication from the FBI last night at all when we ran James O'Donovan's name and we ran his name twice. We could have MS-13 or Al-Qaeda meeting with any one of the 30,000 employees at the White House. We would detect every arrest and conviction listed on their rap sheet, but we wouldn't know if they were the subject of an intelligence related hit. That is unless the FBI contacts us to confirm their presence on their VGTOF list."

"It's an embarrassment to the White House and us," Townes echoed Quinlan's frustration and concern. "What can I do to help, John?"

"Jan, I understand that the VGTOF is subject to strict protocols put in place by the FBI. I get it; it contains highly sensitive information about individuals involved in violent gangs or terrorist activities. But this is the White House. They need to inform us every time they get a silent hit on a name we're vetting for entry."

"I agree," Townes concurred.

"Ma'am," he continued with a concerned tone. "I don't know if there's any connection or significance to this, or maybe it's just a coincidence..."

"What, John!" Townes exclaimed, eager for more information.

He began, "Our Technical Security Division officer working in the Joint Operations Center last night alerted me to the fact that at 7:47 pm, higher than normal radioactivity was detected at an entry checkpoint. "We suspect that O'Donovan had undergone medical treatment which triggered the alarm," he said.

DNSA Townes' jaw dropped, her face contorting into an expression that stayed with him. "You suspect?" she exclaimed. "You mean you didn't question him about the source of the radioactivity or even check if he had a medical waiver?"

Quinlan replied deliberately, "I can explain my actions and reasoning. At 7:47 pm last night, the radioactivity countermeasures were triggered at the checkpoint for the Iftar dinner. I spent hours comparing the video timestamps to the alarm alert time of 7:47 pm when O'Donovan passed through. There's no doubt he set off the alarm. I am aware that these alarms have gone off before at events with similar levels of radioactivity. In each case, the person showing contamination was isolated and interviewed. Every single time, with medical verification, it was found that the person was undergoing radiation treatment for medical reasons, usually cancer. However, I decided not to question him..."

Townes interrupted, "Why?" she exclaimed, throwing her hands in the air. "Is it just a coincidence that O'Donovan is undergoing radiation for cancer treatment and happens to be the same guy the FBI didn't want you to know was under investigation? So, you decided not to detain him because it might, what, tip him off to a government investigation?"

Quinlan hesitated, unsure if the question was rhetorical, but responded nonetheless, "Yes, it was my decision. I considered the slightly heightened radioactivity levels when he entered the White House and deemed them unthreatening. I chose to postpone any immediate action because I didn't know exactly what the FBI had on him and didn't want to draw attention to what seemed like a passive situation. These countermeasures are almost common knowledge, with stories about them on the internet so the FBI might have devised a plan. They would expect us to pull him out and interview him, but we didn't. It could have been their strategy to bypass notifying us about O'Donovan, so they could confirm his medical status. The state of his health is probably relevant to their investigation. If the bureau had conducted a HIPAA-compliant inquiry to obtain his medical status, O'Donovan would have been legally notified, alerting him that the FBI was investigating him."

Townes replied more calmly, "I see, so it was a judgment call on your part? Is it in the memorandum of understanding with the FBI that you would have to share this security alert with them?"

"Yes, if we interviewed O'Donovan about this specific alert and we knew he was under investigation by the FBI, we would be obligated to notify them," Quinlan answered. "Either way, Jan, regardless of the

FBI's reasoning for not informing us about O'Donovan, why is the FBI so concerned about O'Donovan's health? That's the real question."

Just then, Townes held up her hand. "Okay, okay, let's see what Ross has to say when he gets here in a few minutes. Wow, how did things get so screwed up? Alright, listen, John, I was up all-night thinking about your dilemma before hearing the facts as you just laid them out. Here's my thought."

Quinlan listened intently as Townes laid out her immediate plan to prevent similar issues in the future. She suggested omitting the details about the countermeasures and O'Donovan's health from the pending meeting with FBI Agent Ross. She wanted to focus on tightening the security protocols around Room 23. She believed that having a reliable and discreet intermediary from her office would be crucial to addressing any unforeseen access issues. Quinlan, intrigued by the proposal, agreed to the idea. Understanding the sensitivity of the matter, he welcomed the added layer of coordination. Townes would assign her new legal advisor, Lana Miller, as the liaison between Room 23 and her office.

Townes explained that Lana was quickly becoming familiar to the complexities of Washington's political landscape. With a sharp legal mind and a knack for discretion, she was the perfect candidate to serve as the intermediary. Townes had been briefing Lana on the intricacies of Room 23 and its importance in White House affairs. It was not apparent to Townes that Lana's involvement with Quinlan went beyond their tenure at the White House. She was not aware they had a working relationship that went back almost ten years when she was prosecuting his cases in New York City. Townes was definitely unaware of any personal history between John and Lana, or even the possibility of one developing.

Their paths had crossed on many occasions it seemed and yet a new connection had been forming that transcended their professional lives. Quinlan was excited with the prospect of working with Lana again as she was quite adept at navigating conflict. He offered his sincere approval to Townes and expressed his gratitude for the needed assistance.

Since it was Saturday morning, Jan Townes' assistant was noticeably absent from her desk. In the corridor, a man impeccably attired in a high-priced suit waited. Townes pressed the remote locking mechanism under her desk granting access to FBI Supervisory Special Agent Bill Ross. Entering her office, Ross looked refreshed and composed against the backdrop of two exhausted White House security officials.

Townes introduced Ross to Quinlan, remarking, "John, this is Agent Ross of the FBI, and as you know, he also serves as the bureau's representative to the National Security Council Enforcement group."

"Hello, Bill," Quinlan greeted. "I'm too new on the council to say much at the meetings, so I apologize that we're only formally meeting now and under these circumstances."

"No worries, I understand, and I believe I can be candid with you and Ms. Townes on this matter," replied Bill Ross.

Without hesitation, Townes intervened, "It's Jan, Bill, not Ms. Townes," and she winked at Quinlan while making the correction.

"Look, Bill, it's been a long night and an early morning," Townes continued, "we're on the same team, and I want complete transparency regarding our latest Room 23 issue. The issue's name is James O'Donovan."

Bill Ross straightened in his chair, initiating the disclosure, "James O'Donovan has been under investigation by our office for possible money laundering. FinCEN alerted us more than two years ago about suspicious activity related to an overseas bank account in his name. The account is held at the Northern Bank of Ireland in Belfast. Additionally, his nephew, Phillip O'Donovan, along with his 18-year-old son, recently left the United States for Seoul, South Korea with separate itineraries. They both have since dropped off the grid."

"Just like that?" Quinlan questioned.

"Not exactly," Ross replied. "Phillip O'Donovan and his girlfriend, Tara Lee, both held positions at the Bureau of Engraving and Printing. According to their coworkers, Tara and Patrick left for Seoul two weeks ago, though we're still piecing together the exact timeline. It appears Patrick was enrolled in a foreign student exchange program at the National University of Korea. Phillip O'Donovan had mentioned to coworkers that Tara was going to accompany Patrick and then she would split off to visit her relatives in Seoul, South Korea. A few days after their departure, Phillip O'Donovan vanished. He failed to show up for work, and no one at the BEP has had any contact with him since. Colleagues noted that this behavior was unusual, as the man supposedly never missed a day of work at the BEP."

Quinlan interjected, "Were the police notified?"

Ross responded, "Well, no, because no one reported him missing, not really."

Quinlan turned to Townes with a puzzled expression. "What was his role at the BEP?"

"He held the designation of GS-15 Master Engraver. This meant..."

Quinlan cut Ross off, "This means he was one of the few qualified to create the printing plates for our nation's currency!"

Ross, now a bit uneasy, said, "Look John, I know this is all new to you, and you have many questions, but let me proceed with the details of why we suspect his uncle James might have been at the White House and why, we..."

Townes interrupted, "Why didn't you think it was important to inform John and his team that someone flagged on your watchlist was heading to a White House Presidential event?"

Ross, looking sheepish, responded, "Yes, I can't, um, it wasn't my decision to keep you in the dark, per our memorandum of understanding."

Quinlan and Townes now both looked suspiciously at Ross, prompting him to delve into the details.

Ross began. "As John mentioned, Phillip O'Donovan is one of the ten master engravers at the BEP. He is responsible for engraving plates used in the production of our Federal Reserve Notes."

Quinlan chimed in, "In simpler terms, he literally makes money for our country. Go on, Ross."

"Out of the blue, one day he didn't show up for work. DHS confirmed he boarded an American Airlines Flight to Seoul, South Korea. He doesn't have a return flight, and Customs in Seoul verified his passport information and captured his facial image during the entry process."

"Keep going," Townes urged Ross.

Quinlan interjected, "If I may interrupt Jan, this is a complex situation, but I'm starting to see a bigger picture. If I may, can we circle back to James O'Donovan, the uncle. Last night, after everything unfolded, I reached out to the White House Social Office. They informed me they had invited North Korean Supreme Leader Pak Hyun Woo to the Iftar dinner. Following the Peace House meeting at Panmunjom, the White House aims to reciprocate with Pak's administration. They want to maintain a positive dialogue. However, in place of the Supreme Leader, the North Koreans returned James O'Donovan's credentials instead."

Ross continued, "Well that explains why he was on the invite list. Look I have to disclose that the CIA is now entangled in our money laundering case against O'Donovan."

Quinlan, sensing the urgency, inquired, "Do we know why or even how the North Koreans are involved with James O'Donovan?"

Ross explained, "He's emerging as a key figure in the Sinn Féin party and holds a tenured professorship at Tipperary College in Dublin. Though it may seem insignificant, the CIA has discovered a crucial link—the new Supreme Leader of North Korea was once a student under Professor O'Donovan's mentorship, and they have a close friendship even today."

Townes now frustrated, inquired, "Ross, is there a purpose to this revelation? Do we know if there is something nefarious about the relationship between the professor and the Supreme Leader? Is the Supreme Leader manipulating O'Donovan for political gain with Sinn Féin? Does this impact the White House in any way?"

Responding to Townes' plea for clarity, Ross divulged, "There's more to the story. James O'Donovan traces his lineage directly to Ireland. His father, Sean O'Donovan, played a pivotal role in the Irish Republican Army (IRA). He was killed on January 30, 1972, in Derry, Northern Ireland, leading a political protest against the perceived British oppression. British troops, facing mostly unarmed protesters, fired upon the crowd, resulting in the tragic death of 14, including Sean O'Donovan. He was Professor James O'Donovan's brother and the father of Phillip O'Donovan. This incident, labeled 'Bloody Sunday' by the local media, marked the initiation of the Troubles, which lasted for eight years."

Townes and Quinlan both looked on listening intently but hoping for some resolution to the access issue and how this might impact the administration.

"As you're aware, the IRA no longer maintains a significant presence with regard to extortion and violence. They've essentially laid down their arms," Ross explained.

Townes interjected, "We acknowledge the IRA's decommissioning of weapons as part of the Northern Ireland peace process but go on."

Ross continued, "Exactly, Jan. The IRA, in its historical form, has lacked organized leadership since then. Nevertheless, there are still factions in Northern Ireland that align with the Republican cause, operating under various names and ideologies."

"Like Sinn Féin," Quinlan remarked.

Ross affirmed, "Yes, Sinn Féin. In my view, Sinn Féin picked up where the IRA left off. They advocate for Irish reunification under a Republican regime, echoing the IRA's historical goals. Sinn Féin operates within the political system but distances itself from the violence associated with the IRA. It holds influence internationally and is a significant player in the intelligence world. It's crucial to note that although Sinn Féin differs from the IRA in tactics, they are actively working towards the unification of Northern Ireland, excluding the rest of Great Britain, at any cost."

Jan Townes then affirmed, "So, Bill, it is your belief that the professor may be an ally with the new Supreme Leader rather than a pawn. Through him, North Korea might simply be making an inroad with Northern Ireland's political arm? That arm may very well be Sinn Féin's leader, James O'Donovan? Do I have that correct and what about the money laundering and the varying amounts in O'Donovan's bank account?"

Ross answered as best he could, "Yes I do believe the relationship between the Supreme Leader and Professor O'Donovan is genuine. He seems to be extending the same olive branch given to the U.S. during the Peace House meeting, to Northern Ireland. It's true that O'Donovan's bank account has been linked to numerous suspicious activity reports, making him a person of interest. When you add that to his past affiliation with the IRA and his current senior position with Sinn Féin, it's a recipe for our attention. The FBI's Joint Terrorism Task Force has been on him for over a year."

Quinlan, now glaring at Ross with evident frustration, remarked, "So, this information would have been incredibly useful for me last night—or more precisely, four days ago when Room 23 input his name into our access system. You knew then that he was an invited guest at the Iftar dinner. We could have contacted the White House staff and prevented him from being invited. Instead, we allowed a questionable character with potential terrorist ties access to the White House. I suspect his presence at the Iftar dinner furthered your intelligence gathering capabilities?"

"You have every right to be upset with me, John," Ross admitted. "I'm asking for a bit of understanding here because it wasn't entirely my decision."

"Oh, I'll address this at whatever level is necessary," Townes retorted, visibly angry at the clear lapse in judgment.

Ross continued, "There's one more piece of information, and it comes from the CIA. They have a source that we believe is MI-5. This source suggests that the professor and the Supreme Leader's sister, Pak Hyun Mi, are romantically involved. She and her brother, the Supreme Leader, have no friendly relationship whatsoever. In fact, she upholds the political ideologies of her late father. This directly contradicts her brother's new political agenda of peace and transparency. We're not sure how she fits, if at all, into this equation, but we are still collaborating with the CIA on this."

In the tense conversation, Townes interjected sharply, "I want the name of the CIA contact."

Ross continued, "I understand, and there's more unknown than known in this situation. The CIA has shared information with us..."

"The name," Townes interrupted.

"Yes, ma'am. It's CIA Station Chief John Reynolds. He's stationed in London but has been predominantly in Northern Ireland since this all began over a year ago," Ross disclosed.

Townes remarked, "So, at the very least, there is money being funneled into James O'Donovan's bank account in Belfast for purposes we are not yet aware of. Have there been any withdrawals from the account?"

Ross replied, "For the most part there have been no transactions one way or the other. At least initially making this account a depository for illicit funds. However, very recently, a cash deposit of $500,000.00, all in $100 bills, was made. Two days later, an equivalent amount was wired to an overseas account in the Cayman Islands. This wire has been the only monetary fund transfer that we are aware of for this account."

Quinlan interjected, "You mentioned that a deposit was made in $100 bills? As a Secret Service agent, there is an abundance of information I can't overlook that may or may not have anything to do with last night's Iftar dinner. You previously mentioned Phillip O'Donovan, a master engraver employed by the U.S. Bureau of Engraving and Printing. He goes missing and was last seen at Incheon International Airport in Seoul, South Korea. His son, Patrick, who also goes missing and was last seen at the National University of Korea. Let me delve into what could potentially be an entirely different angle in this troublesome matter. I will be looking into the possible connections with the $100 bills and a potential link to North Korea and..."

Ross interrupted, "John, are you considering the possibility of counterfeit currency in this scenario?"

Quinlan replied thoughtfully, "North Korea, a missing BEP master engraver, and a rogue sister of the Supreme Leader? Yes, I am. The Secret Service has long suspected North Korea or the Philippines as the source of the APEX counterfeit note—which we see as an almost perfect counterfeit model. I will forward all of this on to our office of investigations. Again, for now let's get back to Professor James O'Donovan."

Townes inquired with a puzzled look, "Counterfeit currency aside, before the $500,000.00 deposit, there were no withdrawals? If that's the case, where does the laundering come in? Do we even know if Professor James O'Donovan is aware of this account? He could be a pawn in something nefarious from the North Korean side. In my experience, a man in a romantic relationship with a woman can often become a pawn for her interests."

Quinlan inquired, "Do you think James O'Donovan could be a proxy, or I don't know, an arm of the Supreme Leader's sister? She obviously has no working relationship with her brother, but the professor does. Jan, you said, and I don't mean to put words in your mouth, but as you alluded, she is probably manipulating him and his status as a Sinn Féin leader. Even perhaps using his identity to open this bank account and who knows if there are any other accounts?"

Ross responded, "Too soon to tell, but that is where I would go with this."

Townes spoke up, "Gentlemen, we have covered a lot. Agent Ross, you need to be more transparent when working with John's group at the Secret Service, and I mean that!"

Ross spoke up as he rose from his chair, "I wholeheartedly agree, Jan."

He extended his hand towards Quinlan, "My apologies, John. I will make it my personal goal to work more closely with you on White House access issues. We at the bureau appreciate your discretion on this. Why didn't you just ban him from the event when you could have? You could have pulled him aside and questioned him. Why didn't you do any of those things?"

Quinlan replied, "It was a call I made. I was hoping you and the FBI had your reasons for not alerting us when you learned of the silent hit on O'Donovan."

"For us, you made the right call, John," Ross affirmed. "It's to our advantage that he doesn't know he's under any kind of scrutiny. If you had pulled him aside, he might have become evasive. We are still trying to figure out who James O'Donovan is. The Terrorism Task Force has a lot in play right now."

"We'll see, but don't you think he is a bit paranoid now?" Quinlan exclaimed. "Especially after he was given a private tour of the White House by the Chief of Staff rather than a photo opportunity with President Bryce?" This was all Quinlan could offer. Then, out of frustration, staring into Ross' eyes, he said, "Agent Ross, it has been my experience that intelligence agents seem to have a casual relationship with the truth."

Ross let Quinlan's comment hang in the air, refusing to dignify it. The meeting ended, and Jan showed them both to her office door.

"Gentlemen," Townes said, "It has been a trying morning, but I think we all learned a lot. We will need to continue this conversation, maybe before our next meeting of the National Security Council—Enforcement group."

Quinlan and Ross departed the deputy's office, Ross to his car parked on West Executive Avenue and Quinlan to his office two floors down.

Ross turned around to ask Quinlan one final question, "John, did O'Donovan spike for radioactivity?"

"No, why?" was all Quinlan said, then thought to himself, *Now who has a casual relationship with the truth?*

His response, "I hear things John."

Quinlan thought to himself, *Shit, is there a leak in the security team at the White House? Ross, you don't play fair, well neither do I. Besides, I have no idea what I am dealing with here or how deep it goes. I need to figure out what the FBI and CIA are up to, I too, can have a casual relationship with the truth.*

CHAPTER 37

SCI Clearance

Quinlan had navigated the labyrinthine of security clearances, a requisite journey for access to the National Security Council Enforcement meetings. The summit of this clearance mountain was the Sensitive Compartmented Information level. The pinnacle of access in the nation, and it came at a formidable cost. His presence in the Service's Security Clearance Division felt eerily familiar, reminiscent of past predicaments. This time, he was subjected to a national security polygraph conducted by the CIA, a departure from the exhaustive five-hour pre-screening polygraph over a decade ago. The questions now focused solely on matters of national security, concluding in just over an hour with Quinlan successfully passing.

Later that afternoon, SAIC Rick Spencer reached out, inquiring about the ordeal. Quinlan's response held a tinge of weariness, "Good, I guess, as good as a dehumanizing polygraph can go."

Spencer, understanding the toll such processes took, empathized, "Well, I happen to know it went well. No one wins in a world of potential espionage, John, and Room 23 can have its slippery slopes. But you have your clearance now."

"Thanks, boss. I appreciate that," he acknowledged.

Getting to the point, Spencer revealed the next assignment, "To the matter at hand, can you be in DNSA Jan Townes' office tomorrow morning at 8 am for a briefing?"

Quinlan's curiosity was piqued. "Sure, but what am I walking into?" he asked.

Spencer delved further, "It's substantial, John, and it exceeds my purview. The SAIC of the Criminal Investigative Division and the SAIC of the Forensic Services Division, accompanied by their technicians, will be present. Although this matter falls strictly within Secret Service jurisdiction, Jan Townes will serve as the proxy for the National Security Council Enforcement section. Additionally, her legal advisor, Lana Miller, will be in attendance. It seems you've been briefed on DNSA Townes' decision to involve her in all Room 23 matters."

Quinlan couldn't help but experience a slight sense of relief upon learning about Lana's presence. "Yes, Ms. Townes briefed me on Lana's role with Room 23. Thanks again, boss. I'll make sure to keep you in the loop."

CHAPTER 38

A Seat at the Table

Located within the West Wing, the Situation Room stands in close proximity to the President, Vice President, and their advisors, providing the ideal location for swift assemblies of critical staff in times of urgency. Designated as a Sensitive Compartmented Information Facility (SCIF), it boasts surveillance countermeasures reminiscent of DNSA Jan Towne's office. Diverging from her workspace, the Situation Room goes a step further with robust structural fortifications, capable of withstanding explosive blasts.

This chamber is a self-contained zone, possessing its own oxygen source to counteract potential threats of chemical or biological attacks. Its inception dates back to 1961, following the Bay of Pigs invasion failure, when President John F. Kennedy mandated its construction. The specter of leaks surrounding the audacious plan to overthrow Cuba's dictator, Fidel Castro, served as the impetus for its creation.

Initially designed to rectify past errors in judgment, the Room persists in its utility due to the ongoing abundance of crises. It serves as a venue for assembling key personnel to deliberate and coordinate responses to matters of national security and emergency situations as was the case with the events of September 11th. The facility is augmented with cutting-edge secure communications and video conferencing capabilities. It serves as a conduit for real-time decision-making while safeguarding the nation's interests and citizens.

* * *

The Deputy National Security Advisor took command, summoning the NSC Enforcement section to assemble in the Situation Room. A deliberately small quorum, orchestrated by Jan Townes, gathered due to the sensitive nature of Agent Quinlan's imminent briefing.

Townes initiated the meeting by introducing Supervisory Special Agent John Quinlan of the U.S. Secret Service. She conveyed her confidence that the group would find today's briefing, focused on Agent Quinlan's topic, compelling. His presence seemed to captivate the attention of all in the room, their eyes fixated on him.

"Good morning. I am the Secret Service representative to the National Security Council Enforcement section at the White House," Quinlan began. "I've had secure telephone conversations with CIA London Station Chief John Reynolds, who is present today for reasons I will convey shortly. My agency's Criminal Investigative Division recently briefed me on an alarming surge in the production of the best counterfeit $100 Federal Reserve Note ever encountered by the Secret Service. We refer to this note as the APEX note, given its unparalleled quality."

FBI Agent Bill Ross, serving as the FBI's liaison to the NSC, was among the attendees. Quinlan noted his presence, particularly when Ross inquired, "Good morning, John. What sets this counterfeit note apart, and how does it relate to national security?"

Quinlan continued, "The APEX note's remarkable resemblance to a genuine $100 bill is exceptional. It is overtaking all other crude counterfeit currency in circulation. Early in the 1990s our Secret Service Forensic Services Division (FSD) technicians identified various microscopic imperfections that distinguish the APEX note from genuine currency. These imperfections, kept top-secret and compartmentalized, are known only to a select few. Correcting these imperfections would eliminate any discernible features distinguishing the APEX counterfeit note from genuine U.S. currency."

John Reynolds, the CIA Liaison to the NSC, interjected with his words taking the form of a question, "So the counterfeiters are unaware of these imperfections?"

Quinlan responded, "We had always suspected that no one outside of a select few in the Secret Service were aware of these imperfections, especially least of all those making the counterfeit APEX notes. We may have been wrong about that." His gaze swept the room, searching for cues, before declaring, "As of three weeks ago, we have seen a spike in the circulation of the APEX note overseas, and it is starting to trickle into the U.S. The imperfections have been corrected, completely eradicated. The note is perfect and indistinguishable from genuine currency. We know a bank in Belfast, Ireland took in a large quantity of $100 APEX notes a little over a month ago and that is the reason for CIA Chief Reynolds' presence here today. We are still working with his office on those details." Quinlan reminded everyone, "Due to the level of security assigned to the APEX note, the classification is TS/SCI. As you are aware, there is no formal clearance level higher than top secret/sensitive compartmentalized."

FBI Agent Ross interrupted with a shout, addressing no one in particular, "Can someone give us any more on this? Who do you think is behind this, and again, why is it important to the National Security Council?"

DNSA Jan Townes raised her voice, addressing Ross directly, "If I may, we hold a 90% certainty that this is a state-backed operation. Our investigation has narrowed down the list of potential adversaries to include China, the Philippines, Russia, and the Republic of North Korea as the suspected manufacturers of this counterfeit note."

The revelation left those in the room visibly shaken, with some losing their composure and demanding proof. Townes continued, "I have already briefed the National Security Advisor and the Secretary of Homeland Security on the implications of this perfect counterfeit note."

Townes disclosed, "Ladies and gentlemen, I'm not at liberty to discuss why we suspect those countries; however, it is a carefully compiled and intelligence driven list. However, yesterday, John Quinlan's team at the Secret Service provided an extremely convincing briefing. If another country counterfeits the currency of the United States, it will likely lead to significant legal and diplomatic consequences."

"An act of war," a voice rang out. It was FBI Agent Ross.

Jan continued, "No, Bill, that is a common misconception dating back to the Civil War when one-third of the money in circulation was counterfeit. The Civil War had numerous causes, with some historians even suggesting that issues with counterfeit currency played a role. Let me be clear," she emphasized, "we will NOT go to war over this."

She cast a pointed glance at Ross, extending the duration slightly beyond the norm. She effectively conveyed an unspoken directive for him to cease his interruptions and take his seat.

Maintaining a firm grip on the room's composure, she pressed on, "Our focus will be on those countries we believe we can eliminate from the list. Our primary objective is to clear North Korea first. Since the Peace House summit, Supreme Leader Pak Hyun Woo has diligently met every demand we've presented. In fact, we are on the verge of dispatching our weapons inspectors to North Korea, and the Supreme Leader has shown unwavering willingness to accommodate them. Following that, we will scrutinize the situation in the Philippines. Regardless, we will not hesitate to initiate legal action to protect our currency and financial system. The impact of this flawless APEX note will reverberate through international trade agreements, intellectual property, and strain diplomatic relations. Lana Miller, my legal advisor, and her team of NSC attorneys have thoroughly examined the legal implications. I align with them in deeming this act, at the very least, a violation of international law. Let's not mince words; the economic fallout from introducing this impeccable counterfeit note to the global stage would be catastrophic. It would undermine confidence in our currency's value and stability, inevitably paving the way for the economic collapse of our nation."

At this juncture, an undercurrent of anger and desperation permeated the Situation Room, with the earnestness of the news eliciting unwarranted outbursts, some fueled by patriotism.

Townes redirected their attention and pressed on, "Let's center our initial approach on diplomatic channels. Nevertheless, the President is aligned with the strategy that if we definitively identify a country from the provided list—with absolute certainty backed by all available intelligence—we will not hesitate to implement sanctions and trade restrictions on that country and their closest allies."

A silence enveloped the room as the small group absorbed the weight of the revelation, seated in disbelief.

DNSA Townes concluded her presentation by reiterating the top-secret SCI classification of the information. She emphasized that no one, not even supervisors outside the room, were to be briefed on this matter.

Adding a final layer of sincerity, she declared, "As it pertains to this matter, I accept the responsibility of being the beginning and end of your agency's chain of command. Is this understood?"

A collective, albeit hushed, "Yes ma'am," resonated in response, and Townes found solace in the acceptance of her authority.

The meeting drew to a close, and in a measured tone, Townes informally introduced Agent Quinlan to CIA Station Chief John Reynolds. Recognizing the depth of potential discussions, she proposed a reconvening in Quinlan's office.

"I will make myself unavailable for your impromptu meeting gentlemen," she offered, "as I believe you two might have some important matters to discuss."

CHAPTER 39

The CIA

CIA Station Chief John Reynolds exuded a certain saltiness, a trait deeply rooted in his Irish heritage, tracing back to the tumultuous 1970s in Northern Ireland, also known as the Troubles. His family had emigrated from Northern Ireland, specifically from the small city of Londonderry or Derry, depending on one's perspective. At twenty-one, Reynolds became a New York City police officer, and his relentless and aggressive approach to police work earned him his detective shield in just six years—a feat that typically takes ten years or more. His upward career trajectory led him to the FBI-NYPD Joint Terrorism Task Force. From this critical position, the CIA recruited Reynolds as a new case officer, tasked with penetrating the remaining factions of the IRA. Concurrently, Sinn Féin, a burgeoning offshoot of the IRA, was emerging as a political party deeply engaged in the advancement of an independent Northern Ireland. During the 1980s, Sinn Féin was under the leadership of Gerry Finnegan, the party's President, who, at the time, was advocating for a peace process with the rest of Great Britain. Finnegan continued to lead the party until 2012, stepping down after a reasonable agreement was brokered between the Irish Republican Army and the Royal Ulster Constabulary, the armed police contingent of the British Crown.

Reynolds ascended through the ranks of the CIA, always strategically maintaining a considerable distance from Langley. Opting for a post in England, he covertly operated as a CIA case officer under clandestine cover. Seizing the opportunity that seldom presents itself in the CIA, he eventually assumed the role of station chief.

Chief Reynolds accompanied Quinlan to his office in Room 23. Since Quinlan had received his SCI clearance, his office underwent a reconfiguration and was transformed into a SCIF. This space was designated for top secret matters like the impending discussion between the two gentlemen. Chief Reynolds encouraged Quinlan to delve deeper into the details of the APEX note so he could better assess his added value.

Quinlan initiated, "Chief, I understand you're stationed in England, but when you were in the States, when was the last time you carried a $100 bill in your wallet? With credit cards, debit cards, online purchases, digital currency..."

Reynolds interjected, "Yeah, I get it—paper is used a lot less these days," his voice echoing through the room.

Quinlan resumed, "So, it's no surprise that a significant number of $100 bills in our country find their way into international markets without much notice. It used to be that the older notes with a date series of 1990 and earlier were the primary targets for counterfeiting, and hardly anyone noticed. At least, not the average citizen."

Reynolds, seeking clarity on the specifics, reiterated, "So, the $100 genuine note used to create the APEX counterfeit note prior to 1990 lacks all of those security features. That's why this series is the note our target counterfeiters chose when creating the APEX note?"

Quinlan acknowledged Reynolds' deduction with a nod of appreciation before seamlessly transitioning into his own part of the discussion, "Consider, if John Q Citizen acquires a $100 bill. Without a security strip embedded in the paper, even if he's aware of microprinting, another security feature, he'll immediately notice the absence of both." Quinlan began painting a scenario. "He might scrutinize the bill and find the date as 1990. Most people would wonder: where's the strip? Where's the watermark image of some

President? Some might even question the absence of ink that changes color when the bill is moved around."

Reynolds interjected, "They might connect the dots, thinking the old $100 bills didn't have those features and assume the note is genuine. But doesn't the Federal Reserve take those old notes out of circulation?" he queried.

Quinlan responded with a smile, "Every fifteen years. But again, when was the last time you handled a bunch of $100 bills in the states?"

He replied, "Honestly, on a government salary, I don't make it a habit to walk around with a wad of $100 bills."

Quinlan concurred, "Me neither, chief." He continued, "My point is, most of our $100 bills leave the country through international commerce, trade, tourism, and other financial transactions, some legal and some not so legal. Many of these counterfeit notes may not make it back to the Federal Reserve or their final resting place. They stay overseas. Look, chief, the $100 U.S. Federal Reserve Note is part of a currency considered by many to be the most stable in the world. It's no wonder why everyone prefers a greenback over any other currency, and that's precisely why the international markets are flooded with APEX $100 counterfeit bills."

Reynolds appeared somewhat fatigued, attributing it to jet lag after his impromptu flight from London's Heathrow International Airport.

Quinlan pressed on, "It's even more complicated now." Reynolds, showing signs of frustration, questioned, "How?"

He explained, "We used to observe most APEX notes with a series from 1990 or earlier."

Reynolds interjected, "Because notes after 1990 have all those security features added by the BEP—yes, I get that!" His frustration was evident.

"Yes," Quinlan responded. "Shortly after 1990, a security thread and microprinting were added to the $100 note as a security measure. Your average counterfeiter couldn't replicate a clear microprint, and embedding the security strip into the paper was beyond their capability. At that time, we noticed these two crude security updates slowed down the production of the 1990 APEX notes. However, the Federal Reserve quickly spoiled our good mood when they identified a newer version of the APEX note. It seemed the counterfeiter had graduated to the next level."

Reynolds, looking perplexed, asked, "So, the Federal Reserve keeps track of all the counterfeit that comes back to them?"

Quinlan interjected, "And the serial numbers, yes. The one thing we discovered at that time was a random 'country declaration bank stamp' imprinted on the 2013 series $100 bills. A large amount of these new and improved 2013 APEX notes had this stamp. We were working with the Bureau of Engraving and Printing to identify the origin of this country declaration bank stamp. We discovered the banks located in the Republic of North Korea apply such a stamp to any foreign currency that gets deposited into its banking system."

Reynolds continued, "Are you saying you think the North Korean government is involved with the production of the APEX note? Why wasn't that offered up in Townes' meeting?"

Quinlan paused and took a deep breath. "I can't be sure, but yes. I go where the evidence takes me, Chief. An inordinate amount of the APEX notes returned to the Federal Reserve has this stamp. I haven't brought this to DNSA Townes yet because it is still too raw. We are talking major national implications here if I am wrong, and I need your help on this."

"Alright," Reynolds said, "You got my attention. That's what I'm here for."

Quinlan continued, "I believe the 1990 APEX notes underwent upgrades in 2013, coinciding with the enhancements made to the $100 bill by the BEP. The improvements included a security thread and the watermark image of Benjamin Franklin, as well as the existing red and blue fibers. All these elements are introduced to the paper when it is manufactured by the Crane Paper Company. Nevertheless, we observed this 2013 APEX note, featuring all these updated security features, appearing in the U.S. and abroad once again. Even though the counterfeiters flawlessly recreated these enhanced 2013 security features, the notes still exhibited the same microscopic imperfections."

"Well, that's all changed now, hasn't it? They've even corrected the imperfections," Reynolds said, rubbing his tired eyes. "At least we know the same counterfeiter or rogue country is still at the helm."

"You have the right idea, Chief. However, it goes even deeper," Quinlan responded, "The company I mentioned, Crane Paper? It is a company that contracts with the Bureau of Engraving and Printing. They manufacture the paper used to print genuine currency. That paper, in and of itself, is as valuable as whatever denomination is printed on it—maybe even more valuable."

Reynolds asked, "Because of all the security features that are already a part of the paper when it is being manufactured?"

Quinlan continued, "Yes, look, this is a lot to digest, and we are both tired. But I will say that the paper made at Crane is comprised of 75% cotton and 25% linen. It is infused with tiny red and blue fibers, and then the magic happens with the woven security thread and the watermark image of Franklin, and the..." Chief Reynolds held up his hand, implying 'enough.'

"Quinlan, are you going to tell me that there is an insider at Crane Paper dealing out the paper to the counterfeiting plant that is operating somewhere in a hostile country, most likely North Korea? The same country that as of late wants to play nice with the world starting with the good ol' US of A?" Reynolds asked.

"Again chief, I follow the evidence where it takes me, but no. I don't think there is a connection to Crane. I think the North Korean government has even mastered the ingredients used to make the well-crafted and top-secret paper our currency is printed on," Quinlan affirmed.

"So, why should the CIA get involved, Quinlan?" Reynolds asked tersely. "How does this pose a threat to the security of the United States, and why would the CIA be interested in this matter?"

Quinlan, with a hint of exasperation, replied, "Weren't you in the same room as me when the Deputy National Security Advisor presented her case?" He continued, "With the APEX note now perfected, the implications for the U.S. begin with attempts to undermine our economy by inundating it with an undetectable counterfeit note. This APEX note could circulate globally, jeopardizing the integrity of our financial system and the value of American currency. American diplomacy may suffer, and let's be honest, Chief, our international standing as team players is already close to zero on anyone's scorecard."

"Alright, Quinlan," Chief Reynolds summarized after this prolonged day. "I have an idea of how I can contribute to your investigation."

Chief Reynolds knew exactly what he would do next. He was not yet able to convey his intentions to Quinlan. His strategy was born out of a much different world of intelligence gathering than Quinlan's. Reynold's approach would skirt the edges of illegality where there exists a casual relationship with the U.S. Constitution. It was effective and a necessary part of rooting out those that wanted to harm the United States.

If Quinlan was right, Reynolds thought, *and the North Korean government was part of this APEX note, he knew where to start his digging.*

* * *

Reynolds had been handling a motivated asset under the employ of the Russian government. Tatiana Sokolov was a twenty-four-year-old interpreter charged with translating and transcribing all covert communiqués acquired by the Russian FSB. This agency was Russian President Petrov's answer to the now extinct KGB. This CIA asset controlled by Reynolds was extremely motivated to punish Russia.

After all, they destroyed the only thing she loved dear. Her family living in Kyiv, Ukraine fell victim to the first volley of Russian aggression. Although Tatiana was of Russian descent, her mother, father, and two brothers lived together in a modest home in Kyiv. She had moved two years earlier to St. Petersburg, Russia, to follow her dreams of being an interpreter for the Russian parliament. She hoped one day to relocate to New York City and gain employment at the United Nations. Since the war started, all essential Russian personnel were relocated to Moscow and forced to work on the war effort. Little did the Russians know they had a highly motivated CIA spy in their midst. One who had access to a lot of secrets. Her job was to translate and transcribe the conversations between foreign assets and the FSB officers.

Approached under the covert orchestration of a specific CIA station chief, she found herself entangled in a web of espionage. Nestled within this vast array of intelligence were traces of a renegade MI-5 agent's dealings with FSB Officer Sergei Topov. Stansfield Anderson's fingerprints were all over the leaked military preparedness of the Ukrainian forces. Fueled by a thirst for revenge, Tatiana eagerly complied with Reynolds' request. She meticulously recorded interactions between Russian FSB officer Sergei Topov and MI-5 Agent Stansfield Anderson. With thoughts of revenge driving her, she discreetly transmitted the digital recordings to her handler, CIA Chief John Reynolds.

Chief Reynolds, now fully aware of Anderson's compromised status, bided his time, awaiting the right moment to engage MI-5's internal affairs. Despite the precariousness of the situation, the CIA's Counterintelligence Directorate mandated Reynolds to keep the asset operational. Collaborating with the MI-5 Director General, they concocted a scheme to feed Anderson false information, intended to find its way into the hands of the FSB and the Russian Military. This misinformation would inevitably aid the Ukrainian government in protecting their country's sovereignty.

This intricate plan aimed to prompt Russian actions based on the fabricated intelligence, would strategically position Ukrainian forces. Concurrently, Reynolds would extract valuable information to be shared with the Ukrainian Security Service or Sluzhba Bezpeky Ukrayiny (SBU). The SBU, in turn, would utilize this intelligence to enhance their military readiness against Russia and initiate a counteroffensive.

CIA Station Chief Reynolds thought to himself, *What if Quinlan's intuition regarding the North Korean government as the origin of the counterfeit currency was true? This coupled with the unsettling discovery that approximately half a million dollars in $100 APEX notes infiltrated the Bank of Northern Ireland. The two variables together pointed to MI-5 Agent Stansfield Anderson as the most rational starting point.*

This revelation spurred Reynolds into action. He was compelled to shift his focus and mobilize his assets in the field. In the days that followed, Reynolds remained in close communication with Quinlan. He made sure every development was relayed promptly. Armed with this fresh intelligence, Quinlan felt a surge of motivation to craft a strategic plan. After seeking and obtaining approval, he was granted authorization for a temporary assignment in Belfast, Ireland. This move marked the pivotal next step in untangling the complex web and identifying the elusive source of the APEX note.

CHAPTER 40

Belfast

"None of us is as smart as all of us."
—Ken Blanchard

Nearing dawn in Belfast, Ireland, Shankill Road gradually settled into a semblance of calm. The familiar rowdy and inebriated youth spilled out from the bars, stumbling toward taxis and modest flats in the blue-collar enclave of West Belfast. Agent Quinlan, engaged in his customary surveillance routine, allowed his thoughts to meander in the early morning stillness.

Quinlan grappled with an array of concerns that occupied his mind. His persuasiveness with SAIC Rick Spencer had secured his presence in Belfast, a necessity he easily justified. Convincing his boss to approve travel for his long-time colleague, Agent Joe Mackey, however, proved to be a more challenging task. Spencer recognized the seamless synergy of their partnership. This was true especially during intricate investigations such as the APEX case. The complexities of the mission would be relayed to DNSA Jan Townes through her legal advisor, Lana Miller.

Quinlan was jolted back to reality when the sliding door to the van suddenly peeled open. A somewhat disheveled figure of Agent Joe Mackey appeared.

"Q, good morning. Hey, why haven't we met with the embassy personnel yet? We dove headfirst into this without grasping all the details," Mackey inquired, his condition betraying the aftermath of an all-night meeting with dubious characters from the RUC.

The Royal Ulster Constabulary, or RUC, functioned as the law enforcement authority in Northern Ireland, tasked with maintaining order and enforcing a semblance of justice. Mackey coughed up remnants of a night spent with the questionable denizens of the RUC.

"Morning to you as well, Mack." Quinlan sighed; his gaze fixed on the Bayardo Bar along Shankill Road.

Mack questioned their prolonged surveillance, "Why are we still planted here for the second day? What's the deal with keeping an eye on the front of the Bayardo Bar?"

Shankill Road, scarred by some of the fiercest rioting during the Troubles of 1970, had transformed into a hub for illicit activities. It now served as a mecca for drug manufacturing, gun distribution, terrorist financing, and an array of trafficking, including the circulation of counterfeit US currency.

Mack pressed on, "Quinlan, I know you've had the full briefing on the APEX note and its ties to Belfast. Care to let me in on the details?"

Quinlan responded with a playful jab and in a purposeful loud tone exclaimed, "You want the eighty-hour, top-secret version or the condensed twenty-minute need-to-know edition?"

"Easy there, brother. My ball cap is the only thing holding my head together right now," Mack quipped.

Quinlan, raising his voice, asked, "How much did you drink last night?"

Mack admitted, "Enough, Q, enough. It's the cost of doing business in a drinking town like this, isn't it?"

Quinlan concurred, "Indeed, it is."

"Hey, I've got a question," Mack said, pausing for dramatic effect. "What's a Room 23 Supervisory guy like you and a PPD guy like me chasing down counterfeiters? Has there been some kind of breakthrough in this decades-old case?"

Quinlan understood the nature of his assignment in Belfast and the details of the case were classified SCI, a rare designation that often accompanied the words Top Secret. This level of secrecy even surpassed Mack's security clearance, necessitating a certain level of discretion in their conversation.

"Apologies, Mack. Let's just say I'm here, and I've chosen you as my right-hand man on this one," he explained, signaling that he was the primary case agent while Mack played a supporting role.

"Why just you and me, though? Where's the embassy in all of this? Hell, where's the agency? Don't those sneaky CIA spooks want in on whatever this is?" Mack's frustration became evident in his rising voice.

"The agency is the agency," Quinlan replied. "They're CIA through and through, showing up when they see fit. In fact, I have a meeting with the CIA's Station Chief, John Reynolds, later tonight here in Belfast. He's a solid guy, someone you'd get along with."

"It's utter nonsense, if you ask me. We've got no support, or at least none that I'm feeling," Mack retorted.

Quinlan replied, "Mack, this is a Room 23 operation. The CIA has been briefed." He held up two glossy 8x10 photographs one labeled Stansfield Anderson and the other James O'Donovan. He continued, "Our mission tonight is to put these two in pocket and hopefully together."

Attempting to steer the conversation away from sensitive details, Quinlan added, "The embassy has our backs, but for now, we're treating this like any other counterfeit case. My hands are tied on some of the specifics."

Mack cut through the tension in the surveillance van, exclaiming, "Compartmented, yeah, I get it, for fuck's sake."

The air grew heavy with silence, broken only by Mack's probing question for Quinlan, "Do you enjoy being the boss in Room 23 or whatever you do there? And let's be real, you picked me because I've got some compromising photos of your new girlfriend, right?"

He pressed on, reminiscing, "I remember when you were wild, doing reckless things, especially overseas. Like that time, you decided to sneak into Malaysia for some R&R because Brunei was a dry country. Remember that?"

Quinlan responded nonchalantly, "Yeah, I remember that, so, what's your point?"

Mack persisted, "Who the hell walks a mile through a jungle, hops a border fence, and enters a somewhat unfriendly country just for a couple of six-packs? I guess I'm asking, where is that guy now?"

With a wry grin, Quinlan retorted, "I was thirsty, Mack, and besides, your mind is like a dangerous neighborhood. You ought to know better than to go there alone."

In truth, Quinlan couldn't fully bring Mack into the fold on this case, especially concerning the latest developments. He reflected on the unexpected promotion he received over a year ago while on the Presidential Protection Division. Such promotions typically came with a transfer, but Room 23 led him down an unexpected path. Despite reminding himself that it was just a counterfeit case, he couldn't shake the feeling that this was anything but typical. The APEX notes, circulating for over two decades, posed stakes higher than any ordinary investigation. The Secret Service had been close to solving it in the past, but never this close. Quinlan understood the gravity of the situation.

While Quinlan pondered those thoughts, the day transitioned into late afternoon. Professor James O'Donovan was wrapping up his work at Tipperary College's Belfast campus. His destination of choice was the Bayardo Bar on Shankill Road. The West Belfast bar was infamous for the 1975 bombing orchestrated by IRA leader Brendan McFarlane. In the back of the bar, there was a meeting room. Senior-level IRA meetings had transformed into Sinn Féin gatherings. James O'Donovan belonged to this new chapter in the bar's tumultuous history.

"Q, you seeing this?" Mackey exclaimed, his excitement palpable.

Quinlan, busy taking photographs, replied, "I do, indeed." The team watched as Professor O'Donovan strolled down the sidewalk on the opposite side of the surveillance van and entered the Bayardo Bar. It was 5:05 pm on this cloudy Belfast afternoon, and dusk was settling in. However, the special infrared sensors in the night optical camera captured the image clearly. The digital reproductions would be complete with a date and time stamp, ensuring a record of the professor's entrance.

At that moment, Quinlan's cellphone rang, and it was none other than CIA Station Chief Reynolds. A separate surveillance team, led by Reynolds, had been tailing Professor O'Donovan for the past week, but Stansfield Anderson had mysteriously dropped off Reynolds' radar two days ago.

"Quinlan, it's Reynolds. I'm in a gray van four cars behind you. Come back to my van. Just you, though. I need to bring you up to speed," he instructed.

"Coming now," Quinlan responded, a sense of urgency in his voice.

"John, sorry we're meeting like this, but there's been some dynamic shit going on with your case. I'm sure you saw O'Donovan heading into the bar. Anderson is off the grid, or else you would have seen him, too. We suspect he's currently in North Korea, sorting things out with his unofficial handler. She's up to something, and probably behind whatever that something is," Reynolds explained.

"Unofficial handler?" Quinlan inquired.

Reynolds elaborated, "The Supreme Leader's sister, Pak Hyun Mi. She also goes by Akma Deja, we've learned. She acts as an intermediary between Anderson and his Russian FSB controller. I'm pretty sure she's getting a finder's fee for connecting him with the Russians."

Quinlan pressed for more details, asking, "So, you think Anderson is with her? Where, in North Korea?"

"Yes, Pyongyang to be exact. His directorate at MI-5 passed along information that Anderson put in for a leave of absence. He does this shit from time to time citing medical reasons from the injuries he sustained as a result of the blast he was involved in a while ago. The thing is when he does this, he goes off the grid. It doesn't even appear that he said anything to his long-time friend who is waiting for him in the bar."

Quinlan replied, "No worries, we can..."

Reynolds interrupted, "Look our office just received an NSA alert from some asshole analyst that decided to slow walk what I consider to be some life changing intel if you know what I mean."

"I don't exactly but please explain," Quinlan said.

Reynolds proceeded to brief Quinlan on the information sourced from the NSA. He prefaced his disclosure with an ad hoc disclaimer that stressed the sensitivity of the details, emphasizing that the information was for their immediate SCI circle only.

"Several weeks ago, the FBI/CIA Joint Terrorism Task Force intercepted a digital transcription of a 14-minute satellite telephonic conversation between a source in Pyongyang, North Korea, and an address in Anacostia, DC. They were set up on the location because it's some kind of Chinese Triad safe house. Anyway, the coordinates, addresses, times, dates—everything is part of the file. The transcribed conversation reads like a manual on abductions. The two individuals on the phone underestimated the NSA's ability to break their encryption. We believe the conversation involved Akma Deja and someone named Tara Lee, conspiring to abduct Patrick O'Donovan. We think they are using him as leverage to compel his father, Phillip O'Donovan, to come rescue him. You know this already but he's a master engraver with the Bureau of Engraving and Printing. Does all of this, I mean every bit of this, now make sense to you?" Reynolds inquired.

Quinlan, gazing through the windshield of Reynolds' van in confused amazement, responded, "Why did it take so long for you to get this intel?"

"Some disgruntled NSA crypto analyst slow-walked the intel," Reynolds explained. "He faced consequences when my superiors at Langley got wind of it. He's dealing with insubordination internally and might even be slapped with dereliction of duty and nonfeasance related federal charges."

Quinlan inquired, "Were you able to get this information to Jan Townes at the NSC?"

Reynolds affirmed, "Yep, I had a lengthy conversation with Lana Miller, Jan's legal advisor. I sent her a digital copy of the transcription via secured email. Oh, she wants you to call her by the way. I mentioned I would be seeing you today. Something about President Bryce meeting with the North Korean Leader at the White House."

Quinlan found some relief in knowing that Reynolds had taken the initiative to share the new information with Townes and Miller just as he would have done. Seeking clarity, he asked, "Thanks, I'll do that, but where does this leave us now?"

Reynolds responded, "If Stansfield is with Akma Deja in her brother's palace, they're plotting something significant. We need to decide if it's the right time to bring Anderson in and find out what he knows. He undoubtedly has information about your counterfeit plant. My hunch, the counterfeiting is going on here in Belfast, just a hunch."

Considering the options, Quinlan proposed, "I'll maintain surveillance here for a few more weeks with Mackey, monitoring James O'Donovan's movements. Can we hold off on bringing Anderson in? Confronting him might force him to shut down. If he's free to roam, he might lead us to where the APEX note is being manufactured."

Reynolds agreed, "Sounds like a plan, Quinlan. Just so you know, the kind of work we do with spies doesn't allow them to just shut down. We get results, and we decide when they can shut down."

Quinlan acknowledged the instructions with a firm nod, saying, "Understood, chief. Understood."

Immediately, he reached out to Lana, hoping she was still awake at 11:00 pm her time. On the second ring, she answered, exuding a mixture of delight and urgency. Lana wasted no time and informed him that the White House social office had just confirmed the North Korean Supreme Leader's visit on the President's Social calendar. In one week, the event was scheduled to occur at the White House, specifically in the private dining room. She then delivered the second piece of news, "Professor James O'Donovan was designated as his plus one," she revealed.

The news hit Quinlan like a ton of bricks, and he could feel the urgency of the situation. He swiftly made plans to return to DC to start the security preparations for this significant event. He would leave Mackey in Belfast with one of Reynolds' support teams to continue the surveillance. He intended to maintain this setup for at least another two weeks before making any adjustments. Quinlan realized the unique solemnity of the situation—no one in the Secret Service had ever been this close to unraveling the counterfeit APEX note operation, and he was determined not to lose the trail now.

Just as the weight of the situation seemed nearly unbearable, Quinlan's cellphone pierced through the tension with an insistent ring.

"Hold onto your hat, my friend. Our boy, Anderson, is on a flight back to Belfast as we speak," Reynolds' voice exclaimed with urgency. Quinlan leaned in, absorbing every word.

Reynolds had cleverly submitted a notice to the United Kingdom Visa and Immigration Agency under the name Stansfield Anderson. A recent alert had just confirmed that Anderson's diplomatic passport was in process on an Air Lingus Flight from Seoul, South Korea, bound for Belfast International Airport.

"He's got an eighteen-hour flight, giving us time to put together a surveillance plan. But wait, there's more," Reynolds continued, a note of satisfaction in his voice. "My contact at the airport mentioned he parked a green Range Rover with tags DA21 GHD in the hourly lot two days ago. We did a drive-by, and the vehicle is still there."

Quinlan, absorbing the information, asked, "Did we run the tags to be absolutely certain?"

"We did. And the son of a bitch is using his own car. Thanks to you and this APEX case, the CIA now knows it is registered under his name but to a different address—an address neither we nor the British government have on file."

"Go on," Quinlan urged.

Reynolds said, excitement evident in his voice. "It leads back to a commercial building in West Belfast. I've dispatched my surveillance team to stake it out and told them to await further instructions. This could be your counterfeit operation, Agent Quinlan."

Quinlan, thrilled by the impressive police work on Reynolds' part, responded, "Mackey and I are heading to the airport now. Let's follow Anderson to see what he does."

Reynolds agreed, feeling the surge of adrenaline as the urgency of the situation intensified. The case was moving quickly but in the right direction.

CHAPTER 41

Akma Deja's Final Plan

"The greater the power, the more dangerous the abuse."
—Edmund Burke

The illicit operations of the counterfeit plant in Belfast, masterminded by her loyal operative, Stansfield 'Stig' Anderson, unfolded seamlessly under Akma Deja's watchful eye. Stig, her lap dog spy, confided in her about his plans to retire from British intelligence and part ways with MI-5. However, she issued a stern warning, emphasizing the consequences of leaving without her authorization.

Akma Deja possessed a trove of damning evidence, including transcripts and video surveillance, of Stig's meetings with Russian spy Sergei Topov. These recordings showed Stig exchanging classified documents about Ukrainian military readiness with the Russians, which facilitated their invasion of Ukraine. The top-secret information Stig provided allowed the Russians to execute a swift and effective military strategy that would have been impossible otherwise. With this evidence, Deja had significant leverage over her operative.

Deja deftly controlled Anderson by skillfully administering a strategic dosage of opioids and consistently employing blackmail. Yet, his occasional lapses in focus led to inadvertent disclosures of sensitive information. Neglectfully sweeping top-secret data into plastic garbage bags, he would then hand them over to his Russian handler during arranged meetings. The Russians, concerned about his lack of discretion, voiced their apprehensions to Akma Deja. She reassured them of tighter control over Stig.

To divert attention and satisfy her own sinister agenda, Akma Deja directed substantial funds into the bank account of Professor and Sinn Féin Leader James O'Donovan. Unbeknownst to James, he became a pawn in her game. He was blissfully unaware of his newfound wealth. Maintaining her psychological hold, she visited him in Dublin and Belfast, catering to his emotional and sexual needs. In her psychopathic manipulation, she invested in the professor, anticipating returns on her insidious agenda. The depths of her plans remained shrouded in mystery, leaving James oblivious to the unsettling tasks that awaited him.

Opting to retain Phillip and Patrick O'Donovan in North Korea, Akma Deja deemed it a strategic move to keep them on a short leash at Camp 15. This decision stemmed from Phillip's invaluable contribution in rectifying the APEX note's imperfections. Under the watchful eye of Patrick, who had fully recovered, the father-son duo shared a dormitory room initially designated for dissidents of high office. Dissatisfied with members of her brother's cabinet, Akma Deja routinely moved dissidents to Camp 15 for a process she euphemistically termed reeducation. In reality, this meant subjecting them to forced labor under harsh conditions. Some might eventually return home, while others faced a permanent absence.

Operating her own shadow dictatorship, Akma Deja manipulated her brother's political naivety, attributing his obliviousness to the euphoria of new-age politics. As long as she refrained from interfering with his cabinet, she retained the autonomy to execute her clandestine rule.

When her brother, Pak Hyun Woo received an invitation from the White House to attend the Iftar dinner celebrating the end of Ramadan, he sought Akma Deja's counsel due to his unavailability. Swiftly suggesting James O'Donovan as the emissary, she undertook the responsibility of making the arrangements. The recommendation delighted Pak Hyun Woo, believing it would convey a message of alignment between North Korea and Ireland. Akma Deja anticipated her brother's eventual invitation to the White House and began formulating a plan to end his reign. She aspired to replace him as North Korea's New Supreme Leader, steering the socialist republic back on the path of Juche, a self-reliance championed by her late father.

In a diabolical move, Akma Deja planned to orchestrate her brother's demise in a manner that would force the entire Western world to surrender to North Korea. She considered President David Bryce as the ironic collateral damage to her scheme, intending to conduct a test during the Iftar dinner. Aware of James's diagnosis of cancer, she found amusement in the fact that he tried to conceal his illness while undergoing comprehensive radiation treatment. In her warped, psychotic mind, she aimed to exploit the White House's security measures during James's visit, testing the limits of their defenses during the Iftar dinner.

In her realization, it dawned on her that the relatively low level of radioactivity from James might have triggered scrutiny at the White House checkpoint. During a subsequent phone call, James revealed that he never met President Bryce that evening. Instead, he was given a tour by the Chief of Staff, an unusual deviation from the expected protocol. Questioning him about the peculiar treatment, James admitted to being held longer for security scrutiny. This raised concerns, prompting Akma Deja to reconsider the introduction of a radiological weapon into the White House.

Upon receiving James's account, Akma Deja promptly summoned her office of science and technology to convene. While briefing them on the mission's objective, she withheld the crucial detail that her brother was the target. Suspicious of even her loyal followers, she sought an alternative to radiological weapons and leaned towards a chemical-based approach with an aerosol release, confined to a small meeting room.

Her team of scientists worked tirelessly, experimenting with combinations of sulfur yperite, nitrogen, ethylene oxide, and hydrogen sulfide. The trials spanned days that turned into weeks, progressing from rats to pigs and eventually humans. The time had come to bring the testing to a grim climax by involving the worst resident of Camp 15.

This inmate, convicted of murder, had committed a heinous act against a servant girl. After raping her, he callously threw her from a fourth-floor abandoned building. While the fall didn't claim her life immediately, the young girl endured two agonizing days of writhing on the ground before succumbing to internal bleeding, a fractured femur, and exposure. With many more like him in the camp, Akma Deja had patiently awaited the opportune moment to execute this particular convict. The victim in this heinous murder had been a house servant loyal to Deja, and the murderer, Deja's long-time suitor and fiancé. Now, with the testing room set, Akma Deja would subject her prisoner to the harsh realities of her father's Juche. The macabre stage was set for a dark experiment with the condemned man as the unwitting participant. She liked her servant and estranged fiancé both, but she liked the young servant girl more.

Tara Lee stood alongside Akma Deja behind the glass of the control room, joined by the lead chemist upon whom Deja had relied on for years. The naked prisoner, now bound and gagged, faced the security team that secured him to a hoist lowered from the ceiling. Suspended by the hoist, the test subject awaited today's experiment. As the gag was removed, his furious insults echoed, first drawing a smile, then laughter from Akma Deja, who seemed thoroughly amused. Tara Lee, however, questioned her presence, finding no amusement in the macabre display. Voicing her discontent, Lee earned a piercing glare from Akma Deja, realizing she had overstepped.

With a push of the first button, Akma Deja sealed the control room, isolating it from external contaminants. She then instructed Tara Lee to push the second button. Reluctantly, Tara Lee complied.

A slight hiss emanated from the test room as a canister released a brief puff of bluish mist toward the subject's body and face. Almost instantly, his body twisted into grotesque shapes, convulsing as blood flowed from his nose. Froth and blood were expelled from his mouth, and within seconds, his body went limp. While the onlookers in the control room stared in shock, Akma Deja wore an ear-to-ear smile.

Without delay, she turned to her chemist and casually inquired, "How do we make this fit into a device that could be housed in a cellphone?"

Her team embarked on a relentless effort to meet Akma Deja's demand. Developing a potent concentration small enough to be concealed in a cellphone posed a formidable challenge. Every researcher understood the consequences of saying no to Akma Deja—disappearance. The chemical potency underwent rigorous testing on rats and pigs. The correct mixture of mustard-like gas molecules, when concentrated, proved lethal to any biological nervous system. The key was not the volume but the precise combination of chemicals. It was a dark alchemy that brought death to living tissues. The race against time continued as Akma Deja's chilling plans unfolded.

The diluted toxin mixture found another subject in a condemned guest of Camp 15. Akma Deja seized on another opportunity to attend the not so public execution. The prisoner, a former general in her father's administration, had once opposed the late Supreme Leader's wish to continue missile testing over the South China Sea. Out of loyalty to her father, he had been spared from immediate execution and sentenced to a life of imprisonment at Camp 15. His family paid the ultimate price, as his wife and two sons were executed by firing squad outside their home.

Summoning Phillip O'Donovan to join her, Akma Deja brought him into the control room to witness the field testing. Until now, she had paid little attention to him or Patrick.

"I want you to observe something with me, Phillip," she said.

Phillip remained silent until she directed his gaze through the glass into the testing room. The light illuminated a man in his late fifties, naked and hoisted up by a winch. The man was emaciated and crying uncontrollably.

Phillip's body shook, visibly upset. "Who is that? What did they do?" He pleaded for humanity and decency; concepts foreign to Akma Deja. "Are you going to beat him like you did my Patrick," he desperately inquired.

She believed an answer was owed. "It's not important what he did. What he does next is very important. There won't be a beating today, but something much more ambitious, dear Phillip."

This time, the test involved the concentrated chemical mixture, without the cellphone prototype. Phillip observed Akma Deja's face as her hand motioned towards the button. Anticipation played across her expression as she pressed it. A swift mist ejected from the chemical cartridge, the size of a credit card. Akma Deja took delight in this exhibition, much like any psychopath would. The subject contorted and screamed briefly, then, in a matter of seconds, dropped his head while his body stayed hoisted upright by the straps. His lifeless body still convulsed as his nervous system was coming under attack. Frothy blood poured from his mouth and nose. Phillip, forced to watch, shielded his eyes from the horror. Deja led a round of exuberant applause, and her team reluctantly joined in. To her, it was a success. Now, she commanded her team to create the cellphone device that would conceal the deadly toxin.

"Well, Phillip," a triumphant Deja said rhetorically, not expecting an informed response.

He replied, "Please, may I go and see Patrick?"

Akma Deja provided her team with clear instructions on the capabilities the device should possess. The team experimented with different cellphone brands, ensuring the device could make and receive calls and had a digital recording feature. Several prototypes were developed. The triggering mechanism, activating upon an incoming call from a specific number, would authenticate and disarm the chemical awaiting deployment. A four-digit numerical code would activate the triggering mechanism, releasing the mist. All within 30 feet of the device would be dead within seconds. The device would also be capable of video recording in real time. This was Akma Deja's charge to her team. She wanted them to test the prototype on livestock, and when they deemed it ready, she would select the next condemned prisoner.

Only eight days had passed since Akma Deja issued the initial command for the weapon, and now she was about to witness the first prototype. She was quite pleased with the speed and efficiency of her science and technology team. She examined the cellphone prototype, which outwardly resembled any other cellphone of its kind. A team member opened the device for her inspection. She saw a credit card-sized bladder containing the deadly concentrate. The next day, the prototype would be tested on a very special guest of Camp 15.

* * *

Tara Lee had been distant lately, at least from Akma Deja's perspective. She seemed no longer passionate about the cause and indifferent to her purpose. Deja thought it might be a good time to bring the family back together. She arranged for a dinner in the dining room located in her wing in the Supreme Palace. Tara Lee had already settled into her seat when the door swung open, admitting Phillip and Patrick. As soon as they laid eyes on her, anguish contorted their faces, and they swiftly turned physically and verbally aggressive. Phillip lunged at Tara, who was in complete shock. Reacting defensively, she leveled Phillip to the floor. Patrick, defending his father, tried to attack and suffered the same fate. Deja's security team intervened, restraining all three and seating them on opposite sides of the table.

"Now now," Akma Deja said, smiling. "Let's at least communicate our differences. Phillip, you get to ask Tara, or should I say, Soon Min Un, one question. Make it a good one."

He didn't have to think twice. "Did you kill my Annie? Did you kill her? My wife!?"

The contemplative Soon Min Un, almost childlike, replied with a slight Korean accent, "I had to. It was for the cause."

Patrick, again attempting to lunge over the table, was pulled back into his chair by the security team. "Alright, I believe it is time to eat." For the next hour, they were forced to listen to Akma Deja's plan to become the next Supreme Leader when her brother faced his demise. Her company ate in silence. Phillip and Patrick were now fueled by a new sense of purpose—survival for revenge.

The next day, the final test of the device was scheduled. Akma Deja stood in the control room alongside her trusted science and technology team. On the table in the testing room lay a simple cellphone, and hanging from the winch was a subject in a robe with a hood over their head, bound and gagged like the others before.

"Bring in our special guests," Deja commanded. Patrick and Phillip were led into the control room. Phillip immediately looked through the glass, his protective instincts kicking in as he pulled Patrick close, trying to shield his view from what was about to happen. A security officer separated them, forcing their view towards the testing room.

"Dad, what's going on? What are we..."

"Quiet," the evil sister shouted. At that moment, the winch lowered the subject to a standing position. A security officer approached, disrobing the condemned subject, revealing a woman's naked body. Phillip and Patrick, in tears and visibly shaking, did not want to be there. The hood was lifted, revealing Tara Lee, bound by her hands and tethered to the winch. Immediately, Patrick's brow furrowed, his scowl turning into one of disdain. Fueled by emotion, Patrick shouted, "Fucking bitch, I hope they beat you like they beat me..." Once again, Akma Deja commanded, "Quiet!"

She pulled out her phone and dialed a number. The cellphone on the desk below Tara Lee rang twice. Gagged and with her voice muddled, Lee instinctively tried to escape her restraints, she managed to free the gag from her mouth and pleaded for mercy.

Deja handed her phone to Phillip and said, "She killed your wife, she watched with glee while your boy was beaten to within inches of his life. She is the face of your torment, and she is the reason you wound up here. Enter 3-5-2-1, and the same toxin you saw previously will be released ending her life in a very dramatic way."

Phillip trembled, looking at Patrick, who was crying and visibly upset. Neither seemed to find the words to speak.

Then Patrick spoke up, "Dad, do it. Enter the numbers. She killed Mom. She fucking killed Mom!" Akma Deja smiled ear to ear, reveling in the intrigue.

Tara Lee seemingly turned back into Soon Min Un. She cried and mixed her words in Korean and English, "Don't, Patrick, please don't. She manipulated me. She brainwashed me."

Phillip's reach extended to the button, "I need to do this," he said to himself. A long pause ensued, then he reluctantly pushed the phone back towards Deja, relinquishing his involvement in her psychotic pleasures, "I don't have it in me to kill her. Please let me and Patrick go."

He hugged Patrick tighter, saying, "I love you, son. We're going to be okay. We're going to be okay."

Patrick had no words for his father, only a visage of torment and lingering anger.

They watched as Soon Min Un was released from the winch, her body falling to the floor. Still in restraints, she was escorted out of the testing room. She would live, but the fate of the next prisoner would not end the same way. She still had to test the final prototype. Phillip and Patrick watched in horror as another prisoner was hoisted up to the winch and hung from the ceiling. Akma Deja dialed the cellphone. It rang twice, and looking at the father and son, she entered 3-5-2-1. The device worked beautifully.

* * *

Later that day, the Office of Social Affairs for the Supreme Leader called Deja with exciting news. An invitation had been extended to her brother and a guest to join President and First Lady David Bryce in a private gathering at the White House. Deja couldn't help but ponder that such an invitation typically preceded an official state visit. The anticipated date for the private gathering was set for one week from the day. Recognizing the opportune moment, she decided to enlist the services of the esteemed Professor James O'Donovan one final time. Lately, James felt a growing sense of unease with Akma Deja as his attention gravitated towards his ascending role within Sinn Féin. Even his telephone conversations with his nephew, Phillip, were minimal and more infrequent. When they did occur, Deja ensured they remained brief. Whenever Phillip engaged in phone conversations with his Uncle James, each word seemed meticulously crafted and orchestrated. Despite the carefully controlled nature of these interactions, James remained unsuspecting of Phillip and Patrick's captivity.

Phillip's script consistently painted a vivid picture of him exploring South Korea with Tara. He would portray Patrick as a perpetually enthusiastic student immersed in novel experiences abroad. Either way, James remained blissfully ignorant of any hidden agendas. Unbeknownst to him, this rehearsed narrative served as a subtle reminder that Akma Deja held the strings to both Phillip and his son's freedom. She held onto the knowledge that if James ever posed an obstacle, she could readily leverage the freedom of Phillip and Patrick to her advantage. This tactic had proven successful before, a notion she held with a quiet assurance. Despite this, she acknowledged that persuading her brother to select James as his companion for the event would be no easy feat. It was a challenge that she knew would require all her persuasive abilities.

However, Deja, confident in her ability to be compelling, began strategizing on how to navigate this delicate proposition. The stakes were high, and she understood that successfully orchestrating this selection could play a pivotal role in her broader plans. Her counterfeit operation in Belfast was in full swing, creating perfect counterfeit notes. The currency was already saturating the banking system of Great Britain and would soon infiltrate the United States. *Death by a thousand cuts, Papa,* she reflected, recognizing it as his vision. With determination, she vocalized her remaining thought, "I will realign your vision with the final phase of my plan, Papa. I must bring an end to your foolish son's reign so I can initiate mine."

In her opulent palace, she had already beckoned her trusted lapdog, Stansfield, to her side. As he arrived, she wasted no time in unveiling the next phase of her ultimate plan. Seated together in the grandeur of the palace, she thoroughly briefed him on every intricate detail, laying bare the entirety of her scheme, from its inception to its ominous end game. For two relentless days, Stansfield Anderson endured the complete and agonizing exposition of Akma Deja's grand design. By the time she concluded, he found himself utterly speechless, his mind reeling from the magnitude of her ambitions. He was shaken to his core, and physically exhausted from the mental ordeal. She assigned Anderson the delicate task of transporting the lapel camera and the cellphone device to James O'Donovan in Ireland. Given Stansfield Anderson's diplomatic status, she believed everything would proceed smoothly.

CHAPTER 42

Anderson's Return

"The only difference between the saint and the sinner is that every saint has a past, and every sinner has a future."
—Oscar Wilde

Stansfield Anderson sought refuge in the opulent confines of the United Airlines first-class lounge at Incheon International Airport in Seoul, South Korea. He just spent two days at the palace under the thumb of Akma Deja. He was still processing what he just experienced. He found himself entangled in the throes of a perplexing and ominous situation. His third tumbler of Nolet's Reserve Dry Gin did little to unravel the enigma of the past forty-eight hours. It was during this time that Akma Deja had laid bare her malevolent endgame. The solemnity of his own vulnerabilities bound him tightly within her clutches.

The disturbing imagery from the videos lingered in Anderson's mind—three anonymous souls exposed to a sinister noxious gas. Initially dismissing it as an elaborate ruse, the brutal reality seeped in as a group of scientists delivered a macabre presentation, complete with PowerPoint slides detailing the chemical makeup of the deadly gas and the intricate mechanics of the ominous device. Anderson couldn't suppress the thought swirling in his mind: if there existed a psychopath's rock bottom, Akma Deja has surely hit it.

The haunting specter of spasming bodies and blood flowing from noses and mouths haunted Anderson's thoughts. The victims, released in a grotesque display, lay lifeless on the cement floor. Akma's willingness to assassinate the President of the United States as a means to assassinate her own brother bewildered him. Especially when she spoke of resurrecting her late father's North Korea and becoming the Supreme Leader of the Socialist Republic, all captured on film for a global audience.

The revelation that James, his friend, would unwittingly carry the device into the White House struck Anderson like a thunderbolt. She even equipped him with some sort of Bluetooth-connected lapel button camera. *She wants to see everything,* he surmised. Akma Deja revealed a sinister twist—James was dying of cancer and hopelessly in love with her, making him compliant to her demands. She chuckled about a backup plan that involved collateral in the form of an imprisoned nephew and son.

He was now fighting the fog brought on by the pills she had provided to keep him under her control. He found himself at her mercy, swallowing two more opioid tablets to numb the phantom pain. His decision to mix them with the third gin proved imprudent, clouding his judgment even further. Amidst the chaos, he deciphered the mission she had given him: retrieve the counterfeit bills from the Belfast factory, deposit them into O'Donovan's account, and wire an equivalent sum offshore to the Cayman account. *These simple tasks,* he thought, *I can comprehend and execute.*

Trapped by the walls of treason, Anderson wrestled with the unbearable alternatives of life imprisonment or execution. For the first time in his life, he seriously contemplated the possibility of surrender. The eighteen hours in the sky ahead offered a solitary sanctuary for him to grapple with his fate.

Akma Deja tasked him with delivering the cellphone device and lapel camera to James O'Donovan. He knew he must tread carefully. With James, he would need to refrain from revealing Deja's diabolical plans at least until he could figure out an alternative plan. The fog in his brain intensified as he staggered towards the plane. His diplomatic passport afforded him an opportunity to preboard. Nestled in the comfort of the first-class seat, Anderson succumbed to a troubled slumber, cradling the diplomatic pouch that held the lapel camera and the ominous device. As he drifted into sleep, he whispered a prayer—an uncommon gesture for him in a life rife with turmoil.

The flight was uneventful and the aircraft's descent into Belfast snapped Stansfield Anderson awake. His stomach grumbled, having missed all three in-flight meal services. Whether a divine inspiration or a fleeting dream, the notion struck him to secure the lethal diplomatic pouch and its contents in a locker at the Belfast International Airport. There, it would remain safe until he could muster a sober moment to devise a more thoughtful and informed plan.

As he stepped into the bustling terminal, a surge of urgency propelled him to reach for his phone and dial his old friend, James O'Donovan. Words failed him momentarily as his mind grappled with the fog of uncertainty. Seeking clarity, he made his way to the United Airlines lounge, hoping the aroma of freshly brewed coffee would awaken him. After securing a locker with a swipe of his credit card, he stowed away the pouch and its contents before retreating to a secluded corner of the lounge. With a deep breath, he dialed the familiar number of James O'Donovan, his trusted confidant for years.

Meanwhile, Reynolds and his vigilant surveillance team tracked every movement of their target. From their vantage point, they relayed updates to Quinlan and Mackey, as they were covering the parking deck overlooking Anderson's Range Rover.

Mackey's voice carried a hint of nostalgia as he remarked to Quinlan, "Feels like old times, doesn't it, Q?"

Quinlan couldn't suppress a smile of agreement. Just then, their earpieces crackled with the report from Reynolds, "Target in motion, approaching your position, Quinlan."

Navigating through the modest confines of the Belfast airport, Anderson reached his vehicle. Mackey and Quinlan exchanged observations, noting the disparity between Anderson's appearance and their preconceived notions of an MI-5 agent. "Huh, he's taller than I thought," remarked Mackey. Meanwhile, Quinlan maintained a discreet distance as they trailed Anderson's Range Rover. Mackey kept them informed of their whereabouts as the four-car surveillance team initiated their operation. Anticipating a thirty-minute journey from the airport to West Belfast, Quinlan guided the team onto Airport Road, seamlessly merging onto the A57, and finally onto the M2 highway for the ensuing fourteen miles.

Reviewing the map spread across the dashboard, Mackey pondered aloud, "If he veers onto Divis Street, odds are he's heading for West Belfast. This is where Reynolds' guys are already positioned."

Quinlan's response laced with skepticism, "It's never that easy, is it?" Their doubts were unwarranted as Anderson's Range Rover indeed turned onto Divis Street, navigating through urban streets until halting on Wellington Street. From their concealed vantage point, they observed Stansfield's vehicle slipping into a nearby garage beside an unmarked building. Urgently, Quinlan relayed the information to the surveillance team, redirecting their focus to the newly identified location on Wellington Street. Approximately thirty minutes later, the Range Rover reappeared exiting the garage onto Wellington, heading towards the bustling downtown financial district. Enduring a grueling twenty-minute crawl through traffic-congested streets, the team observed Anderson's entrance into the Northern Bank of Ireland, carrying a bulky duffle bag.

Quinlan's thoughts spilled into the air, "We can't confirm if he had that bag when he left the airport, but it's highly probable he acquired it from the factory. And maybe he is now depositing the contents into O'Donovan's account?"

Mackey nodded in agreement, his tone reflecting caution, "It's mostly circumstantial, but those are my thoughts as well. I just wish he hadn't ducked into that garage. Seeing him enter the factory empty-handed and then emerge with that bag would have been priceless."

Anderson exited the bank and departed in his vehicle. The surveillance team followed him back to the Wellington Street factory. Quinlan decided to keep Mackey at the factory address in the van. Reynolds arrived and picked up Quinlan, providing them with an opportunity to discuss their next steps. Both agreed that further discreet investigation at the bank was imperative. It was crucial to identify whether the deposit constituted an APEX transaction or not. This would determine if the Wellington address likely functioned as the hub for manufacturing the counterfeit bills. However, they couldn't shake off their unease regarding Anderson's recent trip to North Korea; it seemed improbable that it was solely related to the APEX note.

Reynolds turned to Quinlan, "Do you believe we have enough grounds for a search warrant if we decide to proceed with the factory?"

Quinlan thought for a moment, his mind racing through legal intricacies before he replied, "I'm fairly confident we do, but I want to speak with Lana first. She's been my legal go-to since our days back in NYC. She used to prosecute all my cases and her perspective is much needed. I'll also see if she can coordinate with a local magistrate here in the UK to see if we have enough for a search warrant."

Reynolds nodded in acknowledgment, his eyes betraying the weight of their predicament. "If we opt for that route, at least we'll have the opportunity to interrogate Anderson regarding his ties to Akma Deja and the reasons for his visit to her palace. There has to be more going on here than a mere counterfeit operation."

Quinlan echoed Reynolds' sentiment, his voice tinged with curiosity and concern, "I couldn't agree more. Who travels on an eighteen-hour journey by plane for a discussion that could easily take place over the phone? Moreover, I'm interested in the disappearance of the O'Donovan duo—Phillip, and his son, Patrick."

That evening, Quinlan's anticipation peaked as he received a response from Lana Miller. Her message carried a glimmer of hope. The bank had confirmed Stansfield's substantial deposit of half a million dollars in crisp $100 U.S. bills. Even more promising, Lana had orchestrated a constructive seizure of the currency without alerting the account holder or Anderson, the depositor.

Mackey responded to the bank and his careful examination of the bills uncovered a startling revelation—each note belonged to the 2013 series. Some of the notes shared identical serial numbers. It was a telltale sign: these were APEX notes. A surge of excitement coursed through Quinlan. He and Mackey bore the responsibility of identifying the source of the counterfeit note that had eluded the Secret Service for over two decades. Moreover, this particular APEX note, once the corrections were made, would be raised to the level of indistinguishable from genuine.

MI-5's interest in Stansfield Anderson simmered beneath the surface, waiting for the opportune moment to address the tangled web he had woven. For now, MI-5's senior management were content to let the CIA and Secret Service take the lead on the counterfeit operation, leveraging the public exposure to bring charges against him. Quietly, they would begin the arduous task of assessing the fallout on UK-Ukraine relations. This would rise to one of the largest diplomatic quagmires ever to tarnish British intelligence. Quinlan pressed Reynolds to expedite the raid the following morning, as he needed to return to DC for the impending visit of the North Korean Supreme Leader. Reynolds agreed, citing the urgency of the situation.

At dawn, Quinlan, Mackey, and Reynolds joined forces with a team of RUC police officers for the search warrant raid. The operation kicked off at 5:00 am with a thunderous breach of the door by the RUC, accompanied by blinding stun grenades. In the chaotic aftermath, Stansfield Anderson was discovered cowering behind a makeshift couch, while another figure, older and of Asian descent, emerged from a rear room. Amidst the disarray, the raid team swiftly identified a printing press positioned near the breached entrance. The room was surrounded by large rolls of uncut paper and ink canisters. It was evident that this makeshift workshop had been hastily assembled.

With Anderson and his accomplice in custody, Quinlan and Reynolds wasted no time in transporting Anderson to Reynolds' clandestine office in Belfast. Tucked away in an abandoned RUC jail, the repurposed facility was acquired by the U.S. Embassy for the CIA's covert operations. This location was a testament to Reynolds' resourcefulness. Quinlan couldn't help but marvel at how Reynolds had transformed such a decrepit setting into a functional hub for their operations, a reminder of the murky world they inhabited.

Anderson immediately confessed his involvement in the counterfeit plant, admitting to collaborating with Akma Deja, to establish her illicit operation. He revealed recent meetings with her, discussing the progress of the counterfeit enterprise. With candor, he confessed to selling secrets to the Russians, attributing it to his desperation and addiction to opioids. His story had layers, intricacies that would require closer scrutiny in due time. However, urgency demanded a focus on his true motives for meeting Akma Deja and the whereabouts of Phillip and Patrick O'Donovan.

In the midst of the interrogation, Quinlan discreetly pulled Reynolds aside, "Did anyone from the surveillance team witness Anderson's actions inside the United passenger lounge at the airport?"

Reynolds shook his head in response. Quinlan pressed on, "We know he made a five-minute call to James O'Donovan, according to his cellphone records but we don't know what he said. We need to press him on that."

They confronted Anderson with their suspicions, but he remained elusive. He insisted that although he had made a call to his friend, James O'Donovan, he merely informed him of his safe return to Belfast and extended an invitation for a drink later that evening. He conveniently left out any mention of the airport locker and its contents. Anderson realized he must have slipped through the cracks of visual surveillance in the airport lounge. It also appears they were not listening in on his call. If they were, they would know of his instructions to his friend James to retrieve the airport locker's contents. He resolved to withhold that crucial detail. For the first time in a long while, a sense of peace washed over him as he partially unburdened himself with the weight of his secrets. He knew his future was bleak, likely confined behind bars for the remainder of his days or maybe facing a more permanent fate. But for now, he found solace in the partial truth, however grim it may be.

* * *

Quinlan made the decision to return to Washington, DC, leaving Mackey behind to handle the coordination of evidence and the initial court proceedings. A specialized team of forensic examiners from Secret Service headquarters had been dispatched to process the evidence, marking what promised to be a definitive victory for the United States Government, particularly the U.S. Secret Service.

Taking up the U.S. Embassy's offer for transportation to the airport, Quinlan seized the opportunity to bid farewell to Reynolds in person and express his gratitude. He was armed with a bottle of Jameson Irish Whiskey as a token of appreciation. He instructed the embassy driver to stop at the satellite office, where he anticipated Reynolds would be.

To his surprise, when he arrived, he was met by an unfamiliar figure dressed in fatigues and a black t-shirt. Inquiring about Chief Reynolds' whereabouts, Quinlan's sense of unease intensified as he was met with silence. After repeating his question, Reynolds finally emerged from a partially open door leading to a back room, revealing a scene of unexpected intensity.

Inside the room, two other unidentified men, similarly dressed, stood behind Reynolds, their sleeves rolled up and sweat staining their shirts. Quinlan's gaze fell upon a slightly inverted table, where a hooded figure lay, the body heaving with exertion. It took only a moment for him to assume the figure was Stansfield Anderson.

"Chief, what the hell is going on here? This looks like a waterboarding rendition," Quinlan exclaimed, his disbelief evident.

Reynolds, his expression grim and determined, revealed the depths of his pursuit. "For the past five years, I've been tracking down leaks to the Russians, and I've always suspected Anderson's involvement," he explained, his voice edged with frustration.

Quinlan attempted to interject, "Yeah, he's confessed to all that."

As Reynolds took his turn to speak, his words carried a weight of urgency and suspicion.

"There's more to this, John. No one travels halfway across the globe just to discuss counterfeit bills. Have you seen Akma Deja? I did some digging online, and yeah she's a piece of ass but I don't care how hot you are, no one travels that far for forty-eight hours for a woman." Quinlan listened intently as Reynolds spoke. "I'm going with a hunch, and I'm getting to the bottom of it NOW," Reynolds declared. "Anderson's involvement with this woman suggests something far deeper than a mere affair or a counterfeit case. You're too fixated on the APEX note to see the bigger picture. Her brother, the North Korean leader, is heading to the White House with James O'Donovan as his date. You see anything wrong with that? Anderson's recent visit to her palace raises more questions than answers."

Quinlan nodded, conceding, "You're right. I may have been missing the forest for the trees on this one. But resorting to these methods isn't the solution."

Reynolds' demeanor remained steadfast; his tone unwavering. "John, you're in my world now. You want the truth, but you're not willing to endure the necessary means to uncover it."

Quinlan let Reynolds' words sink in, feeling the weight of their implications. As Reynolds placed a hand on his shoulder, Quinlan could not help but feel a pang of unease.

"You know what, John? You're a New York City boy. I bet you love your dirty water hot dogs. You know the ones some random guy sells you on the street. They taste so good. Everybody loves those dogs. But there ain't nobody asking how they're made. Don't worry John. I'll get what I want out of him, you'll get what you want out of him, and he will be presented for his arraignment without a mark on him."

Backing away, Quinlan watched as Reynolds and the stranger disappeared back into the interview room. With a heavy heart, he realized that their pursuit of justice had led them into darker territory than he had anticipated. And as he lingered in the hallway, the unsettling feeling persisted, signaling that there were more layers to this case than met the eye.

CHAPTER 43

Assassination at the White House

"These are the times that try men's souls."
—Thomas Paine

In Pyongyang, Akma Deja mindfully orchestrated the arrangements for the impending dinner at the White House through her brother's social office. Personal communication with her brother had become infrequent, reduced to interactions through their respective representatives. She couldn't shake the regret of informing James about holding his nephew, Phillip, and son, Patrick, as her guests in Camp 15. His reaction to the news left him bewildered and infuriated, unable to grasp the desperation of the situation until Stansfield Anderson intervened to provide clarification.

Anderson provided reassurance to James, assuring him that despite the challenging circumstances, Phillip and Patrick were holding up well. He endeavored to explain Akma Deja's motives to his friend, suggesting that they stemmed from a semblance of desperation. Anderson explained to James that she required Phillip's cooperation to resolve issues tied to her late father's money printing operation. Aware that Phillip wouldn't willingly come on his own, she resorted to the drastic measure of abducting Patrick from his college in order to entice Phillip to her side. This scheme appeared as sheer madness to the ailing professor, whose health was deteriorating rapidly due in part to the chemotherapy. He couldn't wrap his mind around the notion of kidnapping his nephew to resolve a matter connected to her late father's counterfeiting scheme. *Utter madness*, he thought to himself. This firm conviction led him to adamantly refuse the White House invitation with the Supreme Leader. He simply would not attend.

"Listen, old friend," Anderson explained, "All you need to do is be present at the White House dinner. It's a small meeting. You need to wear this discreet lapel camera. As you take your seat, simply lay the cellphone on the table. That's the extent of it. Deja intends to view and record the proceedings covertly. Once you've done this, excuse yourself and leave the room to ensure you're not implicated in any way. Her distrust of her brother runs deep, and she's determined to oversee the entire interaction with President Bryce. Afterward, come back to Dublin."

That's how James relayed his conversation with Anderson to Akma Deja when he spoke to her on the phone. "That's good," she said. "I'm glad Anderson explained it to you. Darling, you're doing this for me, and I'll always be grateful," she told him. "I don't trust my brother, and I need to see and hear exactly what transpires at this small dinner. I need you to do this for me, and once this is all over, I'll release your nephew and his son, and we'll reunite in Dublin for a wonderful visit."

"Yes," said James O'Donovan. "I don't understand any of this, but I will do what you ask. I will attend the dinner with your brother. I do it out of love." He concluded the phone conversation with Akma Deja, offering a somber smile to his friend Stansfield Anderson who stood beside him as he made the call to Deja. Then, he handed the phone to the man wearing headphones recording the conversation. James had trapped her. Despite his love for her, bitterness consumed him. He felt betrayed, realizing he would never see her again.

* * *

Back at Camp 15, Akma Deja arranged the control room, ensuring it boasted a luxurious sixty-five-inch flat screen and plush seating for seven. She anticipated relishing the evening's events at the White House. This was courtesy of the strategic placement of two cameras. One discreetly pinned to James O'Donovan's lapel, and another cleverly embedded within a cellphone. Yet, concealed within the depths of that same device lay a potent weapon. She would say it was a credit card-sized bladder brimming with a lethal concoction of freedom. She adjusted for the twelve-hour time difference. She set the stage for her viewing at 8:00 am. Perfectly synchronized with the event scheduled for 7:00 pm at the White House.

She came to the realization that cellphones underwent no manual inspection at the White House checkpoints. She reasoned this was the case during James O'Donovan's attendance at the Iftar Dinner several months prior. This reconnaissance mission proved to be invaluable. It reinforced her reliance on the likelihood of a similar oversight occurring once more. Also, this would be a more intimate setting and given O'Donovan's prominent role within Sinn Féin, she expected no issues.

Gathered for this exclusive one-time viewing were Phillip and Patrick O'Donovan, Tara Lee, Deja's steadfast personal security detail, the chief chemist, the audio-visual aid, and an exhausted Stansfield Anderson who barely made it in time. Akma Deja was acutely aware of Anderson's pivotal role in securing the release of Phillip and Patrick post-operation. She acknowledged his tireless journey spanning two oceans and parts of Europe in service of their cause. Licking her lips, Deja instructed her technical aid to turn on the flat screen. She found immense pleasure in the anticipation. James would activate the video connection on the device as the Supreme Leader's motorcade made its advance to the White House. Anderson found himself unable to tear his gaze away from the monitor. He knew it would unfold as Deja anticipated, so he shifted his focus to her. Her reaction would be more intriguing.

Meanwhile, in Washington, DC, the dignitaries were preparing to arrive at the White House for an intimate evening.

"Castle from Murray, we are a short Bravo. Copy Murray all clear," came the radio transmission. The smaller than usual six car motorcade arrived at the North Portico.

Dignitary Protection Agent Will Murray promptly opened the right rear door of the Secret Service limousine. Agent Stevens followed suit, opening the offside door to allow James O'Donovan to exit. The video froze, causing Akma Deja to jump from her chair in sudden anticipation.

"It's not on our end, madam," her technical aid assured her.

"Fuckin James," she muttered in frustration.

Minutes passed, then the video came to light. It was dark and grainy. James adjusted his lapel pin, and out of the darkness appeared Lt. Colonel Allan Prince. Prince, a proud Marine, hailed from a military family; his father Ronald served in the Army during the Korean War. Ronald Prince was documented as missing in action during the Battle of the Chosin Reservoir, off the North Korean peninsula.

Despite his inherent disdain, Lt. Colonel Allan Prince respected the office and saluted the visiting dignitary. This was a meeting to discuss the plans the new Supreme Leader had in mind to allow United Nations weapons inspectors into North Korea. President Bryce knew what he was doing. He needed a quiet meeting away from the press. He wanted to shake the hand of the man he would look in the eye, to know exactly who he was dealing with.

The White House Usher, Walter Sterling, directed the men to the private residence elevator. The footage now was fuzzy, causing Deja to slam her fist on the desk in frustration. Her team looked on in shock, but her mood lifted when the elevator door opened, and the video showed President Bryce.

Meanwhile, James kept adjusting his lapel camera, causing the lens to falter. "Stop it, stop it. Turn on the phone now, you silly fool," Deja urged, writhing in anticipation as she moved about in her seat.

"Hello, Leader Pak. So good to see you and Professor O'Donovan. I have heard a lot about you. Let's move to the dining area, shall we?"

the President said as they made their way to the private dining room on the 3rd floor of the White House residence. They were invited to take their seats at the adorned family dining room table. The conversation continued, discussing Sinn Féin's growing presence in the UK. Unnoticed by anyone, James had discreetly placed the cellphone on the table. As the video came alive, the 280-degree lens captured every detail perfectly. Deja would finally get to witness her brother's demise in agonizing detail.

James intended to excuse himself when the phone vibrated. Back at the control room, Anderson watched as an evil grin appeared on Deja's face. She made the call to the phone, causing it to vibrate. At that moment, James requested the use of the men's room. Usher Sterling gladly walked him out of the dining room and down the hall. Deja observed as James left the room. Then, at that critical moment, she entered the code, releasing a short burst of the deadly chemical.

She could not discern the mist, however, her brother suddenly stood from the table gasping for air. He clutched his throat. President Bryce stood and motioned to the door, then fell to the floor. Deja was fixated on her brother as she could only see parts of his body blocked by the table. A Secret Service agent stormed in and immediately succumbed to the toxic mist. Blood poured from the agent's nose and mouth. It took only a few minutes. Thrilled to have this recorded memento, she was completely engrossed in the unfolding torment. Unaware, she failed to notice her own security team had left the control room, replaced by Supreme Leader Pak Hyun Woo's own personal guard.

Stansfield Anderson now embraced Phillip and Patrick. "Deja, I will be taking these two now. You no longer have use for them. Do we agree?" he stated firmly.

Akma Deja rose from her perch, paying no attention to Anderson's question. "I am now the Supreme Leader," she declared.

Deja looked at the screen in delight as it went black. With a flick of her hand, she signaled to Anderson, implying she had no further use for them. Silently, he and the O'Donovans departed, flanked by Supreme Leader Pak's personal guard. The guard ensured a discreet vehicle convoy to the DMZ, the rendezvous point where CIA Chief John Reynolds awaited the beleaguered hostages. From there, their lengthy journey homeward would commence aboard an Air Force C-21 bound for Andrews Air Force Base.

Akma Deja, beaming with a wide smile and clearly very pleased, was puzzled when the monitor came back to life. President Bryce, Supreme Leader Pak, and Professor O'Donovan alive and well appeared under the seal of Camp David. The video's time stamp showed that it was a live telecast. Deja's face contorted with bewilderment. She walked to the technical aid, her eyes wide with disbelief, and screamed, "This can't be!" Her expression was one of utter shock and astonishment.

Pak Hyun Woo declared, "Sister, the game is over, and you have been outplayed. You dared to challenge me, setting in motion an elaborate scheme to end my life. But it has come to naught. I have commanded my guards to free those you held captive. Your vision for our nation's future, mired in treachery and shadows, has been rejected. My vision for a new North Korea, one that thrives under the banner of the peoples' rule, will come to fruition. We set forth on a journey toward embracing open democracy, drawing inspiration from the values of the Western world. Once hidden, you schemed deceitfully behind my back, but now your betrayal is laid bare for all to see. You will be brought before a new kind of court, one founded on fairness and justice, where you will be judged in full view of the public. The verdict will be just, and the punishment swift and fitting. A new dawn breaks, sister, heralding an era you sought to prevent."

At that moment, James placed his feeble hand on the Supreme Leader's leg urging him to pause. "Pak Hyun Mi, why? Why?" he implored, seeking understanding in a moment fraught with tension.

Meanwhile, Deja's attention was fixed on one of the sprawling arrays of monitors before her. She spotted Anderson and the

O'Donovans making their way out of Camp 15 under their security escort. Panic surged through her as she pointed at the screen, her voice sharp with urgency. "Stop them, fucking stop them!"

Just then, Tara Lee grabbed Deja by her hair, dragging her into the room where she had witnessed her parents take their final breath. Every soul in the control room stood paralyzed, watching the drama unfold through the glass. Tara managed to close the door behind her using her leg, her arms occupied with intention.

With a swift movement borne of desperation and resolve, Tara tackled Akma Deja to the ground. From her grasp, she revealed a canister taken from the lab some time earlier, its contents were purposeful and lethal. She pulled the tab, and the can released its deadly toxin. Akma Deja and Tara Lee writhed in agony as the mist ignited from the canister. Their faces contorted, blood pouring from their orifices. Tara Lee, realizing her soulless fate, attempted to compensate for the damage she had caused. Deja would join her young protégé in death in mere minutes.

CHAPTER 44

48 Hours Earlier

"I'll get what I want out of him, you'll get what you want out of him, and he will be presented for his arraignment without a mark on him."
—CIA Station Chief John Reynolds

Forty-eight hours earlier, while in Belfast, Quinlan parted ways with CIA Chief Reynolds on strained terms. Despite the rift, Reynolds kept his sights firmly set on extracting vital information from Stansfield Anderson. Determined, he and his team prepared to resume their enhanced interrogation on the MI-5 double agent.

Reynolds was confident that Anderson would quickly succumb. The interrogation techniques, particularly harsh for someone experiencing opioid withdrawal, were poised to break his resistance swiftly. Before the session even began, Anderson's pleas caught Reynolds' attention, prompting him to summon the standby doctor. To mitigate withdrawal symptoms, the doctor administered a medical-grade opioid, easing Anderson's transition from his previous dependency.

Reynolds needed him acute and aware to extract the truth. Then it began. The water was poured, and it was poured gratuitously on Anderson's face. His face was shrouded with a cloth so it would soak him. His body was inverted so the water would elevate upwards through his nose. He couldn't breathe. In that flash of a moment, he recognized what most do. The only thing that really matters in life is oxygen. You can do without many things—but if you can't breathe, you are going to die. Oxygen is what he needed most. Panic ensued. Reynolds knew this state all too well.

His hands flailed against the restraints, a desperate attempt to break free from the confines of his captivity. But for the unyielding ankle shackles, his legs would have been in a frenzied dance of panic. Finally granted a reprieve, Stansfield Anderson was given the chance to speak, and he wasted no time in divulging the sinister plot concocted by Akma Deja.

President Bryce's life hung in the balance, along with that of the Supreme Leader and any other unfortunate soul in the vicinity of the President's private dining room. Anderson's trembling voice revealed James O'Donovan's pivotal role as the courier for the deadly device. A fact of extreme importance given his invitation to be the North Korean Supreme Leader's guest for the dinner.

Chief Reynolds sprang into action, swiftly contacting Secret Service Agent Joe Mackey with the urgency of the impending threat. With the dinner mere days away, time was of the essence. Together, they orchestrated a plan, utilizing Anderson and O'Donovan to ensnare Deja in her own psychotic web.

Professor O'Donovan made a consensually monitored phone call to Deja, objecting to her demands that he attends the dinner as her brother's guest. Reynolds gambled on Deja's reaction, hoping her desperation would force her to reveal her hand. He hoped she would give up the fact that she was threatening the lives of Phillip and his son, held as leverage against O'Donovan's refusal to attend.

Wearing headphones, Reynolds listened intently to the call. To his satisfaction, Deja took the bait, incriminating herself with every word she uttered in the carefully crafted conversation. O'Donovan's genuine anguish for his loved ones only served to solidify Deja's complicit guilt.

With crucial information in hand, Reynolds' mind raced with plans. He needed to relay this intel to Quinlan, who was still airborne in route to DC. Unable to reach him directly, Reynolds called Jan Townes, who was briefing Lana on the unfolding events. With Reynolds on speakerphone, the three gradually pieced together the puzzle and realized the magnitude of Deja's treachery. Their determination unwavering, they prepared to confront a threat lurking in the shadows of power and deception.

* * *

Quinlan, unaware of the recent events, was on final approach to Reagan National Airport in Washington, DC. As the plane was taxiing to the terminal, he started to see several missed calls and text messages scrolling on his phone. Many of them were calls from Reynolds. He also received numerous missed calls from Lana. No one left a message, however, so he knew this was sensitive and timely. He called Lana. She explained the recent developments in vague details because both were on unsecure lines. She told him to get to the Situation Room as quickly as possible. It was Thursday afternoon and traffic into the district was surprisingly lighter than usual.

Quinlan had arrived at the Southwest gate of the White House. He showed his Secret Service credentials to the uniformed Secret Service officer, then sprinted up West Executive Avenue. He swung open the doors of the West Wing and stopped to identify himself to the Secret Service Sergeant manning the Situation Room access desk.

"Hey sir," the Sergeant said, "They are waiting for you, go on in."

As soon as he entered, he saw Jan Townes, Lana Miller, Agent in Charge Rick Spencer, and Chief of Staff Andy Stevens. Despite the intensity of the situation, Lana couldn't help but offer a cautious smile, while Jan's greeting carried both warmth and a subtle challenge.

She said, "Welcome home, John. Congratulations to you and Mackey on solving the APEX counterfeit note case. Now it's time to earn your pay. Have a seat," she said as she offered a wink and a wry smile.

Their attention was directed to the flat screen on the wall. CIA Chief of Station John Reynolds and Agent Joe Mackey were in the middle of their briefing. They were apprising the group on what had transpired over the last several hours in Belfast while Quinlan was still in the air on his flight back to DC.

Reynolds was explaining, "...Anderson led us to a locker at the Belfast Airport where we found the cellphone and lapel camera. We've handed the device over to our Directorate of Science and Technology for analysis. They're working on reverse engineering it so we can link the feed that Lana is creating with her people. If successful, we'll control what Akma Deja sees, replacing her expected feed from the White House dinner with our own fabrication. From what we understand, the original setup demands that the caller initiates the FaceTime function, at which point the phone converts into a video camera, capturing a 280-degree view. It's also equipped to transmit audio."

Special Agent in Charge Rick Spencer directed his attention to Quinlan, "John, I know you are getting caught up and so much has happened in the last twenty-four hours. The North Korean Supreme Leader, Pak Hyun Woo, and his guest, Sinn Féin Vice Leader, James O'Donovan, are coming to the White House in two days' time. Their visit is deemed a private event in the President's third floor dining room. We are learning that James O'Donovan was set up by the Supreme Leader's sister, Pak Hyun Mi, or Akma Deja as she's referred to. Anyway, she is holding his relatives hostage back in North Korea and will only release them after he carries the lethal poison into the event inflicting instant death on anyone that comes into contact."

Quinlan, battling fatigue, attentively focused on his boss's words.

Spencer continued, "The Chief of Staff and I concur that cancelling the event altogether could endanger the lives of the two hostages being held in North Korea. We've already apprised the President of the situation, and he's understandably shaken by the gravity of it all. Both the Chief of Staff and the President are adamant about not endangering the hostages. Their top priority is to prevent any loss of life stemming from this ordeal. I want to hear your perspective on this."

Quinlan suggested, "Why don't we relocate the event to Camp David? If there are hostages held in North Korea, we must proceed with caution, but I agree; hosting it at the White House is out of the question. As for Reynolds' mention of reverse engineering and Lana's involvement, I'm curious to hear more. It seems like there is a plan in motion."

It was Lana's turn, "John, welcome home. I am sorry you are hitting this head on, but I have a colleague. She's a trusted friend who is an attorney to some of the Hollywood industry representatives in LA. Her name is Molly Zurflueh. I want to reach out to her to see about providing an AI generated rendition of the dinner. We see it all the time these days but often we don't see the real thing."

As Lana repeated the details of her plan again, she grasped the challenge of convincing Quinlan to agree with its efficacy. Yet, her plan had already garnered the backing of most of the security council members, with Townes standing out as the foremost supporter. With the assassination plot against the President and the Supreme Leader exposed and thwarted, this intricate game of wits was nearing its climax. Focusing on rescuing the O'Donovans from Akma Deja's grip became paramount.

Quinlan scanned the room with a hint of disbelief, quietly assessing the reactions of those present as Lana's proposition hung in the air. "So, Lana, I'm a bit..." he began cautiously, unsure of how to proceed.

Townes interrupted, her tone resolute. "We've heard her entire pitch, John, and I propose that we obtain a sample of the computer-generated imagery to see what's possible. We should give it a shot. We need to create the illusion that this assassination coup happened so that at least the hostages in her custody have a chance."

Reynolds's voice boomed from the video conference system, commanding attention. "Look, I will accompany Stansfield Anderson to South Korea tomorrow. We will stage at Panmunjom, the DMZ. As you know, it's the dividing line for South and North Korea, and I can't go any further without being detected. Anderson has already been summoned by Akma Deja. She had previously arranged to release the hostages to him once she sees her brother and the President... well, fall victim to this chemical."

Reynolds looking dire continued, "I have to say, our science team has sampled the chemical components. Their first analysis is that it is extremely unstable and a basic mix of potent mustard gas. It's essentially a lethal nerve agent."

Quinlan posed a crucial question. "Reynolds, how do we know Anderson's cooperation is genuine and that he's fully on board with this plan?"

Reynolds responded with conviction, "Well, his MI-5 Directorate has informed him it's the difference between life behind bars in a maximum-security prison or execution by firing squad. They're considering this wartime since his secrets involved the Russian war on Ukraine. He is choosing life."

Jan Townes took charge, steering the conversation forward. "Okay, I think we can all break up into sidebars and move on. Lana, you will look into an AI scenario. John and Rick, if you agree, we can secure this dinner to be held at Camp David. Chief of Staff Stevens, will you please coordinate the new Camp David plan with your staff and, of course, the President, using utmost discretion?" She then shouted to the room, "Hey, what are we doing with James O'Donovan?"

Agent Mackey, standing alongside Chief Reynolds in Belfast, joined the conversation via the video conference system. "I plan on escorting James to Washington, DC tomorrow," he stated. "We can arrange accommodation for him at the Willard Hotel. We will then get him up to Camp David to join President Bryce and the Supreme Leader for the small summit. Obviously, the cellphone device and lapel camera will remain in Belfast, where they'll be worked on by the CIA technicians."

Quinlan seized the opportunity to pose a crucial question. "When do we inform the Supreme Leader about the plot his sister has unleashed?"

Townes offered a strategic suggestion. "Can we arrange this when he lands at Andrews? The less he knows now, the better off we all are. Listen, everyone, discretion is key here. No one else should be informed about any of this, understood?"

A palpable sense of agreement permeated the room, and the group quickly dispersed, each member retreating to their respective tasks. In the hours leading up to the Supreme Leader's visit, Lana reached out to her contact.

* * *

Almost instantly, Lana thought of Molly Zurflueh for such a remote plan requiring swift action. Lana and Molly had formed a strong bond during their time at law school, drawn together by their shared love for books, movies, and TV documentaries—a passion they indulged in long before binge-watching became mainstream. "We're thick as thieves," Molly would often quip, capturing the essence of their friendship. Their shared ideals and passion for practicing law and their equal prowess in the field were warmly embraced at a law firm in Laguna Beach, CA. Together, they honed their skills, pushing each other to excel in the practice. Eventually, Lana would relocate to New York City where she accepted a position as an Assistant United States Attorney for the Southern District of New York. Molly briefly took over Lana's role at the firm before branching out into her own real estate law practice. Molly eventually transitioned her law practice into copyright and patent law, a move that proved immensely successful for her personally and professionally. She thrived in contract law, particularly when she represented two Artificial Intelligence (AI) experts specializing in Computer Generated Imagery (CGI). While AI and CGI were still considered the wild frontier for Hollywood movie production, they were rapidly gaining acceptance as a cutting-edge trend in the industry. This transition not only brought professional success to Molly but also personal fulfillment, as Molly met her husband, Greg, who was considered a tech giant in the industry.

Confident in Molly's expertise and capabilities, Lana felt reassured that she would be helpful in this latest endeavor. After two rings, Molly answered the phone, "Oh my God, my friend. It's been a minute! How are you?"

Molly listened intently as Lana explained the dynamic situation. Lana shared as much detail as possible given the time constraints.

"Let me figure out some things," Molly responded. "Listen, whatever you need. If you're asking for help, I'll do my best to provide it. I need to make some calls. Okay, I'll call you right back."

Molly's swift and supportive response was conveyed by the sense of urgency in her voice. She wasted no time, declaring, "I need to make some calls," which provided Lana with peace of mind, knowing Molly was already exploring possibilities.

Molly reached out to the two AI experts she was currently working with on a Hollywood contract. She informed them that there was a new client, the Secret Service, requesting a time-sensitive training scenario. The scenario would involve an unfortunate plot to assassinate a gathering of three or four individuals in the private dining room of the White House. Armed with a detailed script and sequence of events, they understood the urgency of the task. Molly briefed them on the limited availability of the private residence while the President was away. She accompanied the team as they flew via a special Air Force C-21 dispatched from the Los Angeles Air Force Base near El Segundo.

Quinlan facilitated the entry of Molly and her CGI/AI team into the White House private dining room, ensuring clearance with the White House Usher's office. The two-man CGI team, thrilled to be part of such a prestigious project, eagerly set to work. Molly had assured them that their efforts would be rewarded in the long run, appealing to their sense of patriotism.

They began by meticulously measuring the dimensions of the private dining room and capturing video and still photographs. With enthusiasm, they explained to Quinlan and Miller the versatility of

CGI technology, commonly used in filmmaking to create elaborate scenes and visual effects. They emphasized that much of what moviegoers see nowadays was made possible through CGI.

Due to the time constraints, the technicians worked tirelessly through the night, utilizing video footage of President Bryce and Supreme Leader Pak Hyun Woo retrieved from the Internet. They improvised with what little material they could find on James O'Donovan, mindful of the project's pressing deadline. By morning, they had crafted a digital recreation of the imagined scenario. The video was converted to a digital format and fed to a cellphone cloned from the original device retrieved from the Belfast airport locker. When Deja called the original cellphone, the cloned cellphone reacted in place of the original device. Additionally, the video mimicking James O'Donovan's lapel camera was transmitted via a live cloned camera worn by Room 23 Agent Willie Gonzalez. This footage was prerecorded through a mock motorcade visit conducted the night before. The AI technicians deliberately crafted point-of-view footage of the dinner from the viewpoint of the lapel camera as well, leaving no detail overlooked.

Molly's CGI/AI technicians had no idea of the significance of their work, nor would they ever fully know what had transpired. Their masterpiece ultimately saved the lives of two innocent hostages held in captivity for many months in North Korea as well as the leaders of two countries and possibly many more. Their creation vividly portrayed events that never came to pass, precisely replicating what Akma Deja had witnessed before releasing Phillip and Patrick O'Donovan into the custody of Stansfield Anderson. It was indeed a masterpiece, one that would ultimately save many lives.

* * *

North Korean Supreme Leader Pak Hyun Woo's aircraft landed at Andrews Air Force Base, where his Secret Service detail, Chief of Staff Andy Stevens, and Deputy National Security Advisor Jan

Townes awaited him. They escorted him and his small delegation to the VIP suite within the Joint Operations Building, typically reserved for Generals and high-ranking officials. There, the Supreme Leader received a briefing on the unfolding events in his country, particularly those orchestrated by his sister, Pak Hyun Mi.

Initially subdued, he suddenly erupted, slamming his fist onto the table, and shouting in Korean, causing his immediate staff to recoil. He then turned to Stevens and Townes, his expression intense, and declared, "Does depravity know no bounds? I am indebted to you, and I insist that the meeting with the President proceed."

The Supreme Leader's emotions surged upon learning of the O'Donovans' hostage situation. He emphasized the urgency of a rescue plan. Swiftly, he enlisted his military aide-de-camp, tasking him with devising a strategy utilizing his elite guard unit that remained back in North Korea. Their primary objective was to assist CIA Chief Reynolds and MI-5 Operative Anderson in rescuing Phillip and Patrick O'Donovan. DNSA Townes and Chief of Staff Stevens were comforted by the Supreme Leader's alignment with their views, seeing the hostage situation as a top priority for securing the release of the O'Donovans.

The Supreme Leader was informed that the mini summit would proceed, but at the Presidential retreat known as Camp David, nestled in the Catoctin Mountains of Thurmont, MD. There, he would meet with President of the United States, David Bryce. The meeting heralded the start of a promising journey toward improved relations between the United States and the emerging, soon-to-be free nation of North Korea. They would also confront Akma Deja following her unsuccessful assassination attempt on both of them. This anticipated triumph would dispel any doubts about North Korea's readiness to engage in diplomacy with the Western world.

Epilogue

Sunday morning arrived, and West Executive Avenue lay deserted beneath the morning sun. Quinlan surveyed the empty road, taking note of the vacant parking spots. He relished the quiet. He assumed a familiar catcher's position where he found solace in its familiarity. He grew up playing baseball, always calling the shots behind home plate. His gaze traversed the length of the avenue, a ritual he often performed to gain a unique perspective. They said Secret Service agents had a knack for seeing what others missed. Amidst the turmoil swirling in his mind over the past forty-eight hours, the empty avenue offered a tranquil refuge. Against the competing thoughts vying for attention in his head, he found a semblance of peace here. Those thoughts, however, may have guided him in the right direction and shielded him from harm on numerous occasions. Yet, the near misses and almost happenings went unnoticed, their tally forever obscured.

"Crazy, just crazy," he whispered under his breath, his words scarcely audible. He reflected on what Jan Townes told him that morning during a phone conversation. She recounted to Quinlan how she briefed the Supreme Leader about his sister's death. She described the conversation to Quinlan, "The Supreme Leader listened intently as I detailed the sequence of events leading to his sister's demise. She had tragically succumbed to the poison created by her own scientists under her command." Townes described to Quinlan how he had reacted to the news with an eerie sense of satisfaction. She proceeded to elaborate on her discussion with CIA Station Chief John Reynolds about Stansfield Anderson's future. Reynolds informed her that Anderson's execution had been stayed. Instead, he would serve a life sentence in Britain's notorious Wakefield Prison. Anderson's betrayal of state secrets to the Russians constituted treason and it could have led to the death penalty. However, the United Kingdom considered his cooperation towards the end as a mitigating factor that ultimately spared his life. From that moment forward, Quinlan realized he would perceive the world through a new lens, one that few could understand.

As Quinlan gazed at the Old Executive Office Building, a warmth enveloped his shoulder. "Hey, good morning, Q. Sizing up the playing field?" Officer Doty greeted him. "How was your weekend?"

"Quiet. Just the right kind of quiet." Quinlan kept the events of the last forty-eight hours under wraps. "How was yours?" Quinlan replied, standing upright now.

"The old man opted for Camp David for his summit with the North Korean delegation, so that always brings a bit of relief to the eighteen acres," Quinlan couldn't help but laugh. "We had some Hollywood folks passing through, but not much else."

Doty said. "But you're aware of that; you approved their entry onto the grounds. Nothing particularly crazy." Doty replied in an offhand manner.

Lana emerged from the West Wing, drawing Quinlan's attention with her presence. "Hi, John. How are you?" she greeted him.

"It's cliché, but I'm good now that you're here," he answered, a smile spreading across his face in response to her presence.

"Hello, Ms. Miller," Officer Doty chimed in with his trademark grin.

"Hi Ron. Ron, could you call me Lana?" she requested.

"Of course, Lana," Doty agreed, his grin unwavering. "I can't imagine a better start to the morning than an empty West Executive Avenue. Have a wonderful day, Lana. Q, I'm sure I'll be seeing you soon."

Lana reached down to grab John's hand; he had returned to his comfortable catcher's position. "I'm not calling you, Q. Not ever. You know that, right, John?"

"Understood, Ms. Miller," he conceded, reciprocating her smile. He stood upright and turning to Lana, he posed the question, "What do you think will happen with Phillip O'Donovan regarding his involvement with the APEX note? He corrected the imperfections, and now many flawless notes are in circulation."

Lana responded assuredly, "Yes, but you've taken down the APEX counterfeiting operation. Once those notes have cleared circulation, that will be the end of it. I spoke with the U.S. Attorney's Office, and they are not pursuing prosecution. It was obviously a case of duress and necessity—two formidable defense stances. Both he and his son are undergoing routine medical and psychological evaluations. They should soon be released and safely back home."

"They'll be in my prayers," John said.

"It's all over now, John," Lana affirmed.

Quinlan, changing the subject, said, "I just got word that I'm being transferred to the Charlotte, NC Field Office. I'll be managing a task force. Would you consider coming with me?" he asked.

About the Author

Sean Quarmby is a distinguished figure in the field of security and investigations, holding a Bachelor of Science degree in Criminal Justice from West Chester University in Pennsylvania, and a Master of Arts degree in Education from Seton Hall University in New Jersey. His career with the United States Secret Service began in 1990 when he entered on duty at the New York Field Office. There, he discovered his passion for investigating cases related to counterfeit currency, organized crime, financial crimes, and the collection and dissemination of protective intelligence.

He transitioned to the Secret Service's Financial Crimes Division at Headquarters in Washington, DC. During this period, he worked closely with the Congressional Finance Committee, chaired by U.S. Senator Jon Kyl of Arizona. Together with the Senator's staff, he helped craft the Identity Theft Assumption Deterrence Act, pioneering federal legislation aimed at combating identity theft. During this tenure, he also instructed numerous overseas courses on topics including Interview and Interrogation, Executive Protection, Methods of Intelligence Gathering, Financial Fraud, and Organized Crime.

His career trajectory led him to the prestigious Presidential Protection Division in 1999, where he protected Presidents William

J. Clinton and George W. Bush. Rising through the ranks, he was promoted to Assistant to the Special Agent in Charge, overseeing Room 23 and the White House Access Branch.

After concluding his tenure on the President's detail, he was transferred to the Charlotte, NC Field Office. There, he assumed the role of supervising a dynamic cybercrime task force composed of personnel from multiple law enforcement agencies.

Sean retired from the U.S. Secret Service in May of 2015, and is now an Associate Professor of Criminal Justice Technology at Central Piedmont Community College in Charlotte, North Carolina.

He makes his home in Charlotte with his wife, Lani, along with their three cherished dogs: Ebbitt, Edison, and Ernie, and their grumpy cat, Mocha.

Milton Keynes UK
Ingram Content Group UK Ltd.
UKHW020407021124
450424UK00014B/1479